KU-421-653

Stay
Buried

Kate Webb grew up in Hampshire before reading History at Durham University. She has since spent time living in London and Venice, and now lives in the countryside near Bath, UK. She has written several historical novels under the name Katherine Webb. *Stay Buried* is her first crime novel.

Stay Buried

Kate Webb

QUERCUS

First published in Great Britain in 2022
This paperback edition published in Great Britain in 2023 by

QUERCUS

Quercus Editions Ltd
Carmelite House
50 Victoria Embankment
London EC4Y 0DZ

An Hachette UK company

Copyright © 2022 Kate Webb

The moral right of Kate Webb to be
identified as the author of this work has been
asserted in accordance with the Copyright,
Designs and Patents Act, 1988.

All rights reserved. No part of this publication
may be reproduced or transmitted in any form
or by any means, electronic or mechanical,
including photocopy, recording, or any
information storage and retrieval system,
without permission in writing from the publisher.

A CIP catalogue record for this book is available
from the British Library

PB ISBN 978 1 52942 127 9
EB ISBN 978 1 52942 125 5

This book is a work of fiction. Names, characters, businesses,
organizations, places and events are either the product of the
author's imagination or are used fictitiously. Any resemblance
to actual persons, living or dead, events or locales
is entirely coincidental.

10 9 8 7 6 5 4 3 2 1

Typeset by CC Book Production
Printed and bound in Great Britain by Clays Ltd, Elcograf S.p.A.

MIX
Paper | Supporting
responsible forestry
FSC® C104740

Papers used by Quercus are from well-managed forests and other responsible sources.

For James

1

Day One, Friday

'DI Lockyer?'

A woman's voice, hollow, oddly familiar. For a second Lockyer thought he recognized it. Then silence at the other end of the line, except for the faintest sound of an indrawn breath.

The back of Lockyer's neck prickled. His blurred reflection watched him from the window – a tall, rangy figure, dark hair that needed cutting, a crooked nose and eyes with shadowed rings underneath them. He really needed a good night's sleep.

'Yep. Who's this?'

'It's Hedy. Hedy Lambert.'

Lockyer was quiet for so long that Constable Broad looked up from her computer. Instinctively, he turned away from her curiosity.

'H— Miss Lambert.' He cleared his throat. 'I . . . It's been a while. I didn't expect to hear from you.' There were three empty mugs on his desk and he began to put them together, turning their handles inward so he'd be able to pick them up with one hand. Fiddling, like a nervous child. He made himself keep still.

'No. Well.' Hedy took a breath. 'How are you?'

'Why are you calling, Miss Lambert?' Straight away, he regretted sounding so curt. There was another silence.

'What – no time for a catch-up?' Hedy's tone was dry, but there was a tremor underneath it. Lockyer waited. He might have said more if Broad hadn't been sitting right there, studiously pretending not to listen. 'I need you to come and see me, Inspector Lockyer.'

'What for?'

'It's important. It . . . it could be urgent. Maybe. It's about what happened. It's about Harry Ferris.'

'Do you have new information about the case?'

'Yes. But before you ask, I'm not going to tell you over the phone. I need you to come and see me. Please.' The inflection on the *please* stopped short of begging, but only just.

Lockyer tried to keep his voice neutral. 'I can't promise anything . . .' He searched for a pen among the papers and rubbish on his desk. 'What's your address?'

'My *address*?' That dry amusement again, with its undercurrent of something darker. 'Eastwood Park.'

Lockyer clenched his teeth. DC Broad threw him a pen. Her Majesty's Prison Eastwood Park. Fourteen years had gone by – fourteen years since he'd put Hedy Lambert away, and away she had stayed. Pointlessly, he wrote *HMP E Park* on a scrap of paper. Somehow, he'd thought she must have been paroled by now, but of course not – she'd been handed a twenty-year minimum term. That's what you got for a cold, calculated murder.

'Everything all right, Guv?' Broad asked, once he'd hung up, putting her arms behind her head to stretch her shoulders.

Gemma Broad was short and stocky, which made some colleagues assume she must be out of shape when she was far from it. She did triathlons for fun in her spare time. At a charity obstacle race the Wiltshire force had taken part in the year before, she'd beaten most of the men on the team – though she'd needed help over the bigger walls. She was young, keen and very bright, and ought not to have been stuck on Major Crime Review with Lockyer. She was also naturally very curious, but Lockyer didn't want to talk about Hedy Lambert or the Harry Ferris case – not until he had to.

'Time you got home, Gem,' he said. 'That lot can wait till Monday.'

'Something new for us?'

'I doubt it.' He shook his head. 'Just someone from an old case of mine, probably bored or wanting attention, and . . .' He trailed off, unable to bring himself to lie about Hedy. 'It's probably nothing. Have a good weekend, Gem.'

'You not coming for a drink, Guv?'

'No. Not in the mood.'

'Doing anything exciting this weekend?'

'Just the usual. Family dinner. Working on the house.'

'Party, party, party, right?'

'Non-stop. How about you?'

'Off to Pete's mum's.' Broad stopped just short of rolling her eyes. 'Again.'

'Isn't that three weekends in a row?'

'No.' She stood up with a sigh. 'But it feels like it. She's pitching a fit because the builders have downed tools. God knows what she said to them. I wouldn't mind except she won't have Merry in the house. The poor thing has to sleep in the garage, and then she complains that his crying keeps her awake.'

'Sounds to me like a good excuse to stay at home and let Pete go by himself.'

'Yeah, but . . . Well. He likes me to go with him,' she said, with a trace of embarrassment.

'Have a good one, then.'

Lockyer had met Broad's boyfriend a couple of times, and failed to understand what she could possibly see in him.

When she'd gone Lockyer sat for a while. He couldn't imagine what Hedy Lambert had to say to him, unless it was to vent some anger. Or unless – finally – it was her confession. After a while he turned off the lights and headed across the CID suite, down the stairs and out of the station.

Wiltshire Police Headquarters was housed in an imposing 1960s brick building on the western edge of Devizes. The flag, bearing the police emblem and motto, hung limp and dripping from its pole. *Primus et optimus*. First and best – since it was the oldest county force, outside London. It could also have said *minimus*, smallest, if it hadn't been for good old Warwickshire. Both employed fewer than a thousand officers.

Lockyer walked slowly to his car, parked round the back, thinking about everything he'd done during the past fourteen years – the places he'd been, the people he'd met, the cases he'd worked. And all that time Hedy Lambert had stayed in jail. He'd played a prominent role in the investigation that had put her there. Unease dragged at the back of his skull. It was the same unease he'd felt the year before, on the case that had seen him moved sideways off the Major Crime Investigation Team, to Major Crime Review. Cold cases. He thought he was starting to recognize the feeling – it came on when he was on the verge of doing the wrong thing.

But he already knew that he'd visit Hedy Lambert, just as she'd asked: he was curious to hear what she had to say, and he couldn't shake the sense of owing her something. He'd never forgotten how hard she'd made him wrestle with himself – how he'd lurched from believing her to doubting her ten times a day. And he'd never been sure he'd jumped the right way, not even when she went down for murder.

Hedy Lambert followed Lockyer to his parents' house. *It's important. It . . . it could be urgent.* The case had been closed for so long, he couldn't think how anything could be urgent about it.

Westdene Farm sat by itself, in a slight crease in Salisbury Plain, back from the main road that crossed the grassland from Melksham to Salisbury. Rain blew across the yard in fitful waves as he turned in and parked the car. Black plastic flapped, pulled loose from some discarded bales of haylage, and the wind hummed between the metal pillars of the new barn, which had been new thirty years ago. The air smelt of slurry and smoke, and the dogs started barking at the sound of an engine; the usual detritus lay scattered about – abandoned tyres and machine parts, empty plastic drums, tools and unchecked weeds. Beyond that the land rose up and away, vast and empty.

In the half-dark, in the rain, it was a desolate place. But it was home, the place where Lockyer had grown up. As familiar as it was now subtly depressing.

The farmhouse was square, brick-built, a couple of hundred years old. Lockyer's father had been born within its walls, as had his father before him. Like many of the smaller farms that dotted the plain, Westdene had been in the same cash-strapped family for generations. Water pattered from the blocked gutters onto thick growths of moss below, and the upstairs windows were blank, dark and watchful. But yellow light was coming from the kitchen window, and Lockyer caught a glimpse of his mother inside, slim and short-haired, strapped into a faded apron and wreathed in steam from several pans on the stove. Thank God for her. When he opened the door two brindled grey collies rushed out to greet him, and he was enveloped by the smell of the place, which he'd known from birth – old carpet and smuts, unwashed dog beds, coffee and cooking. A gentle stink that unknotted his shoulders for a while.

Lockyer went for dinner with his parents two or three times a month. They rarely spoke on the phone – none of them liked to. Lockyer worried that Trudy and John were increasingly isolated, increasingly cut off, with only each other and old sorrows for company. He sometimes felt like their last conduit to the rest of the world, and woefully under-qualified for the job.

He called a greeting, then sat down on the hall bench to take off his shoes. The dogs buffeted against him, pushing their noses into his face, and as he straightened up again he caught sight of his younger brother, Christopher, jogging down the stairs in his baggy jeans, with one of his two good shirts buttoned up and tucked in, his blond hair gelled into short spikes. Eyes down, checking in his wallet for a tenner. It was Friday night, of course.

'Off to the pub?' Lockyer said, or thought he said. He blinked, startled, and the moment passed: he hadn't spoken out loud because Chris wasn't there. Of course he wasn't. Lockyer sat still for a moment, waiting for the clench of his stomach muscles to ease.

His parents talked mostly about the farm as they ate, and none of it was very positive – yet more uncertainty due to the weather, falling prices, leaving the EU. John said very little about anything. He looked up from the shepherd's pie only when Trudy badgered him to. It was often shepherd's pie, when it wasn't beef stew, or chicken and dumplings. It was the food they'd always eaten, and Lockyer didn't have the heart to tell his mother that he didn't eat meat any more. He hadn't for years, but felt he'd rejected enough about their lifestyle already by leaving, going to university instead of staying on the farm, then joining the police.

Though they'd come to understand about the police part, he thought.

He sometimes wondered why more farmers weren't vegetarian. He remembered how nervous he'd been about attending his first post-mortem; queasy with anticipation of the controlled violence to come, the alien sight of the inside of a human being, and the very real possibility of humiliating himself in front of colleagues by turning ashen or green. Fainting or throwing up. In the end it had been a good deal less awful than many of the things he'd seen and heard on the farm, growing up. Sheep with fly strike, eaten alive by maggots; cows with bloat, their stomachs bursting; the desperate cries of the dairy cows when their calves were taken away to be slaughtered. He'd lost the ability to see a fundamental distinction between himself and the animals they raised.

'What's up, Matthew? You're only half here,' Trudy said. 'Pass your plate. Have you been sleeping?'

'Not so much last night,' he admitted.

His father grunted. 'Full moon,' he said. John Lockyer didn't sleep much either, and he kept a list of things he blamed for that, as though he needed to have a reason close at hand, at all times. Anything other than acknowledging the real reasons, which they all knew well enough.

Lockyer hated to see the slump of his shoulders, the distracted way his thick fingers roamed his clothes and the table top from time to time, as though searching for something. 'Could have been that,' he said.

'It kept the dogs up,' John said. 'I heard 'em, fretting and pacing half the night.'

'I got a phone call I wasn't expecting just as I was leaving today, Mum, that's all. About a case.'

The pause after his words was a familiar one, loaded with expectation. John's gaze locked on his for the first time that evening, and Lockyer cursed himself.

'Not Chris's case,' he added gently.

'Of course not.' Trudy smiled bravely. 'We know you'll tell us as soon as there's anything.'

As soon as there's anything. It was Lockyer's fault. When he'd moved to cold cases he'd been the one to mention his brother to them; to say that he would be able to take a fresh look at it. The need to catch the guilty party gnawed like hunger, impossible to ignore. He hadn't mentioned that, with his personal connection, he shouldn't touch the case. He hadn't mentioned that, when he had, he'd hit the same dead ends as the original investigation. He'd given them hope, when he shouldn't have. He'd given himself hope, convinced himself he'd find something that had been missed. And he'd spent far longer than he should have done proving himself wrong.

Lockyer nodded. 'It's an old case of mine, in fact. One of my first as a DI.'

'Unsolved?'

'No, no. We got a result.' He saw Trudy register his choice of words. Not *the right result* or *a good result*. 'It's probably nothing. The call I got. It'll probably come to nothing. What's for pudding?'

He didn't want her to worry about him having messed up, or being in more trouble. He knew she did worry about him, in spite of all the other things she had to worry about. Sudden loss did that to people: it made them hold on tightly. He got up to clear the table because Hedy Lambert's case stormed his head again – the memory of turning up to Professor Roland Ferris's house in the glorious light of an early-summer morning. The smell of the jasmine flowering up the wall, and of damp, newly cut lawns. A tabby cat milling about his ankles as he'd thumped on the door. And then, moments later, standing next to Hedy over the body of a man lying dead on the herringbone brick floor of a small barn.

He remembered the way she'd stared at him, unblinking. The way she'd shaken. The way she'd held her bloodied hands away from her, as though they didn't belong to her. Like she didn't want to get blood on her clothes, when they were splashed and smeared with it already. He remembered that, for a minute, his training had gone out of the window and he'd felt every bit as lost as she'd looked.

Fourteen years had passed, but he even remembered that the cat's name was Janus. Every detail. As though it had all been waiting at the back of his mind. As though some part of him had known it was unfinished business, and that, one day, he would have to go through it again.

Trudy followed him into the kitchen with the rest of the plates.

'How's he been?' Lockyer asked her quietly.

'Not too bad.' Trudy pulled a face. 'You know your dad. Everything's doom and gloom, but we soldier on.'

'Come on, Mum.' Too often, she tried to be flippant about it.

'Well.' For a moment her face lost all trace of its habitual smile, and just looked old and forlorn. Lockyer hated to see it. 'It's always worse at this time of year. If only the bloody rain would ease up! Eastground and Flint are already flooded.'

'I saw as I drove in.' The two fields nearest the road, covered with shivering water.

It was on the tip of his tongue to mention selling the farm again. To suggest the two of them moving to some small, warm bungalow somewhere, where there was less mud and grief and work; maybe some neighbours to remind them they were part of a wider society, and that there was more to life than feeding livestock and shovelling out their muck, and the constant scrimping, fixing and teetering on the edge of ruin. Trudy might be persuaded, he thought. She'd grown up in a comfortable terraced house in the small town of Amesbury, not far from Stonehenge. But there had always been Lockyers at Westdene Farm, and the last time he'd suggested leaving, John had actually looked bewildered. *Sell it? And do what?*

And, of course, the farm was where Christopher was, if he was anywhere. They'd emptied his room, not kept it as a shrine, but he was still there. Still there, and at the same time so horribly not. An odd sock of his lurking in the fluff behind the drier; the jar of Marmite that only he had liked, sticky and inedible at the back of the cupboard. Lockyer wondered if his parents saw him around the place sometimes, like he did. A trick of the mind, a memory flaring too brightly, but still a moment, a fraction of a second, when everything felt all right again.

'Will you not think about getting some help in, at least?' he tried. 'A labourer, or an apprentice, wouldn't cost—'

'He or she would cost more than we can afford, Matt.' Trudy reached up into a high cupboard for a new bag of sugar. She winced, pressing her fingers into the thin muscles of her shoulder: the toll of years of farm work. Lockyer felt helpless, then the flicker of an old anger that had no direction to go in. Christopher should have been here to help, instead of cold in his grave. He'd been the one who'd wanted to stay on the farm, and build a career of it. He'd been the one with the talent for forging friendships, and making people laugh.

Trudy gripped Lockyer's hand. 'Don't worry about us so much. We're getting along.'

'Mum—'

'So, this call. Does it mean you'll be looking at the case again?'

'It depends on what she's got to tell me.'

'She?'

'Hedy Lambert.'

'Hedy? Like the film star? She was one of my dad's favourites.'

'I got her sent down for murder fourteen years ago.' He couldn't keep his tone light, however hard he tried.

Trudy glanced up at him, then patted his arm. 'I'm sure it was whatever she did that got her sent down, love, not you. But you're on the cold case squad. Who better to deal with it?'

'Can two people be a "squad"?'

'Of course they can! I like that girl Gemma. She's got her head screwed on.' Trudy stirred four sugars into John's coffee. 'I know, I know,' she said, in response to Lockyer's disapproving look. 'But I have to pick my battles, Matthew.'

'I'll come back tomorrow and sort out the gutters. I've got nothing else on, and—'

'Nothing else other than you need rest. And to get your own place sorted. And, oh, I don't know, maybe think about a social life of some kind? Meeting someone . . .? We'll be fine.'

'I'll come tomorrow and sort it. Don't argue, Mum.'

Lockyer knew he wouldn't sleep well that night either. He knew it as soon as he lay down, a little after midnight, with the wind loud against the walls of his small house and crashing in the bare trees behind it. It was a lonely sort of sound, and one he loved, even though it always made him restless. But it wasn't only that, or the shepherd's pie sitting heavily in his stomach.

His memories of Hedy Lambert kept coming. The dead body lying on the brick floor beside her, the blood on her hands, and the hollow sound of her voice down the phone today, fourteen years later. He wondered how she would look now; whether the years had been kind, or if prison life had taken its toll. When they'd first met he hadn't been able to work out what was different about her. It was only later, once everything about the crime scene had been photographed and sampled and recorded, and she'd been allowed to wash off the blood and get changed, that he'd realized.

Her face had been completely naked. He couldn't remember when he'd last seen a woman – a young one, in any case – without even the least trace of make-up. And her hair had been clean but not styled in any way. It didn't look like it had been cut in a long time, and wasn't dyed either. A mid-brown unremarkable colour, and she'd worn it parted in the middle and tucked behind her ears. Not a single item of jewellery. She'd done none of the things other women did to make themselves more acceptable to each other, to men, to themselves. Old jeans and a baggy T-shirt. Hedy Lambert had looked like a woman trying to be invisible, and she was by no means pretty, at first glance. Her face was slightly too long and narrow, her eyes more grey than blue. And yet Lockyer had found his gaze returning to her, again and again. Like the memory of her returned now.

It was pointless to lie there with sleep so far away, so Lockyer got up. Walking sometimes helped. He stamped his feet into his boots, pulled on a coat and set out. The rain had stopped and the clouds were breaking, showing glimpses of the moon's pale face up in the racing sky; the wind roared in the trees, making a sound like the sea. The driveway outside his place was saturated, churned to mud; all the potholes were full of water. Lights were on in the cottage attached to his, the only neighbour for half a mile or more. It seemed that old Mrs Musprat wasn't sleeping either. Lockyer's life was filled with people who couldn't sleep. He wondered if Hedy Lambert could.

*

Since he was going as a civvy, rather than a police officer, the prison visit had to be booked twenty-four hours in advance. It was Sunday afternoon when Lockyer set off, driving northwards, through villages strung along the road across the plain like beads on a string. He squinted into the pale sunshine and was careful not to think too much about whom he was going to see, or what she might say. Turning west onto the M4, then north onto the M5, not listening to the radio, keeping his eyes and his mind firmly on the road.

Eastwood Park sat just outside the village of Falfield in South Gloucestershire, a complex of low, unlovely blocks behind a green security fence. Lockyer had spent a while on the web that morning. A recent inspection had found three of the closed units unfit for purpose, with some of the inmates confined to their cells for most of the day. Of the four hundred or so women held there, over a third never had any visitors. There were problems with self-harm, drug use and mental illness, and a high percentage of them were homeless upon release. Lockyer had stopped reading.

He waited at a table in the visiting room, apprehensive, curious, knowing he probably shouldn't be there. Some of it was the innate discomfort of being a policeman in a prison, but not all. And then there she was. She'd been twenty-five when she was sent down; Lockyer had been twenty-seven, a new, fast-tracked detective inspector. She was thirty-nine now, and thinner, her cheekbones more pronounced, her hair hanging unkempt to her elbows and still tucked behind her ears. The first strands of grey ran through it at her temples. Her clothes were as shapeless as they'd ever been – tracksuit bottoms and a T-shirt – and her mouth twitched when she saw him. It was nowhere near a smile.

She sat down in silence, and Lockyer fought the instinct to lean back, away from her. As though she might strike. He wondered why his subconscious deemed that a possibility. She studied him with the same clear grey eyes he remembered.

'Thanks for coming,' she said eventually.

'How've you been?' Lockyer said, at a loss.

Now she smiled, with a touch of irony. 'Oh, you know. Terrific. My cellmate took a massive dose of spice the night before last, so I've got a room of my own until she's back on Planet Earth.' She ran her eyes over his face again, and Lockyer remembered that she was clever. However broken she'd been back then, and however broken she might be now, she was clever. 'Not lost your talent for small-talk, then,' she said. 'Do your colleagues still call you "Farmer Giles"?'

'Not as much.'

'I thought they were just taking the piss out of your accent. It took me a while to twig that it was rhyming slang for piles.'

'A pain in the arse,' he said evenly. 'All in the spirit of fun.'

'Really?'

'What did you want to tell me, H— Miss Lambert?'

'You might as well call me Hedy. We're old friends, after all.'

'I'm not here as a friend, Hedy.'

She flinched. 'No. Thanks for that.'

'I meant, you wanted to see me as a police officer, not a friend. Right?'

'Yes. Because you're the officer who put me in here.'

'And you're the person who taught me not to trust my gut. Ever.'

Hedy stared at him, her expression sad. There were tired lines around her eyes. Never beautiful, but still striking. Still something about her that drew him in.

'What if your gut was right, Inspector Lockyer?' she said.

'What's this about, Hedy?'

'Harry Ferris is back.'

'Harry Ferris?'

'Yes. He's come home.'

Lockyer blinked. His heart gave a single hard beat, as if in recognition of something significant. Something big. 'Home where?' he said carefully.

'Home to his father. He's back with Professor Ferris, at Longacres, in Stoke Lavington.'

Longacres, with the jasmine growing around the door, the cat called Janus, and the old barn at the back with the herringbone brick floor. Blood from the corpse had run into the mortar between the bricks, inching out with terrible, geometric precision. At first, they'd identified the dead man as Harry Ferris – Roland Ferris had *insisted* it was his long-lost son, Harry. But then Roland's sister, Serena, claimed that it *wasn't* Harry, that her brother was deluded, and for a while the dead man had had two identities – or none – and the investigation had floundered, tangled up in finding out who the victim was. Lockyer remembered the SIO's face turning crimson when the first set of DNA samples got botched. In the end the fingerprints came back first, with a definitive answer. Not Harry, but a man named Michael Brown.

Later, it was Lockyer who'd worked out that Hedy Lambert had had a motive to kill them both.

'How can you possibly know that Harry's come back?' he said now.

'I still have a friend in the village,' Hedy said. 'It's big news in a place like that. She phoned me.'

'It doesn't . . . it doesn't change what you did. Or what happened.'

'Of course it does!' She spoke with quiet passion, putting her hands flat on the table, fingers splayed. Lockyer noticed scars on her arms that hadn't been there before. Thin parallel pink and silver lines. 'When you first arrested me it was for the murder of Harry Ferris. A man who'd walked out on his father – on his whole life – fifteen years before. Gone without a trace. How can it mean nothing that he's come back now?'

'You still killed a man, Hedy. It wasn't Harry, but—'

'I didn't kill *anybody*!'

The warden looked over at them, and Hedy sank into herself, dropping her hands into her lap and staring down at them. She'd said as much all along. Protested her innocence without wavering, albeit in the strangely deadened, disconnected way she'd had back then. Her demeanour hadn't helped her with the police, or the jury.

'Who's your friend in the village?' Lockyer asked. Hedy brought one hand up to her mouth and chewed at the skin around her thumbnail. A nervous habit she'd never had before – back in 2005 she'd had a certain stillness that prison had clearly obliterated. There were scars on the inside of her wrist as well, and she saw him notice them. She dropped her hand again, frowning.

'I gave it a go,' she said quietly. 'A few years back. But after I'd started it seemed as pointless as living. Dying, I mean. So I changed my mind and shouted for the screws. I got so much stick for it, you wouldn't believe. A lot of people in here would pretty much rather be dead, but you only get respect if you have the courage of your convictions. A cry for help just makes you a laughing stock.'

'You can't have too long left to serve, now,' Lockyer said.

'Really?' Hedy's mouth twisted. 'You think six years in here isn't a long time?'

'Well—'

'It's long enough to be sure I'll never get the chance to have kids. I'll never have a family of my own.' The anger that hardened her eyes was laced with sorrow. 'It's long enough for this thing I didn't do to destroy my last chance of a better life afterwards. A proper life.'

'Who's your friend in the village?' Lockyer asked again.

'Are you going to look into it? Are you going to go and talk to Harry Ferris? Are you going to ask him where he was all that time, and why his dad insisted some stranger was his son?'

'Hedy . . .'

'I know you're on cold cases now. I was surprised when I heard. You were all up-and-coming, back then.'

'Yes. Well.' Lockyer looked away. Most pre-retirement officers would have seen it as a demotion, of sorts. As being sidelined, which of course he had been. Into a career cul-de-sac. But he didn't mind nearly as much as people assumed he must. 'It suits me better. I never was a good politician.' He was saying too much to her, straying into the personal.

'No. I can imagine that about you.' She leant forwards again. 'So treat this as a cold case. Reinvestigate.'

'I look for unsolved cases where new evidence has come to light, or new forensic techniques might help move things forwards, or where I can identify a line of enquiry that was missed. This isn't an unsolved case.'

'Yes, it is.' She stared at him. 'Are you afraid to be wrong? Afraid to prove yourself wrong, I mean?'

'The jury convicted you, Hedy. Not me.'

'You gave them what they needed. But they were wrong, and so were you.'

'I can't just reopen a closed case. Not without good reason.'

'Harry Ferris *is* a good reason!' He heard her rising desperation. 'Doesn't him turning up constitute a new "line of enquiry"? My friend in the village is Cass Baker. She still works in the post office. Talk to her – she's the only one who ever believed I didn't do it. At least, that's what she says . . .' She looked away, shaking her head. 'Even my mum thinks . . . She'd never say so, but I can see it in her eyes – she's not completely sure. Not that I get to see her very often any more. They moved to Spain a couple of years ago, her and Derek – wanted to get out there before Brexit. She still visits once or twice a year.' She was quiet for a beat. 'You *must* want to talk to Harry Ferris. Aren't you even a little bit curious about where he's been for twenty-nine years? Why he went off in the first place, and why he's come back now?'

Lockyer sat silent for a minute. He *was* curious. Harry had fallen out with his father and gone off the rails in his mid-teens – so far, so unremarkable. He'd gone sufficiently off the rails to get expelled from his private school, and at the age of fifteen he'd gone to live with his aunt and cousin instead. At eighteen, having refused any contact with his father for the preceding three years, he'd packed his bags and disappeared altogether. And his father, Roland, had been so desperate to have him back that he'd latched on to a stranger who'd turned up at the house twelve years later, believing him to be Harry. Lockyer said nothing, though. It wasn't enough for him to be curious: nothing he might find out about Harry Ferris would change what Hedy had done.

Hedy waited, and she watched, and at length she spoke. 'You said a minute ago that I taught you not to trust your gut. Does that mean you didn't believe it was me? That at some point in the investigation you thought I was innocent?'

'At one point. Maybe. I think you know that already.' He met her gaze and held it steady. 'But I was wrong.'

'What if you weren't?' she said, quick as a heartbeat. 'What if your gut was telling you the truth?' There was a short silence. 'Whoever killed Michael Brown got away with it, Inspector. And I *know* that's the truth.'

2

Day Four, Monday

Lockyer and DC Broad had been working on a series of robberies from 1997, six in all, of small corner shops and off-licences in and around Chippenham. The last one had resulted in life-changing injuries for the twenty-year-old lad behind the counter, Gavin Hinch. He'd been hit so hard over the head with a cricket bat it had almost killed him; it had taken months for him to start walking and talking again. Swabs of the perp's saliva, flecks that had landed on the counter as he'd shouted his instructions, had been retained, but the technology at the time hadn't been able to raise a DNA profile. They had his profile now, but it hadn't turned up any matches on the database.

Broad's disappointment was almost palpable. She wanted results. She wanted some wins, a clean-up rate – something to show for her time. Lockyer wondered how urgently she wished to be moved off cold cases; she was careful not to show it. They'd spent Thursday and Friday looking for any other avenues they could pursue, and for any other robberies with the same *modus operandi*, but it was time to knock it on the head. Lockyer winced at his own inadvertent tasteless pun. The perp's profile would stay on the database, and if he was ever careless enough to leave his DNA at another crime scene, they'd have him. It was frustrating, but it was time to move on.

Broad came in with two steaming mugs, hers coffee, his tea, the colour of peat. She looked fresh, her blue eyes clear. Her fair, curly hair was scraped back in a way Lockyer didn't think flattered her round face, but there was no Monday-morning sluggishness with her, not ever. Normally she made him feel a hundred years old, but at least he'd slept better the night before. At ten in the evening he'd put on a podcast – an episode of *Making Sense* – and set to work sanding decades of dark brown varnish from the banisters of his staircase: fiddly, exhausting work that made his hands and shoulders cramp, after which he'd fallen into bed at one in the morning, and straight to sleep. He'd left Eastwood Park off-balance, but now he felt steadier. He could think of several significant reasons – and one in particular – not to look at Hedy's case again, but he wasn't sure he could let it go.

He and DC Broad shared a small office in a high corner of the building: two desks, two computers, two phones, a whiteboard they never used, and not a lot else. Green synthetic carpet; desks with metal legs and pale wooden tops. Broad's was in the corner, side-on to Lockyer's and facing the wall, while his faced the room. Her desk was spotless, immaculately tidy, and had a few photos tacked up here and there: Broad and a friend, muddy and flushed, holding up the medals around their necks; her Jack Russell, Merry, on a beach somewhere, tongue curling out; her parents and brother, heads together, pint glasses in their hands, laughing.

There wasn't one of her boyfriend, Pete. When Lockyer had asked about that, Broad had flushed pink, and told him that Pete didn't like to be photographed. She also had an African violet that never seemed to flower. Probably because of the weak, flat overhead lights. Lockyer's desk was a mess, and he had no photos. No personal items at all. Broad's sometimes made him notice the gaps in his own life. The absence of other living things.

She swivelled her chair to face him, cupping her mug to warm her hands. 'So, what's next, Guv?'

She blew on her coffee and sipped it, and he could tell she wanted to know about Friday's phone call. The scrap of paper on which he'd written *HMP E Park* was still on his desk, and she was bound to have seen it. That was just how she was: she saw things without needing or meaning to snoop. He smiled at her briefly.

'Well. Something's come up, but ...' He made a non-committal face.

'Some old perp, wanting you to look at their case again?' she guessed.

Lockyer nodded, though *some old perp* didn't sound like Hedy Lambert. 'It was one of my first cases as a DI, and I was on call so I was first out to it as well. The body was found in the early morning. A murder at a house in Stoke Lavington. The victim's name was Michael Brown, known as Mickey. He was a Traveller, from a group that had pitched up nearby. But for the first few days we thought it was Harry Ferris, the son of the house's owner, Roland Ferris, emeritus professor of medieval history.'

'What does that mean – "emeritus"?'

'It means he used to be a professor at a university – Oxford, I think – and he got to keep the title when he retired. It's a mark of distinction.'

'Why did you think the victim was his son?'

'Because Professor Ferris insisted he was.'

Lockyer outlined the case for Broad, as he remembered it. Hedy Lambert, Roland Ferris's live-in cook and housekeeper, had found the body when she took a breakfast tray out to him, as had become their routine. The victim, thought to be Harry Ferris, had been sleeping in the barn for around six weeks by then, and, at Roland's insistence, she'd taken him meals three times a day. He'd been stabbed through the chest with a large kitchen knife, which Hedy remembered using to chop vegetables the previous evening. She remembered rinsing the knife and leaving it on the draining board. The back door of the house was locked when she arrived for work – she remembered unlocking it, as usual. There was no sign of forced entry. So the killer had been someone with access to the house – or someone from inside the house – who'd been able to take the knife then re-lock the door.

The only fingerprints on the knife were Hedy's, but she regularly used it for kitchen work. There were no useful forensics inside the house – no signs of anyone having cleaned up in any of the sinks, no hastily hidden bloodied clothes or shoes, no mysterious footprints. Just Hedy, covered with blood. She said it had still been quite dark in the barn, so she hadn't seen the body properly at first. She'd slipped in the pooled blood and fallen to her knees. And she'd touched him, to see if she could find a pulse.

The only forensics on the body came from Hedy: her DNA from a couple of hairs, and fibres from a jumper she owned, enough to suggest close physical contact, though she wasn't wearing the jumper when Lockyer first found her. The only footprints were from the rubber galoshes that lived by the back door, which she slipped on to go to the bins or the compost heap. She'd put them on to go to the barn, and had been wearing them when she'd walked through the dead man's blood.

'Sounds to me like the right person went to jail, Guv,' Broad said carefully.

'Possibly.' Lockyer heard how that sounded. 'Probably, yes.'

'But not definitely?'

'The blood on her shoes and clothes *could* have got there the way she described – finding him and slipping in it, checking for a pulse. Panicking a bit.'

'What about spray from the actual stab wound?'

'Pathologist said there wouldn't necessarily have been any. The wound was a single stab, delivered with a lot of force. By chance it missed his ribs and went right through him – he wasn't a big man. It severed a major vein rather than an artery, so he bled to death quickly but the blood went out through the exit wound and pooled, rather than spraying from the entry wound.'

'Christ. How big was the knife?'

'Big. A wooden-handled cook's knife with a nine-inch blade.'

'Was she a big woman? Strong enough to overpower him, and deliver a blow like that?'

Lockyer pictured Hedy's slender arms and tense shoulders; her delicate, bony hands. 'There was no sign of a struggle.' He shook his head. 'It looked like he was asleep when it happened.'

'Right. So not self-defence, then,' Broad said. She cocked her head, giving Lockyer a shrewd look. 'You remember a lot about the case, Guv.'

'It was my first on-call murder. The scene made an impression.' Finding Hedy standing there, bloodied, shaking. Grey eyes locked on his but not focusing, hardly seeing him. 'Then, after we'd brought Hedy Lambert in, she would only talk to me. Refused to say a word to anyone else. So I did all her interviews, and . . . ended up taking more of a hands-on role in the investigation than I might have otherwise.'

'How come she'd only talk to you, Guv?'

'No idea.'

He did know, or thought he did. It made him uncomfortable. At the time, it had made him chase down her guilt even more keenly. He'd been younger then, angrier. More zealous.

'It always seems manipulative to me, whenever a suspect

starts making demands like that,' Broad said. 'Doesn't smack of innocence, does it? Trying to call the shots.'

'No. The SIO said exactly the same thing. She wasn't at all happy about it, but we didn't have much choice, because Lambert had hardly said a word since we arrested her, and we needed her to talk. But if she thought it'd help get her off, it backfired. My interviews helped put her away.'

'So you think maybe she thought she could play you, Guv?'

'Maybe.'

'So why's she popped up again now? This Heidi woman?'

'Hedy. She always protested her innocence.'

'That's not that unusual, though, is it?'

'No . . . It all came down to motive. We had the forensics on her, of course, but to make it watertight we had to come up with her motive.'

'And that's what you did? In the interviews?'

'That's what I did,' Lockyer said. 'We had to figure out why Roland Ferris insisted the dead man was his son, Harry. They'd been estranged, not seen each other in fifteen years. And we had to work out who in that house knew it wasn't Harry, and who believed it *was*.'

'And which was she?'

'Hedy? She said she knew the victim wasn't Harry. But we only had her word for that. The only person who could've confirmed or denied it was the dead man.'

'So . . . why has she popped back up now?'

'Apparently Harry Ferris has come home. For real this time.' Lockyer swigged his tea, and turned to look out of the window. The sky was flat with solid white clouds; a breeze tugged at the police flag. Doubt took hold of him. He didn't trust his own motives for reconsidering the case. He suspected it would lead only to grief of one kind or another.

Broad interrupted his thoughts. 'You mean, he's back home for the first time since before all this happened? Since . . .'

'1990. Yep. According to Hedy's friend Cass, who still works in the village shop.'

'Well, you must want to talk to him.'

Lockyer glanced at Broad, surprised.

'I mean,' she went on, 'I can see that it might not actually be *that* relevant to Lambert's conviction, but for the sake of completeness, might it not be useful to know what went on there? Did you ever get to the bottom of why Professor Ferris insisted the dead bloke was his son? Harry?'

'Not entirely.'

'And why on earth was the victim sleeping out in the barn?'

'I can't remember. But I'm not sure what's to be gained by talking to them again.'

'Well, it couldn't hurt, could it?' Broad suggested. 'I could pull up the file and look through it while you're out. Unless you want me to go with you?'

'No. I've no real reason to pay them a call. Best keep it low key.'

The police division that operated out of the Melksham, Devizes and Bradford-on-Avon stations covered a huge area of Wiltshire, from the A303 in the south to Swindon in the north-east, but it took Lockyer only a quarter of an hour to drive the six miles to Stoke Lavington. The village was a mile off the main road to his parents' farm, but down a small lane that led to the dead end of MoD land, so he hadn't been back through the village once in the fourteen years since they'd closed the case. He felt an odd little jolt in his bones when the first houses came into view.

It hadn't changed – or, rather, the only changes were those made by the season. It'd had the vivid freshness of early summer when he was last there. Flowers in every front bed and hanging basket, and leaves on the trees so brightly new and green they'd hardly looked real. Now there were puddles and churned mud at the sides of the lane, the trees were skeletal, and the houses looked colourless and damp. They were a mixed bag, so typical of the villages of north and west Wiltshire – there was brick and stone and flint, thatch and tiles and slate, some extremely pretty cottages, hundred of years old, and some very ugly post-war builds. Water dripped from eaves and branches. There was nobody about but for a single elderly man, walking a grubby Westie.

Lockyer parked his car – an old four-wheel drive Volvo – in the lane opposite Longacres, and stared.

Roland Ferris's house was the biggest in the village, low, rambling, several hundred years old. The kind that tourists stopped to photograph. Silvered wooden beams ran through its faded brick walls; there was a sundial above the front door, and, to the left-hand side, a gateway leading to a large yard surrounded by barns and stables. By the time of the murder they'd housed classic cars rather than horses. Ferris had collected and restored them as a hobby, and the yard had been pristine, the gravel weed-free and raked smooth. Now it was mottled with moss and shrivelled winter dandelions, rutted and potholed around the gate. The jasmine around the front door had gone, replaced by a low thicket of clematis that was refusing to climb a trellis. Even from across the road he could see that the windowsills were peeling. But other than looking less cared for, the house was unchanged. Smoke was rising from one of the chimneys. Lockyer got out of the car.

The woman who answered his knock was in her late sixties, thin, and extremely well groomed. Her hair was artfully dyed to make it still look ash blonde, but somehow naturally so. He recognized her at once.

'Mrs Godwin . . .'

If he'd expected her to remember him, he was disappointed. Roland Ferris's sister looked him over in a cool, dismissive fashion. 'Yes? We don't buy at the doorstep.' She held the edge of the door tightly, as though preparing to close it, with force if necessary.

Lockyer showed his warrant card. 'Detective Inspector Lockyer. I wondered if I might be able speak to your brother, Professor Ferris?'

'Lockyer . . . Don't tell me you're *that* Lockyer? The one who was here for that ridiculous business with the dead hobo all those years ago?'

'Yes, that's right.' Lockyer didn't smile. He remembered Serena Godwin's sharp tongue, her unfettered opinions. Her *froideur*, poorly masked by cast-iron manners and plummy vowels.

'Still a DI, are you? Oughtn't you to have been promoted by now?'

'May I come in?'

'Is this an official visit? Goodness, don't tell me something else has happened?'

'I'd just like a brief chat with your brother, Mrs Godwin. If he's at home.'

With a sigh through her nose, Serena stood back to admit him. 'You'd better come in while I see if he's awake,' she said. 'He is actually dying this time, I do believe.'

She left him standing in the hallway and went upstairs. Lockyer looked along the corridor that ran lengthways through the house to either side of the central staircase. Framed watercolours and photographs; dark, polished antique furniture; thick carpets and curtains in muted shades. It was the kind of traditional decor that had never been either fully in or fully out of fashion. Classic, perhaps, but all a bit faded and mothy-looking now.

He wandered along the corridor, stopping to look at a montage of photos with the sun-bleached tones of the 1980s. They were mostly of classic cars, gloriously shiny and pristine, with Roland Ferris at the wheel or standing to one side, smiling, a proud hand on a bonnet or an open door. In one, a blonde woman in a blue and white striped dress, her sunglasses holding her hair back on top of her head, was leaning her elbow on a car's roof and laughing at the camera. Lockyer assumed she must be Ferris's wife, long dead before he or Hedy ever came to Longacres. He didn't recognize the car – he was no expert. The emblem on the front was a tiny winged female figure, as far as he could make out. Rolls-Royce, perhaps. The car's sides were a deep, rich red, the roof and wheel arches black. Behind it, out of focus, more cars sat in a neat row in the stables.

Lockyer was about to move on when he noticed something he'd missed – in the driver's seat of the red car, only half lit by the sun. A mop of dark hair, a pair of squinting eyes, peering out, and small hands gripping the steering wheel, all belonging to a boy of around eleven or twelve years of age – Harry Ferris.

He moved on to a sketch of boats in a Cornish harbour, then further, towards the end of the corridor, where the kitchen, which had been Hedy's domain, sat in a large, vaulted extension on the back of the house, at its east end, nearest the barns. She had lived in a converted flat above one of the coach houses. Those had been the boundaries of her world at the time: her flat, the short walk across the gravel to the house, cleaning, cooking. The only time she'd gone out was to the village shop and post office. It was a shrunken, stunted existence that had taken Lockyer some time to understand.

Serena called down from upstairs: 'You may come up, Inspector. My brother will see you now.'

Some people spoke to other people, by default, as though they were staff, and Serena Godwin was one of them. Lockyer remembered almost coming to like Roland Ferris, though.

The professor was lying on a single bed that had been

moved into a corner of his study. He was propped up on cushions but fully dressed, a mustard-coloured waistcoat over a rumpled shirt, and thick cord trousers, baggy at the knees. The bed had been fitted with a grab rail and a wedge-shaped electric lift at the head end, to help him sit up and lie down. Lockyer's glance took in a commode, a walking frame, a reaching aid. The clinical bits and pieces that intruded into a home when somebody grew elderly and frail. There was a faint smell of bodies, and clothes left too long without washing. Roland looked thin and depleted, and far older than his seventy-four years. The whites of his eyes were yellow, and he'd lost all his hair.

Serena didn't stay, and she didn't offer Lockyer a drink.

'Inspector Lockyer. You'll forgive me if I don't get up, I'm dying, you see . . .' The professor paused to cough. 'You remember Paul Rifkin, my *general factotum*?'

Another man, who'd been sitting in one of the two chairs at Roland's enormous desk, stood up and held out his hand. He was short but thickset, with close-cropped salt-and-pepper hair. Lockyer was surprised to recognize him. 'Yes, I do. Hello again.' Lockyer shook Paul's surprisingly small hand, and remembered not liking him at all. His obsequiousness; the showy, self-conscious way in which he did whatever he was told. As though there was something unique and noble in his subservience. He'd been in the army, fought in the Falklands as a teenager, and always managed to drop some reference to it into his conversation. He was that type. 'I'm surprised to find—' Lockyer cut himself off.

'Surprised to find me still here?' Paul finished for him,

smiling too widely. He spoke with a faint Geordie accent. 'Well, I suppose I'm surprised too – some days, in any case! No, I'm only joking. I could hardly desert you now, in your hour of need, could I, Professor?'

'You can bugger off for all I care,' Roland muttered. Paul laughed, but Roland interrupted him. 'And I'm not too ill to fire you if you don't stop talking to me in that *ridiculous* manner. I am not a child!'

'Now then, don't upset yourself. Of course you're not a child.'

'Never get old, Inspector,' Roland said. 'People treat you like an idiot. There's not a damn thing wrong with my mind; it's only my body that's giving up the ghost. The clock is truly ticking down, this time. Did my sister tell you?'

'She did. I'm sorry to hear it, Professor Ferris.'

Roland waved one hand. 'Don't be. I've had so many false starts over the years, I'm actually rather looking forward to finishing the race. If I'm *compos mentis* today it's only because I've just had a blood transfusion. Most of the time I'm a waste of space. But it has brought my son back to me after all these years, this dying business.' Roland's eyes shone. 'So how could I not welcome it?'

'I'd heard that too,' Lockyer admitted.

'Of course you had,' the professor said. 'Why else would you be here? The more interesting question, to my mind, is how you came to hear the news. Paul, fetch us some coffee, will you? And some of those *Pepparkakor* biscuits.'

Once Paul had left the room Roland said, 'That's the other good thing about dying: nobody nags at you about what not to eat. Hardly matters any more, does it?' He shuffled himself a little higher in the bed, and lifted his chin towards Lockyer. 'So tell me, Inspector, how is dear Hedy?'

'Hedy?' Lockyer echoed, surprised.

'I can only assume she somehow let you know Harry's come back. I'm sure the whole village is chattering about it, but I can't think of anybody else who would think to let the *police* know.'

'She asked me to visit her, yes, and told me,' Lockyer confessed.

Roland nodded sadly. 'And?'

'And what?'

'And how is she?'

'All right, I suppose.' Lockyer shifted awkwardly. The scars on her arms, and her wrists. The way she'd chewed at her thumb. The stifled desperation. Like an animal about ready to gnaw off a limb to get free. 'Unhappy,' he said, more honestly. 'Desperate to be out. To reclaim some sort of a life.'

Roland sighed, sinking back. 'Poor, poor Hedy. She was so fragile when she came here – and she'd never talk about why. About what had happened. But I could tell she needed a place to recuperate. I always thought she'd eventually move on to a far better situation, get her independence back. Instead she went the other way.'

'You were fond of her?'

'Still am.' Roland clasped his hands over his middle, eyes distant. 'Like some gangly colt, she was. Not an ounce of elegance about her, but something *better* than elegance, somehow. Something more honest than elegance. We became close. I write to her, you know. Not that frequently, these days, but I still do. I almost wrote to tell her about Harry coming home, but then I changed my mind. Thought it'd stir up the whole sorry business for her. I would have quite liked to see her before the end.'

'Does she ever write back?' Lockyer asked.

'No. No, not once,' Roland said sadly. 'If you see her again, give her my love.'

Lockyer was struck by the word *love*. 'Professor Ferris, do you believe Hedy was guilty of the murder of Michael Brown?'

For a long moment, Roland stared down at his clasped hands and didn't reply. Lockyer glanced around the room – the huge study, which had taken over one of the biggest bedrooms in the house. The walls were lined with wooden shelves, heaving with books and papers. There were piles of books and manuscripts on the carpet as well, concentrated around the vast desk with its two leather captain's chairs, its out-dated computer, its library lamp, odd paperweights and a leather tray of coins and keys and gubbins.

At the time of the murder, in 2005, Roland Ferris had been one of the country's pre-eminent medieval historians, newly retired from Jesus College, Oxford, and quite well known in certain circles. He'd appeared on *In Our Time* with Melvyn Bragg on Radio 4, talking about the social and legal reforms of King Æthelstan after his coronation in AD 925. Several of the books on the shelves had been written by Ferris himself. Lockyer didn't know if historians ever really retired, but given that Roland Ferris seemed to have chosen to die in his study, he supposed the answer was no.

'Well,' Roland said at last, 'your lot ascertained that she was guilty, did they not? Why do you ask?'

'No reason.' Lockyer checked himself. 'Professor Ferris, this isn't really an official visit, but when I heard about your son, I just wanted to—'

'You wanted to ask the same question everyone else has been asking, I assume. Where has he been?'

'Well, yes, among others.'

'These are private matters, Inspector.'

'I know, Professor. But there was so much confusion about who'd actually died out there in the barn, fourteen years ago, before we finally identified Michael Brown. I suppose any clarification of the matter would be . . . would be appreciated.'

'Pah! You're no better than the rest of the curtain-twitchers, Inspector, not one whit better!'

There was a soft knock at the door, and Paul Rifkin came in with a tray balanced on one arm. Coffee cups rattling in their saucers, and the cinnamon biscuits Roland had requested sliding about a plate on a doily. Lockyer was grateful for the interruption: he wasn't sure how to proceed. Paul poured the coffee into the tiny cups and attempted to pass one to Ferris, but the old man batted it away. 'Guests first,' he snapped. Paul's tight-lipped smile didn't shrink as he turned to offer the cup to Lockyer instead, but Lockyer caught the subtle hardening of his eyes.

Lockyer sipped the coffee, even though he didn't really like it.

Roland ate two of the biscuits in quick succession, dusting the crumbs from his waistcoat onto the carpet. 'Well, I suppose whatever Harry is willing to tell you is up to him, Inspector,' he concluded. 'Paul, would you please ask my son to join us? The inspector is all agog to meet him.'

They waited, listening to sounds from elsewhere in the house. Then the study door opened, and for a second it was like seeing a dead man resurrected. Lockyer had to remind himself that the lithe, naked body he'd seen on the pathologist's table fourteen years before, with its scattering of black chest hair stark against the milk-white skin, its many small scars – some of which looked like cigarette burns – and the single neat stab wound below the left nipple, hadn't been Harry. It was never him, even though at the time of the post-mortem they'd all still thought it was.

Harry Ferris came into the room wearing an expression that bordered on hostility. He glanced around from beneath glowering brows, and there were knots at the corners of his jaw. But Lockyer could see at once how a desperate father, having not seen this man in years, might manage to convince himself that Mickey Brown, the murder victim, had been one and the same person. Same height and slender build; same pale skin and inky hair; same dark brown eyes, sharp nose and angular chin.

Harry was wearing skinny jeans with a shirt tucked in; his shoes and watch looked expensive. He left the door open behind him, and stood with his feet braced against the floor, arms crossed, radiating tension.

'What do you want?' he said to Lockyer, without waiting to be introduced.

'Mr Ferris, it's nice to meet you,' Lockyer said evenly. 'After all this time.'

'Harry, my boy, the man merely wanted to set eyes on you. What with all that business I told you about fourteen years ago . . .'

There was little warmth in the look Harry shot his father, and he certainly wasn't placated. 'I'm sure it was all very exciting,' he said, 'but none of it had anything to do with me.'

'It looks as though you've done well for yourself,' Lockyer said, trying to decipher Harry's reaction to him. He was used to being unwelcome, but this was something more.

'That's not a crime, is it? Why shouldn't I have done well for myself? I moved away from home and built a decent career somewhere else. I fail to see what's so very remarkable about that.' His nostrils flared, and he clenched his hands into fists by his armpits.

'I suppose it's because it was all kept so secret from your family,' Lockyer said. 'And because a man was murdered, possibly because the killer thought that man was you.'

An uneasy silence settled over the room. Lockyer saw the way Roland looked down at his clasped hands again, meeting no one's eye, and the way Harry stared out of the window with those knots in his jaw working, and the way Paul Rifkin's gaze flicked back and forth between the pair of them, as if waiting for something.

Lockyer waited a beat longer before he spoke again. 'Can

either of you think of a reason why somebody might have wanted to kill you, Mr Ferris?'

Harry Ferris kept his hard gaze on the window as he answered: 'Don't be ridiculous.' Then he turned, and for the briefest moment his eyes met Paul Rifkin's. 'Of course not. Besides, anyone who knew me well enough to want to kill me would have realized straight away that it wasn't me, dossing out in the barn. Wouldn't they?'

'I suppose that seems likely.'

'Anyway, we know who did it, and presumably you managed to find out why, before she went to prison? Isn't it usually down to money? Or jealousy?'

'Hedy Lambert killed Michael Brown for reasons of her own,' Roland said. 'She's a troubled soul.'

'Even more troubled now, after fourteen years in jail,' Lockyer said.

'Why are you here, Inspector?' Harry turned his angry eyes on Lockyer. 'You want to know where I've been? Well, the answer is London. Big shock. And why I've come back? Because my father's dying, and it's time we worked through a few things. As for why I went, that's none of your damn business.'

'I understand that, Mr Ferris, but it may well be pertinent to—'

'It isn't,' Harry snapped.

'Caesar has spoken, I fear, Inspector.' Roland sounded more amused than apologetic.

'Very well. Nice to see you again, Professor. Thank you for the coffee.'

Paul Rifkin saw Lockyer out, and spoke to him quietly at the front door. 'Come back to kiss and make up, and make sure he gets his inheritance, I'd say,' he said, in a nastier tone than his smile suggested. 'Big-shot city lawyer or not, there's still a lot of money to be had here.'

'Do you know why he left in the first place?' Lockyer asked, since Paul clearly had opinions about it all.

He shook his head. 'Before my time, I'm afraid. Seems to me like something bigger than a normal teenage strop, though. I think he blamed his father for his mother's death.'

'Oh? And *could* Professor Ferris have been responsible?'

'Again, before my time. All I know is that she killed herself, so perhaps Harry thought it was because of something the professor had done. But I don't know.'

'Can you tell me her name?'

'It was Helen.'

Lockyer frowned. Something was bothering him.

'Just then, Harry said he'd come back because his father's dying. But how did he know that, if they've had no contact all this time?'

Paul grinned. 'Exactly, Inspector. Turns out the cousin knew where he was all along – Serena's son, Miles. They got close when Harry went to live there, after he got kicked out of school. They kept in touch the whole time.'

'And Miles never told Professor Ferris his son was alive and well? Not even to put his mind at ease?'

'Nope. Says Harry made him promise not to, but if you ask me he's just a spiteful little sh— so-and-so,' Paul checked himself. 'One of those posh blokes who think it's all a game. A stint in the army would sort him out.'

He kept smiling, and Lockyer could see the cunning in his eyes – the calculation behind that servile façade. 'A pleasure to see you again, Inspector,' Paul said, as he shut the door.

3

The post office and shop was a short walk from Longacres, back into the centre of the village, where there was a triangle of choppy grass with a small war memorial, and a bus shelter to one side. The bell above the door clanged tunelessly as Lockyer opened it. Inside, hard plastic floor tiles in a chequerboard design were worn through to the concrete by the door and at the till, and metal shelves were stacked with everyday essentials. There was a smell of limp vegetables, and a cramped post-office counter guarded by a large, unkempt woman who kept the rows of cheap wine and spirits safely out of reach behind her.

'Hello. I was hoping to have a word with Cass Baker,' Lockyer said.

'Was you now?' She smirked. 'On her break, in't she?' She waddled stiffly to a door in the back wall. 'Cassie! Tall dark stranger asking for you, love – best get yer backside down 'ere!'

'Thank you.'

A thumping of footsteps on stairs and Cass appeared,

somewhere in her thirties and wearing a blue tabard. She had short, badly dyed blonde hair, a pretty face with too much heavy eye make-up, and a gold ring in her nose. She looked Lockyer up and down with swift appraisal, hands on her hips. 'You the copper?'

'Yes. That's right.' Lockyer found himself on the back foot.

Cass nodded. 'Hedy said you might come to have a word. She wasn't sure though – said she'd have to convince you. So I guess she did.'

'Well, I—'

'Mind if I smoke while we talk?' Cass didn't wait for a reply, grabbing her cigarettes from the counter and heading out the front.

Lockyer waited while she lit up, refusing when she offered him one.

'Best we talk out here. Maureen's a nightmare for spreading stuff around, almost none of it right. By the end of today half the village will have heard that we're sleeping together, and I'm your informant now because you got me off a drugs charge, or something like that.' She rolled her eyes.

'Right. Well, Hedy told me you were still in touch, and that you'd let her know Harry Ferris was back. Can I ask how you found out about it yourself?'

'One of Roland's carers, Debbie,' Cass said. 'Not the brightest. She always comes in here for chocolate and a Coke after she's been in to see him in the morning, and she was there the day Harry showed up. Witnessed the whole big reunion scene, and was only too keen to tell someone about it. It was Maureen she told, so I expect they'd heard about it in Swindon by lunchtime.'

Lockyer wanted to hear about that scene: what Harry and Roland had first said to each other after nearly thirty years, how they had reacted to one another. He took out his notebook. 'What's Debbie's surname?'

'Sorry.' Cass shrugged. 'Don't know. That dodgy butler of Roland's would probably be able to tell you. Or the hospital. So, are you reopening the case? Is Hedy going to get out?'

'No. The case is closed,' Lockyer said carefully.

Cass stared at him. 'So what you doing here, then?'

'Just ... tying up loose ends. Regarding Harry Ferris's disappearance.'

'So, what? You still think Hedy killed that other bloke?'

'You don't?'

'Course not. I *know* her. Poor cow. And, yeah, we were friends when she was living here, but it's not loyalty making me say it, it's *knowing* it.' Cass took a long drag and exhaled a plume of smoke into the chilly air. 'She isn't the killing type. And that nonsense they had in the papers, that she was after Roland's money when he died, that was grade-A bollocks. I never met anyone less interested in money in my life. And what would she spend it on, anyway? Never went shopping, never went out. She never even bought a lottery ticket or nothing.'

'She may have had a different motive.'

'Yeah, I know. The one you lot pinned on her, when you found out about that bastard Aaron. Her ex-boyfriend. I read that in the paper, when the trial was on. That was bollocks too.'

'How can you be so sure?'

'She just wasn't the killing type. Wasn't then and isn't now, and it doesn't say much for your detecting skills if you haven't figured that out. Besides, she loved the professor – God knows why, he's a grumpy old bastard, but she cared about him, anyway. Wouldn't have done anything to hurt him. Sure as hell wouldn't have killed the bloke he thought was his son, would she?'

'I don't know, Miss Baker.'

'Well, I do.'

'She'd been through a very traumatic time with Aaron Fletcher. She may well have had feelings she kept hidden – anger or vengeance. Or fear.'

'The only thing Hedy was scared of was never getting back on her feet. Never getting back to her *old self*, she told me once.' Cass shook her head. 'How was stabbing some bloke then waiting around to get arrested ever going to help her do that?'

'Not all decisions are rational, Miss Baker. And not all actions are the result of a conscious decision.'

'Well, you won't ever get me to believe she lost it enough to stab that guy. She had no reason to.'

Lockyer looked away across the village green as he thought about it, to a field gate where two wet ponies were standing, waiting patiently to be taken somewhere less muddy and cold. 'If you hear anything else you think might be relevant . . .'

Cass dropped her cigarette and stamped it out as she took his card. 'If you ever want background on Harry

Ferris – when he was a kid, I mean – you should talk to Maureen. She used to babysit him.'

'I'll remember that. Thank you.'

Lockyer drove slowly back to the station, turning the short visit to Stoke Lavington over in his mind. The years since Hedy's arrest seemed to have shrunk: he'd somehow imagined the protagonists of her story scattering when the case was closed; moving on, or even fading out of existence. It had suited him to put it all behind him, Hedy included. To try to. But Roland Ferris was still ensconced in his study, still dying, and his sister was staying again. His manservant was still serving, still doing a fair impression of a man not boiling with resentment inside. It had been claustrophobic in there, crowded with unsaid things.

And now Harry Ferris was back as well, in the house where he grew up. An unhappy home, it must have been, and he seemed to have grown into an unhappy man – unless it was simply being back there now that was affecting his attitude. Lockyer replayed the things that had struck him particularly, making sure he'd missed nothing, making sure he would forget nothing important. *Anyone who knew me well enough to want to kill me would have realized straight away that it wasn't me.* The cold looks that Harry Ferris had given his father, and Paul Rifkin. The cogs turning behind Rifkin's tight smile. *Hedy wasn't the killing type. She had no reason to.* None but the reasons Lockyer himself had dug out of her.

And the fact that Miles Godwin, Serena's son, Harry's cousin, had known Harry's whereabouts all along. Ever since he'd left home. All that time they'd wasted thinking that the body was Harry's, then scrambling to catch up when the fingerprints and DNA proved it wasn't ... And besides the murder, all those years of anguish for Roland Ferris that Miles could have alleviated with a word, yet hadn't. The six weeks that Mickey Brown stayed in the barn at Longacres, and Roland believed him to be Harry returned home, and Miles had said nothing. *One of those posh blokes who thinks it's all a game*, Paul Rifkin had called him. One thing was for certain: Lockyer wanted to talk to Miles Godwin.

As he crossed the car park at the station, lost in thought, a big, fair-haired man emerged and strode towards his car. Their eyes met and, for a hung moment, neither spoke or blinked.

'Steve,' Lockyer said, trying not to sound stiff.

'Farmer Giles,' the man replied, without humour.

Since joining the police, Lockyer had found he could take any amount of stick. He'd heard again the jibes and piss-taking he'd thought he'd left behind in the school play-ground. It was part of the job, and it was mostly done in fun. Jokes about his Wiltshire accent, his farming background, his quietness and loner-ish tendencies. But hearing it now, in Steve's scathing tone, was something else. The two men had been friends – work friends, at least – for years, until recently.

DI Steve Saunders was an extrovert, loud and ambitious. He hadn't been to university, he didn't have a degree; he'd made it to DI the long way, working steadily upwards from uniformed PC. Buying drinks for the right people, doing all the shitty, boring jobs his superiors didn't want to do. So he had nothing but contempt for officers who'd been fast-tracked, and Lockyer knew better than to dismiss that out of hand. There was a lot to be said for the experience that grafters like Saunders accumulated over the years.

Working together had been tricky to begin with, since their personalities were polar opposites. But slowly, gradually, Steve had come to respect Lockyer. Perhaps even to like him. So maybe that was why his animosity was so powerful now: Lockyer had let him down. However much Lockyer regretted that, he also knew there was nothing he could do about it.

In the aftermath of the case that had got Lockyer taken off the MCIT the year before, there'd been some who'd called for him to be officially disciplined. Demoted, even. Steve had called the loudest, and he'd almost succeeded. But no, Lockyer corrected himself. Like his mother had said of Hedy, it was what he'd done that had almost got him demoted, not Steve Saunders.

'How's life in the slow lane?' Steve said.

'Fine, thanks.'

'Glad to hear it. It seems to suit you. Suits the rest of us, too. Best you stay put, mate.'

Lockyer carried on walking. There was just no point in getting drawn into it.

Until that spring, the two of them had been on the same Major Crime Investigation Team, sharing duties with the Avon and Somerset and Gloucester forces, part of the joint task force initiative that had come about thanks to repeated budget cuts. They'd rubbed along, made a pretty good team. Then they were called out to an arson, a suspected insurance job at a pub called the Queen's Head, and Lockyer had immediately informed the SIO that he knew the family involved. He'd been taken off the case at once.

But Steve had asked for his help anyway *because* Lockyer knew the family involved, and had been to the Queen's Head more times than he could count. And Lockyer had helped. But he hadn't helped the investigation: he'd helped the old friend who was a suspect in the case. He'd had a clear choice; he'd acted of his own free will. When the moment came, he chose to do what seemed fair and right, rather than what was required of him by the law. He'd shocked himself. It had run contrary to everything he believed about policing and the law, and everything he'd been taught. He'd thought himself incorruptible.

Afterwards, Lockyer was neatly sidelined into Major Crime Review, with DC Broad to help him, and a detective superintendent above him reviewing current major investigations that weren't progressing. It really could have been a lot worse.

He got himself a tea, and a coffee for Broad, as he went back up to the office. Broad was hunched over her desk, a thick case file in front of her. She looked up with a smile as he came in.

'Thanks, Guv,' she said, taking the coffee. 'How did it go? Anything interesting?'

'Yes, and no.' Lockyer sat down. 'How far have you got through that file?'

'Mostly the highlights so far, but . . .' She hesitated. 'It does seem like it was a bit of a self-solver. Like Hedy Lambert was the first, last and best suspect.'

'She was. We did pursue other avenues for a while, but it was the forensics.'

Broad nodded. 'The knife was the only real . . . smoking gun, wasn't it? Like you said before, a lot of it *could* be explained the way she told it, apart from the knife. There being no other prints on it but hers, and her prints being . . .' she leafed back a few pages to find the report '. . . "faint in places but undisturbed". So it didn't look like anybody, even wearing gloves, had handled it after she had. I mean, that's pretty damning, isn't it?'

'Yes.' Lockyer turned his chair to stare out of the window. The horizon had always helped him think, even if, from the office, it was built up and not very far away. He looked at the sky through the uppermost twigs of a naked ash tree. 'Did you notice who was SIO of the original investigation, back in 2005?'

'Yes. DCI Considine.'

She was now Detective Superintendent Christine Considine, and she was still Lockyer's boss. 'Let's keep this to ourselves, as much as we can. For now. Not that anyone's very interested in our caseload.'

'So we're going to look into it again?' Broad sounded keen. This was exactly what she wanted to work on – a murder, a miscarriage of justice. Something big.

Lockyer didn't answer at once, caught by the same self-doubt from fourteen years before: doubt in his own ability to make the right call. He didn't usually feel any such thing. *Are you afraid to be wrong?* Hedy had asked him. It wasn't that, exactly. More that he suspected he *was* wrong. Wrong about something. And if there had been a miscarriage of justice, he had pushed it over the finish line. The thought turned him cold.

He took a slow breath, shaking his head. 'We need more to go on. Some forensics – it can't all just come down to a hunch. Most of the same players are still there – it's weird. Back in 'oh-five Miles Godwin was there as well, and I definitely want to talk to him. And Professor Ferris had a research student at the time . . . I can't remember her name. But the big three were all there today. Ferris, Serena and the dodgy butler.'

'There's a dodgy butler? Well, case solved, Guv,' Broad said. 'He's bound to have done it.'

Lockyer smiled. 'Serena's still playing lady of the manor, Roland's still dying. It was strange, going back there. And there's *something* not right . . .'

'What's he dying of?'

'I can't remember exactly – one of the blood cancers. It's come and gone over the years, I guess. I didn't like to ask.'

Broad leafed back through the file again. 'Chronic lymphocytic leukaemia,' she said. 'Sounds nasty.'

Lockyer nodded. 'There was no break-in. No signs of anyone jimmying any of the locks. Whoever got the knife from the kitchen and went out to the barn had keys, or was inside the house already and unlocked the back door using the key that hung next to it. Whoever it was knew where to find Mickey Brown. It was someone in that house, I'm sure of it, so let's— No,' Lockyer interrupted himself. 'No. We start with the knife. Let's get it re-examined. What do "faint" prints mean, anyway? Surely a woman gripping a knife hard enough to drive it right through a man's chest would leave pretty definite prints. I want a second opinion. If there's absolutely no chance whatsoever that anybody else touched the knife after Hedy did, then we can stop right there.'

'It'll be hard to keep that quiet,' Broad said.

'You're right.' Lockyer sank inside. 'Fine. I'll talk to Considine. I'd have had to anyway, sooner or later.' He took a long breath. 'Might as well be sooner.'

'Have to be tomorrow, Guv – she's at that second PM over in Flax Bourton the rest of today.'

'Right – of course.'

'What do you want me on, Guv?'

'Keep reading through. See if you spot anything, anything at all, that doesn't sit right with you. Witness statements. Crime-scene notes. Anything that might have been missed. And see if you can find any references to, or details about, Roland's wife, Helen. She killed herself – the dodgy butler reckons that's why Harry hates his father and left. I'd like to know when it happened and, if possible, why.'

'I'll get on to the coroner's officer.'

Broad was already turning back to her desk, her attention on the matter in hand. She reached for her coffee cup without looking up, as if she had radar. Lockyer felt lucky she'd been assigned to him. She might not have wanted to be there, but she always gave a hundred per cent, and he was never in any doubt that if he asked her to keep something quiet, quiet would be how she kept it.

Lockyer took the transcripts of some of the early interviews from the 2005 investigation home with him. He stopped at the Co-op on the way and bought bread, milk, a bag of carrots that had turned bendy, and a box of Tunnock's tea cakes. It was November, and the sun set earlier every day. His home, one of a pair of Victorian brick cottages, sat along a muddy track outside the village of Orcheston. The small rear gardens backed onto a copse of beech and oak, which was what had sold the place to Lockyer. He'd viewed it on an unsettled summer's day, and the roar of the wind through those trees had been mesmerizing. He'd made an offer on the spot, even though the place hadn't been modernized since the 1940s. The loo had still been in a hut at the end of the slippery garden path. Dank, spidery, very dark.

Lockyer had lived in a borrowed caravan for the first six months, while he gradually plumbed a bathroom into the smallest bedroom upstairs, and updated the kitchen from the existing few grubby old cupboards and battered cooker, which shorted out the electrics if he tried to use it, to something he could actually cook meals in. Mrs Musprat, who lived next door, grumbled all the while about the noise, and that the cottage had been good enough for Bill Hickson, the previous occupant, who'd lived there since the war. Lockyer guessed they'd been friends, and that Mrs Musprat missed him. She'd been the one who'd found Bill's body during a spell of freezing winter weather. His little electric heater – which he'd taken around with him, room to room – had packed up. A sad, lonely death that gave Lockyer a kick in the gut whenever he thought about it.

Lockyer had the place liveable and weatherproof now, but there was still a lot to do. Evidence of his labours lay scattered around outside: a workbench with sawdust all around it, a skip that needed emptying, a pallet of reclaimed bricks he'd found at a salvage yard – a perfect match for the cottage's walls. All his comings and goings had made the driveway even muddier and more rutted, which was another thing Mrs Musprat complained about, not that she ever went out or owned a car. She was ninety if she was a day. Once a week she hauled her ancient tartan shopping trolley onto the bus to the next village, which had the small Co-op she depended on for all her groceries. He was struck now by the similarity between the way she lived and the way Hedy Lambert had been living before her arrest. Separate from the bustling majority of the population.

As he pulled up outside, Lockyer noticed that Mrs Musprat's front door was ajar. It was cold, and drizzle sifted through the beams of his headlights, vanishing when he switched off and got out.

'Mrs Musprat? Are you in?' he called. Hearing nothing, he pushed the door open further, and stepped inside. 'Mrs Musprat?' The place was floor to ceiling with stuff. Furniture lined the walls: shelves and corner cabinets and dressers, each piece groaning with lamps and boxes and ornaments, and all of it covered with dust. The corridor was a narrow strip of bare rug, picking a pathway through it all. Mrs Musprat had run an antiques and curios shop in Devizes, once upon a time. It looked as though she'd brought all of the unsold stock home with her when it closed.

'What do you want?' she said, appearing at the top of the stairs. 'What are you doing, coming in, putting mud on the carpet? Be off with you!'

'I'm on the mat, Mrs Musprat,' Lockyer pointed out. 'Your door was open. I was just checking you were all right.'

'Checking I'm all right? Ha! Checking I've not dropped dead, like poor old Bill, I know.' She thumped down to him, shooing him out, surprisingly quick on her feet. She was a scrawny wire of a thing, her ankles perhaps half the circumference of Lockyer's wrists. 'Can't wait to get rid of me and have my cottage too, I know.'

'Not the case. I've brought you some tea cakes. And carrots for Desiree.' He held out the offerings, which Mrs Musprat took with a frown. Desiree was her goat, kept tethered in the back garden. Mrs Musprat occasionally presented Lockyer with homemade cheese, which he didn't dare to eat. He hadn't had a lifetime to build up the right immunities, like Mrs Musprat had.

'You don't need to be buying me things! What are you after, eh?' she muttered.

'Just thought you might like them. They were in the "last chance" bin. I didn't think they should go to waste.' He'd learnt that this was the only way Mrs Musprat could reconcile herself to a gift.

'Ah, well, right you are, I suppose.' She beetled away

towards the kitchen at a surprising rate, but paused by the door to the living room and went in.

'I'll be off, then, Mrs Musprat. You have a nice evening.'

'Just you hold your horses, boy!' came the sharp reply. A moment later she returned, carrying a small glass paper-weight with a purple thistle inside. 'Here,' she said, pushing it into his hand, keeping her eyes down. 'For your trouble.'

Lockyer smiled, not that she would see it. Her eyes were bright, watery, a washed-out blue, always moving, always flitting from one thing to another. She rarely held his gaze for more than a few seconds. Not since she'd found out he was police. It made him wonder how above board her past antiques dealings had been. She had high cheekbones with deep hollows underneath them, and her hair was coarse, iron grey. Her fingernails were stained with dirt. Lockyer strongly suspected that her bluster was all front. 'Thank you, Mrs Musprat. Does this mean I can call you Iris?'

'No. It doesn't.'

At home, he worked on the banisters again for a while, then ate dinner and sat down with a beer and the transcripts.

It had been chance that he'd been on call at the time of Mickey Brown's murder. Fluke that he'd been awake and dressed anyway, and lived nearby. He had almost beaten uniform to the scene. Serena Godwin had called it in – she'd been getting dressed when she'd heard a crash coming from the barn, which turned out to be Hedy dropping Mickey's breakfast tray. Serena had gone out to see what was going on, found Hedy standing there, next to the body, and had run straight back into the house to call the police and lock the doors. Hedy, it said in Serena's statement, had looked 'deranged'.

But she also stated that she'd been woken in the first place by the sound of Hedy getting the breakfast tray ready. And the pathologist estimated that Mickey had been dead for at least three hours by then – there'd been the beginnings of rigor mortis in the neck and jaw. He also suggested that the killer wouldn't necessarily have much of the victim's blood on them, given the nature of the wound and the lack of a struggle. No traces of blood were found inside the main house, or in Hedy's flat, so the theory was put forward that, having killed him cleanly, she had simply gone back inside, then come out again later with the tray to 'discover' the body, deliberately slipping in the blood to explain away any small traces that were already on her hands or clothes.

Thinking about all their interviews made Lockyer strangely uncomfortable. Just him and Hedy, facing each other across a desk in a small room. Intimate, despite the one-way window. Considine had wanted it wrapped up: she'd wanted a result, and everything had pointed to Hedy. Getting her motive – or, better yet, her confession – would be the final nail. How big and important he'd felt, to be singled out by a suspect like that; to be charged, obliquely, with building the case by himself. He'd been embarrassed by those thoughts, but he'd had them all the same. He'd tried to stay professional, impartial and aloof, when inside his blood had been rushing.

He'd interviewed Hedy for around eighteen hours over

the course of a fortnight. He'd learnt her body language. He'd learnt her face, its every line and contour. The fall of her hair. Her composure, and how hard she'd fought to keep it. After a while, she'd started to turn up in his dreams.

He flicked through a couple of pages, then started to read Hedy's words:

> I . . . I'd slept straight through that night. I don't, usually. I overslept a bit, even . . . I had to hurry to get the breakfast ready – that's probably why I made more noise than usual. I usually try not to wake anyone. But the professor likes his breakfast tray taken up at seven fifteen, and he said I should take Harry's out to him first. He said his son had always been an early riser.

OFFICER 724 DETECTIVE INSPECTOR LOCKYER: *Why was Harry Ferris sleeping in the barn?*

RESPONSE: *I . . . I'm not sure. It was like a test, when he first came back. There was never much said about it.*

DI LOCKYER: *What do you mean, a test?*

RESPONSE: *Well, he turned up that first time – slept the night out in the barn, and one of the gardeners found him in the morning and went and told Professor Ferris. Straight away he – Roland – was weird about it, because it was Harry's birthday, twelfth of May.*

DI LOCKYER: *Why was that significant?*

RESPONSE: *Well . . . that he'd chosen that particular day to come back, I suppose. He'd left on his fifteenth birthday, after all, Harry had, to go and live with his aunt. Hadn't even opened any of his presents, or had any of his cake. He just left, that's what the professor told me. It . . . He was really sad about it. Heartbroken. So,* well, his birthday cake was all ready and waiting for him this time too. Roland had asked me to make it the day before. Strawberry and vanilla layer cake. I made one last year, too.

DI LOCKYER: *You made a birthday cake for Harry Ferris last year?*

RESPONSE: *Yes. It was a bit strange, but I thought Roland must have been expecting him to show up. Then Paul told me there'd been a cake every year. He'd made it himself a couple of times. Then they'd switched to ordering one from a bakery, but he always preferred homemade and I quite like baking. And Roland got him presents and a card every year too. Even though he never showed up for them.*

DI LOCKYER: *Every year since he was fifteen?*

RESPONSE: *Yes. In case he came back, I guess.*

DI LOCKYER: *What happened to the cake? And the presents?*

RESPONSE: *The cake went in the bin. I don't know about the presents. It was just so . . . sad . . . The professor went off into his study in the evening and didn't come out or let any of us in all the next day. I wanted to . . . you know, help, somehow. Try to cheer him up. But I didn't know what to say. So I . . . I didn't say anything. And then there he was, Harry, this year, right on his birthday.*

DI LOCKYER: *What did you mean about him staying outside being a test?*

RESPONSE: *Well . . . Roland came down and saw him, and I'll never forget his face. He was crying, and so happy at the same time. He was just . . . overwhelmed, it seemed like. And he kept saying, 'You've come home,' and that sort of thing. Only his sister, Mrs Godwin, she was a bit less certain. More suspicious of him — that's just how she is. She asked Roland how he could be so sure after all this time, and with Harry looking so . . . unkempt. They argued about it for a while, and Harry never said a word . . .*

DI LOCKYER: *So, there was a test?*

RESPONSE: *Not deliberately, I think, but . . . Roland said to Harry, 'Come inside, my boy,' or something like that. He took his arm and led him over to the house, but Harry wouldn't go inside. He just wouldn't, and he seemed a bit freaked out. Professor Ferris looked confused but then he seemed to understand. 'You're a man of your word, then?' he said to him, and Harry nodded. And that was that – even Mrs Godwin was convinced, I think. Turns out it was the last thing Harry ever said to him, you see, on the day he left. He swore he would never set foot inside that house again. That's what he said when he left, and then no one saw him for however many years.*

DI LOCKYER: *But Mrs Godwin didn't recognize Harry at first?*

RESPONSE: *Well . . . she just wanted to be sure, I think. But, then, I suppose he must have looked very different. Twelve years had gone by – fifteen, since Roland had actually seen him. He'd grown from a boy into a man, and he . . . he'd obviously fallen on hard times. His clothes were filthy, and he hadn't washed or shaved for a while. He didn't have any belongings or a bag with him or anything.*

DI LOCKYER: *But Mrs Godwin was satisfied, after this 'test'?*

RESPONSE: *Yes. Well . . . you'd have to ask her. But he certainly knew his way around.*

DI LOCKYER: *You said he wouldn't go inside.*

RESPONSE: *No, but . . . outside. Like, he knew where the gardener's loo was – it's in a little brick hut right over in the corner behind the walled garden. You wouldn't know it was there, unless you'd been before. He just took himself across to it, didn't need to ask where to find it. And when the professor told him to come to the kitchen window and I'd pass him out a cup of tea, he knew exactly which window it was. Serena couldn't argue with that.*

Lockyer pictured Harry Ferris, the real Harris Ferris he'd just met, who'd clearly done the opposite of falling on hard times, and had either forgotten his sworn vow never to re-enter Longacres, or had broken it without a qualm. It was odd that Mickey had seemed to know his way around. At the time of this interview they'd still thought the dead man was Harry Ferris, but Serena Godwin had argued loudly to the contrary, and they'd been trying to get to the bottom of that. Soon afterwards, in the clamour of finding out that the dead man was Michael Brown, his seeming to know Long-acres had been forgotten. But, then, perhaps Mickey had stumbled upon the outdoor toilet the night before, when he'd first arrived in the Ferrises' garden. And then made a lucky guess at the kitchen window.

Lockyer stared at Hedy's words and heard her voice, clear in his memory: calmer by then but still subdued, still shocked. Still expecting to be let go at the end of it, back to Longacres, to comfort Roland on losing his son for a second time. He remembered the way she'd held his gaze while she spoke, not looking around or looking away like people did when they lied – unless they were very good at it. She'd looked at him as though she trusted him.

He'd trusted her too, at first, until the forensics report on the knife came back. He'd trusted the shudders gripping her body, as she'd stood next to the dead man, how shocked she'd looked, how pale and stunned. *It's all right*, he'd said to her. *I'm here. You're safe now. It's going to be all right.* He'd spoken on instinct, as a man, not as a police officer. Her eyes had flickered to meet his, and she'd swallowed convulsively. Perhaps that was where it had started. *You're safe now.*

Had her shock been real? Had it been an act, or had it merely been the chickens coming home to roost – her realization of the finality of what she'd done? Beyond those first few blood-scented hours he couldn't remember ever being sure he knew the answer to that. So he'd chosen a side – the side his SIO was on – and he'd stuck to it. Guilty. He'd talked and talked, asked question after question, until he'd got them her motive.

He read until late, but it only left his thoughts more restless than before. So he decided to walk before going to bed, and set off through the trees, following the bridle-way that ran up onto the high ground of Orcheston Down, between knotted hedges of blackthorn and elder, past ancient burial mounds, the sleeping bones of long forgotten warriors.

There was no moon so he wore his head torch, but turned it off as soon as he was sure of the path. He didn't like the way it blinded him to everything but his own feet and the patch of ground in front of them. He didn't like the way it announced his arrival to the landscape, and separated him from it. He wanted to belong there, not feel like an intruder. The rhythm of his long strides calmed his thoughts. He breathed in time. The wind nudged across the plain, as restless as he was, ignoring him and every other living thing. Somewhere to his right, a barn owl shrieked.

He'd always walked, even as a child. His brother, Chris, hadn't understood it, dragging his feet as he came along behind, eight years old to Lockyer's twelve, complaining, asking constantly where they were going. He didn't get that they weren't going anywhere in particular, they were just going. Chris didn't see the point, but that was what he'd been like: never lazy, but always keen to expend the least energy necessary. He worked like a Trojan on the farm, but as soon as the work was done he'd throw himself down in a heap in the nearest comfortable spot and then not budge. Even his grin was languid.

But however much Chris had hated walking, he'd always wanted to be where his big brother was, and do what he was doing. On the Saturday night nearest to his birthday, three days after he'd turned eighteen, Chris had planned a big night out in Chippenham, where several of his friends lived. The pub crawl would start at the Bridge House by the river, then make its way up the hill via the Rose and Crown, the Flying Monk and the Bear, and end with takeaway curry and chips from the Taj Mahal, to be eaten on the street, probably messily. Then they'd stagger back to sleep on a floor or a sofa somewhere.

Even at the age of twenty-one, Lockyer could think of few things he'd like less.

'Oh, come on, you old git,' Chris said, shouting over the racket of the tractor. He was stacking bales of plastic-wrapped haylage in the new barn, face flushed from the exercise, blond hair a scruffy mess. He was a heavier build than Lockyer, but not as tall. 'It'll be a laugh!'

'You don't need me there,' Lockyer said. 'You'll have all your mates.' They'd already celebrated Chris's birthday at home, and he hated the rowdiness of the town pubs. How crowded they got on a Saturday night – the heat of other people pushing in, the naked appraisal in their eyes. He knew his antipathy to such occasions marked him out – it had all through university. But he didn't mind being marked out, if it meant he didn't have to go.

'Joanne'll be there.' Chris grinned. 'You know she fancies you.'

'Two pints down the line you won't even notice I'm not there.'

'That's not true.' Chris stopped grinning. 'Come on, Matt. Just this once. It's time for sibling revelry!'

'But the trip's all planned.'

'Right. Walking. By yourself. On Dartmoor. Have you *seen* the weather forecast? And who exactly will you be letting down if you move it to another weekend?'

Lockyer didn't reply. He felt himself wavering, his desire to please Chris as strong as his desire to be anywhere but in a pub in Chippenham on Saturday night. He pictured the emptiness of Dartmoor, and going to sleep under the stars in his one-man tent with cold air in his lungs, versus passing out in a fug of alcohol and junk food on a sofa that'd be too short for him – they always were. Not to mention waking up there the next morning, feeling like shit.

But if Chris didn't cave, he knew *he* would. Chris opened

the throttle, raised the fork lift. 'Ah, forget it, boring old fart,' he said, smiling again.

'Sorry,' Lockyer said, as relieved as he was guilty. 'You'll have a brilliant time, I know you will.'

'Forget it. I'll tell Joanne you're gay.' Chris went on stacking the bales, and Lockyer let his relief win out.

Sibling revelry. Chris had come up with it, aged eleven, sitting at the dining-room table as a roast lunch was devoured. It was one of those phrases that sticks, becomes part of the family vocabulary. Their grandparents had been there for Sunday lunch, and Nan commented on the lack of infighting. The boys didn't battle one another for space or attention or praise, unlike their cousins. Unlike most kids.

'Well, they're too different, aren't they?' Trudy said. 'They like different things. Move at different speeds, think different thoughts.'

The two boys had looked at each other, rolling their eyes. They didn't feel different from one another at all – not in any way that mattered.

'What's the opposite of sibling rivalry, then?' Nan said. ''Cause that's what you two have got.'

'Sibling revelry?' Chris said.

'Ha! That's it. Lucky little buggers. My brother put me down the well, once.'

'Uncle Tom put you down the well?' Trudy was incredulous.

'Too right he did. Left me down there for hours, sitting in the bucket. I was only six. Wet me pants, I did.'

This set the boys laughing.

'I'm sure he loved you really, Mum,' Trudy said.

'Did he hell. If he'd thought he could get away with it, he'd've drowned me like a runt.'

Sibling revelry. If Lockyer had gone out with his brother that Saturday night – his last night on earth; if, just for once, he'd put up with the noise and the banter and the too-short sofa, and done what Chris had wanted rather than what he'd wanted. If only . . .

Lockyer pushed the thoughts away, smothered them down. They made him so angry he could hardly breathe. Angry with himself. Angry with Chris. Angry with the world.

He deliberately slowed his pace, and made himself think about Harry Ferris instead. *Anyone who knew me well enough to want to kill me would have realized straight away that it wasn't me.* Wasn't that an odd thing for him to say? Didn't it imply that he could conceive of someone wanting to kill him? Wouldn't most people have simply said, 'No'? Hedy had loved Roland Ferris, Cass said, and Roland had clearly been fond of her. They had grown close, during the time she worked for him. Lockyer wondered how close; whether it had been close enough to have talked about his wife's suicide, or the reasons Harry had left. As far as Lockyer knew, nobody had ever asked Hedy about it.

He would have to talk to her again.

4

Day Five, Tuesday

'Please tell me you're joking, Matt.' Detective Superintendent Considine tapped her fingers on the arms of her chair. She dropped her chin to stare at Lockyer. 'You're winding me up, right?'

The DSU was well into her fifties, and her auburn hair had mostly faded to grey now. Lockyer had worked with her for nearly twenty years, and secretly approved of her decision not to dye it. There'd always been something defiant about her that he liked. She had a strong face, all cheekbones and jaw, and a penetrating gaze.

'No, I—' Lockyer tried.

'You want me to approve the re-examination of evidence from a case *I* closed – with a conviction – fourteen years ago, and waste budget we really don't have, because "something's not quite right there"?'

'Ma'am, Hedy Lambert was the obvious suspect—'

'Yes, she was. Because she was guilty. As her trial concluded – as *you* helped the jury to conclude.'

'By majority, only. What if . . .' He hesitated, looking up at his boss.

Considine liked him, he knew she did. She was a big part of the reason he'd ended up on cold case review, rather than demoted, after the Queen's Head fire. But, still, he was pushing his luck and he knew it. 'We wanted a result and we wanted it as quickly as we could get it,' he said. 'We had to go hunting for a motive because she didn't really have one—'

'She *did* have one. And nobody else in that house did, not once we knew it wasn't Harry Ferris who'd died . . .'

'What if we had tunnel vision?'

The silence in Considine's office rang for a few seconds. She stared hard at Lockyer and he struggled not to look away. She took a slow breath. 'There was no forensic evidence whatsoever to suggest that anyone other than Hedy Lambert was in the barn that night or had handled the murder weapon,' she said precisely. Then something occurred to her. 'How did you even know about Harry Ferris being back?' Her frown deepened. 'Have you been in touch with Lambert? Jesus Christ, Matt!'

'On my own time, ma'am,' he said.

'What are you thinking? You're supposed to be keeping your head down, clearing up some old cases, mending some fences!'

'That's exactly what I'm *trying* to do,' he said, failing to keep the tension out of his voice. He rubbed one hand along his jaw, searching for the right words. 'There's no room for hunches in an investigation any more, I know that. Not in the face of hard evidence. But this one *never* sat right with me, ma'am. I didn't say anything at the time because ... well, because I was still just starting out. Inexperienced.' And because Considine had wanted a result, and fast. 'But it strikes me now that the main reason we went after Hedy Lambert was because we couldn't find any reason anyone else in that house might have wanted to kill Harry Ferris – or Mickey Brown.'

'Or any other forensic evidence, Matt, and we did find *her* motive.'

'I've got doubts, ma'am. And I know I was the one who put her motive together. That's part of the problem.' He looked up in appeal. 'What if we got it wrong? What if *I* got it wrong? There's an ambiguity in the forensics report on the knife. It says Lambert's prints on it were "faint in places but undisturbed".'

'"Undisturbed" is not ambiguous at all.'

'Please let me get it looked at again. If the lab tells me there's absolutely no chance anybody could have handled that knife after Hedy did, then I swear I'll drop it.'

Considine took another breath, shaking her head. 'You've got an obsessive streak a mile wide, Matt,' she said. 'You're like a dog with a sodding bone. I used to think that was a good thing in a detective, but you're beginning to make me change my mind.'

Lockyer didn't reply. He waited in silence.

'You know what happened with the Queen's Head case. You know where you went wrong. Don't you?'

'Too involved. Lost impartiality,' was Lockyer's curt reply.

'Yes. Lessons supposedly learnt. So why do I get the feeling you're doing it again now? How much of this is just about Hedy Lambert?'

'It's about catching a killer.'

'Are you sure? Because I think Hedy Lambert got under your skin back in 2005. I wonder if she's still there now.'

Lockyer jolted. Was he that transparent? 'All I know is that I had my doubts then, and I've got them now. I didn't have the guts to say anything at the time. And if I was responsible for sending an innocent woman to jail, while a killer walked free . . . . I don't want that on my conscience, ma'am.'

'If she's innocent – which she isn't – you'll just have to live with it. It's been fourteen years.'

'But at least I can fix it now. I can . . . put it right. Some of it.'

Considine stared at him a while longer, then leant away with a sigh. 'All right. I regret this already, but get the murder weapon looked at again. On one condition: if there's no ambiguity about it, this case gets put back to bed where it belongs. Permanently. I mean it.'

'Yes, ma'am.'

'And stay away from Hedy Lambert. I mean that, too.'

Lockyer decided he would go to the forensic archive in Birmingham the next day, collect the murder weapon and take it to the Cellmark pathology lab in Abingdon himself. Continuity in the chain of custody of physical evidence was crucial. He was filling out the request form when he saw something on the forensics submission list that made him pause. There was precious little on the list that had belonged to Michael Brown – his clothes, his boots, the sparse contents of his pockets. He seemed to have turned up at Roland Ferris's barn with little more than what he was wearing. But, in the top pocket of his battered old blazer: *Audio tape cassette, without case or inlay card, commercially sold music.*

He stared at the listing, his sense of unease increasing. He'd forgotten about it, but remembered now. The strangeness of it. It was one of the things he hadn't spoken up about back in 2005, one of the anomalies he hadn't pushed back on, or chased hard enough. Why on earth would the victim be carrying a tape around with him, when he didn't own a stereo, or a car, or any other means of playing it?

'Found something, Guv?' Broad asked.

'I'm not sure. A tape in Mickey Brown's jacket pocket.'

'A tape? Like a tape measure?'

'No.' Lockyer looked up. 'A music cassette. Please tell me you remember them.'

'Not from personal experience.' Broad grinned. 'I've heard of them, of course. Like I've heard of dinosaurs, and the Battle of Hastings.'

'Just you wait. It'll happen to you, too.'

'What will? Obsolescence? Technological, I mean.'

'Course you do,' Lockyer said drily.

'What was odd about it, then?'

'He had no means of playing it. And in 2005 it was already

obsolete – properly obsolete. Tapes didn't even keep an underground following, like vinyl did. Probably because they were crap. So it was an odd thing for him to have, when it didn't seem like he had much else.'

Broad thought about it. 'Michael Brown was of no fixed abode, right? A Traveller. Maybe he just picked it up some-where.'

'That's what we decided in the end. Not significant to the investigation.'

'So what didn't you like about it?'

'What I didn't like about it was that there were almost no fingerprints on it. Something that must have been handled a lot, in its lifetime. And the fragments we did manage to lift didn't belong to Michael Brown.'

'So . . . somebody else put it into his pocket. Or he picked it up somewhere, wearing gloves at the time?'

'It's one possibility. Except it was summer.'

'The lining of the pocket might have rubbed it clean. Was it even his jacket? I mean, couldn't he have got it second-hand, or borrowed it?'

'We'd no way of knowing – not then or now. All we know is he was wearing it when he turned up at Longacres.'

'What tape was it? What music, I mean?'

'It was . . .' Lockyer searched his brain. 'What was it? It's on the tip of my tongue.' He gave up. 'Can't think of it.'

'Probably not relevant, in any case. But you could always add it to the forensics request.'

Lockyer was sorely tempted. But he decided against it, at least until the murder weapon had been re-examined. The last thing he needed to do was irritate Considine any more than he already had.

However keen he was to talk to Miles Godwin, Serena's son, about why he'd kept Harry's whereabouts a secret all these years, Lockyer knew he had to wait.

DC Broad picked two more possible lines of enquiry out of the file: first, an elderly lady, out walking her dog in the middle of the night, had seen a white vehicle parked in the lane just outside the village, near Longacres. She thought it might have been an SUV or a small van, with writing on the side, a logo maybe, she wasn't sure: it had been too dark to see it clearly. She'd walked that way every night for years and never seen it before, which was why she'd noticed it. A Mrs Hazel Peterson, aged eighty-two. Now, sadly, almost certainly deceased.

The Scene Of Crime Officers had found fresh tyre tracks in the location she'd described, but had been able to identify them only as a common, low-cost brand. There'd been no other follow-up, and Lockyer could understand why. *Was it rocking?* he remembered one of the DCs asking, and getting a laugh. It had most probably been a couple of horny teenagers with nowhere else to go. There were no traffic or CCTV cameras anywhere near the village and, in any case, they'd been looking for someone from *inside* the house. Someone with keys, who knew where to find the victim.

Second, there was the bruising on Michael Brown's body. Moderate bruising to his torso and arms, plus faint finger-marks on his neck, perhaps a week old, layered over older, more severe bruising, mainly to his intercostal muscles. There were corresponding fractures to two of his ribs, healed, but recently – perhaps a month or two old rather than days.

'Someone beat him up before he was murdered. Twice,' Broad pointed out. 'Those older bruises, and the ribs – those could have been done before he arrived at Longacres. But the newer ones happened while he was staying there. Did you ever find out who attacked him? Or why?'

'No. I don't think so – if it's not in the file.'

'Was Hedy Lambert the beating-up type?'

'I wouldn't have said so. But, then, I wouldn't have said she was the stabbing type either.' Lockyer thought for a moment. 'I wouldn't say she was physically strong enough to inflict bruises like that on a young, relatively fit man. Not unless he literally just stood there and took it.'

'Fibres from a jumper she'd been wearing earlier that week were found on him, implying close contact between them.'

'Yes. She had an explanation for that. It was what helped put her away.'

Broad was obviously curious, but Lockyer didn't expand. He wanted her perspective on the case to be as fresh as possible. As unencumbered by pre-existing impressions as he was overloaded with them.

'So, somebody was pissed off enough with Mickey Brown to give him a good hiding. Possibly two different people. Could be worth trying to find out who they were, do you think?'

'Keep it up, Gem,' he said.

Lockyer finished the day feeling less sure of himself than before he'd spoken to DSU Considine. When they'd charged Hedy Lambert fourteen years ago, he remembered thinking she'd almost had him. Almost taken him in completely. He'd explained away all his misgivings about the case with the idea that she'd deliberately manipulated him. What if she almost had him again now? What if she was like a magnet to a compass when it came to his judgement?

As he left the station he got a text from an old friend. *Fancy a pint?*

Lockyer frowned as he read it. Kevin hadn't been in touch for months. Lockyer had told him not to be, and he hadn't specified a timescale. He didn't know how long he'd meant. It had been a knee-jerk thing to say, a reflex reaction, mostly in shock at how badly he'd screwed up, how close he'd come to ruining his career. But he'd known Kevin since primary school, and shutting him out had felt wrong. Kevin's father, Bob, had been the landlord of the Queen's Head; he was now serving four years for arson and attempted insurance fraud. That Kevin hadn't been charged as an accessory was solely down to Lockyer.

Kevin, of all people, knew where Lockyer was from. Turning up to school with muddy shoes and too-short trousers, sometimes with ringworm, usually with a runny nose; never having any of the latest toys or games or holidays; learning to fight dirty at a young age, because it was that or always coming off worst. Huddled on the school bus in their grimy coats, not wanting to get off because it was warmer there than it would be at home.

They'd stuck together, kept out of trouble, entertained themselves, when they weren't working for their dads, with dens and homemade weapons and collections of random things. Bird skulls, napped flints, cereal box freebies. It was pure chance that Lockyer's family business was a farm, whilst Kevin's had been a failing pub, a wrecking yard, and various get-rich-quick schemes that had walked a very fine line between the legal and the criminal. And frequently stumbled over it.

The only times Lockyer had got into fights as a kid were when Kevin – short and skinny then – was in trouble. Or when Chris got picked on. Lockyer had understood being picked on, and he understood somebody picking on Kevin, who always chose the wrong moment to crack a joke. But not Chris. Anybody who'd want to pick on Chris must have something wrong in their head, and Lockyer made it his mission to knock it out of them.

It had got him suspended once. Seeing boys from his own year pushing Chris around, scattering his packed lunch across the playing field. Swinging him around by his tie. Lockyer didn't remember having a single thought in his head except stopping them. No, more than that, *punishing* them. He knocked out several teeth and gave two bloody noses before he was tackled to the ground. Two weeks suspension, but his father had patted him on the shoulder when he heard how it had happened. Now, when he thought of the man who'd killed Chris, that same blind urge to punish rose up, unchanged after all these years. After all the growing up he'd supposedly done. Some things were hard-wired in.

Lockyer sat in his car and stared at Kevin's message for a while. Eventually, he replied: *Dog and Gun, 8 p.m.*

Kevin replied at once: *Didn't think you meant 8 in the a.m., bellend.*

He went home for something to eat first, and watched Mrs Musprat mucking out Desiree's stall in the back garden, one painful shovel of manure at a time. She might be fit for her age, but how long could she carry on alone in that ramshackle place? Lockyer lived in dread of coming home and finding her dead on the floor one day, just as she'd found his predecessor. It wasn't his business, he reminded himself. She was managing. Still, the urge to interfere – to help – was strong.

The sight of her slowly shovelling, bending painfully, wearing old wellingtons and a thready rain mac over trousers patched at the knees, while the brown nanny goat pottered around at the end of her tether, gave him a strange feeling. Like a premonition of sorrow, or nostalgia for a life it seemed neither of them was destined to live. Family, kids, grandkids, god-kids, nieces and nephews. That extended clutter of company and love other people seemed to have and to acquire so easily.

Newly motivated to see a friend, Lockyer headed to the pub.

Kevin was already there, hunched over a half-finished pint. Not tall, scrawny but for a slight paunch that was coming on with middle age. Thinning brown hair, kind eyes; a face habitually pinched with worry. He looked up when Lockyer arrived, and Lockyer hated to see the tentative way he smiled. What happened hadn't been Kevin's fault. His father had always been the boss. The Slater family had always had to deal with the fallout from its patriarch's crap decisions. And the decision to lie, to protect Kevin during the arson investigation, had been Lockyer's alone.

'All right, Matt?' Kevin said. 'Thanks for coming.'

They both heard how formal, and therefore how stupid, this sounded.

Kevin grinned sheepishly. 'Sit down, mate, you're making me dizzy.'

'How've you been, Kev?'

'Oh, you know. Bit shit. Lisa's finally kicked me out. I'm dossing down at Carl's and he's driving me nuts. Times me in the fucking shower, he does.'

'Sorry to hear that.' Lockyer didn't ask what had been the final straw for Kevin's long-suffering second wife.

'Don't blame her. I'm a shit husband.' Kevin's tone was light, but suddenly Lockyer could see the stress of it all, and the grief, in the new lines on his face. 'That's it for me.' He held out one hand, palm facing the table top, and slowly lowered it to the wood. 'I've given it two goes. I'm not cut out for it. No more weddings for me.'

'I'll believe that when I see it,' Lockyer said. Kevin had got engaged twice before he was first married. He'd been fourteen the first time he'd asked a girl to marry him. Craving security, Lockyer had always thought.

'She's letting me see the kids, no arguments. So at least I can still try to be a good dad.'

'And what about . . .' Lockyer waited for Kevin to fill in the blank. The girl he'd been seeing.

Kevin raised his eyebrows. 'Jen?' He shook his head. 'Nah. She didn't last. Went back to that ex of hers – you know, the squaddie. Built like a brick shit-house, so I didn't make too much fuss. Shame, though. That body of hers — I still dream about it.'

Lockyer looked at his friend, still seeing the thin whip of a boy he'd been inside the careworn man in front of him. There but for the grace of God, he caught himself thinking. Was this how his life would have played out if he'd never left home? Finished school at sixteen and followed into the family business? Married the first girl he'd got pregnant, and the next as well? Worked and worked and worked all his hours and days and never got anywhere? Lockyer checked himself. It wasn't as though he'd got particularly far. He'd known, even before Chris's death, that he couldn't stay on the farm, but he still belonged to it, and to the windswept fields of the plain. He didn't feel he fitted in anywhere else.

But at least he'd gone away, and come back, and there was satisfaction in his work. He loved his job, and hoped he didn't have Kevin's air of exhaustion, and despair.

'What about you?' Kevin asked. 'Sam been around lately?'

'Sam? No.'

'You finally given her the heave-ho?'

Lockyer shrugged. He and Sam had been together for a year at university. At twenty, feeling like a proper adult, he'd produced a ring, and Sam had laughed for five minutes straight. She still came to see him sometimes, off and on, for long enough to chip her way back into his heart, to make him wonder if she'd stay this time – and if he wanted her to – then left again. She was like a rash that wouldn't quite clear. Painless, infuriating at times. But impossible to forget about altogether.

'I've not seen her for the best part of a year now,' Lockyer said. 'She sends the odd email.'

'Still married to that lawyer?'

'Divorced. Big mess, from what I could gather.'

'Ah.' Kevin grinned. 'Pity.' He finished his pint in two big gulps. 'Still reckon she's the one for you?' he said, not without sympathy.

'I doubt it.'

'Then you need to get out there! Plenty of women about, but you're not going to meet any of them holed up in a house in the middle of bloody nowhere every night, are you?'

'Probably not.'

'Hopeless.' Kevin stood up. 'Another?'

'You carry on.' Lockyer had barely touched his own drink.

A minute later, Kevin sat back down with a full pint. 'It's good to see you, Matt,' he said. 'I wanted to test the water. Thought I might still be in the doghouse.'

'It was never that, really.'

'Still. I owe you.'

'No. Let's be really clear about this. You *don't* owe me anything.'

Kevin stared down into his pint. 'Feels like I do. Wasn't good for your career, was it?'

Lockyer didn't reply at once. It was by chance good timing that the retired DCI who'd worked Major Crime Review out of the Bradford-on-Avon station had had a heart attack and retired completely, around the time of the Queen's Head fire. Lockyer had been shoehorned neatly into the vacant role. He'd been allowed to continue working out of the Devizes station, perhaps as an extra punishment, because he'd still see his CID colleagues every day, busy on live cases. Progressing. Lockyer was careful not to let on how much he didn't mind.

'I'm fine with it.'

'Not going to get promoted, though, are you? Not from what I've heard.'

'Maybe I don't care about that.' Lockyer took a mouthful of beer as he thought about it.

'Come off it, Matt.'

'I mean it. When did it all get to be about advancing, constantly trying to wrestle your way to the top of the tree? I can still do good work – valuable work. The satisfaction of catching a criminal who thinks they've got away with it . . . giving closure and justice to a family who've long since given up on either. It's every bit as rewarding as catching someone quickly. If not more so.'

Kevin looked at him shrewdly. 'Because of Chris?'

'Because it just is,' Lockyer said. 'Because people shouldn't be allowed to get away with things. They should pay for the damage they cause.'

Kevin searched Lockyer's face for a moment, then looked down at his pint.

'Yeah. They should,' he said. 'Anything new? On Chris's case?'

Lockyer all but ignored the question. If he thought about it too often it'd make him angry again. Angry like he'd been as a young man, a newly recruited police officer. It had given him a zeal like something hard and metallic he could almost taste. He didn't like the feel of it. 'The way we investigate . . . it's changed so much since I joined the force,' he said. 'It's a machine now. Everyone has their one function to perform, and they perform it, and it all goes into the computer to help the SIO join the dots. These days, a detective inspector is in the office, making sure the DCs are doing the right legwork. Twenty years ago we'd have been out, talking to witnesses, interviewing suspects . . .'

'Back in the good old days?'

'Yeah, right,' Lockyer said wryly. 'The good old days. One of my first big cases, as a DC, the SIO turned up drunk, trampled the crime scene, and later on beat up the suspect. Who turned out to be innocent.'

'Jesus. So which is better?'

'We solve more crimes now. We're more accountable. A lot less racist, far less likely to plant evidence. Or do a favour for a friend.' He glanced up at Kevin. 'That kind of thing.'

'Sounds like progress, I suppose.'

'Without a doubt. But I miss the way we used to work an investigation. Well, some of the ways. On cold cases I get to do some of it again, off my own bat. So,' he waited until he'd caught Kevin's eye, 'no harm done.'

'Right.' There was relief on Kevin's face. 'Last time I went to see Dad he said to say thank you. For keeping me out of it. Said he'd like to say it in person, if you wanted to pop by. I said you were more likely to sprout wings and fly.'

'You got that right.'

'Well, I guess you get to work alone now, right? You always did want to be a one-man army. "Not really a team player" – wasn't that what Twatface Thompson wrote on your report that time? I don't know how you do it.'

'How I do what?'

'Do everything by yourself. Live. Work. Go to bed. Aren't you lonely as fuck? I'd be lonely as fuck. Well, I *am* lonely as fuck, and I've got a load more people in my life than you have.'

Lockyer didn't reply. He drank again. There was no way to explain to somebody who depended on the company of others how it felt not to. And yet. Perhaps something was missing.

Kevin sensed the change in mood. 'I still can't believe you're a detective frigging *inspector*, Matt.' He grinned. 'You! The boy I once had to rescue from my auntie's Yorkshire terrier! God help us.'

'That dog was mental.'

'Yeah, well, they can smell fear, mate, that's the problem.'

The cottage seemed extra quiet that night. The wind had dropped, and there wasn't even the muffled sound of the TV coming through the wall. It had been Lockyer's, but he'd donated it to Mrs Musprat when her vintage box had packed up. Her suspicion of gifts did not extend to going without a TV, and Lockyer had come to realize that he preferred reading or listening to the radio, to podcasts, audio books or music. He could listen while he renovated the house, and it didn't stop him thinking.

He fetched another beer from the fridge and roamed from room to room, looking at the things that still needed doing. From replacing rotten skirting boards to cleaning years of paint and screed from the quarry tiles he'd found under the rat-eaten dining-room carpet; from working out why the chimney wouldn't draw to repairing the ceiling in the second bedroom, which had come down with a gleeful shower of plaster, dead flies and crap from the attic when he'd tried to change the light fitting. He didn't feel like tackling any of it right now.

It felt too empty, and he blamed Kevin's questions for that, until he realized it wasn't Sam he was thinking about. He went to bed, early for him, with a fistful of transcripts from the Michael Brown/Harry Ferris case. He told himself it was work, but it was Hedy Lambert's voice he wanted to hear. Not because it was a comfort, not because he wished she were there, but because it was like pressing on a bruise. Painful, but irresistible. He read from a few days into the investigation, when they'd still thought the body was Harry's.

DI LOCKYER: *Why were the others there at the house, at the time of the murder? Professor Ferris's sister, Serena Godwin, and her son Miles?*

RESPONSE: *They often came to visit. Well, Serena did. Miles a bit less.*

DI LOCKYER: *More often, would you say, since Professor Ferris's illness was diagnosed?*

RESPONSE: *Yes, I suppose so. But that's to be expected, isn't it? Serena was only staying with us when Harry first came back because the professor had just heard about his test results. There was a bit of a panic. People hear 'leukaemia' and think they've only got weeks to live.*

DI LOCKYER: *But you didn't think that?*

RESPONSE: *It sounded really bad at first, but I did some research and found out he wasn't going to suddenly fall down dead – he most probably still had years left ahead of him. I mean . . . it was still scary. For him. But it could have been worse.*

DI LOCKYER: *Did you share what you'd discovered with Serena and Miles? Did Professor Ferris?*

RESPONSE: *I didn't. Serena doesn't talk to the staff, unless it's to ask them to do something – and by ask I mean tell. I'm sure Roland will have spoken to them about it, though. It all calmed down a bit after the first shock of it.*

DI LOCKYER: *Still, it's a serious illness. Do you suppose Professor Ferris turned his thoughts to getting his affairs in order?*

RESPONSE: *I don't know.*

DI LOCKYER: *Did you think it likely?*

RESPONSE: *I don't know. I suppose he might have. Wouldn't you?*

DI LOCKYER: *Did you?*

RESPONSE: *You're asking me if I started to think about Professor Ferris's will?*

DI LOCKYER: *Did you? You rely on him for your job and your home, after all.*

RESPONSE: *Yes, I do. And I was worried about having to move on,* if he had to go into hospital or whatever . . . I was worried about what would happen in the future. But I didn't think about his will.

DI LOCKYER: Why was that?

RESPONSE: Because it was none of my business. I don't expect to be left anything.

DI LOCKYER: Why not? You've been with him for eighteen months now.

RESPONSE: As an employee. I'm not family, I'm staff.

DI LOCKYER: So you're not fond of him at all?

RESPONSE: I am fond of him, yes.

DI LOCKYER: And he's fond of you? It seems as though he relies on you a great deal.

RESPONSE: You'd have to ask him. There are plenty of other house-keepers out there he could hire. I don't think I'm special.

DI LOCKYER: Yes. Plenty of other housekeepers. In fact, it seems that Professor Ferris hired and fired four other women in the seven months leading up to when he hired you. Why do you suppose that is? Why do you think you succeeded where those others failed?

RESPONSE: I don't know about those other women. I . . . He can be grumpy. Bad-tempered. He doesn't mean anything by it, though, that's obvious. He's a kind man, inside. But perhaps they didn't get on with him. Perhaps I'm . . . quieter than the others. He prefers that.

DI LOCKYER: Would you say you had a special bond with him, then? It would be easy to become close, working in someone's house, day in, day out. Living under the same roof.

RESPONSE: We're not under the same roof. I have my own flat, above one of the garages.

DI LOCKYER: Yes, of course. But your whole life is spent there,

with Professor Ferris. From what I understand. It would be easy
to get close to somebody, under those circumstances, wouldn't it?

RESPONSE: I suppose so. Yes.

DI LOCKYER: It must have been hard for you, then, when Harry
came back. The long-lost and much-loved son. That must have
been difficult, seeing how happy Professor Ferris was? Perhaps
you felt a bit . . . sidelined? Miss Lambert? Did you resent Harry
for turning up the way he did, just as you were getting settled in?
And getting close to the professor? Miss Lambert?

RESPONSE: [pause] No.

KATE WEBB

5

Day Six, Wednesday

Lockyer spent most of the next day driving. The two and a half hours up to the forensic archive in Birmingham to collect the knife with which somebody had killed Michael Brown, the hour and a half down to the Cellmark lab outside Abingdon, and a further hour and a half back to the station. Going himself, he put as few new links into the chain of custody of the evidence as possible. It was as important to any future trial as to his own peace of mind.

The knife was their only hope, forensically speaking. The blood on the blade was now old and brown, flaky and delicate. An ordinary kitchen knife, the huge blade visibly worn down from years of being re-sharpened; a wooden handle, smooth from use. He was careful not to touch it at all, even through the plastic evidence bag. The original examination had found no prints but Hedy's – not unexpectedly, since she'd done all the cooking. But if some of the prints were disturbed ... if somebody else *might* have held it, albeit wearing gloves ...

Lockyer didn't know what he hoped to hear, or what would be worse – confirmation or refutation. He could picture that same knife clearly, jutting out of Mickey Brown's chest. *It's all right*, he'd said to Hedy. *I'm here now. You're safe.*

'How soon do you need this?' asked the lab technician, who signed the knife over from him.

'Come on,' Lockyer said. 'You know the answer to that.'

'As soon as possible?' The girl smiled.

'As soon as possible.'

As he walked away he felt a tingle of anticipation.

Back in their poky office, Broad had finished reading through the paper file.

She swivelled her chair as Lockyer came in, stretching back her shoulders.

'Anything else shout at you?' Lockyer asked.

'Not exactly shout, no. I thought for a while about the possibility of somebody from outside the household putting a wire through the door somehow, and hooking the keys that way. But even if there'd been a cat flap or a letterbox – which there wasn't – there's no way they could have hung them up again the same way, once they'd been in for the knife.' She twisted her chair to and fro. 'If I'd been the SIO, I think I'd have wanted to know who'd beaten Mickey up before he died.'

'Considine did want to know. But nobody was forthcoming and it didn't seem crucial, given the forensics on the knife, and on Hedy Lambert.'

'Of course, Guv.' She looked chastened.

'It's totally fine for you to say things like that, Gemma,' he reassured her. 'I don't think . . . I don't *think* the first investigation had major holes in it. I just think it was a case of . . . horses not zebras.'

'You mean, if you hear hooves, think horses not zebras?'

'Exactly. Everything pointed at Hedy. We went with it.'

'But you think there might be a zebra lurking somewhere?'

'Well. The knife's at the lab. If it isn't hiding one, we're done.'

'Right.'

Broad didn't sound that convinced. She'd got the bit between her teeth, Lockyer could tell. It was as much their job to disprove a suspect's guilt as to prove it, after all. He looked at the clock. 'See if you can find out where Miles Godwin lives or works. Perhaps we might pay him a visit, regardless. If he's not too far away. Just to discuss the way he impeded the original murder inquiry.'

'Okay. Shouldn't take too long. Can't be that many Miles Godwins out there.'

'His middle name's Cuthbert.'

'Course it is.' Broad swivelled back to her desk with a roll of her eyes.

She ran the search, and before long they had his home and work addresses: an old rectory in Manton, a village near Marlborough, and a shopfront and office in Marlborough itself. Miles owned a small chain of high-end eponymous estate agencies. The kind that offered a *bespoke service*. 'Oh, he's *that* Godwin. That's not what I was expecting,' Broad said. 'I was thinking lawyer or banker, or politician. Isn't that what all those Eton types go into?'

'A lot of them. He went to Marlborough College, not Eton – I remember now. He obviously didn't fly very far upon release. But there's money in selling houses to rich people.'

'There's money in selling *anything* to rich people.'

'Exactly. Come on.'

'Are you sure you want to get back in the car?'

'I'll already be seeing white lines when I shut my eyes later. Another half an hour won't make much difference.'

The drive took them north-east of Devizes, where the road had a long view across acres of waterlogged farmland. Shafts of failing sunlight glanced silver from the flooded ruts in every gateway. Rooks scattered the sky above copses of beech, and most fields seemed to have a prehistoric earthwork of some kind, a tumulus or barrow, that the farmer had either fenced off or simply ploughed around. The road crossed the path of the Wansdyke, a ridged earthwork that snaked thirty-five miles through Wiltshire and Somerset, built either by the Britons to keep the Anglo-Saxons out or vice versa.

'I hiked that last summer,' Broad told Lockyer.

'What – you and Pete?'

'Just me. And Merry, of course. Took me three days, and next time I'm doing Airbnbs, not lugging a tent the whole way.'

'But it was good, right?' Lockyer was envious. It had been too long since he'd done a walk like that. Since he'd had the time, and the freedom.

'Yeah,' Broad said. 'Loved it.'

'I used to hike a lot. Proper hiking, I mean.'

'Why not now?'

'You know. Work. Renovation.' He didn't mention the guilt that had lingered ever since he'd chosen Dartmoor over his brother that one catastrophic time.

'Those don't sound like very good reasons, Guv. Come with me next time.'

She said it lightly, but Lockyer hesitated too long before answering, and in the end didn't.

Miles Godwin's office occupied an elegant Georgian building on Marlborough's wide, affluent high street. It was surrounded by independent shops, high-end chains, restaurants and cafés. As soon as Lockyer saw the shop-front he realized he'd seen Godwin's for-sale signs all over the county, without making the connection. On houses he would never be able to afford, houses like Longacres. Almost all of the properties for sale in the agency window had seven-figure price tags. Broad caught Lockyer's eye as she pushed open the door, and raised an eyebrow.

A young and extremely glossy woman immediately got up from her desk to greet them. She was suited, and her hair, a dark swathe held back in a clip without a single stray, shone under the spotlights.

'Good afternoon.' Her eyes swept over them, taking in the age gap, the difference in height, Broad's ill-fitting trousers,

Lockyer's mud-flecked shoes. Her face betrayed nothing. A very telling nothing. 'Can I help you at all?'

'We'd like a word with Mr Miles Godwin, if he's here.' Lockyer showed his warrant card, and watched her friendly veneer turn brittle.

'Do you have an appointment?'

'No.'

'I'll just see if he's available.' She reached for the phone.

'Surely you know if he's here or not,' Lockyer said.

'Well, yes, but—'

'We'll follow you, then.'

He hated being treated like an inconvenient cold-caller. Even if, a lot of the time, that was what the police were.

The woman blinked, pressed her lips together and turned without a word. She led them between other desks where nobody was sitting, through a door and upstairs. Their footsteps made no sound on the thick, crimson carpet. She knocked on the door of a room at the front of the building, and they followed her in before she had a chance to introduce them. Lockyer knew they were being rude. He didn't care. Something about the place was bringing out the worst in him.

'Mr Godwin,' he said, as he and Broad showed their ID again. 'I'm Detective Inspector Lockyer, this is Detective Constable Broad.'

He liked to watch people's faces when first confronted with the police. The little tell-tale flickers that might betray all sorts of things – guilt, resentment, a love of drama. In Miles Godwin, it betrayed impatience, and something close to scorn.

'Yes. I'm actually expecting rather an important call,' he said, not getting up.

Serena's son had inherited her fair hair and narrow shoulders, but that was where the similarity ended. Miles was rounded and soft in body and face, where his mother was all angles. He had the beginnings of jowls, his hair was thinning and he had pink cheeks – there would have been something babyish about his face if it hadn't been for eyes that were slightly too small, and too hard. Lockyer knew he was a year older than Harry Ferris, which made him forty-five.

His office was a high-ceilinged room with elaborate plasterwork, floor-length curtains and a vast antique partner's desk, behind which Miles sat in an ergonomic executive chair. Racing green, to match the desk's inlay. The rest of the furniture was sleekly modern and minimalist. An extravagant display of pale flowers was arranged impeccably on a side table; the paintings on the walls were abstract, originals.

'Well, in that case, we'll get straight to the point,' Lockyer said. 'You'll be aware, no doubt, that Harry Ferris has recently returned home – after twenty-nine years – to be reconciled with his father, your uncle, Professor Roland Ferris.'

'This is about *Harry*?' Miles said, and Lockyer thought he saw a tiny flicker of relief.

'In a way. This is about the murder of Michael Brown at your uncle's house in 2005.'

'Oh, right.' Miles leant back in his chair, clicking the button on the top of his pen. He had definitely relaxed.

Lockyer wanted to know what he'd been nervous about. 'I rather thought that was all settled a long time ago.'

'The case was concluded, yes.'

'The housekeeper, in the barn, with the kitchen knife. Just like Cluedo.' Miles looked pleased with his joke.

'However, that investigation was initially hampered by the misidentification of the victim. It was several days before we established that it was not in fact Harry Ferris, and could then correctly identify him. During which time, crucial evidence may have been lost, and the killer might have been given time to disappear.'

Miles Godwin stopped clicking his pen. He narrowed his eyes. 'But she didn't disappear, did she? And you had enough evidence to convict her. So,' he smiled, 'no harm, no foul.'

'Were you aware of Harry Ferris's whereabouts during the time he absented himself from his father, and the rest of the family, between 1993 and the present time?'

'Yes.'

'You were at Longacres in 2005, when the man claiming to be Harry Ferris first arrived. You were also there several times after that, prior to Michael Brown being murdered.'

'In fairness to the fellow, I don't think he ever actually *claimed* to be Harry. Uncle Roly did that for him.'

'You must have known as soon as you saw him that he wasn't Harry Ferris,' Broad burst out.

'Yes. That's correct.' Miles fixed her with a steady gaze that refused to be rebuked, least of all by a young woman.

'So why didn't you say anything?'

Miles shrugged. Lockyer couldn't tell if his nonchalance

was real or feigned. 'My mother tried to tell Roly, but he wasn't having any of it. Didn't want to know.'

'But *you* could have convinced him. You were in touch with Harry, after all. And, more importantly, you could have told the police when Mr Brown was murdered. Why let the charade continue?'

'The thing is, Officers, I made a promise. And I keep my promises.'

He looked from Broad to Lockyer and back again, as though waiting for them to respond. When they didn't, he looked impatient. 'Harry and I were close, growing up; closer than a lot of cousins, especially after he came to live with us. When he told me he planned to cut them all off – all but me, as long as I never told anyone we were still in touch – what choice did I have? It was up to him what he did, after all. Wasn't it better that I kept my word, and knew where he was and that he was okay, than that I broke it and lost touch with him?'

'And you never spared a thought for his father's feelings, all those years?' Lockyer pressed.

Miles pulled a dismissive face. 'Harry didn't want his dad to know anything about his life. He didn't want to see him, or speak to him, and he never asked me for news about him. He was well within his rights with all of that, I'd say.'

'Had you seen Harry at all, during the years he was absent?'

'Yes, of course. Really, the only place he was absent from was Longacres, and the only people he was absent from were Uncle Roly and my mother. I often saw him, especially while I was still in London. He was living a normal life – studying, then working his way up a law firm. Girlfriends, gym membership, the lot.'

'Yet you never let it slip, not even by accident.'

'I try not to have accidents, Inspector.'

'Obstructing the police is a serious offence, Mr Godwin, particularly when it's prolonged and determined,' Lockyer told him. 'You could have told us in confidence, instead of watching the investigation go off in the wrong direction.'

'Well.' Miles looked down, with a smirk that told Lockyer he'd enjoyed watching the police do precisely that. 'You got there in the end. If I'd told you straight away it would have come out, and then what? My mother always suspected I knew where Harry was. She'd have been on to me in a flash, and he'd have cut me off.'

Lockyer caught himself disliking the man intensely. *One of those posh blokes who thinks it's all a game.* 'So you didn't tell her either?'

'I never told anyone. My word is my bond.'

'You should have told the police what you knew,' Broad said.

'*You* don't look old enough to have been a police officer at the time,' Miles replied. He looked at Lockyer. 'But I remember you, of course. The thrusting young yokel detective. Quite the figure you cut. The prime suspect developed something of a crush on you, as I recall . . . Perhaps it was mutual.'

'Why did Harry want to cut his father off so completely?' Lockyer asked.

'You'd do better to ask Harry that.'

'I'm asking *you*, Mr Godwin. And I'd hate to think you made a habit of hiding things from the police.'

The remark hit the spot. Miles looked put out – tense again. 'I don't know, really. Aunt Helen's suicide can't have helped – he would never talk about it. Harry, I mean. I know there were problems before that as well, but any mention of her put him into a fury. He gave me a bloody nose over it once – all I did was ask if he thought it'd hurt. Not the most sensitive of questions, but I was a callow youth at the time. She hanged herself, you know. Out in the barn, same place where that chap got stabbed. If you believed in ghosts, that barn'd be a place to avoid.'

Lockyer thought of the laughing woman in the photo on the wall at Longacres, leaning on the car, sun in her hair, a glint of white teeth. Her little boy in the seat by her hip. 'Do you believe in ghosts, Mr Godwin?' he said.

'No, of course not. I'm not an idiot.'

'Did Harry blame his father?'

'Like I said, he wouldn't talk about it. But when a woman hangs herself, it doesn't cast the husband in a good light, does it?'

'What was Helen Ferris like?' Broad asked.

'Like an auntie,' Miles said. 'Kind, softly spoken, wore flowery dresses, that sort of thing. I don't really know. I was just a boy. She never shouted – she only ever gave us the meekest of tellings-off, which we always ignored. Not like my own dear mother, good grief. Helen wore pearls for dinner and probably never had an original thought in her life, and she doted on Harry. I don't think he was meant to be an only child, I think she wanted more, but Harry was all she got, and she adored him.'

'Odd, then, that she should take her own life while he was still so young.'

'Well, I guess when you've gotta go, you've gotta go.' Miles's phone began to ring. 'Now, if you don't mind, I really must take this.'

'Well, we'll let you know,' Lockyer said, with a nod.

'About what?'

'Whether we decide to press charges for obstruction.'

'Really, Inspector.' Miles raised his eyebrows. 'Haven't the police got better things to do with their time?'

Lockyer and Broad went back to the car without saying a word to each other.

'God!' Broad exclaimed, as they got in, cheeks flushed.

'I know.'

'Was he that full of himself during the original case?'

'Worse, I think.'

'Can we charge him with being a smug wanker?'

Lights were coming on along the high street as the sky darkened. Lockyer stared across at the pristine windows of Godwin's Estates for a bit longer, before starting the car and pulling away. 'He certainly thinks he's a lot cleverer than everybody else. That's often a useful way to catch someone out.'

'You think he has something to hide?'

'I'm certain of it. Whether it has anything whatsoever to do with the case, I'm less sure about.'

They were out of Marlborough, and driving fast back along the A4 towards Avebury before Broad spoke again. 'Guv, what he said about the main suspect having a crush on you . . .?'

'Yes?' Lockyer spoke more curtly than he'd meant to. The question made him feel exposed. He waited, but Broad had taken the hint. And yet he found himself answering. 'She didn't. I don't think she did. It's just that . . . I was the on-call detective, and when I got there she was still in the barn, standing next to the body. Uniform had told her to stay put until the SOCOs got there. So she was just standing next to the corpse, covered with blood and shivering. She was . . . in a bad way. Upset, obviously. I was the first to go in and talk to her.' He stared at the road as it rushed towards them so he wouldn't see Hedy's face again, or her wide, frightened eyes. Wouldn't catch the smell of blood in his nostrils and, underneath it, the smell of her skin and hair and clothes. He fiddled with the heat setting in the car. 'Like I said, after that she would only talk to me.'

'So . . . there was a kind of . . . connection?'

'There was . . .' Lockyer thought about shutting the conversation down. Denying it. 'There was *something*. She seemed to trust me.'

'Trust you to do what?'

'I don't know.' He realized how true that was. 'She was either deeply manipulative and playing with my ego or else she . . . needed a friend.'

There was a long pause. The peculiar silhouette of Silbury Hill slid by outside the window, a huge and enigmatic prehistoric mound that was so familiar to them that neither of them truly saw it any more.

'I don't really think of you as having an ego, Guv,' Broad said. 'If you don't mind me saying so.'

'Well, perhaps I did back then. Do you know any men in their twenties who *don't*?'

'No. So what's next? Are we going to go after Miles for obstruction?'

'Not worth the effort – he was right about that. But we know where he is, if we get the chance to make ourselves annoying to him again.'

Lockyer saw the flash of Broad's smile in the dark.

'I wonder if Harry Ferris would give *you* a bloody nose if you asked about his mother's suicide?' she said.

'You may yet get the chance to find out. But we have to wait.'

'Forensics on the knife.'

'Yes.'

What Lockyer didn't say was that, if Miles Godwin was telling the truth about knowing where Harry was all along – and it seemed likely that he was, given that he'd contacted Harry to let him know how ill Roland was now – then it put Miles out of the frame for the murder of Mickey Brown. He could have no possible reason to kill a blameless Traveller who was unknown to him. Not unless he *had* known Mickey somehow. But that would imply that he had a whole other life that they didn't yet know about.

And then there was Harry Ferris, living his normal life for twenty-nine years, during all of which time Roland Ferris stayed at home, missing him, wondering. So desperate for his son to come home that he made him a birthday cake every year, like some latter-day Miss Havisham. *Working his way up a law firm. Girlfriends, gym membership, the lot.* If Roland had been so desperate to find his son, it sounded as though a few simple searches would have done the trick. Certainly, a private detective would have had no trouble unearthing him, and Roland was hardly short of money to pay for one. So why did he never try?

'Weird, isn't it, two violent deaths happening in the same place like that?' Broad said. 'The barn, I mean. Mickey Brown being murdered, and Helen Ferris hanging herself.'

'I suppose so.'

'Do you think they're connected?'

Lockyer wanted to say, *Yes, I do.* He had never believed in coincidences. Assume nothing; believe no one; challenge everything. It was the ABC all police officers were taught. But he didn't want Broad getting in too deep yet. Not if they were going to have to pull the plug.

'We need to wait for the forensics,' he said.

Lockyer got the phone call from the lab two days later. His pulse picked up when he realized it was one of the Cellmark scientists on the line, a woman called Susan Jones to whom he had spoken many times but never actually met.

'I've emailed you the full report – you should have it now. But I wanted to talk through a couple of things with you.'

'Something interesting?' Lockyer asked. Across the room,

Broad looked up. Lockyer turned his face to one side. He didn't trust his reaction to whatever was coming, and wanted to keep it to himself.

'Potentially. I found many latent prints, layered on the handle of the knife, but none at all on the blade. That's to be expected. Some of the latents were intact, some had been damaged by overlaying prints and subsequent handling. All that were good enough for comparison matched your suspect, as identified at the time, Hedy Lambert.'

'The previous report noted that some of the prints were faint. What do you make of that?'

'I was just getting to it. It's a confused picture. Some of the prints are indeed fainter than others, which is not that remarkable in itself. Older prints, prints made by fleeting contact, you might expect them to be partial, or less distinct. What the previous report didn't seem to pick up on was that it was the *newest* prints that were generally fainter, in places.'

'What does that mean?'

'The handle of the knife is very porous. It's hardwood, but years of use have raised the grain and worn off any wax or varnish it might have had when it was new. That's why so many prints made at various different times have survived. And, of course, it can't have been washed thoroughly after each time it was used.'

'No, it was only used for vegetables. Lambert said she often just held the blade under the tap for a few seconds to rinse it.'

'Right. Well, I also found something else the first examination didn't. I'm surprised it was overlooked, but perhaps it was more hidden by the blood when it was fresh.'

Susan paused. Lockyer shut his eyes briefly.

'I found a tiny fragment of plastic caught in the small gap between the blade of the knife and the handle.'

'Plastic? What kind of plastic?'

'A thin, clear PVC film.'

'Cling-film?'

'That would be my best guess. It might not be relevant at all – I sometimes use a knife to cut cling-film. Nevertheless, given how porous the wood of the handle is, and how good, therefore, at retaining latent prints, it is possible that, if somebody wrapped the handle tightly in cling-film, making sure there was no movement of the film *across* the wood, causing friction, they could then have handled it briefly, and left the existing prints intact enough to imply that it hadn't been touched. Partial transfer to the plastic film would account for the top layer of latents appearing fainter. This is not a proof positive at all, you understand. It's a theory – one I plan to investigate further when I can.'

Lockyer was silent for a beat. He pinched the bridge of his nose, hard. 'Are you saying that somebody not only took steps not to leave any prints on the murder weapon, but that those steps were designed to preserve Lambert's prints, and implicate her?'

'I couldn't possibly speculate on this potential third party's motives, DI Lockyer. And as I stress in my report, this is not proof positive of the involvement of any such person.'

'But it's enough that Hedy Lambert's defence team might have been able to raise sufficient doubt to prevent a conviction, had they been aware of it.'

'They could certainly have given it a good go.'

'Thank you, Susan. You've been extremely helpful.'

'Is this good news or bad news?'

'I have no idea. But it's certainly news.'

Once he'd hung up, Lockyer took a moment before turning to Broad. He ran one hand through his hair and down along his jaw. Centring himself.

'That sounded important, Guv,' she said.

Lockyer nodded. 'I need to talk to the DSU.'

'Do you think it's enough for us to carry on with?'

'I think so. I hope so. That's what I need to find out.'

He got up without another word. He couldn't work out what he was feeling, whether it was anger, or guilt, or hope. A potent mix of all three. It made it hard to keep still. He clenched his fists impatiently while he waited for Considine to finish a call, then knocked and went in. 'Can I have a word, ma'am?'

As briskly as possible, he relayed what the scientist had told him. Considine listened in apparent total calm. Only a crease between her eyebrows betrayed that she might be troubled by what he was saying.

'This proves nothing, Matt,' she said at last.

'It raises doubt.' Lockyer jabbed her desk with one finger, then quickly retracted it. 'Which, coupled with Hedy Lambert's continued protests of innocence . . . I think it's enough, ma'am. Enough for me to take another look.'

'How sure are you that you don't simply *want* Hedy Lambert to be innocent?'

'After putting her away for fourteen years? I'm not sure I want that at all, ma'am.' It was true: the idea felt like a fist in the stomach. 'But if she is, I want her cleared. We *have* to clear her.'

Considine looked at him steadily. 'There is still no forensic evidence that anyone else was involved, Matt. We certainly don't need to trouble the CPS with this just yet.'

'But the prints on the knife were the only cast-iron forensics we had on Lambert! Everything else could be explained the way she described it. The fibres, the blood . . . If the print evidence on the knife *isn't* cast iron, then . . .' He spread his hands, looking up at his boss. 'We worked the case as best we could, and we trusted in the forensics on the knife. But I *know* you, ma'am. Well enough to know you'd rather admit a mistake than let a killer walk free. Or leave an innocent person in jail.'

'*Christ*, Matt!' Considine burst out, reacting at last. She gripped the arms of her chair as if she'd like to propel herself out of it, out of the room, away from the news Lockyer was giving her. She dipped her chin, staring down at her desk for a moment. 'Fine. What's your strategy?'

'It was someone inside that house, or who had keys to get in and get the knife,' Lockyer said. 'Harry and Roland Ferris are hiding something. I'm sure of it. But the other people in the house at the time too – Roland's assistant, Paul Rifkin; Miles Godwin, and Roland's research student . . . It's going to come down to who thought the man in the barn was

Harry, and who knew he was Mickey Brown. And who had a motive to kill either of them. I need to talk to them all again. I need to do some digging. And I need to talk to Hedy Lambert. This could have been deliberate. A deliberate, malicious and successful campaign to frame her. And I'd like all the forensic evidence looked at again.'

'Well, you'd better get on with it, then, hadn't you?'

'Thank you, ma'am.'

'Matt? Keep it to yourself. For now. If I'm going to look a twat in public, I'd rather know when it's coming. And I'd rather you were one *hundred* per cent sure first.'

6

Day Eight, Friday

The hope on Hedy's face was unmistakable. Lockyer noticed it as soon as he saw her, waiting at one of the tables in the private room they'd been allocated now that he was there on official police business. Rain was hammering at the windows and the room was lit by sickly yellow strip lights, but Hedy's eyes were bright as he approached. She sat up straight, shoulders back, hands in her lap. Like a child on her best behaviour – as though that might somehow make him deliver good news. Something to cling to. She'd piled her hair on top of her head in a messy knot; long strands escaped and hung down around her shoulders. Lockyer knew he needed to be very careful. Careful of himself. Careful not to raise her hopes too much.

At the same time, he was reluctant to disappoint her.

'Inspector Lockyer,' she said, with the same bright tension in her voice. 'You've found something. Haven't you?'

'Miss Lambert.' Lockyer chose his words carefully. 'I've been to see the Ferrises and—'

'You met Harry Ferris?'

'Yes, I did.'

'What was he like? Did he say why he'd run away for so long? How was Roland? I bet he was over the moon—'

'Hedy, please . . . Can you just listen to me, and answer a few questions?'

Hedy blinked, and sat back from him a little.

'I know it must be very difficult to be patient,' he said.

'Not at all. You have to get good at it in here or you'd go mad inside a month.'

'I did see Harry Ferris, yes. He's a lawyer now, living in London. Done very well for himself. Roland was obviously delighted to see him, but I can't say the feeling appeared to be mutual.'

'A lawyer? So, not living rough, not struggling with any . . . issues, then?'

'He didn't seem to be. Other than that he was obviously angry about something.'

'So he just . . . went and lived his life elsewhere? Poor Roland.' Hedy shook her head. 'Whatever he did to deserve being cut off like that . . . I don't think he *can* have done anything that bad. If he made mistakes . . . well, I don't know. But he's not a bad person.' She chewed her upper lip, eyes fixed on the middle distance. Picturing him, Lockyer guessed. Picturing him as she'd seen him last.

'He's come back because Professor Ferris is very ill,' Lockyer said.

'The CLL?'

'Yes. I don't think he has much time left.'

'I suppose he didn't do too badly. Fourteen years after first diagnosis, at his age, I mean. Poor Roland,' she repeated. 'I'd have liked to see him again.'

'He said the same thing about you.'

'Did he?' The ghost of a smile.

'We've found out that Miles Godwin knew exactly where Harry was all that time.' Lockyer watched carefully for her reaction. 'They'd stayed in touch, but Miles was made to swear he'd never disclose Harry's whereabouts to the rest of the family. That's how Harry found out his father was dying. Miles let him know.'

Hedy's stare turned hard, and Lockyer saw a muscle twitch in her cheek. It looked like the suppression of a dangerous outburst of emotion. 'That little shit,' she said quietly.

'You didn't like him?'

'You've met him, haven't you? Miles is not the kind of person anyone can like. Even Serena doesn't *like* him – she might have to love him but she doesn't actually like him. He's a selfish pig. I think he might actually be a psychopath or a sociopath, or whatever. He can't conceive of other people being real, let alone caring about them. We're all just cardboard cut-outs to him. He can't comprehend a world outside his own bubble, where anything could be more important than him winning. I met some of his friends once – they came to the house – and they were all the same. Competing to be the loudest, the richest, the most daring or wacky or clever. And everything – *everything* – is a way of keeping score.' Her voice was laden with disgust.

'He's an estate agent now,' Lockyer said.

Hedy tipped her head back and laughed, properly laughed. 'Priceless,' she said. 'Thank you, Inspector. That's made my day.'

Lockyer couldn't help smiling. He realized it was the first time he'd ever heard her laugh. 'Are you surprised he knew where Harry was all that time?' he asked.

'Not at all. I'm sure he loved it. Knowing something nobody else did – that's a win, isn't it? I'm sure he enjoyed not telling Roland.' She looked down at her hands. 'At least Harry cared enough to come back now his father's actually dying. That's something, I suppose.'

'Hedy, do you have any idea why Harry went away in the first place? Did Professor Ferris ever talk to you about that? Did *he* know the reason? Or have suspicions?'

'No. I mean, I did ask him, once or twice.'

'You asked Ferris?'

'Yes. And I asked Harry when he came back – well, I asked the person I *thought* was Harry.'

'You mean, you asked Mickey Brown?'

'Yes.'

'What did he say?'

'Oh, something vague.' She folded her arms defensively, not meeting Lockyer's eye. He was reminded of the second motive that had helped get Hedy sent down. Her motive for killing Michael Brown.

'Like what?'

'Like . . . oh, I don't know. He was always saying something and nothing. He might have said "I just needed to be somewhere else," or "There are many places to call home, and many people." That kind of thing. Pseudo-philosophical stuff.' Her voice had gone flat. 'Ultimately meaningless. But ambiguous enough that poor Roland could read into it whatever his heart desired, I suppose.'

'You never heard him say anything that it seemed like only the real Harry would know?'

'Well . . . not to me; but then, I didn't know the real Harry. There was one time I overheard him talking to Roland, and there was something more . . . definite. What was it?' She squinted, trying to remember. 'Something about school. That was it, yes – the headmistress at school. About her being the wicked witch or something, and they laughed about it.'

'Really? So Mickey did know things?'

'I think so, yes. But, like I said, I wasn't normally around when he and Roland were talking, and to me he was always just . . . vague.'

'And what about Professor Ferris? Did he ever say anything to you about why Harry left?'

'Nothing specific. Once, before Harry – Mickey – arrived, he told me he wasn't to blame.'

'For what?'

'I don't know, exactly. I'd said something like "I'm sure he'll come back one day, when he's ready," that sort of thing.'

'Could he have meant he wasn't to blame for his wife's suicide?'

Hedy looked up at him steadily. As though trying to work out what he knew. How much. Lockyer felt again the unease she often caused him. That blurring of truth, when to trust and when to be wary. 'He might have. And of course he wasn't.'

'No?'

'No. Mental illness causes suicide.'

'Can't people – relationships – or situations, cause mental illness?'

'I suppose so.' She leant towards him. 'But for every bad situation, there's someone who refuses to help themselves. Like an unhappy marriage – it only stays unhappy because, on some level, both people involved choose to stay in it.'

'And was theirs an unhappy marriage?'

'I don't know, Inspector. She'd been dead for more than a decade when I went to work there.'

'Professor Ferris never gave you an impression of what it was like?'

'He loved her, I'm sure of that. Maybe he was a bad husband at times – too caught up in his work, his books. I can imagine that. And I'm sure he could be a bully, perhaps to her, perhaps to Harry, too. But sometimes I'd see him look at her picture – there are pictures of her all over the house, did you notice? And the sadness would be . . . *radiating* out of him. And he goes and lays flowers on her grave on her birthday. Every year.' Hedy chewed at the skin by her thumbnail again. 'Once I brought in some peonies from the garden, pink ones, a big bunch. He looked at them, smiled, and told me they'd been Helen's favourite. And there was so much sorrow in his eyes. That's love, surely. No man would remember a woman's favourite flowers and smile when he saw them if he hadn't loved her.'

Lockyer was inclined to agree with that.

'Inspector Lockyer.' Hedy leant towards him again. 'Have you found out something that's going to help me get out of here? Please, tell me.'

'I can't discuss it with you at this stage, Miss Lambert. Hedy,' he said. 'But certain things have come to light . . . I'm looking into the case again. That's all I can tell you.'

Hedy shut her eyes. 'Please, Inspector. Is there something concrete?'

Lockyer wasn't sure how best to answer. 'I'm having some of the forensic evidence looked at again. At the moment there's no concrete proof that anybody else was involved in Michael Brown's death.'

'But they *were*! Someone else *was* involved! Ask Harry – he's at the heart of all this, I'm certain of it!'

'Hedy, please. I'm reinvestigating. You need to be patient, and tell me anything – *anything* – you can think of that might be relevant.'

'I . . .' Hedy spread her hands. 'I've been inside for fourteen years, Inspector. What could I possibly know now that I didn't tell you fourteen years ago?'

'Did you ever . . . did you ever use a knife to cut clingfilm?' It was one of those things you either did or didn't do, he suspected. A habit, a way of doing something, like using a fork to juice a lemon instead of a squeezer, or crushing garlic with the flat of a blade.

'What? I . . . No. No. It's always got those tear strips on the box, hasn't it? Why are you asking that? What does that mean?'

Lockyer didn't answer. He hated to ask his next question. There'd be no getting the idea out of her head once he'd planted it there. 'Can you think of anybody who would want to harm you, Hedy? Or any reason why somebody might?'

'Harm me?' She looked baffled, before realization dawned. 'You mean ... someone did this to me? Don't you?' Her voice shook, and Lockyer saw the anguish fill her face, tears glinting in her eyes. 'Someone killed him and made it look like it was me. Why? *Why*? I was ... *nobody*! I was nothing! Just a housekeeper, working there ... I didn't do anything to anyone that might make the—' She broke off, taking a deep breath, visibly trying to keep hold of herself.

Lockyer waited, watching thoughts chase across her face. If she was an actress, she was an extremely good one. One of the best he'd ever seen.

'I can't ... I can't think,' she said.

'Do you ever hear from your ex-boyfriend, Aaron Fletcher?'

'What?' Her face came up in an instant, eyes flashing. 'Aaron? No! Of course not. Not since he ... not since ... Have you found him?'

Her hands on the table top clenched into fists, shaking with the strain.

'No.'

'You can't think he'd have anything to do with this? That he'd want anything more to do with me? He got what he wanted after all. How would he even have known where I was?'

'Did he have any family members who might ...' Lockyer trailed off because she was already shaking her head.

'No – well, I say no, because that's what he told me. He said he was an only child and his parents died when he was little. He was brought up in care. But who knows if anything he ever told me was the truth? I doubt any of it was.'

'No. You're possibly right.' Lockyer thought about him for a moment – about Aaron Fletcher, who'd taken everything from Hedy. *I'm not who I used to be*, he remembered her saying to him, during the original investigation. He had looked into her naked eyes, her oddly immobile face, and believed her. Yet again.

He got up to leave. 'If you think of anything else from back then that might help me, anything at all, about anyone in that house, then call me with it. Please.' He gave her his card. The one with his personal mobile number on it.

Hedy nodded. 'Do you have to go already?' she said.

Lockyer didn't really want to. But what could they possibly talk about, other than the case, which they'd exhausted for now? How could he make small-talk with a woman he'd helped lock up, a woman who might be innocent? The stakes were too high. *But there was a connection?* Broad had asked. One way or another, Hedy Lambert might turn out to be the worst mistake he'd ever made. But something else did occur to him.

'Did Aaron have a birthday while you were with him?'

'I . . . Yes. Of course. Why?'

'It's something people don't generally think to lie about. Do you remember when it was?'

'It was on New Year's Day. He always used to joke that the only present he ever got was a hangover.'

'How old is he – or was he?'

'He . . . I . . . we had his thirtieth while we were together. In 2002.'

'Thank you.'

'Please . . .' She stood and reached out quickly, put a hand on his arm. It was only for a second or two: she let go before the guard had a chance to tell her to. 'Please come back soon. Keep asking me things. Keep looking,' she said. 'Please.'

Lockyer said nothing. He turned to go, trying not to notice that he could feel the warmth of her fingers through his sleeve, lingering on his skin.

Lockyer took Broad for a drink at the British Lion at the end of the day. They'd both spent so many hours going through the original case notes that Lockyer's thoughts were refusing to stay straight. Sometimes beer helped. Or, at least, helped something rise to the top, as a starting point. The walk to the pub took them along the main road into Devizes, past the huge duck pond, where the murky water was crowded with swans and geese and moorhens, and past the Bell By The Green, where they were more likely to encounter colleagues. Including Steve Saunders. The British Lion was the only pub in Devizes still run by an owner-landlord, the only one that didn't serve food, or have a TV or any frills of any kind. It was just a boozer, plain, simple, and perfect.

Lockyer got himself a pint of Mad Hare, a bag of crisps to share, and a Diet Coke for Broad, who never drank a drop if she was going to be driving. Lockyer knew he ought to follow her example. They settled into a corner away from the draughty doorway.

'Keep in mind that the forensics don't prove Hedy Lambert *wasn't* the killer, just that she *might* not have been,' he said, determined to do it right this time. To assume neither that she'd done it nor that she hadn't. 'What do you make of her motive?'

'I think the second one you came up with was better than the first, Guv.' Broad flushed, a mottling of colour creeping into her cheeks. Lockyer pretended not to notice.

'I know. The inheritance thing was a stretch – we established that quite quickly at the time, when we asked Ferris about his will. Lambert wasn't mentioned in it. But we thought they might have discussed it, that perhaps Ferris had told her he'd take care of her, and Harry was a threat to that. And we thought she was a woman on the edge – at times she gave every appearance of it.'

'Couldn't that have been shock?'

'Partly, it could. But it was more than that – anyone who spent any time with her could see it. There was something bigger under the surface. Some trauma.'

'Aaron Fletcher.'

Lockyer took a long swig of beer. 'Lambert doesn't think he'd have had anything to do with it – or would've known where she was. But I don't think we should discount him altogether.'

Broad sipped her Coke. 'Perhaps I could come with you next time you go to Eastwood Park. I'd like to meet her. You know, get a feel for her myself.'

'Not a bad idea,' Lockyer said.

'Sounds to me like she was a bit . . .' Broad spread her fingers, searching for the right word '. . . not naive. Credulous. That business with Fletcher, I mean. All that money! And she never thought to check up on him at all.'

'He was very credible. That's how con artists make a living. And they were together for nearly a year, don't forget. She loved him. She thought he loved her. He's clearly very good at what he does.'

'You think he's still at it?'

'I don't think there's any chance at all that Hedy Lambert was his first mark. And he came away with close to two hundred grand, so I don't see any reason why he wouldn't want to give it another go elsewhere.'

'Bastard.' Broad shook her head. 'And there were no grounds to go after him?'

'Only for the Allegro. Which was never recovered.'

Hedy's 1973 Austin, spearmint green. Known, fairly or otherwise, for being the worst car ever made. Complete with quartic steering wheel – universally hated by early users – original upholstery and a boot opening too small to take a suitcase. It had been an eighteenth-birthday present from her grandfather, having sat rusting in his garage for a quarter of a century, and Hedy had restored it herself, with her stepfather's help. It had been her pride and joy, and the only thing she'd managed to refuse Aaron Fletcher was putting him on the insurance. *He asked and asked, but the way he drove . . . there was no chance,* Lockyer remembered her saying. *Slipping the clutch, cornering hard. Seeing if he could get the needle up into the red. No way. That car needed a gentler touch.* Lockyer remembered tears welling in her eyes, dropping onto her clasped hands; her quiet, intense fury as she'd said: *That was my fucking car.*

Stealing it, when he broke cover and ran, was the only crime she could report Aaron for, legally speaking. It should have been one of the easier stolen cars to recover, but it hadn't been. Like any other getaway car, the police had expected it to be dumped, maybe torched, but it didn't turn up. Around half of all cars stolen in the UK never make it back to their owners. New plates, a respray, an over-stretched police force and a change of county . . . Hedy's car, like Aaron Fletcher, had vanished without trace.

'It must have counted as obtaining money via false representation, surely?' Broad said. 'Couldn't they go after him for that?'

'She borrowed the money in her own name and gave it to him freely. Transferred it to a joint bank account. She thought she was topping up his contribution to the venture, but she only had his word for that. Once it was in the joint account, the money was legally as much his as hers. And she was liable for her debts.'

'They were going to set up a physiotherapy clinic, right?'

'Yep. He'd found the perfect premises. It was going to be state-of-the-art, all the latest gadgets – infrared machines, body scanners, I don't know what – the two of them in partnership. Except he wasn't even a physio – he just mirrored her. Went out "to work" every day, fake website, fake clients, the whole shebang.'

'How did she even manage to borrow that much? It's not like her salary was that good.'

'Those were the bad old days of self-certification, Gem, back before the crash in 2008, when banks would basically lend you what you claimed you could afford to pay back.'

'They sound like the good old days to me. I might have had a shot at being on the property ladder before I retire.'

'Yes, you would've. And plenty of people got into a lot of trouble that way.'

Hedy had taken out a 95 per cent mortgage on her grandfather's little terraced house in Swindon, which she'd inherited. She'd also taken out personal loans totalling seventy-five thousand pounds, and maxed-out several credit cards. All of it had gone into the joint account, which she believed was holding the fund for the new premises Aaron had found, just until money from the sale of his house came through. Then the mortgage on Hedy's place would be paid off, as well as a chunk of the loans. The rest they would earn back within three years. They'd done the maths. They'd rent out Hedy's house in Swindon, and live in the flat above the new clinic. Aaron had come up with the plan. Aaron had been so fired up, so excited, so in love.

When he'd vanished, Hedy had been frantic with worry. She'd thought something terrible had happened to him, an accident or something more sinister. She reported him as a missing person. Reported her car stolen, because she couldn't put the pieces together – couldn't believe that Aaron would have taken it. Would have taken all of it, and left. She struggled to keep everything going, contacted the estate agent with whom their new premises had been on the market, only to be told that Aaron had never put in the offer. The solicitor he said he'd engaged had never heard of him. She checked the joint account and found it empty. Spent another two weeks or so desperate for word from him, certain he'd been the victim of a crime of some kind – blackmail or extortion.

Slowly, she'd started to realize what he'd done, and that it had been entirely deliberate. Right from the very start. Choosing her, meeting her as if by chance, making her fall in love with him. The house he'd claimed to be selling to provide his half of the money had been a rental. He'd banged a stolen *SOLD* board into the ground whenever she'd gone round. Understanding came with the feeling that her insides were filling with concrete.

Two months later she'd had no choice but to file for bankruptcy. Her grandfather's house was repossessed. She moved back home with her parents, lost her job because she couldn't turn up for work – could hardly get out of bed in the morning. And still she'd waited for him to come back. It took a lot longer for her to accept what had been done to her. After eighteen months she'd taken the housekeeping job at Longacres as a way to get back on her feet – a return to independence, and an income to start, slowly, to live again.

Lockyer and Broad had both read the transcript of his interview with Hedy:

DI LOCKYER: *How do you feel about him now?*

RESPONSE: *How do I feel about Aaron? [pause] How do you think I feel?*

DI LOCKYER: *I'd like to hear about it in your own words.*

RESPONSE: *I feel . . . I can't describe what I feel. He took everything. I don't mean the money, I mean . . . Everything I was. Everything I thought about myself, about other people . . . all of it . . . he took it. Broke it. But you tell me he didn't break the law.*

DI LOCKYER: *It's very difficult to prove fraud in certain circumstances.*

RESPONSE: *Like it's difficult to prove rape.*

DI LOCKYER: *Are you saying that he raped you?*

RESPONSE: *[pause] Not with physical force. But what do you call it when someone you're sleeping with isn't who they say they are? When they're actually a stranger? What do you call it when everything they've pretended to be, to think and to feel, to get there in bed with you, was a lie? When everything they've ever said to you has been a lie? Isn't that rape?*

DI LOCKYER: *I think—*

RESPONSE: *Because that's how it feels.*

DI LOCKYER: *Please try to remain calm, Miss Lambert.*

RESPONSE: *[upset] Staying calm is going to help me, is it? He's probably doing it to someone else right now, don't you think? Behind him is this trail of . . . of broken pieces that used to be lives. That used to be people. And on he goes. On to the next. More lies, more stealing, more rape.*

DI LOCKYER: *[pause] Michael Brown was a liar, wasn't he?*

RESPONSE: *What?*

DI LOCKYER: *Michael Brown – Mickey – the victim. He was a*

liar. A fraudster, you could call him. Claiming to be Harry Ferris.
Lying to you, lying to Professor Ferris and his family, possibly for
financial gain.

RESPONSE: *Yes. I suppose he was.*

DI LOCKYER: *You must have been very angry with him when you*
found out?

RESPONSE: *[no response]*

DI LOCKYER: *Please answer the question, Miss Lambert. Were you*
angry with Mr Brown when you found out he'd been lying about
his identity?

RESPONSE: *Yes. I was.*

Broad was staring into her notebook of scribbles, frowning in thought. Eventually, she shook her head.

'It'd make no sense at all for Aaron Fletcher to have come back for more.' She looked up, reached for her glass and swilled the remains of the Coke around in the ice melt. 'Would it? Why on earth would he track Lambert down again — and risk exposing himself — to do something as mad as kill a man to frame her?'

'No. I know,' Lockyer agreed. 'If it wasn't Hedy, it was someone else within that household. Had to be.' He finished his drink. 'Still, I'd quite like to trace Mr Fletcher, if we can.'

'What for, Guv?' Broad looked puzzled.

'Just to see if we can make life a bit less easy for him. It pisses me off when people get away with stuff like that. And if Hedy killed Mickey because of what Aaron Fletcher did to her, then isn't he at least partly to blame?'

'Legally?'

'Of course not legally, but *actually*. Morally.' Lockyer turned his empty glass in his fingertips. 'We could at least get him for the car. If we could find him – and he's still got it.'

'Okay.' Broad looked unconvinced. 'It's not really relevant to the investigation, though, is it, Guv?'

'It's all part of the same picture, Gem. I'm not suggesting we make Fletcher a priority. Just put out a few feelers, would you? He'll obviously be using a different name, but we have the photo Lambert provided back in 2002, when it all hit the fan for her – and we have his date of birth, first of January 1972. He told her he grew up in care.'

'It's not much to go on, Guv.'

'No. But it's not nothing.'

'So, what's our priority?'

'I'm going back to talk to Professor Ferris. He needs to know we're looking into all this again, and there isn't much time left to question him about it. Then I'm going to talk to Maureen, and you, DC Broad, are going to locate Tor Heath for me.'

Broad leafed through a couple of pages of her notes. 'The intern?'

'Research assistant. She was helping Professor Ferris with his book, and she's the only person who was at the house at the time of the murder who isn't still there – or thereabouts – now. Not counting Hedy Lambert, of course. See you tomorrow, Gem.'

Lockyer was standing in Sainsbury's, trying to decide whether to buy a curry or Chinese for dinner, when his mother called. Foreboding immediately crashed through the faint blur of beer in his head. She never called unless she needed him.

'Mum? What's happened?'

'It's your father . . .' Trudy sounded tired and frightened. For a second Lockyer thought of Helen Ferris, Harry's mother, hanging herself in the barn. The unthinkable horror for those who'd loved her. He was already putting down his basket of shopping and striding towards the door. 'I'm sorry to bother you, Matthew. I just can't get him to come inside,' she finished.

'What do you mean?' Lockyer stopped in the middle of the car park until someone pipped their horn at him.

'He's been out in Highground since lunchtime, and now it's getting dark but I . . . I can't get him to come in.' There was a pause. 'Silly, really . . .' she said, trying for levity.

'Well, what's he doing?'

'He's just standing there. He's been standing there for hours. I've tried talking to him, and taking him out a coffee, but I wondered if you might come and have a go?'

'I'm on my way.'

He drove too fast, teeth clenched, swung into the yard with a spray of puddled water. Trudy was waiting for him in the porch, her cardigan wrapped tightly around her, arms folded, face heavy with worry.

'I'm sorry to call, Matthew,' she said.

'Don't be ridiculous. Of course you should call me.' Lockyer kissed her cheek.

'Take the quad bike,' she told him.

It was the end of a bitter day, the first flecks of rain in the breeze. The western sky was the coldest of blues. 'What the hell are you playing at?' Lockyer muttered, fronting up to his own fear. The racket of the quad engine filled his ears and his face ached in the wind, eyes streaming as he rode out along a rutted track behind the house, curving westwards and rising to one of their biggest fields, which straddled the top of a long hill. Lockyer slowed to a stop, eyes raking the land in the failing light until he spotted John's thick-set figure against the skyline, wearing the same wide boots and shapeless coat he always wore. Lockyer killed the bike's engine and walked over to him, his work shoes slipping on the wet ground.

'Dad? Are you okay? What's going on?'

John didn't move, or turn towards him. He was staring into the distance, his face red raw from the cold. He had a piece of old baler twine in his hands that he was twisting and rearranging. The slow, steady work of his fingers, and his hair catching in the wind, were the only parts of him that moved. That looked alive. Lockyer took hold of his arm. 'Dad?' he said again, squeezing it hard. Still no response. He shook the arm, then shook it harder. 'Enough of this, Dad! I know you can hear me! There's nothing wrong with your bloody ears.'

Without blinking, John half turned his face. A thin, silvered trail of wet ran from his nose to his upper lip. It caused a sudden dart of love and pain to pierce Lockyer. He had to get hold of himself before he could speak again. 'You're scaring Mum, and I'm freezing my bollocks off, Dad. Let's go in.'

'What?' John's voice seemed to come from far away.

'What have you been doing out here all his time, Dad?' Lockyer noticed the blue tinge to his lips, the shivers starting to grip him.

'Trying to think, Matthew. Trying to work out . . .'

'Work what out?'

'What . . . what to do. About it all.'

'You mean the farm?'

'It's all over, son. You were right to leave, and do something different. I just can't see a way. It's all . . . it's all just . . . I'm no use. None at all.'

'That's not true.' Lockyer searched, desperate for the right thing to say. 'Look, Dad, change doesn't have to be for the worse. Right? Perhaps . . . perhaps it's simply that nothing lasts for ever.'

John blinked. He finally seemed to focus on his son, eyes roaming his features as though trying to make sense of them. Make sense of anything. It scared Lockyer, that questing gaze.

'Come on, Dad. Let's go in.' He took John's arm and started to tow him towards the quad bike. 'Just try not to worry about it now. All you need to do is whatever comes next – right now that's come down to the house, have a bath and eat the hot meal Mum's cooked you. Okay?'

'Change?' John said. 'What change?'

'Come on, Dad!'

John took a couple of stiff steps then stopped. He stared up at Lockyer, eyes wide, glinting in the last of the light.

'Have you found him yet, Matthew?' he whispered, like he hardly dared to be heard. 'Have you got him?'

Lockyer knew exactly who he meant, of course. 'No, Dad. Not yet.'

They were both quiet for a moment. The wind streamed past them.

Then Lockyer spoke. 'It . . . it would have been better for the farm if Chris had still been here, wouldn't it? He'd have had ideas. Made a difference. But I can't, Dad. I just . . . I can't.'

It was true, and they both knew it. By now Chris would have thought of some way to turn the farm around by specializing or innovating. Raising some rare-breed sheep and making cheese from the milk. Setting up farm stays, or yurts for glamping, or rewilding some of the land. If Chris had been there, if he'd lived, he'd have kept the farm alive and made it thrive, whereas his older brother felt powerless to do a damn thing.

The farm was home, it always would be. It just wasn't *his* home any more. But he would always be drawn there; some days he longed to be back, and he always liked to visit. Seeking to feel again the way he'd felt as a kid – the rightness of its four solid walls, his parents, his brother, their animals, all safe and where they were supposed to be. But even before Chris's death, he'd known he couldn't stay forever. He wasn't a farmer, and the thought of trying to be one made him feel suffocated. The thought of never moving away, of living the same life for the rest of his days. Now, however much he tried not to let it happen, being there turned him into the version of himself he liked the least. Out of step with his family, and their way of life. Lacking, in some fundamental way.

And since Chris's death, the farm just reminded him all the more viscerally of his brother – his brother's absence – and the fact that nothing Lockyer ever did could bring him back, or unmake his decision not to go with him that night. Walking by himself on Dartmoor, while Chris bled to death on a pavement in Chippenham. He could never fix it. He had unfinished business with the man who'd killed Chris, and there was a chance that, one day, he might bring him in. But the business he had with himself would never be finished.

John was still staring up at him, his face moving in eddies of emotion so powerful that Lockyer flinched.

'Better that Chris was still here?' John said. 'Of course. Better that we'd lost you instead? Is that what you're saying to me?' He ground out the words.

Lockyer didn't reply. He couldn't.

'Don't you *ever* say that. Don't you ever even *think* it, you hear me, boy? Well?'

'I hear you, Dad.' Lockyer's throat was tight.

John gave a single curt nod. They said nothing else as they crossed to the quad bike, and clambered on board.

7

Day Nine, Saturday

Arriving at Longacres, Lockyer was distracted by voices and the gunning of an engine from the gravelled yard, so he let himself in through the side gate instead of knocking at the door. A low-slung, silver sports car was parked in front of the converted stables with its bonnet propped up. A man was leaning over the engine while Paul Rifkin sat behind the wheel, revving on demand. He was wearing leather driving gloves, Lockyer noticed, with an unfair frisson of scorn.

Paul got out when he saw Lockyer, leaving the car running. His beige chinos were slightly too tight around his sturdy thighs, and his checked shirt was buttoned right up to his Adam's apple. His hair was a severe short-back-and-sides, black bristles against the thick skin of his neck.

'Problem with the car?' Lockyer said.

'Selling it, if he doesn't quibble on the price,' Paul replied. He gazed back at the vehicle. 'Pity. It was always my favourite.'

'Why don't you make Professor Ferris an offer?'

Paul shot him an amused look. 'That's a fully restored 1968 Mercedes-Benz 280 SL Pagoda,' he said. It meant nothing to Lockyer. 'That's getting on for two hundred grand's worth of automobile, Inspector.'

'That much?' Lockyer was surprised. He'd never really understood the fascination some people had with cars. If it got him from A to B through all weathers, he was content.

'Mr Laidlaw over there has had his eye on it for a decade or more. He's another collector – a rival, I suppose you could say. He gets in touch three or four times a year to ask whether it's for sale yet. This time the professor decided to let him make an offer.'

'Generous of him.'

Paul chuckled. 'You've no idea how generous, by his standards.'

'I need to talk to him again.'

'Must you? He's not having a good day.' Paul looked across the yard again. Mr Laidlaw had got into the driver's seat, on the left-hand side. 'It's a bit sad, really. In the good old days that meant you'd get your head bitten off ten times before lunch. Now he hasn't got the energy. Though he did call this morning's carer a "cretinous oaf", which I took to be a good sign, poor bloke.'

'What's his actual medical prognosis?' Lockyer asked.

'There's not much else they can do. The chemo isn't touching it any more, so he's in palliative care. We need to be very careful that he doesn't get any infections – his immune system's shot to pieces.' Paul delivered this news in a softly respectful tone that Lockyer didn't quite believe. 'He could go into a hospice, but he wanted to be at home. Can't say I blame him.'

'How long has he got?'

'It's not an exact science. Weeks or a few months, if he keeps well. Days if he catches an infection that takes hold, or gives him pneumonia.'

'Do you have the contact details of his carers? I'd like to get in touch with one called Debbie. Do you know her?'

'Possibly,' Paul said. 'I've stopped keeping track, if I'm honest. Seems to be a different one every time. I don't have contact details for them individually, no. But I can give you the switchboard number.'

'Thank you.'

'What's Debbie done, then?'

'Nothing you need to concern yourself with, Mr Rifkin.'

'Well, that's put me in my place, hasn't it? Follow me, then, Inspector. I'll take you up. He'll tell you when he's had enough, but please try not to get him riled up. He tires easily these days.'

Roland Ferris looked like the last leaf on the tree. Limp and bloodless, slumped back against his pillows in the study. Lockyer was shocked at the change in him in just a few days. He seemed to have no substance at all, to barely make a shape beneath the sheet. His face had a sheen of sweat, though it was chalky pale rather than flushed with fever.

'Ha!' The professor managed to say. His voice was as reedy and thin as the rest of him. 'You need to work on your bedside manner, Inspector.' He paused to catch his breath. 'By the look on your face, I gather that I look quite as bad as I feel, today.'

'Sorry, Professor.'

The old man waved away the apology. From outside came the sound of the engine again, and he gave the ghost of a smile. 'Purrs like a kitten, that Merc,' he said.

'What made you decide to sell it?'

'Ah, well. The man's been begging me for years. I might have sold it to him before, if I weren't so bloody-minded. Can't drive the thing any more, can I? Might as well take his money.'

'Two hundred thousand is worth having.'

'Paul told you?' Roland rolled his eyes. 'The man is obsessed with price tags. He's worse than the *Daily Mail*. I find it rather off-putting.'

'How many cars do you have, Professor?'

'Seventeen, if Laidlaw takes that one. And before you ask, no, they aren't all worth that much. Some of my favourites could be had for a quarter of that, but that's never been the point, for me. What is it you want?'

'To ask you a few questions, Professor.'

'Hedy?'

Lockyer pulled a chair up to the bedside, keeping a tactful distance. 'You'd better make it quick,' Roland said. 'Time in which to extract answers from me grows short.'

'What answers can you give me, Professor?' Lockyer said.

The old man twitched a shoulder, a movement that might have been a shrug if he'd had more energy. 'Rather depends what questions you ask, Inspector,' he whispered.

'I've had the knife used to kill Michael Brown re-examined. The original pathologist appears to have missed something. It's thrown doubt on whether Hedy was the last person to handle it, or whether somebody else might have done so after her.'

Professor Ferris's face was so still it was like he hadn't heard. His eyes focused on a spot somewhere past Lockyer's left shoulder. At length, he made a slight murmuring sound in his throat. 'Well,' he said. 'Well, well.'

'Are you surprised?'

'I don't know what to think, Inspector. It would be a terrible, terrible tragedy if it turned out poor Hedy has been locked away all this time for no good reason.'

'Yes. It would. So, I'm reinvestigating, and will need to speak to everyone who was in your household at the time.'

'And, of course, it'd be no small black mark against yourself, Inspector. The police, and you specifically.' The dying man stared coldly at Lockyer.

Lockyer chose not to answer. 'Hedy Lambert is still our chief suspect—'

'Rubbish.'

'I just need to be sure.' Lockyer tried not to sound wrong-footed.

'Tosh. You don't think she did it any more than—'

'Any more than you do, Professor?' Lockyer said. 'Then I'd be very interested to hear who you think *could* have been responsible.'

'Haven't a clue. It was probably someone else from the pikey contingent – that was where he'd come from, wasn't it?'

'Could someone from the Travelling community, having located Michael, have unlocked the door to this house, taken the knife, then somehow locked the door again behind themselves?'

'Buggered if I know. But they're a canny lot.'

'Professor, you don't have a lot of time, as you yourself have just pointed out. Sorry to speak so plainly.'

'If you're trying to coax me into some kind of deathbed confession, I fear you'll be disappointed. There's nothing I need to get off my chest.'

'Why did you identify Michael Brown as your son?'

'Because I believed it was him! At the time ...' A small shake of his head. 'Now that I've seen my Harry, I realize I would have known him in an instant, of course, but ...' he gazed up at Lockyer '... sometimes a desperate mind will see what it wants to see, Inspector. And, oh, I was *desperate* to have my boy back! It *could* have been him. There were similarities ...'

'But it must have been obvious that he didn't speak the way Harry had, surely? That he didn't know anything about you, or his childhood.'

'The way a person speaks can change, given ... extreme circumstances. Trauma. That kind of thing.'

'What trauma would that be?'

'And, besides,' the professor went on, ignoring the question, 'he *did* seem to know things! He seemed to know the house. To know me and ... and ...'

'Hedy told me about a conversation she'd overheard. Something about his school days.'

'Yes! Yes, there was that ... Things about his teachers. Other things.'

'How do you suppose Mickey could have known anything specific about Harry's childhood?'

'I have no idea.'

'Are you absolutely certain you'd never met him, or heard of him, before we informed you of his identity?'

'Quite positive, Inspector. He wasn't— His background, as we found out ... Well, he wasn't the sort of person we would have known. Different circles. I don't know ... Perhaps I *gave* him the information. Asked leading questions. At the time ... You must understand, at the time, I was completely convinced.' The professor was quiet for a moment, staring into the past. 'But, you see, he'd just come back to me, my son, or so I thought. And it was obvious he wasn't quite ... stable. Emotionally. I didn't want to frighten him off. So I didn't dare *press* him on anything – press him to answer questions he didn't want to answer, or to talk about things he was reluctant to talk about. I dreaded him simply vanishing again.'

'What didn't he want to talk about, Professor Ferris?'

Again, the old man ignored the question. 'I didn't want to upset the apple cart,' he murmured.

'Professor, why did your son cut contact with you in the first place?'

'None of your damn business.' The sick man's chest rose and fell with short, shallow breaths, and his eyes fixed on Lockyer's with a strange intensity.

'I will get to the bottom of it, Professor. It would just be a lot quicker if you told me.'

'Why? It's not relevant to any of this.'

'Why did you never try to find him? He wasn't in hiding, just living and working in London – hardly the other side of the world, is it? I'm sure you could have tracked him down, if you'd wanted to.'

After a long pause, the professor swallowed. 'Wouldn't have done any good.'

'What do you mean?'

'He didn't want to come back. Didn't want to see me. I . . . I didn't look for him because I knew he didn't want to be found.'

Lockyer sensed the profound pain behind those words. 'I'm sorry to have to ask about these things, Professor, I really am, but if I'm to clear Hedy's name then I need to find the real perpetrator.'

'Ask then, damn you.'

'Did Harry get on well with his mother?'

'Stupid question. What small boy doesn't get on with his mother? He and Helen were devoted to one another.'

'And yet your wife took her own life while Harry was still very young. Do you know what caused her to do such a thing?' There was a silence. 'Did she leave a note?'

'No.' A single, choked syllable.

'You mean, no, there was no note?'

'How can Helen possibly have anything to do with that man's death, Inspector?'

'I don't know yet. Call it a hunch.'

'A hunch? A blasted *hunch*, you son of a bitch?' Roland

struggled to sit up, but soon gave up and lay back, shutting his eyes.

Lockyer hesitated, wanting to push on but not push too hard.

'Please leave,' the sick man whispered.

'You must have some idea why Helen took her own life, Professor. Please.' Lockyer spoke as gently as he could, not really expecting Roland to reply.

Eventually the professor cleared his throat, took a breath. 'There are certain things about a person that should only ever be known by someone who *loves* them, Inspector. Someone who will understand, and not judge.'

After that he seemed to drift into sleep. Lockyer got up to leave, noting the swift movement of a shadow underneath the door. He guessed that Paul Rifkin had been listening to everything they'd said. There was no sign of him when Lockyer opened the door, and no sounds of movement. So it seemed Paul could be quick and quiet when he needed to be. His army training or battlefield experience, perhaps. Both of which, Lockyer realized, meant that he had possibly killed a man, or men.

Lockyer glanced around the upstairs hallway as he went across it, and at the pictures hanging in the stairway as he went down. More faded photos of Helen, Harry, and of the professor as a young man, but by far the most common subject was the classic cars. Pictures taken at shows and rallies; montages depicting the before and after of a restoration; photos with Roland posed at the wheel. It was always summer in those pictures; the sky always high and cloudless, Roland often wearing a narrow-brimmed Panama hat.

Lockyer found Paul in the kitchen, assembling a tray of coffee. There was a small saucer on one side, onto which he was carefully counting pills from a variety of pots and blister packs.

'I think I put him to sleep,' Lockyer said.

'Doesn't take much these days,' Paul replied.

'Mr Laidlaw changed his mind?'

'Hardly, but I told him he'd have to wait. It's coffee time.' He reached for a slip of paper, held it out. 'Here – I wrote down the number of the care coordinator. She should be able to contact Debbie for you.'

'Thank you.' Lockyer took the note, then looked around the kitchen. The ceiling was high, an inverted V of wooden beams lit by spotlights; the cupboard fronts were oak, the floor reclaimed flagstones, the worktops a dark reddish marble that Lockyer found deeply unattractive.

'Who took over all the housework and cooking, once Hedy had gone?' Lockyer asked. 'Did Professor Ferris find another girl to move in?'

'God, no. Not after what had happened. Don't underestimate how shaken up we all were, Inspector, especially the prof. He'd trusted Hedy – *liked* her. Do you know how few people he actively *likes*?' Paul smiled. 'It really made him doubt himself.'

Lockyer was reminded of what Hedy had said about Aaron, and her own broken trust. Her own doubt. *Everything I thought about myself, about other people.*

Paul poured boiling water into a cafetière from a showy height. Glancing up, he caught Lockyer's expression. 'It cools the water slightly before it hits the beans,' he explained. 'Stops them scorching.'

'Right. So, you do it all, now?'

'Not all, no. We've got a woman who comes twice a week to clean and do the laundry. I do the ironing and cooking. Not quite what I signed up for but, to be honest, I'm happy to have something to do.' He glanced at Lockyer again. 'Except when his sister's in residence, of course. She says I could ruin a boiled egg, which I find a bit unfair. Anyway, when she comes, she cooks for the two of them – not for me, mind.' He smiled tightly. 'Burnt eggs all the way, for me.'

'You don't like Serena?'

'I don't like her attitude. Or the way she forgets I work for her brother, not for her.'

'Where is she now? And Harry?'

'Serena went home yesterday. She's got a house down in Dorset, near Shaftesbury. I expect she'll be back next week, if she can fit it in around her busy schedule.'

'Oh?'

'She's on a lot of committees, or so I gather.'

'And Harry?'

'Back in London and at work – business as usual. He's due here for Sunday lunch tomorrow, but I don't know how much he's enjoying his homecoming. Or rather, I do, and the answer's not very much.'

'Not an instant reconciliation, then?'

'Not at all.'

'And what will you do, when the professor isn't around any more?' Lockyer watched Paul closely as he put a teaspoon on the tray, then picked it up again, peered at it, reached for a cloth to buff it.

'I'm not a million miles from retirement age myself, Inspector. I'll have to take stock as and when the sad day comes, of course. But I hope to have some time off. See a bit of the world.'

Lockyer nodded. Paul Rifkin's world was, in some ways, as small as Hedy's had been. He had the nanny flat in the basement, and he'd lived and worked there for twenty years or more. Roland Ferris was bad-tempered, and rarely showed gratitude. Lockyer wondered what had kept Paul there all that time – had he been paid over the odds? Had he grown fond of his employer? Lockyer had seen no sign of that – at least, no sign he'd mistake for being genuine. Was Rifkin just institutionalized, after such a long tenure? Or was he playing the long game, and expecting to be taken care of when the old man died?

'Longacres has been your home for a long time,' he said neutrally.

'I've been very lucky.'

'Has Professor Ferris ever spoken to you about provision being made for you in his will?'

This, finally, bothered Paul. He'd opened the fridge for milk, but stood there a few beats too long, staring into the lit interior as though he'd forgotten what he'd gone for. He turned to look over his shoulder, and Lockyer couldn't quite read his expression. But his smile had gone. 'No, Inspector. He hasn't. Not to me, at any rate.'

'Do you hope to be left something?'

'I'm not sure what you're getting at, but all right, I'll admit it. After twenty-two years working for him, I hope to get a mention at least. But I'm sure as shit not banking on it, Inspector. You've met him. He's changeable, and he's secretive. So I've been salting money away for years. Investing. I've been looking after my future, as well as him, all this time.'

'Prudent of you.'

'So if you're angling for a reason for me to want to knife Harry Ferris, you won't find one there.'

'Did you believe the man in the barn was Harry Ferris?'

'Course I did. I'd never met him before, and he's just a kid in all the pictures. If his own dad said it was him, then of course I believed it. Harry being gone, not having any idea where he was, or how he was . . . It'd plagued the professor, properly plagued him, all the time I'd known him. Small wonder he latched on to the first likely candidate to come along in decades. He *loved* that boy. Now that I finally meet him . . .' Paul shrugged '. . . can't say he seems to deserve it.'

'Can you think of any reason someone in this house at that time might have wanted to hurt either Harry or Michael Brown?'

'No. I don't know of anything.' He spoke flatly. 'Now, if you'll excuse me, the professor likes his coffee hot. I'm sure you can see yourself out.' He left Lockyer in the kitchen.

Lockyer went out through the back door and found

himself facing the barn where Michael Brown's body was found. Where he'd first seen Hedy. For a second he expected to smell the summer morning air again, the jasmine and cut grass, then the blood. He took a breath: nothing but damp earth and leaf mould. He walked along the paved path to the entrance.

The barn was built of wood, which had been rich with creosote fourteen years ago but was now faded and splintering; the pan-tiled roof had a thatch of moss. It wasn't large, only about twenty feet by fifteen or so. The doorway wasn't wide enough for a car, and there was no vehicular access from the yard, so it had never been used as a garage. He went inside, glancing instinctively at the floor where the corpse had lain. *I'm here. You're safe now.* There was no trace of it, of course. The blood had been scrubbed away. Still, Lockyer crouched by the spot and stared hard at it. Then he looked up.

There was only one small window, high in the back wall. The glass was filthy with dead insects and green algae. The roof beams were a good fifteen feet above him, but there were two horizontal cross beams much lower down. It must have been from one of those that Helen Ferris had hanged herself. Lockyer stood, reached up, and was nearly able to touch one. She'd have needed a stepladder. A scratching noise made him look up sharply. Birds on the roof.

The far end of the barn was littered with junk, dusty and cobwebbed: old deckchairs, reels of hose, tea chests. A half-empty box of tiles, a wooden stepladder, speckled with worm holes. *The* stepladder? Nearer the door were things that were clearly still in use – a ride-on mower; a Henry Hoover; a furled parasol and stacked garden furniture. Nothing remotely out of the ordinary.

Lockyer let his mind roam freely for a minute. It came up with a question, and a realization. Why on earth had Mickey stayed out in this barn, when he could have had a cosy room in the house? Harry Ferris might have had a reason not to go indoors – albeit the flimsy one of a childhood vow – but what had Mickey's been? And the realization was that if someone had wanted to kill Harry Ferris back then – wanted it badly enough to go through with it, only to find out soon afterwards that they'd killed the wrong man – there was a good chance they'd still want to kill him. And now he'd broken cover, and come home.

Lockyer phoned Broad on the way back from Longacres, and left a long message outlining what he'd heard that morning. It could have waited until Monday, when she was at the station. Lockyer knew he was avoiding giving himself room for personal thoughts, as much as he possibly could. As soon as there was a gap in his mind his father appeared, standing in that field, slowly freezing himself to the bone. Looking for answers to questions that had none: loss, old age, the steady death of past livelihoods and past ways of living.

Now and then Lockyer caught himself thinking that if he could only find the person who'd killed Chris his parents could be happy again. Whole again, like they'd used to be. He'd looked at the case – of course he had. He'd even got treacherously excited when the lab had managed to raise a DNA profile of the killer, and lift one good thumb print from the handle of the knife, a short-bladed pocket knife that was found two streets away in a bin, nothing like the one that had killed Michael Brown. But then he'd hit the same dead end as he had with the 1997 robberies he'd been working on, just before Hedy's call about Harry's return. Whoever the print and DNA belonged to, they weren't in the database. And unless they did something else to put themselves on there, he was never going to find them.

There'd been no motive. Just a stupid, short, pointless scuffle outside one of the pubs on Chris's big night out, which he had been trying to break up, by all accounts. But then someone had landed a punch on him and he'd shoved back. The police had only had the disjointed and sometimes contradictory accounts of the mostly drunk participants and bystanders to go on – the pub's CCTV had been ancient, the images so poor it was impossible to tell people apart from the grainy, juddering images. Three lads had run off into the night at the end of it. Christopher had leant against the wall for a minute or two while people fussed around him. Then he'd sunk slowly to the ground.

Those involved in the fight hadn't even been mates of Chris's, but it was just like him to try to sort it out anyway. Not because he was a hero, but because he was stupid, in certain ways. He'd always thought everything was just a laugh, and would turn out fine. Hadn't really believed bad things could happen. Sometimes Lockyer was as angry with his little brother as he was with himself, and with whoever had used the knife. And, of course, finding that person wouldn't help. Not really. It wouldn't bring Chris back. It wouldn't take that loss away, or restore their family. It wouldn't cure John's depression, or mend Trudy's broken heart, or make the farm prosper. It wouldn't let Lockyer off the hook.

Still, the sheer mundanity, the *pointlessness*, of Chris's death made Lockyer want to howl at the sky in fury. The need to find his killer, and to punish them, permeated his mind like an indelible stain.

On Monday morning, Broad heard back from the coroner's officer.

'Not that it tells us much we didn't already know. Helen Ferris died, aged thirty-eight, from asphyxiation caused by hanging.' She swivelled back and forth on her chair as she told him, her feet hooked under the desk. Lockyer noticed that she was wearing mascara, which was new. It looked nice. He knew better than to say anything about it.

'And it was definitely suicide?' he said.

'Yep. No sign of foul play.'

'But no note?'

'No. None was ever found. And they looked high and low because she had ink on her right hand.'

'You're kidding?'

'Nope. A thin line of blue ink, from a biro or similar pen. But there was a blue biro on the kitchen planner, where she'd recently added a few things to the shopping list. So it could have been from there.' Broad stopped swinging, put her hand on the computer mouse and tapped her fingers instead. Full of restless energy.

'Is there somewhere else you need to be, Gem?' Lockyer asked.

'No, Guv.' She sounded far too innocent.

'Well. She's hardly going to have put apples and bread on the list right before hanging herself, is she?' he said. 'Don't people about to kill themselves have other things on their mind?'

'I really don't know, Guv.'

There was movement underneath Broad's desk, something other than the fidgeting of her feet. Broad's face fell, but she didn't let her gaze falter as a small dog stuck its head out between her ankles to peer up at Lockyer. The Jack Russell from the photo on her desk.

'Gemma . . .' he said.

'I know, I know! I'm sorry – the dog-sitter's on holiday this week, and Pete was supposed to take him but then he had to visit a client . . . I couldn't leave him home alone all day. I'm really, *really* sorry—'

'All right, all right.' Lockyer held up his hands. 'He's not going to pee anywhere is he?'

'No, I *promise*. He won't bark, either.'

'Just don't make a habit of it – and don't let anyone else see. How did you even get him in here?'

'He fits quite nicely in my backpack.'

'Right.' Lockyer tried to pick up where they'd left off. 'Maybe there *was* a suicide note. And somebody took it.'

'Maybe. Or maybe there was no note. She could have got

the ink on her for any number of reasons. Or even the day before, or something.'

'True,' Lockyer conceded. 'And Harry found her?'

'Yes, when he came home from school. The twelfth of May 1990 – and get this: That's Harry's birthday. He turned fifteen that day. Poor kid.'

'Are you sure? Jesus. Awful.' A pause. 'That has to be significant, don't you think? Or she must have been out of her mind. Do you think she forgot the date?'

'I don't think mums do that.'

'No. So, Harry finds her, and then alerts his dad? How long had Helen been dead?'

Broad skimmed the report again. 'Several hours. As many as eight or ten, and no fewer than six. Though obviously it was only an estimate.'

'So maybe all day. And in all that time Roland Ferris didn't notice his wife was absent from the house?'

'Apparently not, no.'

'Does that strike you as odd?'

'I don't know. I've never been married. Perhaps he was working on his book, or whatever, had his head down and didn't stop for lunch. Or perhaps he thought she'd gone out.'

'Possibly. Still. He kept on working upstairs while she went out to the barn and hanged herself. Doesn't look good, does it?'

'Why the barn, do you think?'

'Convenience,' Lockyer suggested. 'It has good, strong, reachable beams.'

Broad was silent for a while, considering this. Then she

shuddered. 'I just can't imagine doing that to myself. I mean, actually *doing* it. Feeling like that was the best and only thing to do.'

Lockyer thought of his father. He couldn't help it. *I'm no use. None at all.* A twist of fear that he bit back. 'That's something to be glad about, Gem.'

'Too right.'

Lockyer turned his own chair to the window and stared out of it. Trying to move the pieces around. 'If you could unpick a lock, you could pick it closed again after you, right?' he said.

'I think so, yes. If you knew what you were doing. But there were no stray prints on the door, and no signs of it being wiped down. Gloves, maybe?'

'Habitual criminal, then. Professional, even. Calm, considered. Done it before many times. Highly skilled.' He thought again of Paul Rifkin. His army training. But he'd have had keys, no need to pick the lock.

'I suppose so. It was a good Yale lock. You fancying an outsider then, Guv?'

'No. I don't think so. Surely a professional would have brought his own knife with him. Why risk breaking into the house, even to frame Hedy, or misdirect us? But Professor Ferris did bring up the idea of someone who'd known Mickey attacking him. Finding out he was there, somehow, and coming for him. Someone from the Travelling community. And there was that unidentified vehicle parked in the village that night.'

'That would . . . open the field, somewhat.' Broad sounded wary.

'It'd be a nightmare,' Lockyer agreed. 'But we can't discount it. The older bruises on Mickey's body, and the cracked ribs – he got those before he turned up at Longacres. And what was he doing in that barn in the first place? Why not go into the house when he was invited, and take advantage of the plumbing? Plus he had a perfectly good caravan sitting empty not four miles away.'

'Hiding?'

'Hiding.' Lockyer agreed. 'I need to get in touch with PC Tom Williams. He was the SPOC at the time, if I'm remembering right.'

'Single Point of Contact? What – for Travellers?'

'We don't have one now, but we did back then. Tom's retired now, but there's a slim chance he might remember something more. Most other lines of enquiry were shut down once we had Hedy Lambert.' Lockyer thought about it. 'I think I've still got Tom's phone number somewhere.'

'I've found Tor Heath for you as well, Guv,' Broad said. 'Wasn't too hard. She's a professor herself, these days, and she got married. She's Professor Tor Garvich now.'

'Please don't tell me she's at Edinburgh University, or somewhere miles away?'

'No, much closer to home. Bristol. History lecturer, currently teaching units on women and power in early medieval Europe, and the economics of the Black Death, in the undergraduate programme, according to the website. Want me to get in touch with her?'

'Good. Yes, please. Arrange a convenient time for us to go and talk to her.'

Lockyer found Tom Williams's number after a bit of rummaging in an old address book – one that pre-dated his smart phone. He called and left a message, asking to come by and see him. He'd only just hung up when the phone rang again, and he picked it up with a slight start. 'Tom?'

'It's Hedy – Lambert,' the caller said, as though there were other Hedys it could have been.

'Hedy. Miss Lambert.' Lockyer hated the way he immediately felt on edge. Conspicuous. Like he was doing something he shouldn't. Broad swivelled her chair to face him. He forced himself not to turn away, but stopped short of putting the call on speaker. 'What can I do for you?'

'What can you *do* for me?'

He thought he could hear her smile, but perhaps it was only sarcasm.

'You can get me out of here, for starters.'

'I'm working on it.'

'I've thought of something. I mean, I've remembered something.'

'Oh?' Lockyer picked up a pen, moved some important papers aside to find a scrap he could write on.

'You said it could be anything, even if it was small?'

'Yes. Go on.'

'Okay. After the initial excitement of Harry – I mean, Michael – turning up in the barn, and the professor saying it was Harry, and Serena saying, no, it wasn't, well, after that it all calmed down again. For weeks, I mean. We got into a routine, me taking out food for him, him coming and going a bit, but mostly staying put in the barn. We all stopped trying to get answers out of him – where he'd been, what he'd been doing. In fact, after a while it was only ever me and the professor who bothered with him at all. Going out to talk to him, I mean.'

'Go on,' Lockyer said, listening hard to every word, trying to catch the things she didn't mean to say along with the things she did.

'Then one day, I saw Paul go out there. To the barn.'

'Paul Rifkin?'

'Yes. Him.' There was something about the way she said *him*, some tone or inflection. Lockyer tried to identify it. 'He was in there maybe five or six minutes. I was doing the washing-up – you remember the sink is in front of the kitchen window? So he was only in there the length of time it took me to clear up after lunch. But this is the thing – when he came out, he looked *furious*.'

'How do you mean?'

'Red in the face. Glowering at the ground. Looked like he was chewing a wasp. He was . . . stomping, you know? Not walking in a relaxed way. And his clothes were a bit messed up. Shirt half pulled out, that kind of thing.'

Lockyer met Gemma Broad's eye in silence as this sank in. The newer bruises on Michael's body, the finger marks on his neck.

'You're sure about this, Miss Lambert? Why didn't you say anything about it before?'

'I just . . . didn't think of it. It was days before the murder.

I saw Michael later that day, with his dinner tray, and he was fine. I think he was, anyway. Then, with all the shock of – of what happened, it went out of my mind. It's probably nothing, but you did say to think of anything I could.'

'I did. Keep at it, Hedy.'

He felt little chinks appearing, little cracks in the case against Hedy. In the idea of her being a killer. He tried not to grab at them too quickly, in case they slipped away, but they made him clench his fists. These were the things that had troubled him in 2005, the things he'd ignored, and not questioned. The things he'd let go. The ways he'd fucked up. Most things in life, once done, stayed done. He was old enough to know that. Just a rare and precious few things could be put right, and he was going to make this one of them. He couldn't give Hedy back the fourteen lost years of her life, but he could give her the rest of it as a free woman. And he could catch whoever thought they'd got away with Mickey's murder.

8

Day Eleven, Monday

Late in the morning, Lockyer managed to catch Debbie Marshall, Roland's carer, on the pavement beside her parked car in Amesbury. She was young, overweight, and looked terrified the second Lockyer showed his warrant card. Her dark hair was scraped back into a tight ponytail, and she had wide eyes of an arresting pale green.

'I've got to get to my next client,' she said wheezily. Scraps of exhaled breath hung around them, quickly vanishing. Debbie scrabbled in her bag, fetched out an inhaler and took a puff.

'I understand that, Miss Marshall,' Lockyer said. 'But I'm investigating a murder, and I only need two minutes of your time.'

Debbie stared at him, her bottom lip hanging softly open in shock. 'Who's been murdered, then?'

'A man named Michael Brown. Miss Marshall,' he hurried on, before she could declare that she didn't know him, 'I understand you help to care for Professor Roland Ferris, in Stoke Lavington, on a rota.'

'Yes?' Her forehead creased in consternation.

'I've also heard you were present in the room when Professor Ferris's son, Harry, came home to be reunited with him. I believe it was the morning of the twenty-sixth of October.'

'Yeah, I was.' Debbie relaxed a bit.

'Can you tell me what they said to each other? How they were?'

'Well, it wasn't like you'd expect,' she began. The look in her eyes changed from fear to excitement – something almost greedy. 'Not like on *Corrie*, or whatever, where they'd run into each other's arms and hug and say they're sorry and that.'

'No?'

'No. First that butler bloke comes in – normally he knows not to while I'm getting Roland washed and dressed and that but, anyway, he comes in and says, "There's someone to see you," only he says it in a bit of a weird voice, which I notice but I don't think Roland does. He just waves his hand and says he doesn't want any visitors, but the butler bloke says, "I think you'll want to see this one," or something like that. Anyway, before he can say anything else the younger bloke – you know, the son?'

Lockyer nodded.

'He comes up the stairs behind the butler bloke and into the room, and then they just stare at each other.'

'And . . . how did they seem?'

'It was weird. For a second I was dead scared that they were going to go for each other – that's what it seemed like. I was trying to think of how to get out the way but the young one was standing in the doorway, so I couldn't. Anyway, then Roland starts to cry – proper tears running down his face – but he still doesn't say anything, and I can't tell if he's happy or scared or what.

'So we all stand there for, like, *ages*, but then the young one takes a big breath in, like he's been holding it, and he says, "Hi, Dad," serious as anything, and he goes over to the bed, and the old man's holding out his hand to him, but the son doesn't take it or hold it or nothing. And that's when the butler bloke says to me that we should clear off and let them have a moment – though I think he mostly meant *me*, not himself.'

'And how did *he* seem?'

'The butler?' Debbie thought for a second. 'Now you come to mention it, he did seem to have his nose out of joint. He was really rude – practically threw me out. Good job the younger bloke hadn't shown up ten minutes earlier, else he'd've had his big reunion with me still sponge-bathing his old dad. Would've been even more awkward, that.'

Lockyer was disappointed. 'So you didn't hear what they said to one another after that? Nothing at all?'

'No. Sorry. What's this got to do with the dead bloke?'

'Did Paul Rifkin – the butler – say anything else to you as he showed you out?'

'Not *to* me, exactly, but he was muttering away to himself. Like he was cross, I suppose.'

'Muttering? Did you catch any of it?'

'Not really. He was all like "The progidal one returns," and "Well, well, well," that kind of thing.'

'Prodigal son?'

'Yeah, like I said.'

'Thank you, Miss Marshall. Did anything else happen that morning that you can think of? Anything out of the ordinary?'

Debbie thought for a moment. 'Well . . .' She squinted at the sky.

Lockyer waited.

'No. Sorry.'

Driving back to Stoke Lavington, Lockyer tried to glean anything of use from the interview. She'd described the reunion pretty much the way he'd imagined it, but her story *had* served to confirm that the bad atmosphere between Harry and Roland Ferris was long-standing, not the result of arguments since his return, or the presence of the police. Harry Ferris had been cold and angry from the outset. It also confirmed that Paul Rifkin was not pleased about Harry's return. Not pleased at all.

It was one more thing Lockyer could use when he brought Paul Rifkin in for a formal interview. Before that, he wanted to be sure he had all his ducks in a row – he'd put Broad on it. A full and detailed background check, everything she could possibly find out about him, and she would look much harder than the original investigation had. It was no longer a formality, a box to be ticked. Paul Rifkin was now a suspect.

*

He went from one gossip to another, calling in at the shop in Stoke Lavington and asking after Maureen. She wasn't working that day, but he got directions to her house from Cass Baker, who cast a shrewd eye over him and demanded to know if he was reopening Hedy's case. Lockyer gave her no answer.

Maureen, whose surname turned out to be Pocock, lived in a small, terraced cottage at the far end of the village. In the front garden an old tin bath was planted with woody herbs, and there were gnomes. Lots of gnomes, most with chipped paint and the faded, manic grins of washed-up clowns. Maureen opened the door to Lockyer with a knowing sort of smile, and Lockyer tried not to let it irritate him.

The cottage was cramped and low-ceilinged. It smelt strongly of cigarette smoke and last night's cooking, but was otherwise clean and cosy. A fire licked steadily at the window of the log burner.

'Sit yourself down there, Officer,' Maureen said, indicating one of two armchairs either side of the hearth. 'I'll get us a cup of tea, shall I?'

'Thank you. That would be good.'

While he waited, Lockyer looked around the room for evidence of a Mr Pocock. No slippers or shoes by the door, no angling or car magazines, but there were framed pictures of what he took to be grandchildren on the sideboard, so he guessed there must have been one. An elderly tabby cat plodded into the room and jumped into his lap without checking him out first. It settled down at once, and started to drool. Lockyer took a mug of too-milky tea from Maureen, and accepted a biscuit from a family assortment.

'I hope you don't mind cats?' Maureen said. 'You'd be amazed how many people do. Mind them, I mean. I've never been able to get my head around it. Cold? Snooty? Nonsense. That there's the soppiest creature in the world.'

Lockyer smiled briefly, choosing not to mention he was more of a dog person.

'Cass mentioned to me that you used to babysit for the Ferrises,' he said. 'Back when Harry was a little boy?'

'That's right. I've looked after most of the kids in this village at one time or another. Lived here all my life, I have.' Maureen settled her substantial figure into the chair opposite. 'I did try to call in on Harry the other day, to say hello, see if he remembered me, but I was turned away.'

She shrugged, but Lockyer could see that she minded.

'He was such a dear little lad, back in the day. I suppose they've got things that need sorting out between themselves.'

'It's those things I'm interested to hear about, Mrs Pocock. Can you tell me anything about the feud between Harry and Roland Ferris?'

Maureen stared into space, eating her biscuit. 'Can't say as I can, I'm afraid.'

'Right. Well. Can you tell me about Harry as a little boy? And about the family, as you knew them then?'

'That I can do.' She repositioned her backside. 'What's this all about? You digging the dirt on the Ferrises? You can tell me, I won't breathe a word. Going to get the house-keeper off the hook, are you, like Cass is always on about?'

'Just tying up a few loose ends, Mrs Pocock.' Lockyer regarded her steadily. 'Young Harry? And the Ferrises?' he prompted.

'Yeah. Well, they were just like any normal family when I first started there. 'Cept rich, of course. They always had lots of money – I think it was in Roland's family before he even got to be a famous professor. And Helen was from money too. That type always marries one of its own, don't it?'

'A lot of people do, I'd say,' Lockyer said. 'Not just the wealthy.'

'Yeah, I suppose.' Maureen looked at him slyly. 'What about you, Officer? You married to another copper?'

'I'm not married at all, Mrs Pocock.'

'Well, well. Who'd've thought it, handsome man like you?' She squinted at him. 'Who broke your nose for you?'

'My brother.'

'Ha! Sounds about right.'

Lockyer smiled. He didn't bother to explain that it had been an accident. The winter before Chris died, he'd been going through an American punk-rock phase, listening to The Offspring, spiking his hair and hanging a long key chain from his waistband when he went out. There'd been a spell of icy weather, and they were trying to free a frozen drop bolt, both of them heaving on it, hands numb, teeth gritted, steam rising from them like it did from the cattle. And when it finally surrendered Chris's fist landed in the middle of Lockyer's face with a crunch.

'Shit! Matt!' he cried, while Lockyer was distracted by the sudden pain, the rush of hot blood over his mouth. That metal taste.

'Fuck,' he mumbled, thickly.

'Fuck,' Chris echoed. Then laughed. 'Sorry! Mate . . . that looks . . . I don't know.' He flexed his hand. 'Ouch . . . think I've cracked my knuckles.'

'Well, I'm very fucking sorry about that,' Lockyer said, but couldn't keep a straight face. He was giddy with adrenalin by then.

'Jesus – please don't smile.' Chris shuddered. 'The blood in your teeth . . .'

The A and E doctor said: 'Nasty break. How did this happen?'

'I punched him,' Chris told her, grinning. 'Sibling revelry.'

Lockyer left a pause he hoped Maureen would fill.

She did. 'Where was I? Right, yes. Nice people. Happy enough. Roland was always quite strict and formal, not the warm and friendly type. I don't know if he was a very *fun* dad. If Helen was busy he certainly wouldn't come out of his study to look after the boy. That's when they'd call me. He always wanted Harry to go off to boarding school, but Helen was adamant she wanted him at home with them. She wouldn't have a nanny either, not even when he was a tiny baby. So he was a day pupil at Dauntsey's, with all the other posh kids. But he was sweet as anything, back when I first knew him.'

'How old was he then?'

'When I first sat for them? Dunno. Four? Five? But you'd

have thought he was younger – he was small for his age. A skinny little thing, sweet but ever so shy. Wouldn't say boo to a goose.'

'Do you remember him ever having a friend called Michael Brown? Or Mickey?'

Maureen eyed him shrewdly. 'You mean the bloke who got stabbed? No, 'fraid not.'

'It seems that Mickey knew enough about Harry's early years to be able to convince Professor Ferris he was Harry. Was he a school friend, maybe? Or here in the village?'

'Not that I know of.' She shrugged. 'Harry's best mate was little Jasper Coombes, though I think they drifted apart after Harry moved up to big school.'

'So, Roland was strict? What kind of strict?'

'He was forever telling Harry off. Helen kept telling him he was too hard on the lad.'

'Telling him off for what?'

'Oh, all sorts of things. School marks not good enough, not getting his swim badge – that was one. He wasn't allowed to play around the cars at all, unless Roland was there to supervise him. You know – the fancy old cars? So if he ever got caught climbing on them he got a right good bollocking. Floods of tears when I got there sometimes, poor little mite.'

'And did you ever—'

'I don't mean it to sound like Roland didn't love Harry. *Course* he did. He was just the old-fashioned type. Kids should be seen and not heard – or better still neither, especially if he was working. I suppose that's how he was brought up himself, see?'

'I understand.'

'And I think they were happy, for the most part, Helen and Roland. In spite of the rows, I think they were happy. Though I did used to wonder if Helen wasn't a bit lonely. I mean, she was quite a lot younger than him. I *heard* she was one of his students, back in the day. But she had Harry, I suppose. They were always thick as thieves. When he was little, anyway.'

Lockyer was trying to reconcile this picture of Helen – clever enough to go to university, bold enough to run off with her lecturer, and fight for her son's upbringing – with Miles Godwin's description of her. *Wore pearls for dinner and probably never had an original thought in her life.* He suspected, more strongly than he already had, that this said more about Miles than it did about Helen.

'When he was little, you say,' he said. 'Did that change, then?'

'Oh, yes. Harry turned thirteen and it was like this.' Maureen snapped her fingers. 'I mean, it was almost funny. Suddenly he's a moody teenager. A problem child. Shuffling about the place in silence, hands in his pockets. You were lucky to get a grunt out of him, let alone a conversation. "What's it all about, Harry?" I said to him. "You can always talk to me, if someone's getting at you." Tried to help, I did, but not a word from him. Wouldn't be hugged any more. Off his food. Rebellious, you know?' Maureen shook her head. 'Got himself suspended from school for telling a teacher to eff-off. Then the rows really picked up.'

'Between the Ferrises?'

Maureen nodded. 'The police even turned up one day. I was coming along the lane and I saw the car pull up, and I could hear the shouting from back there – Helen and Roland. I 'spect the whole village could hear them, and I thought, someone's only gone and called the filth – pardon my French – thinking they're going to kill each other. Turns out the visit was about something else altogether, can't remember what, but I wouldn't have been surprised if someone *had* called them to break it up. Harry was sitting out on the step when I arrived. "What's it all about?" I asked him. He just got up and ran away. Over the gate across the road and into the field. Ran away from *me*. Just about broke my heart, that did.'

'Did you ever find out what was making him behave like that? Or if it was just hormones?'

'No, I never did. Could have been hormones, I suppose, but . . . seemed like there was more to it, to me. There was a time when I wondered whether . . .'

'Go on.'

'Well, he was such a sweet, fey little boy. I wondered at one time if he wasn't . . . you know, a fairy. Batting for the other side.'

'You thought Harry might be gay?'

'That's the kind of thing that can cause upset between a boy and his dad, isn't it? Least, it was back then. And it's the sort of thing that shows up around the same time as the hormones.' Maureen paused. 'Then Helen ups and kills herself! The kid had no chance after that.'

'What makes you say that?'

'If his *mum* hadn't been able to sort him out, how on earth was Roland ever going to manage it? He sent Harry off to board at his school, but he soon got himself expelled. Then he went off to live with his aunt and I think it was probably for the best, if you tell me he's turned out all right now. A lawyer, I heard?'

'That's right, yes.'

'And they've made up, have they? Him and his old man?'

'They've been talking, as I understand it.'

'That's something I suppose. Sad, it was, what happened to that family.'

'It does seem . . . extreme, to me, for Harry to cut all contact with his father for so long. Wouldn't you say?'

Maureen frowned as she dipped another biscuit into the dregs of her tea. 'Here's what *I* think, Officer. I think sometimes, when someone goes off like that and doesn't get in touch, it's not because they don't want to see the people they've left behind. Not always. It's because they don't want to *be* seen.'

'You mean . . . he was punishing *himself*, not his father?'

'Could've been.'

'Do you think Harry blamed *himself* for his mother's suicide? Blamed his disruptive behaviour?'

'Whatever else he was, or turned into, he was a sensitive child. He *felt* things. So, yeah, I reckon maybe he did. And, tragic as it may be, who's to say he wasn't at least partly right?'

Shortly afterwards, as Lockyer stood beside his car brushing cat hairs from his trousers, he decided Maureen could well be right. And if Harry *had* blamed himself for Helen's death, perhaps other people had blamed him too.

That evening, Lockyer called the farm to check all was well with his parents. Trudy told him they were fine in a tone of voice that suggested she had far better things to be doing than answering pointless questions on the phone.

After dinner, he spent a while tackling the wallpaper in the second bedroom. It was old and brittle, but seemed to have been fixed with some kind of permanent cement. After soaking, it came away in damp, sticky flecks that attached themselves to his skin and clothes as readily as they'd previously attached themselves to the wall. To Lockyer's dismay, Bill, the house's previous owner, had seen fit to paper the ceiling to match the walls.

He tried listening to a podcast as he worked but soon gave up. He wasn't taking any of it in: he was thinking about Harry Ferris's guilty conscience. Could that really be what had sent him into exile for so many years? Lockyer knew a bit about guilt. His own pernicious guilt about Chris. Having not protected him from life – or from death – as an older brother was supposed to. Not finding his killer. His guilt about lying during the investigation into the Queen's Head fire – or, rather, his confusing *lack* of guilt about that, which was what he felt most guilty about. Guilt could tie you in knots.

He tried to imagine what it might be like to feel responsible for a parent's death. If his father tried to kill himself, or – God forbid – succeeded, would he blame himself? Would he feel guilty? He knew he would. He knew he'd blame himself for leaving the farm, for not doing enough to help them, for not forcing John to seek help for his depression, performing an intervention of some kind. It would be unbearable. Unshakeable. But would he let it separate him from his mother for decades? Until she lay dying herself?

He knew it wouldn't, even if she blamed him too. Some part of him would listen when he was told it hadn't been his fault – would listen, and at least try to believe it. Had Harry Ferris not tried? Had he not managed to set down that terrible burden? It seemed extreme, to Lockyer. A distraught teenager might blame himself for his mother's death, but surely an adult would come to understand that no mother ever killed herself solely because her child was badly behaved? That there had to be more to it than that? Underlying mental health issues, or another ongoing situation he simply hadn't been aware of.

But perhaps it was only Lockyer who was still unaware of that ongoing situation.

A loud knock made him look up, startled, because it came from the door to the bedroom rather than the front door. Mrs Musprat was glaring at him from the threshold. 'Will you stop that infernal scratching!' she said.

'Sorry?' Lockyer was tired. It took him a second to get out of his own head.

'Well, it's no good being sorry. Sorry's not going to help me sleep, is it?'

Lockyer cupped his ear. 'Mrs Musprat, I can hear your TV through the wall. I don't think you were trying to sleep.' He looked at his watch. 'It's only half past nine.' She'd wanted to see what he was doing, he guessed.

'Well, I'm struggling to *hear* the telly, aren't I? With you scratching away like a plague of locusts!'

Lockyer had been working on the party wall. He dropped his scraper and picked at the itchy shreds of paper on his hands. 'Fine,' he said. 'I'll call it a night. But it's got to be done sooner or later.'

'It was good enough—'

'For Bill,' Lockyer interrupted. 'Yes, I know. Everything all right, Mrs M? Apart from me interrupting the TV, of course. Do you need something?'

'No. No.' The old lady remained in the doorway, peering around. Never quite meeting Lockyer's eye. There was something furtive about her, he realized. Something almost shifty. Yet she seemed unwilling to leave.

'Clearing out everything of Bill's,' she muttered. 'Sweeping it all away like it counts for nothing. He was a good man, you know.'

'I'm sure he was,' Lockyer said gently. 'And it's not *him* I'm clearing away. Just his home decor. Got to make the place my own, haven't I?'

'Well, you're doing that right enough.' The old woman gazed up at the ceiling for a minute, her lips pressed tight. 'Closest I ever came to hearing Bill swear was when he was papering that ceiling,' she said.

'Why on earth did he want to do it in the first place?'

Mrs Musprat took a long time to answer. 'Storm brought a branch through the roof one night. The rain got in and left a dirty great mark. He reckoned paper was the best way to cover it.'

It sounded very much like a lie, but Lockyer decided to let it go.

'Well, he put it up good and solid, that's for sure,' he said.

'Put a little something in the paste, he said. Something with a bit of grab.'

'That explains a lot,' Lockyer said, still picking at his hands.

There was another loaded silence, and Lockyer was surer than ever that she wanted to ask him something. Or tell him something. 'I'm off duty, you know,' he said. 'Not a police officer at this precise moment.'

Mrs Musprat glanced at him, her expression at once suspicious and dismissive. 'Not a police officer? *Course* you are,' she huffed. A pause. 'Always listening to some *programme*, aren't you?' she added. 'Always reading about *something*. Learning God knows what. Too good for a bloody telly, even.' She poked a finger at him. 'You'll never make yourself any better than you are, you know.'

With that, and a nod of satisfaction, Iris Musprat turned and headed back downstairs.

'Goodnight, Mrs M,' Lockyer called after her.

He took Hedy's transcripts to bed. The ease with which he could summon her to mind as he read her words worried him. Her long hair, tucked carelessly behind her ears, the stony grey of her eyes. The exact texture of her skin, chalk-pale after so long in prison. The way she'd sat up straight, shoulders squared, when he'd returned to see her – because he'd given her hope. There was his guilt again, gnawing at the back of his mind. If he didn't manage to clear her name now, and even if he did, would he ever be able to think of Hedy without guilt? The thought that it might taint everything between them, forever, troubled him more than it should.

DI LOCKYER: *Fibres from a pink jumper taken from your flat have been found on Michael Brown's clothing. Can you explain how they got there?*

RESPONSE: *Yes. They . . . he . . . he was still Harry Ferris when they got on there. That's what I thought, anyway.*

DI LOCKYER: *When was this? And how did it happen?*

RESPONSE: *It was . . . I suppose it was three nights before he . . . died. I hugged him. I gave him a hug.*

DI LOCKYER: *You hugged him? Why?*

RESPONSE: *He was upset.*

DI LOCKYER: *What was he upset about?*

RESPONSE: *The whole . . . the whole situation, I think. He told me he'd done a bad thing. I didn't know what he meant. He said he had to come clean, and that it had gone on long enough.*

DI LOCKYER: *Did he mean the situation of him being there in the barn?*

RESPONSE: *I didn't know then. I suppose so. He said he was scared, and started to cry, so I hugged him and told him nothing could be that bad. That, whatever it was, I was sure it could be fixed. That his father would help. That sort of thing.*

DI LOCKYER: *What did he say?*

RESPONSE: *Nothing for a while. Not till he'd calmed down a bit, and stopped crying. Then he kind of laughed. Like a disbelieving laugh. It went a bit . . . weird, you know? It started to seem kind of . . . manic. And that's when he told me.*

DI LOCKYER: *Told you what?*

RESPONSE: *He said he wasn't Harry Ferris. He told me his name was Michael. He said he couldn't believe how long it had gone on, or what a stroke of luck it'd been, him finding the barn that night. He . . . he laughed!*

DI LOCKYER: *Would you like a tissue, Miss Lambert?*

RESPONSE: *No. Thank you. So, that was it.*

DI LOCKYER: *And how did you react to hearing that?*

RESPONSE: *I was . . . I was shocked. I thought we were . . . I don't know . . . becoming friends.*

DI LOCKYER: *You must have talked a lot in all the times you took food out to him?*

RESPONSE: *No. That's just it. He never said much and I . . . neither did I. And a lot of what he did say was very . . . out there. Mysterious, or trying to be. I guess now I know why that was.*

DI LOCKYER: *And yet you became friends?*

RESPONSE: *In a way. He . . . I . . . I thought I understood him. Hiding in there, not wanting to see anyone, or talk to anyone. Not wanting to be . . . in the world. I thought he was like me.*

DI LOCKYER: *A kindred spirit?*

RESPONSE: *Yes. Someone in the same boat as me, in any case. But it was just more make-believe. Lies.*

DI LOCKYER: *Did you tell anyone what Michael had confessed to you?*

RESPONSE: *No.*

DI LOCKYER: *Why not?*

RESPONSE: *It would . . . I knew how gutted Professor Ferris would be. He . . . it had changed him, having his son back. Thinking he had his son back. Like something hard inside him had cracked, you know? Or mended – perhaps it was mended, not cracked. Whatever, I knew he'd be devastated. Finding out it was all lies.*

DI LOCKYER: *But he was going to have to be told.*

RESPONSE: *Yes. I told Harry – I mean, Michael – that he had to come clean. That I wasn't going to do it for him.*

DI LOCKYER: *And what was his reaction to that?*

RESPONSE: *He said he would, but I had to give him a few days to figure out where he was going to go. 'Put out some feelers' were his exact words.*

DI LOCKYER: *And you agreed?*

RESPONSE: *I agreed.*

Even after fourteen years, Lockyer remembered the way she'd flicked her eyes up to meet his when she'd said *I thought we were . . . I don't know . . . becoming friends.* The trace of embarrassment that went with an admission of feeling, of vulnerability. Of having got somebody very wrong. Again. He remembered having the impression that Hedy was the kind of person whose trust had to be earned, and constantly kept. A person who had been burnt more than once. Like a wild animal – the kind that shrank back from your hand. He'd been so eager to win her trust, and so pleased when it seemed as though he had. And then he'd felt edgy and exposed, because his pleasure hadn't only been to do with solving the case.

But he also remembered how flat her voice had gone by

the end of that interview, when she'd spoken about Michael revealing his true identity. How deadened, and cold. Sometimes frightened animals also lash out.

Retired PC Tom Williams called Lockyer back first thing Tuesday morning, as Gemma Broad sat at her desk, scrolling through a list of names with a look of intense concentration. Tom's voice was grizzled from years of boozing, his Wiltshire accent thicker than Lockyer's.

'Tom, I'm looking at the Michael Brown murder again. You were the SPOC at the time of the original case, weren't you? Back in 'oh-five?'

'Ah, got yourself bumped onto Major Crime Review, didn't you? I'd heard a rumour.'

'I'm sure you did.'

Tom chuckled. 'Don't you worry. I never got promoted above PC, but I like to think I still made a difference out there.'

'You did, Tom.'

'Now then. Michael Brown . . . Brown . . . Oh, I know – the Traveller in the barn in Stoke Lavington?'

'That's the one.'

'Yeah, bit of a weird one. How come you're looking at it again now?'

'Something came up with the forensics. I want to make sure we didn't let anybody slip through the net.'

'Right, right. Housekeeper got sent down, am I right? Slip of a girl. Didn't seem the type.'

'You always said that about slips of girls.' Tom was an old

school copper: not a bad one, but possessed of an out-of-date attitude towards women, and drinking on the job.

'Not all of them,' Tom qualified. 'Some were right murderous harpies.'

'It says in the file you visited the camp on a byway near Larkhill where Michael Brown's caravan was parked up, but you couldn't get any information on him from the others there.'

''S right.' Tom cleared his throat. 'Trouble is, they don't like chatting to our lot at the best of times, as you know well enough. Chuck in a murder, and one of theirs having broken some code or other and run off—'

'He'd broken a code? What code?'

'Oh, I don't know. There's always something, with them. Usually comes down to honour, money or somebody's sister. Or some combination of the three. And the head man there – well, unofficial head man, you understand – was a right psycho. Not one you'd want to cross.'

'Oh?'

'Yeah. Name of Sean Hannington. Thorn in my bloody side the whole of the nineties and noughties, he was. And I expect wherever he is now he's a thorn in someone else's side. Now, I know better than most that the majority of the Travelling community are just getting on and minding their own business, but at one time that man was responsible for a good percentage of Wiltshire's violent crime and burglaries.'

'You've no idea where he might be now?'

'Nah, sorry, Matt. Quite happy to say I haven't a clue. He dropped right off the radar about eight years back. Buried in concrete somewhere, for all I know – if there is a God.'

'So, if Michael Brown had crossed Hannington, he'd be in trouble?'

'Worst kind of trouble, I'd say. People had a habit of vanishing around Hannington. Not that we could ever pin anything on him, mostly due to all those who *hadn't* vanished suddenly going deaf and blind, or having never heard of him. People were that scared of him, see.'

Broad half rose from her chair and turned towards him with an urgent look on her face. Lockyer held up a finger to stall her for a minute.

'Right. Can you remember anyone else who was living at the camp at that time, or where they might be now? Sorry, Tom, I know it's a big ask.'

'It's certainly that.' Tom gave a low whistle. 'Leave it with me. I'll go back through me notes – stir the old brain around, see what floats to the top.'

'Thanks, Tom. I appreciate it.'

Lockyer hung up. Broad's eyes were bright, cheeks flushed, like on the mornings she cycled into the station, the seven miles along the canal towpath from her flat in Semington. 'Tell me,' he said.

'Paul Rifkin did time, twenty years ago. A short stretch for embezzlement.'

'Yes. That's in the file.' Lockyer remembered Paul squirming in his interview in 2005, begging them not to tell Professor Ferris. He hadn't divulged his criminal record when he'd applied for the job, or that it was a pre-vious employer he'd stolen from.

'He served eighteen months of a two-and-half-year sen-tence up in HMP Northumberland. Let out early on licence for good behaviour in 2001.'

'So?'

'So guess who else was there at the time, doing a stretch for dealing?'

Lockyer's pulse picked up. 'Michael Brown?'

'The very same.'

9

Day Twelve, Tuesday

Lockyer updated their findings to DSU Considine, who agreed that they should bring Paul Rifkin in for interview. She gave him a dark look before he left her office. 'Shit and damnation, Matt. How did we miss that the first time around?'

Lockyer wasn't sure how best to answer. 'Thought it had solved itself, didn't we?' he said eventually. Tactfully, he hoped.

'And we had good reason to think that,' she called after him, as he left.

He sent Broad and a PC in a squad car to pick Paul up, knowing how much the man would hate it. The publicity, the disruption. He told himself he wasn't *only* doing it to take Paul down a peg or two for his own satisfaction. It was also to put him on the back foot, unsettle him before the interview. Unsettled people always gave more away.

He also left Paul in the interview room for a good hour

after Broad got back with him. Just to let him stew. Lockyer guessed Paul was the type to get angry when he was kept waiting. The type who thought his time important.

'Just a bit longer, Gem,' he said, to her repeated anxious glances.

On their way down to the interview room, they bumped into Steve Saunders.

'Lockyer,' he said. 'Exciting break on your case?'

'Could be,' Lockyer replied.

'So that's an actual real-life suspect in there, is it?' Saunders raised his eyebrows. 'I'm impressed.'

'Was there something you wanted, Steve?'

'Nothing in particular. You've found holes in the original investigation, have you?'

'Potentially. The forensics—'

'Weren't you *on* the original investigation, Lockyer?'

Lockyer frowned. Nobody was supposed to know what they were working on. Not yet. But Saunders clearly did, and there was no point in dissembling. 'Among others,' he said.

'Right, right,' Saunders agreed. 'Including DSU Considine, if I'm not mistaken. Your champion.'

'Your point being?'

Saunders smiled. 'So, you're basically cleaning up your own mess? Something most people have learnt to do by the age of ten. But well done, all the same. Baby steps, right?'

Lockyer was silent for a beat. Waiting until he trusted himself to speak.

'Come on, Gem,' he said then, angling past Saunders. 'Ignore him, if you can,' he added quietly.

'Guv,' she said. Her cheeks were burning, her jaw set.

Again, Lockyer wondered how much she minded being saddled with him.

'How did he know we're working on the Michael Brown case?' he said.

'I don't know, Guv. But it wouldn't have been hard for him to find out.'

'Well, I wish he'd mind his own bloody business,' Lockyer said. 'Considine won't be pleased.' He looked down at Broad again, and she didn't quite meet his eye. 'Are we set?' he asked, one hand on the interview room door.

Broad nodded, and they went in.

Paul Rifkin didn't look half as angry or rattled as Lockyer had hoped. He was leaning back in the chair with his arms folded, shirt neatly tucked into his belt, perfect creases ironed into his chinos. Sensible lace-up shoes the right side of stylish, but only just. Squeaky clean. He looked up as Lockyer and Broad came in and sat down opposite him. 'You took your time,' he said. 'While you're faffing me about, a dying man isn't getting any lunch, you know.'

'We've arranged for one of Professor Roland's carers to wait with him while we conduct this interview.' Broad looked up from her files. 'I'm sure she'll manage to make him a sandwich.'

Lockyer was struck by the change in her demeanour. They hadn't had the chance to interview any suspects since they'd started working together, and she was doing a good impression of a hard-arse. She pressed the button on the tape recorder.

'Interview with Paul Rifkin on the twelfth of November 2019. Present in the room are Detective Constable Gemma Broad . . .'

'. . . Detective Inspector Matthew Lockyer . . .'

'. . . Paul Ian Rifkin.'

'You're being interviewed under caution and have refused legal counsel,' Lockyer said.

'I don't need a lawyer. I haven't done anything wrong,' Paul said.

'Well,' Lockyer said, 'let's discuss a few things before we leap to that conclusion, shall we? The thing is, Mr Rifkin, when you lie to the police, the police get suspicious.'

'I haven't lied.' Paul's eyes flicked back and forth between the two officers. Measuring, trying to guess. It was exactly the way Lockyer had seen him look at people before, most recently at Roland and Harry Ferris. Paul was a schemer, of that Lockyer was utterly convinced. Whether or not he was a killer remained to be seen.

'You have, so let's not waste time,' Lockyer said.

'You're the ones wasting time. I—'

'When I spoke to you at Professor Ferris's house last Saturday, the ninth of November, about the murder that occurred there in 2005, I asked you whether you had believed the man sleeping out in the barn, later the victim of the murder, was Harry Ferris, Professor Ferris's son, as the professor claimed him to be.'

It wasn't a question, and Paul didn't answer.

'For the recording, please could you confirm that the conversation DI Lockyer is describing took place?' Broad said.

'It did.' Paul drummed his fingertips on the table.

'Well, that was a lie, wasn't it?' Lockyer said. He nodded to Broad, who placed a police mugshot in front of Paul. It was twenty years old, and in it Michael Brown was a young man with a swathe of dark hair over his forehead, a thin, straggly beard, and wide, hunted eyes. Completely unaware, of course, that he had only a handful of years left to live.

'In 2000 you were sentenced to two and a half years' imprisonment for the embezzlement of funds from your then employer, Colonel James Crofton, resident of Audley Park, Morpeth,' Broad said. 'You served eighteen months in HMP Northumberland alongside this man,' she tapped the photograph, 'Michael Brown. He was imprisoned there for drug dealing.'

Paul's cheek twitched. 'There were a lot of inmates,' he said. 'I kept my head down. Hardly knew any of them.'

'Come off it, Mr Rifkin.' Lockyer tried to hold the man's restless gaze. 'I've never believed in coincidences, not where serious crime is involved. Put simply, I don't believe you. And I'm sure it wouldn't take us too long to find someone else who was at HMP Northumberland at the time who would testify to the two of you knowing each other.'

'Well, I wish you luck with that.'

Lockyer continued to stare at Paul, and he stared defiantly back. 'Constable Broad?'

Broad checked her notes for a second. 'We have a witness statement from somebody who saw you go into the barn where Mr Brown was . . . dwelling, only a few days before he was murdered. And who saw you coming out again a short while afterwards, in a state of disarray. Can you tell us what happened between the two of you on that occasion?'

'Who?' Paul leant forwards. 'They're lying, whoever they are!'

'Why would they do that?'

'It was Hedy, wasn't it? *She's* saying she saw me. She's trying to shift blame off herself and she's got you eating out of the palm of her hand.'

'You're not doing yourself any favours, you know, Mr Rifkin,' Lockyer said.

'I've done nothing wrong.'

'We know that someone attacked Mr Brown in the days before he was killed. He had fresh bruises on his body and neck, as though someone had put their hands around his throat. We suspect, given the strength required to inflict such injuries, that this person was a man.'

'Well, it wasn't me.' Paul leant back again. He put his hands behind his head in a show of nonchalance, but only for a second before he changed his mind.

'You're very careful not to let the people around you see who you really are, aren't you, Mr Rifkin?' Lockyer said. 'But you're not as good at it as you think you are.'

'You've considerable sums of money set aside, haven't you, Mr Rifkin?' Broad said.

His face registered shock.

'We had our financial investigators take a look.'

'You had no business ... I *earned* that money! It's *my* money.'

'Could be,' Lockyer said. 'Or you could've been up to your old tricks.'

'It was quite a neat scheme, wasn't it?' Broad said. 'You dealt with all the tradespeople, household utility bills and, crucially, all builders and groundsmen on behalf of your ex-employer, Colonel Crofton, who trusted you implicitly, what with you being a fellow ex-serviceman. Then all you had to do was either take a backhander to determine who was going to get a particular job, or else make adjustments to written tenders and keep the difference for yourself.' Broad looked at Paul steadily. Only Lockyer could see how hard she was concentrating on staying cool. 'The colonel was making significant improvements to a large country estate at the time. Rather a lot of money went through your hands, didn't it, Mr Rifkin?' She checked a note again. 'And over a hundred grand of it ended up in your bank account.'

'It was a mistake. I was a different person, back then. The army . . . messed me up. I had PTSD . . . I needed to feel safe. Secure. But I did my time. You can't use it against me now.'

'We're not using it against you, Mr Rifkin. But it does pose some questions about how you've now managed to amass three-quarters of a million pounds while working in a position that pays twenty-four thousand pounds a year.'

'Good investment,' Paul said. 'And few outgoings.'

'Well, if that's true our financial boys will soon be able to tell us so,' Lockyer replied. 'It might take them a little while, but it's amazing what they can uncover, even with the most skilled embezzlers. Which I suspect you aren't.'

'I'm telling you, it's all above board. They won't find *anything*!'

'Michael Brown knew you were a thief and a liar, didn't he, Mr Rifkin? You see, I think you recognized him immediately when he turned up at Longacres. I think you kept your distance, kept your head down, hoped he'd move on again.'

'But he didn't move on, did he, Mr Rifkin?' Broad said.

'So you went to have a word with him,' Lockyer said. 'Maybe to find out what he was up to, whether he intended to alert Professor Ferris to who you really were. And perhaps you thought you'd give him a bit of a scare, let him know he really ought to be on his way. Did you threaten him, Mr Rifkin?'

'No.'

'And then what?' Lockyer went on. 'A few days later, when it was obvious he wasn't going anywhere, you decided to make sure he couldn't jeopardize the new life you'd built there. So that night you took a knife from the kitchen and got rid of the problem.'

'It wasn't me!'

'The murder was quick, efficient. Cold, even. The way a soldier might kill somebody.'

'Are my prints on that knife?' Paul demanded.

'Forensic re-examination suggests that the killer's prints may well not be on the knife.' Lockyer stared again. 'It was quite a clever trick, that. The sort of thing one might hear about from other criminals. In prison, for example.'

'You can start to see why we might have doubts about you, can't you, Mr Rifkin?' Broad said.

'You've got it all wrong!'

'Have we?'

'Yes! I didn't kill him! You're – you're barking up the wrong tree, Inspector.' Paul was clearly trying for outraged incredulity but falling short.

'Are we?' Lockyer spread his hands. 'Maybe. I think there are two possible scenarios. One, you did everything I've just described. Two, you only did some of it. Because I *know* you're lying to me, Mr Rifkin, and I *know* you recognized Mickey when you saw him. I strongly suspect you were the one who roughed him up, and you'd definitely have wanted him to leave before he lost you your job – and maybe even landed you back inside, if you *had* been on the take. I'm willing to be persuaded that you weren't the one who killed him, but if you want to convince me of that you'd better start talking. Right now.'

There was a pause. Neither Lockyer nor Broad moved a muscle. Paul was looking down at his hands, his lips moving as he muttered silently to himself. Lockyer and Broad exchanged a look. They had him.

'Look, I didn't kill him, all right? I'm not a killer.'

'You were in the army, Mr Rifkin,' Broad said. 'You fought in the Falklands.'

Paul let out a sigh. 'The thing is, if you look further back than 2000, you'll discover that I . . . I wasn't actually in the army.'

'Oh?'

'Look, it was a line I spun to get me the job with the colonel, all right? Army types always stick together. I thought it might tip the scales in my favour, and I was right. After that, people always seemed impressed by it. So I . . . you know . . . went with it.'

'We know, Mr Rifkin,' Broad said. 'We did look further back than 2000.'

'That just proves you're a habitual liar and a thief, though, doesn't it?' Lockyer added.

'But it proves I'm telling the truth now. And you can't paint me as some . . . some hardened killer!'

Paul leant forwards, spreading his hands on the table. It was a position of supplication, but Lockyer knew better than to put too much trust in body language. Some criminals were fluent in it. Paul took a deep breath. 'I recognized him, all right? I knew who he was. I knew he could get me sacked if he started chattering about prison, and why I was inside. But, look, I didn't kill him. And he *couldn't* have landed me back in jail because all that money's legit, okay? It's my nest egg. So, all he could have done was get me fired, and you can't think I'd kill anyone over that? Of course I bloody wouldn't! But I did . . . I did thump him. Picked him up by the scruff and gave him a bit of a shake. Told him to make tracks.'

'And did Mr Brown say that he would move on?'

'Did he hell. He just laughed. Well, sort of giggled, really. I think he'd fried his brain over the years, I really do. All that shit he used to take.' Paul shook his head.

'That must have made you angry,' Broad said.

'It wound me up, yeah. But, truth be told, once I'd calmed down a bit I wasn't as worried as I had been. He was shot to bits. Nobody would have believed a word he said, even if he'd decided to say something. And since he was quite enjoying being Harry Ferris, I didn't think he *would* say anything. Couldn't without giving away his true identity, could he?'

Broad glanced across at Lockyer.

'Hedy Lambert attested at the time that Michael Brown had confessed his true identity to her some days before he was killed. She gave him the ultimatum that if he didn't tell Professor Ferris the truth, she would,' Lockyer said.

'Right. Well. I didn't know anything about that.'

'Might have made him more of a threat to you, though, mightn't it? If the game was over anyway. Mickey might have taken you down with him, so to speak.'

'Look, I just said I didn't know anything about it!' A fine sheen of sweat had appeared along Paul's top lip. He rubbed at it with a hand. 'I like my job. I like living there. It's my *home*. But would I kill the lad to stay there? No. Because I'm *not* a murderer. I'm not the career criminal you're making me out to be. I *hated* being inside. Hated it. I've been straight as a die ever since, and that's the God's own truth. The reason I knew Mickey from inside was because he was one of the good ones. Don't get me wrong, he was always a bit out there. Damaged at an early age, I reckon. But he never meant anyone any harm. He wouldn't have *wanted* to "take me down with him." He was . . . gentle, I suppose you'd say. Almost like a bairn in some ways. Whoever killed him . . . Whoever killed him was a heartless bastard. Now, I might be a liar, and once upon a time I was a thief, but I'm not a heartless bastard, Inspector.'

'You were heartless enough – and worried enough – to

leave the imprint of your hand around his neck,' Lockyer pointed out.

'I know.' Paul looked down at the table. His body was hunched, shoulders curling forwards. So different from his normal puffed-up posture. 'I'm not proud of that. But, I swear, that was as far as it went.' He looked back and forth between them again, in mute appeal.

Lockyer tried to see if they were being played. If Paul was checking that they were swallowing his story.

'Get your people to look at the financial stuff, and you'll see,' Paul said. 'I earned that money, and I invested it. I've been following that old sod around like a golden retriever for the past twenty years so I can spend the *next* twenty with my feet up somewhere sunny, not back inside.'

Lockyer told the same PC to drive Paul Rifkin back to Longacres.

'Do you believe him, Gem?'

Broad pulled a rueful face. 'Annoyingly, I think I do, Guv.'

'Me too. But let's check out the money, just in case. Money's what drives that man, that's for sure. Perhaps he's just a *really* good liar. And he's definitely holding out for Professor Ferris to die. Probably counting the days.'

'Do you think he'll be left anything?'

'No idea. Maybe.' Lockyer leant back in his chair. 'It'd be churlish not to leave him *anything*, after all these years. But, then, Ferris is the churlish type. I reckon Rifkin's secretly hoping for the house, but I also reckon he's going to be disappointed there.'

'Can we look at Ferris's will?'

'No. It won't be a matter of public record until after probate. Before that – well, depends on the solicitor. Some are more willing to be leant on than others. But we can certainly ask Ferris about it – he might tell us.'

'Have I got time for a sandwich before we head off?' Broad asked.

Lockyer checked his watch. 'No. But we can stop and get something on the way. Come on. Traffic never gets any better in the centre of Bristol.'

They were driving to an appointment with Tor Heath, now Professor Tor Garvich, the research student who'd been working with Roland Ferris at the time of Michael Brown's murder. Lockyer remembered her. She'd been in her early twenties during the original investigation, fresh-faced and . . . luscious, in a way that was hard to ignore. Voluptuous lips, soft, buoyant hair, clear skin, and a curvy figure that she dressed in tight roll-neck jumpers and pencil skirts. She'd been the kind of young woman who liked to catch people checking her out, so that she could dismiss them. Never overtly flirty, but very aware of her effect on men – and how best to make use of it.

Lockyer remembered feeling undermined by her. Knocked off his stride. A slight sinking feeling whenever he had to talk to her, because he could tell she enjoyed making him uncomfortable, even though she wasn't his type at all. But they'd both been so young, back then. Not that he'd had to talk to her many times – they'd discounted her as a suspect early on. She had no motive, and she didn't stay in the house overnight. She'd gone home at the end of the after-noon the day before, and her flatmate had dropped her off for work the next morning to find Longacres in disarray, taped off, police everywhere.

Lockyer had re-read her statement earlier, and remem-bered her making it. The way she'd leant forwards over her crossed knees. *All a bit exciting, isn't it? A murder?* Something close to amusement dancing in her eyes, not taking it at all seriously. Loving the drama, in fact. He even thought she'd been a bit disappointed not to be more involved in the investigation. *Is that it? Don't you want to lean on me a bit, Inspector? See if I'll crack?* He remembered saying: *This isn't a game, Miss Heath*, then wincing at how pompous he'd sounded.

Lockyer took them along the A420 to Bristol, instead of up to the M4. There was always more to look at along the way. Once they'd made it past Chippenham's traffic lights and roundabouts the road skirted the southern edge of the Cotswolds, leaving Wiltshire for South Gloucestershire. It cut a gently winding line between shallow hills, past huge fields of pasture dotted with sheep, surrounded by drystone walls; past ancient farmsteads and roadside pubs all built of buff-coloured stone. Then, west of Marshfield, the villages got steadily closer together, the buildings ever newer and more densely packed, until they finally blurred into the hin-terland of Victorian terraces, car showrooms and massive retail sheds on the outskirts of the city.

'Here you go,' Lockyer said, pulling in at a Tesco Express in St George. 'Lunch.'

'You bring me to all the fancy places, Guv,' Broad said. 'Want anything?'

'Just a sandwich, thanks. Anything veggie. Except egg.'

'So ... cheese, then?'

'Thanks.' He handed her a tenner.

They were seeing Professor Garvich in her office at the history department of Bristol University, in a large Victorian house on a spacious, leafy road between Clifton and the city centre. The sun was shining coldly, and a brisk easterly wind snatched the last leaves from the plane trees and swirled them extravagantly to the ground. Other humanities departments were in the houses to either side, and students were everywhere, coming and going, wrapped up in massive scarves and seeming ridiculously young. Lockyer realized that meant he was getting old. It all looked very rarified, but once they were inside the building they were greeted by the familiar synthetic carpet, stale coffee and printer-ink smell of underfunded institutions everywhere. The decor was a dowdy beige, and a passing student directed them up the narrow stairs to the second floor, where they knocked at Professor Garvich's door.

'Come!' she called from inside.

Broad rolled her eyes. 'Teacher will see us now,' she murmured.

Tor Garvich looked up from her desk as they came in. Her face showed a moment's confusion before she smiled. 'Ah! You must be the police? I'm so sorry – I forgot what time it was.'

'Professor Garvich, thank you for seeing us,' Lockyer said.

They showed her their warrant cards, and he waited to see if she would recognize him. She gave no sign of it. He was clearly a lot less memorable than she was.

'Well, one doesn't say no to officers of the law, does one? At least, that's how I was brought up.' Her speech was oddly accent-less, precise in diction but not especially upmarket in delivery. Lockyer wondered if she'd once had a regional twang she'd worked hard to lose. She came out from behind the desk and shook their hands, then cocked her head. 'Oh, that was rather odd of me, wasn't it? Should we have shaken hands? Is that what one does?'

'No harm done.' Broad smiled.

'Oh, good. Do sit. Shove those on the floor – here, let me.' She picked up piles of books and papers and slid them onto a corner of her desk, freeing up a pair of wood-framed armchairs with tough upholstery, of the kind common in staff and waiting rooms. The other furniture had the same kind of cheap functionality – metres of shelving, desk, filing cabinet, chest of drawers with a plastic kettle and a jar of instant coffee on top. There was no polished mahogany, no antique globe or decanter of whisky.

Lockyer watched the professor closely, noticing all the things that had changed and all the things that hadn't. In her late thirties she was still very attractive, and not at all a professor of the moth-eaten cardigan variety. Her fair hair had no grey in it, and was piled messily on top of her head in something that was halfway to being a pony-tail. Fastened with a pencil, of course. Her curves were more pronounced, her face a little fuller, but unlined.

Soft red lipstick on her mouth, long silver earrings. She was wearing round, wire-rimmed glasses, a leather skirt and knee-length boots. Lockyer noticed a family photo on her desk: husband and two little girls, gap-toothed and grinning.

'Now,' the professor said, settling herself back behind her desk. 'To what do I owe the pleasure?'

'Professor Garvich—' Broad began.

'It's Garv-*ick*, actually. A hard *ick* sound at the end.'

'Oh. Sorry.' Broad cleared her throat. 'We're reviewing the investigation into the murder of Michael Brown, at Long-acres, in Stoke Lavington, in 2005. Do you remember the incident?'

'Christ – remember it? Of course I remember it. Shocking.'

'We've reason to believe the initial investigation may have been incomplete, so we're talking to everyone who was involved with the Ferris family at the time. Just a few routine questions, if you don't mind?'

'Fire away, by all means. Incomplete? Does that mean . . .'

'We're simply making sure nothing was missed. You were working for Professor Ferris at the time, as a research assistant?'

'That's right. For two or three days a week. I was doing my own doctorate as well. Our subjects didn't cross over *that* closely, but it helped me pay the bills. Plus, you know, Roland Ferris was a bit of a celeb in medieval history. If you can imagine such a thing.'

'Was?' Lockyer said.

'Well, *is*, then. Though he hasn't published much in recent years.'

'Professor Ferris isn't a well man,' he said.

'No. Of course. I'd forgotten about that. Poor old stick.' Garvich conjured up a sympathetic smile.

'How long had you been working there when Michael Brown arrived?' Broad went on.

'Well, I first went there in the spring of that year ... March, I think it was. I can't remember exactly when the fellow in the barn turned up, but I must have been there two or three months by then, I suppose.'

'Did you recognize him?' Broad asked.

'No, not at all. I hardly saw him after the first day. He arrived and there was all the drama. I certainly didn't go out and introduce myself or anything like that. None of my business. My place was at that desk of Ferris's, up to my eyeballs in tenth-century agricultural surveys.'

'So when Professor Ferris said that the man was his son, you believed him?'

'Of course. Why wouldn't I?'

'Weren't you at all curious about the situation? It must have been quite ... out of the ordinary?' Broad said.

Professor Garvich gave an exaggerated shrug. 'A little, possibly, to begin with. But then it was business as usual, really. It certainly wasn't my place to go asking Professor Ferris personal questions, and I very much doubt he'd have answered them if I had. You've met him, I'm sure.'

'Did you think it strange that the person you thought was

Harry Ferris stayed out in the barn, rather than coming into the house?' Lockyer said.

'Well, yes, it was odd, but I didn't dwell on it. I wasn't really that aware of what he was doing, Inspector. I turned up for work at nine, and left again at three, and Professor Ferris made sure he got his money's worth out of me in between.'

'Did you discuss the situation with anybody else in the house? Serena Godwin, for example, or her son Miles? Or the *general factotum*, Paul Rifkin?'

'Oh, that one,' she said, pulling a face. 'No, indeed. I spoke to him as little as I could. *General factotum*. That's new-Latin for dogsbody, you know. *Do everything*. Apt.'

'You didn't like Mr Rifkin?'

'Not really, no. Not terribly likeable, is he? He was *everywhere* in that house – you couldn't go to the loo without bumping into him. Forever listening at doors. And that infernal *smirk* of his, like he wants the world to think he's laughing inside, because in fact he's *so* much better than his job, and it's all part of his master plan.'

Lockyer thought of the three-quarters of a million Paul Rifkin had accrued: his smirk wasn't as far wide of the mark as Garvich thought. So long as the money was legit, of course. But she was right about him not being very likeable.

'I bet he still works there, doesn't he?' she asked, then laughed when Lockyer and Broad nodded. 'I knew it!'

'The day before the murder, Professor Garvich, that was Tuesday, the twenty-eighth of June 2005,' Broad said, 'you left Longacres at what time?'

'Well – and I can't remember the specific day you're talking about, but I always left at three to catch the number two bus at ten past, from the middle of the village. That took me all the way to Salisbury, where I was living then.'

'And did you take the bus to work in the mornings, too?'

'Some of the time, but the schedule wasn't ideal. My flatmate worked around Trowbridge and Westbury some days, so he would drive me in when he could. Ah, those were the days – cadging lifts and arguing with the bus driver over the correct change.'

'What did your flatmate do?' Broad asked, though it wasn't really relevant.

'Mobile dog-groomer. Gaz . . . I've not seen Gaz in *years*.'

'Did you not have a car of your own, then?'

'I didn't drive at all. I do now – you have to, with kids. As soon as they're born you turn into a taxi service. I'm *terrible*, though. Hopeless, really, and I can't park straight to save my life. I'm every cliché you ever heard about women drivers, to my shame.' She smiled self-deprecatingly.

'Did you notice anything unusual at all in the household in the weeks leading up to the murder, the time immediately preceding it, or at any time afterwards?' Broad went on.

'Unusual . . .' Professor Garvich mused. 'Christ, if I did, I certainly can't remember now. But I would have said at the time, if I had. I can't think of anything, though.' She pursed her lips. 'I mean, obviously it was *all* a bit odd – Ferris saying, "This is my son," and his sister saying, "No, it isn't" . . . And the nephew, Miles, walking around either sniggering to himself or with a face like a smacked arse. And that odd little housekeeper girl ferrying food out to him on a *tray* . . . It wasn't a normal set-up, by any means.'

'How well did you know Hedy Lambert?' Lockyer asked.

'Barely. Hard to get to know somebody who doesn't speak and won't look you in the eye.' Garvich shook her head. 'They do say it's the quiet ones you have to watch, but who knew she had it in her? I suppose he must have done something to set her off. Bit of a ticking time bomb, she turned out to be.'

Broad shot Lockyer a quick look. Seeking direction.

'So you weren't surprised when Hedy was arrested? And convicted?' Lockyer said.

'I was very surprised. I was surprised about all of it – surprised someone had stabbed a man to death at my place of work. It's the kind of thing one imagines only happens on TV, really.' Garvich spread her hands. 'But who knows what's going on inside other people's heads? I remember thinking – Gosh, what an odd thing for me to remember! – the cat there was called Janus. Did you know that? After the two-faced Roman god. I remember thinking that was like *her* – Hedy Lambert. Two-faced. One half barely alive, the other half a killer.'

'What do you mean, barely alive?' Lockyer said.

'Well, she was hardly making the most of the gift she'd been given, was she? Life, I mean. Moping around that house, trailing a duster behind her, looking like some kind of perambulating laundry pile. Never talking, never going out. Such a claustrophobic, blinkered existence. You can't really call that *living*, can you?'

'Miss Lambert had been through a very traumatic experience,' Broad said.

'Had she? Oh. Now I feel evil. Poor her.' Garvich didn't sound overly sorry. 'Still, I can't stand self-pity, and it's no excuse to go around stabbing people, is it?' she added.

'No,' Lockyer agreed. 'You didn't follow the case in the press, then? Hedy Lambert's trial and conviction?'

'No. I mean, I knew she'd been sent to jail, whenever it was. But I moved on soon after it all happened. Another opportunity presented itself, and I'd had enough of Roland's temper by then.'

'Opportunity?' Broad asked.

'Private tutor to a boy in Salisbury. Hated history, but he needed four A grades for Cambridge. His parents paid considerably more per hour, and I didn't have so far to travel.'

Lockyer allowed a pause. Professor Garvich was leaning on her elbows on the desk, her ankles crossed neatly below. She looked at them frankly. There was no tension in her, no unease or impatience. Outside in the corridor a door banged, and young voices went chattering down the stairs.

'How did you come to hear about the job with Professor Ferris?' Lockyer asked.

Professor Garvich blinked once, took a quick breath. 'Gosh, now you're asking. I can't remember exactly, but it will have been one of the usual ways – a notice on the board at the university, or a small ad in the back of one of the journals.'

'Which university would that have been?'

'Southampton, where I did my PhD.'

'That was quite a commute for you, living in Salisbury.'

'Not too bad. There's a good train service, and I certainly didn't have to do it every day. You're largely left to your own devices at that stage of study, aside from taking the odd undergrad tutorial. Plus I wanted to be near my mum – she was having a rough time.'

There was a knock at the door. Professor Garvich jumped a little, and looked up at the clock. 'Ah – that'll be one of my MAs. Sorry, Officers, I may have to end our chat there, if that's all right with you?' She walked unhurriedly to the door, opened it and spoke to whoever was on the other side. 'Would you mind hanging on for one minute, Jenny? I'll be right with you.'

Lockyer and Broad got up.

'Thank you for your time, Professor.' Lockyer handed her his card. 'If anything occurs to you about the incident, or your time at Longacres, anything at all, however small or seemingly insignificant, please let us know as soon as possible.'

'I certainly will,' she said, with a brightness that implied she didn't expect to think of anything, and would probably put it out of her mind as soon as she closed the door.

Lockyer and Broad walked down to the end of the street before returning to the car, just for the crisp fresh air and the change of scenery. Past more university buildings, old and new, into Royal Fort Gardens, along a wide tarmac path narrowed by banks of fallen leaves. The air smelt very different there, in the city, than further east in Wiltshire. It was a brief and welcome change.

'Not a bad place to work,' Broad said, looking around. 'Sort of makes me wish I'd gone to university.'

'Why didn't you?'

'Didn't need to,' she said. 'I only did A levels because my dad kept banging on about giving myself options. But I didn't think I needed options. I wanted to be a cop, and I wanted to start at the bottom and work up. Old school.'

'And now?'

'Well, now I see that another three years of being a kid might not have been such a bad thing.' She smiled. 'Still, no regrets. It's all going according to plan.'

'I hope so,' Lockyer said.

She looked up at him briefly, the remains of her smile lingering. 'What about you, Guv?'

'What about me what?'

'You went to university, right? Did you already know you wanted to join the police?'

'Not straight away, no. I studied geography, not criminology or psychology or anything like that. Law enforcement was one of a couple of ideas I had as I got towards the end of the final year. All I knew was, I wasn't a farmer.'

'I heard that—' Broad cut herself off.

'What did you hear?'

'Well. That you went into the police because of your brother. Because of what happened to him. And I wondered if you'd wanted to be on cold case to be able to ... you know ... keep looking for his killer.'

'I'd already applied to the police when Chris died.' Lockyer heard the way his voice changed at the mention of his brother. Even after all the years that had passed, it was no small thing to talk about him. He didn't think it would ever be a small thing. 'And the decision to move to cold case was made for me.'

'Yeah. I heard something about that, too.'

Lockyer decided not to ask. They walked in silence for a while.

'I'm really sorry,' Broad said eventually, 'about what happened to him. What was he like?'

'Chris? He was ... he was better than me. He was full of chat, and smiles, and daft thoughts that he blurted out the second he had them. Total opposite to me.' In truth, Lockyer had been all but silent in comparison, when they were kids; unable to say what he thought or felt. 'Chris loved people, and he was the one people were always happy to see. He was going to stay on the farm, take it over one day.'

'I'm sure people were happy to see you too, Guv,' Broad said awkwardly, not looking at him. 'He sounds like a good guy, though.'

'He was. No malice in him. Bit rash sometimes, I suppose. Didn't always think things through. But, then, he was still just a kid.'

'I really hope we catch the person who attacked him one day.'

Lockyer didn't reply. What he felt about it went too far beyond *hope*.

Broad changed the subject. 'What did you make of Garvick, Guv? Was she like you remembered?'

'Yes. Well, more of a grown-up now, obviously. She had an ... edge, back then. Hard to describe what I mean. You could see she was thinking things about you that she wasn't saying. That kind of thing. But I guess she grew out of it. You?'

'I suppose I quite liked her,' Broad said. 'Not that that's really relevant, I know, but she seemed like what she is, I suppose. A busy history professor who happened to be on the edges of an incident a lot of years ago.'

'Yes. I got that impression too.' They walked in silence. 'Quite keen to distance herself from the incident, and from Michael Brown, though, wouldn't you say? No opinions about it at all, really, when she certainly had opinions about everyone else in the house.'

'But Michael wasn't *in* the house, I guess,' Broad said. 'And it sounds like she was fairly well confined to Ferris's office.'

'That's true.'

'Plus it was a murder. I'd want to distance myself too.'

Lockyer glanced at Broad. Catching her identifying with, even sympathizing with, a witness. So Tor Garvich still had that seductive quality, that ability to draw people in. Was it that, and her obvious ease in company, her obvious confidence, that put Lockyer's back up? People disliked in others what they disliked in themselves, he knew. And what others made them notice about themselves. Lockyer had always despised his envy of those with that same social ease, those who drew others to them, and connected with them without even trying.

So that was probably the source of his nagging unwillingness to drop Garvich from the investigation. Or perhaps it was simply that he didn't plan to drop *anybody* from it this time around. There'd been far too much of that the last time.

10

Day Thirteen, Wednesday

Lockyer called Cellmark to check on the progress of the additional forensics, only to be told that they weren't quite the bottom of the pile, but nearly. There'd been a horrific accident on the A34, with multiple fatalities. It was a tragic mess, and Lockyer couldn't argue with his reinvestigation being sidelined while they attempted to unpick it.

'Do me one tiny quick favour, would you, please?' he said, to the impatient scientist.

'What is it?'

'One of the items I gave you is a cassette tape. Remember those?'

'I remember seventy-eights, Detective Inspector.'

'Could you look at it quickly? Not examine it, just tell me what it was – the music? It's annoying me that I can't remember.'

'I'm really—'

'Please. It might be important.' He doubted it, and felt bad for saying so. 'Then I won't pester you for at least a week, I promise.'

'Hold on.' The line clicked as Lockyer was put on hold. There was no waiting music. A minute or two ticked by. 'DI Lockyer?'

'I'm still here.'

'Your tape is a single, "Voyage Voyage" by Desireless on the A-side. Not one that I remember at all. Curiosity satisfied?'

'Thank you. Yes.'

Lockyer wrote it down on a scrap of paper. It rang a vague bell from the original investigation, but he couldn't remember how it went. Broad was away from her desk, liaising with the tech team about something. He picked up his mobile, found the song in Apple music and hit play.

Eighties synth, French words sung in a smooth female voice, fast enough to dance to, but with wistful overtones. Lockyer dug about in his schoolboy French for the meaning of some of the lyrics, but came up very short. Something about travelling and never returning was as far as he could get. Broad returned while it was still playing, and Lockyer was tapping his pen along in time. She listened for a moment, smiling.

'What *is* that?' she said.

'The tape that was in Mickey Brown's top pocket. It was a massive hit in the late eighties. Number one, I think.' He took in her sceptical expression. 'Back when you had to go out to a shop to buy a record if you wanted to hear it. Madness, eh?'

'Utter madness. Do you remember the song? Dancing to it at the discothèque, perhaps?'

'I *was* only ten at the time, you know, in spite of my extreme old age now. But I do remember it. Vaguely.'

Broad sat down, obviously waiting to speak to him, so Lockyer killed the music.

'Do you think it's significant?' she asked.

Lockyer thought about it. 'I can't see how. But it's still weird. Unexplained. Anyway, what have you got?'

'I found some of Aaron Fletcher's early records. Turns out he *was* brought up in care. He wasn't lying to Hedy about that.' She passed him a few pages of printout.

'You mean Fletcher is his *real* name? I'm amazed.'

'Not exactly. I got Clare to search the care order records for anyone called Aaron or Fletcher with his date of birth.'

Lockyer looked at the paper he'd been given. 'Aaron Bates,' he read.

'Made the subject of a care order and placed at Kipling House near Wellingborough in September 1978, at the age of six, when his mum was given a two-year term for possession of class As. His dad doesn't seem to have been in the picture at all.' Broad waited while Lockyer scanned the documents. 'Kipling House wasn't too bad, by all accounts. Still, not the kind of place you'd want to grow up in, given the choice. Aaron didn't come out till he was sixteen, and then he dropped off the radar.'

'What happened to his mum?'

'Accidental overdose in prison.'

'So he's using assumed names. Could be anywhere now, calling himself anything.'

'He could be,' Broad agreed. 'But look at this.' She handed Lockyer another piece of paper, a grainy copy of Aaron's birth certificate. 'He was calling himself Aaron Fletcher when Hedy knew him, right? Look there.'

'Fletcher was his father's name.'

'Exactly. So he wasn't that imaginative with his choice. We're looking for any other family members or associates whose names he might be using now, or could have used in the past.'

'Good thinking. Are there any?'

'Not many yet. We've found reference to a maternal aunt, applying for visiting rights while he was in care, and we're trying to find out where she is now. And we can keep digging.'

'Good work, Gem.' Lockyer stood. 'Come on.' He reached for his coat. 'It's time you saw where all this happened. And met Professor Roland Ferris.'

Broad's eyes lit up.

Paul Rifkin's smile was tighter than ever when he opened the door to them. Lockyer noticed the hint of panic that flew across his face, saw the way he hesitated, itching to slam the door again. Lockyer would never want to cause an innocent man grief, but it was preferable to the man's usual smugness. And, besides, like Miles Godwin, Paul could have told the original investigation straight away who the man in the barn was. He could have saved a lot of confusion. He could have saved Roland the disappointment of believing his son was home, and being wrong. And he'd had the nerve to criticize Miles for the exact same thing.

'Mr Rifkin,' Lockyer said, with a thin smile of his own. 'We've come to make further enquiries of the professor. If it's a convenient time.'

Paul frowned, but stood back. 'Not really,' he said. 'It would be so much better if you called first and made an appointment, Inspector.'

'This is murder inquiry, Mr Rifkin.'

'Yes, I know it's a bloody murder inquiry. But the man's *dying*, for Christ's sake. He has times of the day when he'll be more awake and feeling better, and times when he can't cope with anything. There are strict routines with his medication, and when he can and will eat . . . And it's not made any easier by you barging in any time you fancy.'

'All right,' Lockyer conceded. 'Point taken. We'll call ahead next time.'

'Thank you. Go up, then. I'll bring coffee.'

'Tea for me, please, strong as you can make it,' Lockyer said.

Paul made a non-committal sound as he walked away.

Roland Ferris was propped up on pillows, with a huge hardback book on a straddle-legged lectern across his lap, the pages held open by weights. His eyes travelled over the words, his focus not changing when the police officers entered his room.

'Professor Ferris,' Lockyer said. 'This is my colleague,

Detective Constable Gemma Broad. We'd just like to ask you a few more questions, if we may.'

The old man put his finger on the page to mark where he'd read to, and looked up at last. 'There are so few days when I have the energy to read, Inspector, and here you are to spoil it for me. Hello, young lady. Can't say I'm *that* pleased to meet you, but I'm sure you're delightful,' he said to Broad. 'Ah, look! I made you blush. I apologize, Constable . . . what was it?'

'Broad.'

'Ah. How unfortunate,' he murmured, then raised the fingers of one hand. 'More apologies. I can be terribly rude, I'm told.'

'May we sit down, Professor?' Broad asked, with admirable nonchalance.

'By all means.'

'What are you reading, sir?'

'This? S. A. J. Bradley's translation of early Anglo-Saxon poetry. Since you ask.' He made a short sound of amusement. 'Have you read it, Constable Broad?'

'Can't say I have,' she replied. 'Been meaning to. It's been on the pile by my bed for months.' She smiled, and Roland Ferris gave a weak laugh.

'Ha! Good girl. Never neglect your source material.'

'The very motto I live by, Professor.'

'Well. Is Paul bringing drinks?'

'He said so, yes.'

'I'd check yours for spit, if I were you, Inspector,' he said to Lockyer. 'Goodness me, the mood he was in when he got back here. Crashing about the place like a rhinoceros, reeking of stress and outrage. What on earth did you uncover about him?'

'It might be better if you asked him, Professor.'

'Oh, I have. He's being very stubborn about telling me, however. Nothing I ought to worry about? Not been harbouring a killer all this time, have I?'

'Not as far as we know, Professor,' Broad assured him.

'Good.' The old man stared at them. 'Still, there's something, isn't there?' Another beat. 'But you're not going to tell me. How irritating. I find I enjoy suspense so much less these days. Hopefully I'll live long enough to hear the full story.'

Paul arrived with the tray of hot drinks, and Lockyer noticed that standards were slipping. His mug had a chip in the base, and the biscuits were still in their packet: no plate, no doily. He studied the tea Paul had made him in dismay. It was so weak and milky it was almost colourless. Undrinkable. Paul smiled as he left the room.

'Once we have the full story, we'll disclose it,' Lockyer said. 'And we'd get there much faster if you were open and honest with us, Professor Ferris.'

'Don't hector me, man.'

'Time is short. For you and for Hedy,' Lockyer said.

'He does so love to prod at my guilt, see if he can't get it to wake up,' Roland said to Broad.

'What are you feeling guilty about, sir?' she asked.

'Ha! Not what you suspect, I think. Just the usual things a man of my age and state of decline feels guilty about. Past mistakes, things I did, things I didn't do and should have done. Things I should have done differently, and better.'

'Where's Harry now?' Lockyer asked.

'Still up in London. He has a job, you know. He's busy and important, as lawyers tend to be. He took a week's leave when he first came to see me, but then he had to go back.'

'Are you expecting him at the weekend?'

'Yes, he said he'd come.'

'And you're still not prepared to tell us what took him so long?'

'As I said before, Inspector, it was his decision and only he can tell you his reasons.'

'Then please tell him to phone me as soon as he can to arrange a suitable time for us to talk.' Lockyer felt a flare of impatience at the old man's soft, derisive *hmm*. 'Or we could send a car to bring him to the station instead, as we did for Mr Rifkin.'

'Very well, very well. Don't get your back up.'

'We'd like to ask you about your will, sir,' Broad said. It was clumsy, and she flicked an apologetic glance at Lockyer.

'Would you indeed,' Roland said.

'We believe questions about inheritance could have motivated the attack on Mr Brown. Especially if the killer believed him to be your son, Harry.'

But as she said this, Lockyer realized that the only people who'd still believed Mickey was Harry by the day of the actual murder were Tor Garvich and Serena Godwin. And Serena was only a maybe. And Garvich couldn't possibly have hoped to benefit from Roland's will. By the time of the killing, Paul Rifkin, Miles Godwin and Hedy had all known Mickey's true identity, as had Sean Hannington, the Traveller who'd most likely cracked his ribs and forced him into hiding. Lockyer pinched the bridge of his nose.

Even if Roland had gone to his grave insisting that Mickey was Harry, and even if Mickey had tried to go along with it and claim the inheritance, it would never have held up. The real Harry, tipped off by Miles, would surely have made a swift reappearance. And Serena would have insisted on a DNA test, had she been in any doubt – or about to miss out. So, could thoughts of protecting their inheritance *really* have been in any of their minds?

'Everything okay, Guv?' Broad said.

Lockyer looked up at them both. 'I just had a thought,' he said. 'I'll tell you later.'

'Hmm. Didn't look like a good thought, did it, Constable Broad?' said the professor.

'Did you make any changes to your will as a result of your son apparently returning home, fourteen years ago?' Lockyer said.

'No. Why would I?'

'Are you sure? You didn't discuss it with anyone? Nobody could have got the impression that the will would be changed, as a result of Harry's reappearance?'

'Why on earth would they? Not that it's any of your business, but my will is the same now as the day I made it, God knows how long ago.' He waved his hand weakly. 'I kept waiting for Miles to produce some grandchildren for me, but he hasn't so far. Neither has Harry. They still have time, of course. Unlike me.'

'Do you mind telling us who benefits?' Lockyer said.

'I do mind, but since this is a murder investigation ...' Roland Ferris fixed Lockyer with a sharp, considering look. 'Since Helen ... died ... the house, the cars, and the bulk of the liquidity goes to Harry. Serena gets some shares and the place near La Rochelle. It's where we used to go as children. Our parents took us sailing ... I used to have a boat, too, but I sold it. Used the money to buy a particularly lovely 1965 Daimler 250 V8 saloon.' He smiled fondly. 'Gorgeous thing. Cherry red leather seats, walnut dash and panelling.' He sighed. 'Helen suffered terribly with *le mal de mer*, so we never used the boat anyway.'

'How much does a car like that set you back?' Broad asked.

'Ah, well, most of thirty grand. But she was a beauty. I used to prefer to buy them in poor condition, neglected, some only held together by the brambles growing through them. Then I'd set about restoring them, over a number of years. Coaxing them back to life. I got quite a name for myself, in certain circles, so from time to time I found myself working on other people's cars as well. But that was always more frenetic. People are so impatient. I didn't enjoy it as much but it was lucrative.'

'Hedy Lambert had a car she loved that she restored herself,' Broad said.

'Yes, she told me about it. An Austin Allegro – ha! Bless her. I never saw it, of course – that crooked bastard made off with it before she came here.' The old man shook his head. 'But she understood the joy of bringing a wonderful machine back to life. Rare in a woman.' He sighed. 'Can one call the Austin Allegro a wonderful machine? Bit of a stretch, perhaps.'

'Do you still have it? The Daimler, I mean.'

'Of course. I've had to sell several of the others over the years, sadly, in fallow times. But one doesn't part with a sweetheart like that.'

'May we see it?' Broad asked. She sounded keen, and Lockyer didn't have the heart to point out that it wasn't relevant to the case.

'Yes.' Roland sounded surprised. 'By all means. Paul will give you the keys. I should so like to see them all again myself, but I simply haven't the energy.'

'You could ask Mr Rifkin to bring them out, and then you'd only have to go to the window,' Broad suggested.

'Have *Paul* drive my cars?' Roland sounded appalled. 'Good grief, Constable, don't even *whisper* it. And I must ask that you be *very* careful around them. Look, but don't touch.'

'And nobody else is mentioned in the will?' Lockyer said.

'Well, there's some cash and shares for Miles. We're a family of only children, Lockyer. Funny how that happens, sometimes. There aren't too many people to share the sum of me around.' He stared into the middle distance. 'Perhaps I *should* make some adjustments, though,' he murmured. 'Before I go. Some provision for faithful retainers, perhaps.'

Lockyer made a mental note that Paul Rifkin owed him one.

'The cars must be worth quite a bit of money,' Broad said. 'How many do you still have?'

'Seventeen. And I know them all very well, Constable Broad, so don't go thinking you can pinch one without my noticing.'

'Oh, go on, sir. I only need a small one . . .'

'You should bring her with you every time, Inspector,' Roland said. 'She's far better company.'

'Yes.' Lockyer looked across at Broad. 'I know she is.'

As they got up to leave, Lockyer said, 'One more thing, Professor. I spoke to Maureen Pocock recently. She told me about an occasion when the police came here to talk to you.'

'What? When? She was probably talking about that highly conspicuous car you sent for poor Paul.'

'No, this was a long time ago. Harry was still a boy – twelve or thirteen, she thought.'

The professor said nothing. He stared at Lockyer, his face immobile.

'Mrs Pocock thought it was because you and Helen had been overheard arguing loudly. She thought a concerned neighbour had called them, but that it later turned out to have been about something else. Can you tell me what, Professor?'

'Haven't a clue,' he said tersely. 'You're talking about thirty-odd years ago, man! Whatever the reason, it was insignificant enough for both myself and Maureen Pocock to have forgotten it. And that woman is an elephant, in more ways than one.'

'Right, then. I'll ask Harry when we see him. Perhaps he'll remember. Thank you, Professor.'

'Good day to you,' the old man muttered, already staring at his book again, but blindly, with a frown hiding his eyes.

Lockyer got the garage keys from Rifkin and led Broad past the small barn. While she stared up at the shadowy beams, he told her what he'd realized about the inheritance being a possible motive.

Broad looked dismayed. 'I can't believe we didn't twig that sooner.'

'I know. Money is so often a motive, but not this time.'

'That does kind of narrow the field, doesn't it?'

'Possibly.' Lockyer was cautious. 'He was lying about not remembering that police visit.'

'Yes.'

'Thirty years back. What are the chances of it still being in the system somewhere?'

'Slim to nil.' Broad puffed out her cheeks. She knew what was coming. 'And paper files from that far back are like hen's teeth.'

It was true. So many old police buildings had been abandoned or sold off, and there was a limit to what could be stored, and for how long. Thousands upon thousands of old case files had been lost or destroyed.

'And if it was a routine or speculative visit, and the Ferrises weren't actually involved in the case ... Needle in a haystack.'

'Yes. It'll be difficult to chase down.'

The main run of stables was built of brick and beams, like the house, but the large barn was wooden, the same style as the one in the back garden, albeit considerably bigger. Lockyer unlocked that door first.

The air inside was frigid, and loaded with the smells of engine grease and petrol, which always seemed to get into the very fabric of a building. At one end was an inspection pit with a powered ramp above it, surrounded by racks of tools, cans of oil, sprayers, rags, and posters of cars, car shows and car-parts suppliers. Goodyear, Castrol, Michelin. *Le Grand Prix de Pau Historique, 2001.* Light streamed in through high windows, their vertical bars casting patterns on the concrete floor. At the far end, where the original cobbles were still intact, the first of the cars were parked in three rows, two deep.

Some were covered with dust sheets, others not. Broad walked between them, arms folded against the cold, and peered in through the window of one that was uncovered. They could smell leather, metal and rubber now.

'I can see why people like them,' Broad said. 'Have them for their weddings and that. There's something about them. Really old cars, I mean. Relics of bygone glamour, I suppose.' She looked over at him with a quick smile. 'Back when glamour was actually glamorous.'

'I suppose so.' Lockyer wasn't really interested in the cars. Not even when Broad identified the Daimler saloon Roland Ferris had been rhapsodizing about. His mind was churning through the shrinking group of people who had an identifiable motive for killing Mickey Brown.

'Guv . . .' Broad started. 'That stuff about the police coming round . . . Could that really be relevant? I mean, it was ages before Helen Ferris killed herself, even – a good year or two. So it's probably nothing to do with that. And Harry Ferris was just a little kid . . .'

Lockyer bit back a sharp reply. He knew she was right. And he knew his immediate flare of impatience stemmed from desperation. He didn't want to think too hard about that. 'It might not be relevant,' he conceded. 'But there's *something* going on here. Roland and Harry Ferris are lying about something. Could be completely unrelated, but it might not be. And I want to know what it is.'

'Yes, Guv.'

'We dropped the ball on the original investigation, Gem. We had an obvious suspect and we stopped looking at anyone else. I won't do it again.'

'I understand, Guv. It's just . . .' Broad looked uncomfortable. 'None of that means you didn't get the right person first time around. Maybe the fact we can't find anyone else with a motive is because . . . there isn't anyone.'

'We haven't looked at everyone yet. We haven't looked at everything.'

He couldn't stand the thought of not solving it. Of not being able to fix it. All his past mistakes. Broad must have heard the pent-up feeling in his voice: she said no more.

They went briefly into the coach house and the stables, where the partitions had been removed to create one long space for another single row of vehicles to be parked, side by side. Most of them were shrouded, and sank into shadow the further from the door they were. Broad fingered one of the covers speculatively, but Lockyer didn't want to spend too much time there. 'Look, don't touch, remember?'

He examined the key ring Rifkin had given him. A silver Yale glinted among the big, old-fashioned mortice keys for the barn and stables. 'Come on.'

Broad followed him to the rear of the coach house, where steps led up to the loft apartment. The Yale opened the door, as he'd suspected it would.

'Hedy Lambert's place?' Broad asked, as they went inside.

Lockyer nodded.

The air inside was stale, warmer than the garages but only just. Kitchen, bathroom, bed-sitting room. Beige carpets and walls, cheap kitchen units with the bare minimum of mod cons: a washing-machine but no drier, no dishwasher. The furniture still looked quite new, and all smacked of IKEA, apart from the stuff that had obviously come from the main house. A cherrywood coffee-table that had lost a chunk of its decorative trim; a standard lamp with an ugly tasselled shade. Lockyer thought back, picturing it as it had been in 2005. He remembered a few things – alarm clock, stripy oven gloves, a bottle of bubble bath, a photo of her parents – but Hedy had brought precious little with her. Thanks to Aaron Fletcher, she'd had precious little left.

His attention, that last time, had been almost entirely focused on Hedy. Shivering, her freshly washed hair dripping dark spots onto her sleeves. Sudden spasms of emotion had stormed her face now and then, twisting it for a second before the glassy emptiness returned. Lockyer remembered trying to work out what those spasms were – guilt, anger, grief, fear? He didn't feel he was any closer to knowing now than he had been then.

'Who came and cleared out all her things?' he wondered aloud.

'Her family, I suppose,' Broad said, looking around. 'I hate attic flats like this. I could never live in one.'

'Oh? Why's that?'

Broad pointed at the ceiling, which sloped steeply on either side of the room, and met at a sharp apex about eight feet above their heads. 'Nothing but skylights. No proper windows. You can't really see out.'

'What was it Professor Garvich said? "A claustrophobic, blinkered existence."'

'Perhaps she was right,' Broad said.

Lockyer didn't reply. He remembered something Hedy had said to him, in one of their many interviews. *No, I like the flat. It's small but it's more than enough for me. And I like to look up at the sky at night. I like to know nobody can see in. Nobody's watching me. I'm just invisible.*

'Come on,' he said, trying to ignore the pang the memory gave him. Something like sorrow. 'We should head back. Let's try to get Serena Godwin in for a chat. Who knows what might lie beneath that permafrost? There could be whole worlds of bad feeling we don't know about yet. And I'm not clear how convinced she really was, at any point, that Mickey was Harry.'

'Plus the theory was that the stabbing was a woman's crime, right?' Broad said. 'Killing him in his sleep so there was no chance of being physically overpowered.'

'Right.'

They walked back out to the car in silence.

'Course,' Broad said tentatively, as they reached it. 'There is another type of person who might want to avoid a fight.'

Lockyer stopped and turned to face her.

'An older, weaker man. A man who knew he'd lose if it came to a struggle. Perhaps a sick man . . .'

'You're talking about Roland Ferris.'

'Like you said, Guv, there were a lot of people who, by the end, knew that Mickey was Mickey, not Harry. What if one of them told the professor?'

'And broke his heart,' Lockyer said.

'Strong emotions often manifest as anger, in blokes,' Broad said. She looked away. 'Or, at least, they do in some of the blokes I know.'

Lockyer glanced at her. 'Do they?' he said.

'Well. Yes.' She looked back briefly, then down at her hands, colouring faintly. 'Not *you*, Guv. I didn't mean . . . You're the least like that of anyone I . . .' She trailed into an uncomfortable silence.

'Pete?' Lockyer asked, feeling a flare of outrage at the thought. It would be so easy to bully somebody like Gemma Broad. So easy, and so wrong. 'Does he ever—'

'Oh, no!' she said hurriedly. 'No. Strong emotions aren't really Pete's problem. Not that he *has* a problem, it's just . . .' She trailed off again, and took a sharp breath. 'Forget I said anything, Guv.'

She looked stricken, and they got into the car in silence. Lockyer couldn't tell what it was, exactly, that Broad had been trying to tell him. He focused, and for some reason found himself saddened by the thought of Roland Ferris as the killer. He glanced at Broad.

'And there I was thinking you'd liked the professor,' he said, as he turned the key in the ignition.

'I do.' Broad nodded. 'But that doesn't mean he didn't snap and stab the guy, all those years ago.'

'You're right. It doesn't.'

And if he had, Lockyer thought, then the one person Hedy had grown to care for, the one person she'd come to trust after Aaron Fletcher ruined her life, had let her be jailed for fourteen years for a crime she hadn't committed.

11

By the time they got back to the station Lockyer had missed a call from Tom Williams. He rang him back immediately.

'Got something for you.' Tom cleared his throat with a rattle. 'Now, she may or may not want to talk to you, I can't promise anything, but I've found Kim Cowley. She was Sean Hannington's missus back in the day – around the time we were looking for him, anyway, and into the noughties. Could be she was still his missus at the time of your murder. Maybe she can tell you something about what went on with Mickey.'

'That's brilliant, Tom. Thank you so much. How the hell did you find her?'

'Last time I saw her we talked a little bit. She asked me – on the quiet, like – about getting a council flat. She wasn't from a Travelling family, see. She met Sean at an impressionable age and ran off with him, and I think she'd had enough. So I called in a favour at the council, a mate who works in housing, and bingo. She and her son Kieron have got a flat in Westbury. Want the address?'

DSU Considine put her head around the door. 'Matt, a word, if I may.'

'Tom, I've got to go – can you text it to me?' Lockyer said. 'Thanks for this. I owe you a pint.'

'Well,' Tom chuckled, 'I'll be up to Devizes to cash it in before you forget.'

Lockyer rang off and got up to follow Considine, ignoring Broad's look of mild trepidation.

'Shut the door, Matt. Have a seat,' the DSU told him, as he arrived at her desk. She spoke lightly, but didn't smile. 'I'm keen to hear where you're at. Did you get anywhere with Paul Rifkin?'

'You'll have read my report, so you'll know he lied to the original investigation – he knew Mickey Brown of old, and he assaulted him in the days leading up to the murder.' Lockyer wanted this to sound like progress, but it would only be progress if he thought Paul was the killer. Reluctantly, he explained why he didn't. And that they'd discounted the inheritance of Roland's wealth as a motive. And that their chat with Professor Tor Garvich had been unenlightening.

'So, where are you going next? What are your thoughts?'

'We've managed to locate a woman called Kim Cowley, who was the partner of a man from the Travelling community. Sean Hannington ran the camp where Mickey had been living, and by all accounts he was not a man to cross. He could well have been the reason Mickey had gone into hiding at Longacres. Could've been the one who gave him the broken ribs.'

'So you're going to talk to this Cowley woman? See if she knows where he is?'

'Yes.'

'I thought we'd established that the killer had to be someone from inside the house, or someone with keys? And does this Hannington sound like the kind of man who'd make a swift, clean kill while the victim was asleep?'

'I just don't know yet. Maybe, if he'd had time to get control of his temper. And maybe he was good with locks . . .' Lockyer dried up. It sounded thin. 'We've only ever had Hedy's word that the knife was on the draining board the evening before. That was where she said she left it, but it's not like she would have checked it was still there before she went bed, is it? What if it somehow made its way outside before the door was locked?'

'How could that possibly have happened, Matt?'

'I don't know . . . Maybe she took it out with his dinner tray by mistake, and it was in the barn, ready for the killer to find it. Maybe she threw it onto the compost heap with a pile of scraps. Things we do every day, like leave a knife by the sink . . . she could have been remembering any one of a hundred other times.'

'And the killer thought, "I know, I'll just go and look on the compost heap for something to stab that bloke in the barn with"?'

'Probably not,' Lockyer conceded. 'But someone *could* have got into the house earlier in the day, before the doors were locked, and taken the knife then. It's possible.'

'But unlikely.'

'A lot of what people do is unlikely. Until they do it.'

'Christ, you're as stubborn as a mule, Matt.' She shook her head.

'Constable Broad identified another possible suspect earlier on today.'

'Do tell?'

'Roland Ferris.'

Lockyer explained Broad's idea.

Considine listened. 'I find that a lot more plausible than the compost-heap idea.'

'I do too. But I don't want to discount Hannington yet. I don't want to discount anyone.'

'Unlike the last time?' Considine's tone cooled.

'Roland Ferris is definitely lying to us. Or not telling us everything, at any rate. Someone could still have thought they were killing Harry Ferris with that knife, and I think the reason why might lie a lot further back . . .'

'What makes you say that?'

'It's just a—'

'A hunch?'

'A hypothesis.'

'Right.' Considine pressed her lips together for a second. 'Look, Matt, it seems to me you're no closer to understanding who the killer thought they were killing, let alone why they did it, or who the hell it was. *If* indeed it wasn't Hedy Lambert.'

'We're making progress, ma'am. Even if it's to rule people out—'

'This can't go on for ever, Matt. You can't spend the next

six months ruling people out. You need to rule someone *in*, and God knows the forensics aren't going to help you with that. Unless, of course, she's guilty.'

Lockyer said nothing. It wasn't a question. Considine studied him. Then she waved a hand. 'Well, go on then. Carry on. But I want to see progress, Matt. And soon. Something new, not just a list of people who didn't do it.'

'Ma'am.' He got up to leave.

'How are you getting on with Gemma Broad?' Considine asked.

'Fine,' he said. 'She's quick. Lacks confidence, maybe, but she's good.'

'Great,' was all Considine said, already focused on her paperwork.

Lockyer asked Broad to keep trying Serena Godwin's number between brief visits to Paul Rifkin and Miles Godwin, then to start searching for any record of the Ferrises' involvement with the police from thirty years ago. Any whiff of a hidden past, or a criminal incident. She looked deflated as he left.

He drove south before turning west along a narrow road that skirted the edge of Salisbury Plain. The grassland rose steeply on his left; a vast, green escarpment, rumpled like a velvet cape. In summer, paragliders launched themselves from the ridge, circling on thermals above the flat patchwork of fields below. It was on Lockyer's bucket list to try it. Be alone in all that sky with a distant, three-sixty horizon. Before long he passed below the Bratton white horse, one of the eight still visible on hillsides across Wiltshire. Giant carvings exposing the gleaming white chalk beneath the turf. Lockyer had always found them beautiful, fantastical; the horses caught for ever mid-stride, mid-flight, or else standing four-square and implacable, as men had marched below with feet of clay, one century through to the next.

He was taking the cross-country route to Westbury, unsure whether he was wasting his time or not. Considine's points about the knife were valid. It was so much more likely to have been taken out to the barn by someone from inside the house for the purpose of killing the man sleeping there. He wanted to talk to Hedy again, find out how certain she was she'd left the knife where she said she had. Broad would want to come. She *should* come, he told himself, and see what she made of Hedy in person. Yet he couldn't shake his nagging reluctance to let her.

Westbury was a small, unlovely and ungentrified town; a workaday place of pubs, takeaways, and small Georgian shops that changed hands regularly. Kim Cowley's flat was on the ground floor of a neat, low block in the centre, with communal grounds that consisted of tarmac parking and a muddy lawn. In response, Kim had crammed as many different-coloured flowerpots as possible outside her front window. Not to mention plastic windmills and charms that caught the light, bird feeders and small resin statues of animals. She answered Lockyer's knock by opening the door three inches and peering out through the gap, so he saw only part of her thin face and one huge eye, sooty with mascara.

'What?' she said.

'Kim Cowley?'

'Who wants to know?'

Lockyer held up his warrant card. Kim's visible eye widened.

'There hasn't been any trouble, Ms Cowley, I'd just like to ask you a few questions about a case I'm working on.'

'Questions about what?'

'Sean Hannington.'

Kim stared at him for a moment, saying nothing. Then she opened the door wider.

'Ain't seen him in months,' she said. Lockyer nodded. So she had seen Hannington relatively recently. He wasn't buried in concrete somewhere.

'If I could have a few minutes of your time, I'd very much appreciate it.'

'All right.' She glanced outside, then opened the door wider.

Kim was a tiny bird of a woman, who looked more care-worn than aged. She wore bright colours – a purple T-shirt with an elaborate Hand of Fatima motif, over red leggings – and lots of jewellery. The inside of the flat was cluttered with little things, much like the space outside the window. Wall hangings and crystals and dream-catchers and potted plants sought to defy the building's abject lack of character. The sweet smell of cannabis hung in the air.

As if suddenly noticing it herself, Kim lunged at an over-flowing ashtray, cupping her hands over it as she spirited it through to the kitchen and tipped it into the bin. 'Do you want tea?' she said. 'I've got a pot on the go.'

'That'd be lovely. Thank you.'

He never said no: it was good manners, and helped put mistrustful people at ease. It meant he had to accept whatever he was given, but the cup Kim poured him was strong without being stewed, just as he liked it, and he smiled. 'That's the best cuppa I've had in a long time,' he told her.

Kim relaxed a little, but her expression stayed taut with suspicion. 'My nan taught me how to make a proper brew. Warming the pot and not leaving it too long, and buying proper leaves instead of cheap bags full of floor sweepings. Some things are worth paying a bit more for.'

She sat at one end of a sagging sofa, and motioned Lockyer to an armchair. 'What's he done this time, then?' she asked.

'I'm actually looking at an old case.' He watched her closely. 'The murder of Michael Brown in 2005.'

Kim went a shade paler. 'Mickey . . . It was Sean, wasn't it?' she whispered. 'I always thought it must've been him . . . Even when they put that woman away for it.'

'Well, that's what I'm trying to find out. We really don't know yet, Ms Cowley—'

'Kim. Please. I've always hated Cowley. You can guess what I got called at school.'

'I was hoping you could fill in a few of the blanks about Mickey's time in the camp with you and Sean. How well did you know him? Mickey, I mean.'

'How well did I know him?' A sad little half-smile. 'I knew him pretty well.' She pointed at a photo propped on a shelf on the far wall. 'That's his son, right there.'

'I'm sorry – your son, Kieron, is Mickey's son?'

Kim looked down at her restless fingers. 'I reckon he is. No way to know for sure, of course. As far as Sean's concerned, Kieron's his. He said there's no way Mickey's spunk could have out-swum his. Prick.'

'You think he's wrong?'

'Got to be. Kieron's nothing like Sean. He's got a good heart, you know? I don't see how a bastard like Sean can have been his dad.' She looked up, and Lockyer understood that it was fear that had worn her down. Habitual fear. 'Still comes around to see him, he does. Not that often these days, thank Christ. Says he's got a right to see his kid.'

'Couldn't you get a paternity test done?'

'Costs money. Besides, Sean says there's no way anyone's taking his DNA.' She snorted. 'The amount of evil shit he's done in his lifetime, probably best for him if he doesn't. More's the pity.'

'So Kieron's more like Mickey? Mickey was kind-hearted?'

'Soft as butter,' Kim said sadly. 'Just wanted everyone to be happy and get along, you know? He'd do anything to please you. Like a bloody puppy, he was.' She sipped her tea, not meeting his eye. 'That's how it started. Him and me, I mean. After being with Sean for years, God, I'd have fallen for anyone who was kind to me. Gentle with me.'

'Was Sean ever violent towards you?'

'Just a bit,' she said sarcastically. 'Actually, after the first few pastings he hardly had to bother. That's how he operates – makes people scared, then they're easy to control.'

Lockyer looked again at the size of her, her fragile build, and felt hatred for Sean Hannington rise up, bitter, in the back of his throat. He'd never understood men who beat up women. He had no idea how such a man must think or feel about himself. 'How long had Mickey been living at the camp with you?'

'A year or so, I guess. He just wandered up one day, and Sean grilled him for a bit. Marked him as easy prey, I 'spect. Easy to boss about. Mickey'd been on his own before that, just parking up a night here, a night there. Been travelling all round the country, but he told me this was home – round here, I mean. He was down here for a bit as a little kid, before his mum took him up north. Darlington, I think it was.'

'Did he ever mention where exactly he grew up?'

Kim shook her head.

'He never mentioned Stoke Lavington? Or a family called Ferris?'

'Where he got killed, you mean?' she said, her voice small. 'No.'

'So, Sean found out you and Mickey had been seeing each other?'

'Hard to keep things like that quiet when you're all living on top of each other. I thought we were being careful, but . . . I thought Sean was going to kill him. He *would*'ve killed him, I know he would.'

'How did Mickey get away?'

'It . . . Luck, mostly. Sean started laying into him, and I was yelling at him to stop, and then Sean . . . stumbled. He'd been sinking cans all afternoon – I mean, it takes a lot to get a bloke his size pissed, but he was at least halfway there.

He lost his footing and went down and Mickey was away. He wasn't strong but, by God, he could run. Learnt that at a young age, I reckon.'

Lockyer pictured Mickey's sinewy body on the mortuary slab, with its cigarette-burn scars, and could believe it.

'Sean had no hope of catching him,' Kim went on. 'Bloody great lumbering ox, he is.'

'And you think Sean would have carried on beating Mickey if he hadn't got away?'

Kim nodded. 'I seen it happen once before. Some bloke who'd been cutting the coke Sean was dealing, and selling it on the side. He kept kicking him and kicking him, like a bloody machine.' She shut her eyes. 'Just out the back of a pub it was. Not scared of being seen or caught or nothing.'

'What happened to that man?'

'No idea. Sean told me to bugger off and he never had to tell me twice. Never saw the other guy again. Wouldn't shock me if he was dead.'

'How did you get involved with Sean Hannington in the first place, Kim?'

'Fifteen years old and thick as mud, wasn't I?' She shrugged. 'I met him at the pub, thought he was the bee's knees. A *proper* man, not like the boys at school. He bought me drinks and jewellery, cheap stuff, and said he loved me. Hook, line and bloody sinker.'

'But you got away from him in the end. That must have taken a lot of courage.'

'Yeah, right.' She rolled her eyes. 'I was with him seven years, and in the end I got too old for him. He brought some new little slapper back to the van. I made a big scene like I was broken-hearted, and off I went. Couldn't believe my luck.' She smiled her quick, sardonic smile again. 'Felt sorry for the poor cow, of course. 'Spect she's regretting her choice by now, same as I did. But that's the other thing that makes me sure Sean's not Kieron's dad, right? Seven years I was with him and we weren't that careful. I couldn't always get the pill and he'd never put on a johnny. But I never got pregnant – not till Mickey.'

'Do you know where Sean is now?'

'No. And I don't want to. Though it might take the shock out of it when he turns up next if I did.'

'If he's still abusive towards you, Kim, you should report—'

'Yeah, yeah, whatever. You don't get it. How can you?' she said wearily. 'You're a bloke. And a copper.'

Lockyer had to concede the point. It seemed so unfair that the onus for ending abuse like Sean's had to come from the victim – reporting them, pressing charges, dealing with the fallout, or else uprooting their entire life. 'Did you see Mickey again after he ran off?'

'No. I thought . . .' She took a breath. 'I thought he'd got away. I thought he'd put some miles between them, gone back up north or something. Then later that summer someone spotted that picture of him in the paper, asking for information about a murder victim.' She stared at the carpet, her focus in the past. 'Hiding in a fucking barn not four miles away. What the *fuck* was he thinking?'

'Perhaps he thought it would blow over.'

'He might have been away with the fairies, but he weren't

that daft. With someone like Sean you knew it weren't ever going to *blow over*. Sean sets off all the warning bells in the back of your brain. Same way a rabbit knows to run from a dog. I just hope Mickey didn't stick around because of *me*.' Her voice wobbled.

'I think Mickey thought he'd found the perfect place to hide,' Lockyer said. 'Perhaps he only planned to stay one night, and get some sleep, but Professor Ferris welcomed him in, and fed him . . .' He spread his hands. 'So he stayed. Kim, forgive me for asking about something so difficult. Mickey was killed by a single stab wound, probably while he was asleep. Does that sound like Sean's work?'

'I dunno. Nothing would surprise me. But the Sean I know . . . He's got so much rage in him, he'd be more likely to pick up whatever first came to hand and smash his head in with it.'

'Right.'

'Still, nothing I know's more likely to get you killed, one way or another, than pissing Sean off.'

Lockyer thought for a moment. 'It always puzzled me that Mickey stayed out in the barn. He was offered a room in the house – and it's a nice house, all the creature comforts.'

Kim was shaking her head. 'In and out of institutions and juvy his whole childhood, he was. He never talked about it but I reckon he was fiddled with. You know, sexually. Mickey was messed up. That's how he ended up on the road – he wouldn't go inside anywhere with brick walls or locks on the doors. Not even a pub – someone always had to fetch his pint out and he'd drink it on the pavement.'

Lockyer stood up to leave. 'You've been a huge help, Kim. Thank you.'

'You finally going to put him away, then? For good, I mean? Be about bloody time.'

'Believe me, if I can, I will.' Lockyer paused. 'There is one other way you could help. You and Kieron. And maybe it would help you too.'

'Yeah? What's that?'

'We have Mickey's DNA on file from the investigation into his death. If Kieron was willing to give us a sample, we could find out for certain whether Mickey was his dad. If you knew for sure he was, it might put a stop to Sean's visits.'

'It might,' Kim said, not sounding at all sure. 'Or it might just piss him off.'

'Forgive me for asking this, Kim, but are you absolutely sure Kieron's father was either Mickey or Sean?'

'Yes. I'm absolutely sure.'

'Then . . . if it turns out Sean *is* Kieron's father, we'd have a close family DNA profile on file. It might help us put him away for any of the other crimes he's committed.'

'I don't know . . .' Kim squeezed her fingers together, shaking her head. 'If he found out . . .'

'If he asked, we'd say that your son's DNA had been taken for elimination purposes as part of a different investigation. I promise that your and Kieron's voluntary input would never be made known to him.'

'I don't know,' she said again. 'I'd have to ask Kieron. It's up to him, isn't it?'

'Yes. Absolutely.'

'I'll ask him when he gets home from school.'

'We wouldn't even have to send anyone here to take the sample, if you don't want. Just get Kieron to wrap his toothbrush up in a plastic bag and send it to me.' He handed her his card. 'Please, Kim. It could be very important.'

Kim didn't answer. She stared down at his card, and her hands were shaking as she closed the door behind him.

Back at the station, Broad had been to see Paul Rifkin and Miles Godwin.

'Both of them swear blind they didn't tell *anyone* else what they knew about Mickey not being Harry, let alone tell Roland,' she said.

'Right. So that leaves Hedy.'

'Or Mickey himself. Or Roland finding out some other way, accidentally or otherwise.'

'Yes, true,' Lockyer said. 'Or Serena? Maybe she went snooping, and found something. Something Harry had sent Miles – some correspondence?'

'I asked Miles that, and he's certain there was no evidence for her to find, unless she hacked his phone or email, which seems unlikely. She doesn't even like to use an ATM, by all accounts.'

'Have you managed to get hold of her?'

'No. I've left about twenty messages.' Broad pulled an exasperated face.

'Let's keep trying. Hopefully all the calls are annoying her, at least.'

'What are you thinking about this Sean Hannington guy, then?' Broad asked.

Lockyer told her what he'd found out from Kim. 'He's a brute, that much is certain,' he said. 'But the stabbing . . . I don't know. It doesn't really sound like his style. And the knife would have to have been there already, to hand. Picking locks, finessing doors and evidence . . . That seems unlikely.'

'Yeah, he sounds more the kick-the-door-in-and-break-some-heads type,' Broad agreed. 'Plus there was no other DNA on the body, was there? Only Hedy's hair. Could he have been that careful, and not left any?'

'It's possible, I suppose. Besides, some of the clothing fibres on the tapes could have been his, but there's no way of proving that now, fourteen years after the event.'

'And maybe the SOCOs missed something,' Broad suggested. 'Think they'll give us a DNA sample?'

'Might do. She wants him out of their lives, and who can blame her? Course, she'll be hoping that Mickey is Kieron's dad, and we'll be hoping the opposite. I feel a bit bad about that.'

'Not if it puts Hannington in jail.'

'No. True.' Lockyer sat down, swivelled his chair to the window and stared out at the tree tops. 'Mickey grew up round here, Kim says. I wonder if he knew the Ferrises, somehow. Maybe he went to that barn deliberately. Maybe that's how he knew enough to convince Roland Ferris.' He paused. 'I'm going to call Eastwood Park. Book in to see Hedy again tomorrow.'

He could feel Broad's anticipation. 'Come with me this time, see what you make of her.'

'Yes, Guv.' Broad turned back to her screen.

That evening Lockyer started on the wood-chip ceiling in the spare room. It made the muscles in his back and shoulders burn, but he'd soon uncovered what he thought must be the stain Bill Hickson had been trying to cover up. It didn't look like rainwater had been the issue, though. There were no concentric rings, and it wasn't the right shade of tea-brown.

Movement outside the window caught his eye, and he looked down to see Mrs Musprat heading back along the path from the goat shed. She looked up, saw Lockyer watching her and froze, staring up at him, her face expressionless. Lockyer supposed he was silhouetted by the ceiling light behind him, but she would be able to see, of course, which room he was in. Something about her stillness struck him as odd. He was about to open the window and call down to her when she stirred, hunching into herself, and carried on towards the house. It was hard to tell in the dark, but she seemed to shudder.

When he'd had enough of work Lockyer made dinner, and was sitting on the stairs eating a pile of chilli noodles when he heard an engine outside, then footsteps and a knock. He was surprised. Visitors to his place were rare. He still had his dinner in one hand as he opened the door.

'All right?' Kevin attempted to kick some of the wet mud off his trainers, then kicked off the trainers instead. 'You really need a security light out there. It's pitch sodding black. Sorry – thought you'd have finished eating by now. Hang on,' he looked at his watch, 'it's half past nine ... We're not in Spain, are we?'

'I lost track of time,' Lockyer said.

Kevin held up a six-pack of beers as he came in, looking around at the mess and the piles of tools and boxes and roughly swept sawdust and scraps. 'It has to look worse before it can look better, right?' he said.

'Thanks.'

'No, seriously. I can see progress.'

They picked their way through to the living room, where a single armchair was currently in use, albeit still covered with a dust sheet so that Lockyer could collapse into it whenever, without worrying about having wet paint or muck on his clothes. He gestured Kevin towards it and perched on the windowsill, carrying on with his noodles. Kevin opened a beer and passed it to him, then got one for himself. He cocked his head, listening, and made a face. 'What the hell are you listening to?' he said.

'Oh – hang on. Just a podcast.' Lockyer fumbled for his phone and hit pause.

'About maths?'

'Economics. I know, I know,' Lockyer said, to Kev's dubious expression.

'Thinking about a career change?'

'No, not at all. I've never understood any of it. Thought I'd give it a go.'

'Christ, Matt, you get any more like a monk and you'll have to shave that stupid hole in your hair.'

They both smiled.

'Tonsure.'

'You what?'

'That's what the stupid hole in your hair's called. A tonsure.'

'Oh, right. Learn that in a podcast, did you?'

'Yes, actually.' Lockyer grinned. 'Anyway, monks don't drink.' He took a long pull of his beer.

Kevin did the same, then pointed a finger at him. 'You're wrong. Monks invented champagne. And Benedictine. Know where I learnt that?' He paused for effect. 'The back of the bottle.'

He looked around the room again, though there was precious little to see. His fingers fidgeted with the ring-pull of the beer can. Lockyer knew him well enough to sense his unease. The edginess he'd so often had as a kid. And he knew well enough not to push him to talk, though he wished he would. Lockyer was tired. He wanted to go to bed so that it could be the next day, and he could get to Eastwood Park and talk to Hedy. Maybe inch closer to solving the case.

'So, what you working on, then?' Kevin asked, still framing his visit as a purely social call. 'Are you allowed to talk about it?'

'A bit.' He outlined the bare bones of the case, and why he was looking into it again. When he'd finished, Kevin was grinning at him. 'What?'

'Oh, nothing, nothing,' Kevin said. 'I just understand a bit more about why you're not out there on the dating scene, now.' He took a drink. 'Nice-looking, is she? This Hedy girl?'

'She's hardly a girl any more. And she looks like you'd expect someone to look when they've been in jail that long.'

'Which is?'

'Pale. Knackered.'

'Huh. Bit like you, then.' Kevin studied him for a moment, still smiling. 'So, you don't fancy her? No . . . inappropriate feelings?'

'Fuck off, Kev.'

'No daydreams about getting her out and, I don't know, helping her rehabilitate back into society . . . and other things?'

'Seriously, fuck off,' Lockyer said.

'All right, all right.' Kevin laughed.

'Believe it or not, I'm actually pretty professional at work,' Lockyer said. 'Usually.'

Kevin's face fell. 'I know you are.' His eyelids fluttered, a series of staccato blinks. He twitched his head and it stopped. 'Can I ask you something? Not as a copper, but as a mate?'

'Course.'

Kevin stared at the black glass of the window behind Lockyer, where the reflection of his face and the spartan room were the only things to see. Lockyer cast a glance over his shoulder. 'Sorry. Not got around to curtains yet.'

'My old man's been in touch.'

'Right.'

Lockyer had the same feeling he'd always had whenever Kevin's father came into the room. The unease of being around a bully, a man of unpredictable moods and temper. A growing sense of foreboding as to what Kevin would be made to do next. It had been the same since they were kids. *He sets off all the warning bells in the back of your brain.* Just as Kim Cowley had said. But they weren't kids any more, and they weren't defenceless, or at the mercy of his whims. Or, at least, they shouldn't have been.

Was that what he'd been doing when he'd lied to the investigation into the pub fire, Lockyer wondered. Had he been trying to cut the ties between Kevin and his father? He should have known it wouldn't be that easy, but the sinking feeling he had now told him he'd hoped it anyway.

'He sounded chipper,' Kevin said. 'Enjoying himself. He's been making some new friends inside.' He looked down at his beer again, turning and turning it before taking a sip. 'He's told me some of them might call round. Bring some stuff for me to store. That kind of thing.'

He looked up at Lockyer with weariness in his eyes.

'Tell him no,' Lockyer said. 'No – don't shake your head, Kev! Tell him no.'

'I thought . . .' Kevin trailed off. 'They're just going to turn up, these blokes. I guess. I'm pretty sure they're not going to like it if I say they've got the wrong house.'

'You tell them exactly that, Kev! For fuck's sake, whatever they bring round, don't take it. And don't let them in. Christ, I wish you weren't telling me this.'

'I wish I didn't have to, Matt.'

'What are you asking me, Kev? What am I supposed to do with this?'

'I don't know. I'm sorry, Matt. It's just he's my *dad*. And you know what he's like.'

'You can't . . .' Lockyer changed tack. 'You're going to have to get out from under his thumb sometime, Kev. Now seems pretty good to me, with him locked up.'

'Matt—'

'If you go along with this, and get involved with who the hell knows what, you'll probably end up inside, with him, and I won't be able to help you. And you can't expect me to.'

'I know. I know. I just thought . . .' Kevin looked up, desperation in his eyes. 'He says I owe him, since you got me off and he took the rap for the fire.'

'The fire was *his* idea – and he started it. You don't owe him a thing.'

'Couldn't you talk to the prison? Maybe tell them what's going on, what's being planned.'

The silence filled every corner of the room.

'Just tell him no, Kev. Tell him you want no part of it,' Lockyer said. 'That's the only thing that'll make a difference. Not me talking to the bloody prison.'

'And if he sends these guys anyway?'

'If you feel threatened, call the police.'

'Christ, Matt.' Kevin sighed. 'You just don't get it.'

Lockyer thought about Kim Cowley again. Her tiny frame and startled eyes, the tremor in her hands when he'd asked her even to consider going against her oppressor. He knew it took courage. He knew that at least Kim was trying.

'I do get it – no, listen. Bob's not my dad and it's not my situation. It's not me he's had under the cosh all my life. I know it won't be easy. But I do know the *only* way it ends is if you end it, Kev. That's the only way, because he's never going to change, and he won't give a shit if you end up in prison too.'

Kevin's answer was the smallest of nods. Lockyer couldn't tell if he was agreeing to try, or simply accepting the truth of it. He finished his beer and left.

Kevin's visit had ruined Lockyer's chances of sleep. Not even the echo of Hedy's voice in his head could settle him. His friend's remark about wanting to free her so he could help her back into society had hit a nerve, so now, as he read one of the old transcripts, he grew even more restless.

DI LOCKYER: *What made you apply for the housekeeping job at Longacres?*

RESPONSE: *Well, I needed work. A place to live. Once I was . . . up and about again, I couldn't go back into physiotherapy. I just couldn't. I needed a job where I wouldn't have to smile. Or be seen.*

DI LOCKYER: *But why Longacres?*

RESPONSE: *I wanted . . . I wanted to go back to the beginning, I suppose. Start over. I grew up not far from there. It felt like . . . a chance to start over.*

Hands deep in his pockets and a hat low over his forehead, Lockyer walked along the driveway, through the sleeping village and out the other side, across the main road and up, up onto the pitch blackness of Maddington Down. In summer, the tracks cutting across the high meadow there were blindingly white with chalk, and sent up puffs of dust with every step. Now the ground was a mess of treacherous grey mud, and the wildflowers that had blazed brightly against the golden grass were dead, brittle, broken off.

The breeze picked up as the land rose, rolling endlessly over the plain, hissing through dry stems of hogweed and thistle, and bringing the occasional reek of fox. Lockyer was soon warm, simultaneously soothed and wakened by the effort of the climb and the cold touch of the air on his face. He tried to imagine Hedy at his place. Making her something to eat. He didn't think she'd mind the mess, the improvisation, or a meal made from the odds and ends in the fridge. He couldn't think of anybody less demanding.

He pushed away the thoughts, angry with himself. It was fiction, and dangerous fiction at that. How well did he really know her? Would he want her there, in his house, in his space, if she turned up tomorrow? He had no idea. He thought about Kevin instead, but it ruined the peaceful feeling he'd been striving for. Frustration boiled up inside him, caused by caring about somebody who simply would not – or could not – do what was best for themselves. Someone who was stuck in a seemingly unbreakable pattern of self-destructive behaviour. He was being unfair, and he knew it. He had no idea how hard it must be.

So he went back to Hedy. To how hard it would be for her when she came out of prison. For she would come out – sooner, if he could prove her innocence, or later, at the end of her stretch. She'd barely been a whole person when she went in: how could she hope to be a whole person when she came out? *Broken pieces*. That was how she'd described herself, in one of her interviews. Broken pieces of the person she'd been before. If she was innocent – *if* – could anybody be expected to recover from the wrongs that had been done to Hedy Lambert? How could a life that had been so comprehensibly shattered ever be reassembled? It was ridiculous to think he might ever be able to help. Considine was right about one thing, though: Hedy Lambert had got under his skin.

12

Day Fourteen, Thursday

Lockyer noticed the shift in Hedy's expression as she was brought into the private room and saw Constable Broad sitting next to him. She stopped for a second, a shadow of doubt dulling the anticipation in her eyes, then tucked her hands into the sleeves of her hoodie and slid into the plastic chair. Her eyes flicked uncertainly between the two of them.

'Hedy, this is Detective Constable Gemma Broad. She's been helping me look at the investigation.'

'Nice to meet you, Miss Lambert,' Broad said.

Hedy cleared her throat self-consciously.

Lockyer thought how few new people – people from the outside – she'd have had the opportunity to meet over the past fourteen years. He noticed that her shoulders had slumped again, and there were dark rings under her eyes. Her hair was tied back in a heavy, limp ponytail at the back of her neck. Kept out of her face, but otherwise ignored.

'How are you?' he asked.

Hedy looked wary. 'Fine, thanks.'

Her eyes flicked to Broad again, then away across the room. Lockyer wondered if he should have come alone. Hedy looked uncomfortable, like she was shutting down. Or possibly revising what she would say.

Broad glanced at Lockyer.

'Well,' he said, 'we've been talking to various people who were at Longacres at the time of the murder, and we have a few more questions we'd like to ask you, if that's okay?'

'Course.' Hedy chewed the inside of her mouth and looked down at her hands.

Lockyer cursed inwardly. It was the same blank front she'd worn throughout her trial. A defence mechanism, he could see now.

Broad leant towards her and smiled. 'I hope you don't mind me coming along with the inspector,' she said. 'It's really only so I can hear whatever you've got to say from the horse's mouth, so to speak. In your own voice, not filtered through DI Lockyer's . . .' She glanced apologetically at Lockyer. 'We're both doing our level best to get to the truth about what happened back then.'

Hedy looked up at them, then straightened her back. 'Sure, okay. Thanks.'

'We've discovered that Mickey'd had a falling-out with a man, another Traveller, called Sean Hannington. We believe it was Sean that Michael was hiding from in the barn at Longacres, and we're looking into the possibility that Sean somehow found him there.'

A flicker of interest returned to Hedy's face. 'Was that

who beat him up? When he first arrived, he was obviously injured . . . he had a cut lip, and kept holding his ribs, and moving really gingerly . . .'

'Yes,' Lockyer said. 'Almost certainly.'

Lockyer caught himself wanting to tell Hedy more about Mickey, wanting to reassure her that he'd been a nice person, by all accounts; damaged, but kind. That she hadn't been wrong to like him. But he needed to stick to the facts, and tell her the bare minimum to get unbiased and unguarded answers from her. 'There's a problem with the theory that Sean was responsible for Mickey's death, however,' he said. 'Well, a couple of problems.'

'First, how did Sean find out where Mickey was hiding?' Broad asked.

'Well . . . he did go out a bit,' Hedy said. 'Not much, but there were a few times I went to see him and he wasn't there. I was worried the first time. I thought he'd left for good, so I walked into the village to look for him, and he was sitting on the war memorial drinking a can of lager. Must have got it from the shop, though I've no idea how he paid for it. Or if he did.'

'How often did he go out, would you say?' Lockyer asked.

'I don't know.' Hedy thought about it. 'Not often. Maybe . . . four or five times over the six weeks? Hardly at all. He was obviously . . . I mean, it was obvious there was *something*. It wasn't normal, the way he stayed in the barn like that. And he was always . . . nervy. You know, twitchy.'

'From what we hear about Sean Hannington, he isn't the type you'd want to cross,' Broad said.

Hedy looked past them. 'So he was just scared, that whole time. Poor man.'

'It's possible, then, that somebody could have seen him in the village, recognized him and told Sean. Maybe even followed him back to Longacres,' Lockyer said. 'The Traveller camp where he'd been living was only about four miles away.'

'Seems possible, Guv.'

'The next problem is the knife.' Lockyer looked Hedy in the eye. 'Hedy, please think very carefully. You rinsed the knife when you'd finished cooking with it the night before, and you left it in the drainer.'

She nodded, wide-eyed.

'How certain are you that it was still there when you locked up for the night?'

'Well, I . . . Nobody would have moved it, that's the thing. But it wasn't me that locked up. It never was. After making supper for the professor and Paul, and taking Harry's out to him, and doing the washing-up, I was finished for the day. I usually left by about eight o'clock. Paul would stack their plates in the dishwasher and make coffee or whatever, and then he'd lock up last thing, before he went down to his flat.'

Lockyer could feel Broad's eyes boring into the side of his face.

'The knife was there when I left after dinner,' Hedy went on. 'I mean, I can't remember exactly, now, but it would have been there because it was my favourite, the one I always used. It'd go into the rack to dry at the end of the day, and then I'd pick it up again in the morning to cut the fruit for breakfast, so it never got put away. Paul was really keen on us sticking to our job descriptions, and the washing-up and all that was *my* job.'

'But somebody could have moved it after you went home, and before Paul locked up?' Broad asked.

Hedy spread her hands. 'They *could* have. I said so at the time. Didn't I? I'm sure I must have done . . .'

She looked at each of them, not seeming sure at all.

Lockyer ran a hand along his jaw. Broad tapped her biro on the scribbled page of her notebook.

'Right,' Lockyer said eventually. 'Thank you, Hedy. That's useful.'

'Ask Paul – he'll tell you he locked up. And he would have done it – definitely. I might not have liked him much, but he was always thorough. Methodical, I suppose. I guess it was his army training.'

'Something like that,' Broad said.

'Who else have you spoken to?' Hedy asked. 'What about Harry Ferris? I mean, he must have some idea what it was all about, mustn't he?'

She spoke with the same eagerness as when she'd asked about Harry before. Lockyer wondered about that. 'We will be speaking to him again, yes,' he said. 'Think back, Hedy. How sure are you that, at the time Mickey was killed, Roland Ferris still believed him to be his son?'

'Well . . .' Hedy seemed confused, as if she was trying to unpick the question even as she searched for her answer. 'I'm sure.'

'Completely sure? There was no change in the way Roland spoke or seemed to think about the man he thought was Harry? He never said anything to you, or seemed troubled by anything? Or angry?'

'No . . . no, he was—' Hedy stopped, and stared across at Broad's notebook.

'You're sure you didn't let anything slip, by accident, after you found out the truth yourself?' Broad asked.

'No.' Hedy was emphatic.

'Or perhaps Mickey spoke to Roland and told him the truth?'

'No. He . . . I mean, I know he said he was going to, and I'd told him that he had to, but I didn't really think he *would*. I thought he'd just disappear one night. Truthfully, that was what I thought would happen, and I'd be left to break it to Roland. But I'd have known if he'd told him – Roland would have been so upset. Well, you saw how upset he was when he *did* find out, from the fingerprints . . .'

Lockyer remembered it well. He'd been at Considine's side when she'd told him, and could picture the way Roland's face had crumpled, turning ashen. Soon, tears had dripped from his jaw onto the knees of his trousers. Lockyer had seen Roland's bewilderment, unable to tell whether he was feeling grief or anger or relief. But given a couple of hours to assimilate, relief had won. Overwhelming relief, to know that his son might still be alive, and that the body they had in the mortuary wasn't his.

But there was still the possibility that either Paul Rifkin or Mickey had told Roland the truth after Hedy had left for the night.

'I swear I didn't tell him,' Hedy said. 'Do you think I should have? Straight away, I mean?'

'It's okay, Hedy—'

'I think I should have,' she said sadly. 'It was only being a coward that stopped me. Knowing how upset he'd be, and not wanting to be the one to do it.'

'We've also spoken to—'

'Why are you asking about the professor, anyway?' Hedy interrupted Broad. Her eyes narrowed. 'You can't think he'd have had anything to do with it?'

'We're looking at everyone and everything, Hedy,' Lockyer said. 'It's the only way we might find something that was missed before.'

'I . . . I understand that,' she said, chastened. 'But there's no way it was Professor Ferris.'

'You sound very sure,' Broad said.

'I'm more sure he didn't do it than I am *I* didn't.' Hedy smiled nervously. 'The very idea of it is ridiculous.'

There was a moment of quiet, a regrouping. Lockyer watched Hedy's restless fingers on the tabletop, fiddling with her cuffs. Long, elegant fingers. *Not elegant*, Ferris had said about her. *Something better than elegance*. His stomach gave a strange jolt. Could Hedy and Roland Ferris have fallen in love? Was that possible, given the huge gap in age? But, then, it would hardly be the first time.

Hedy broke the silence. 'What were you going to say, Constable? I interrupted you.'

'I . . . er . . . I was going to say, we've also spoken to

Professor Tor Garvich. Or Tor Heath as she was when she worked for Roland Ferris that year.'

'*Professor* Garvich?' Hedy's smile was a little cynical. 'Well, I always knew she was ambitious.'

'Did you get along?' Broad asked.

Hedy pulled a face. 'I suppose. I hardly had anything to do with her. I think she worked out quite quickly that there was nothing to be gained by making friends with me, so she didn't bother.' Hedy looked at Broad. 'You know the type,' she said. 'Probably says she doesn't have many female friends because they're all jealous of her, or don't trust their husbands around her.'

Broad smiled briefly. 'So you didn't really like her?'

'Not really. I mean, I didn't *dislike* her . . . I got a bit fed up with having to wipe her fingermarks off all the pictures. But she hardly noticed I was there. We didn't exactly get to know each other.'

'What do you mean, "wipe her fingermarks off all the pictures"?' Broad sounded puzzled, as though it might be a euphemism for something.

'Exactly that. She was always snooping about the place, picking things up and putting them back wrong. Leaving smudges on the glass of the photos of Helen. Roland hated any marks on them.'

'Garvich gave us the impression that she kept to Professor Ferris's study for the most part,' Lockyer said. 'That she didn't have much to do with the rest of the household.'

'Well, that's not how I remember it. Maybe she didn't see me – *literally* didn't see me – but I saw her. Going into rooms she had no business being in. Having a good look around. Skiving off whenever she could. I remember being surprised about it, because from the way she'd flirted her way in that first time, you'd think Roland was her absolute *idol*, you know?'

'"Flirted her way in"?' Lockyer echoed. 'You think she got the position by using her feminine wiles?'

Hedy raised her eyebrows. 'I *know* she did. I was there, I heard the whole thing. She knocked on the front door one day and said she was a huge fan of the professor's and she was looking for work to help her through her PhD, and did the professor need a research assistant, because she wouldn't charge much for the honour of working for him, and all the rest of it. She laid it on pretty thick.' Hedy's mouth twisted. 'Literally batted her eyelashes at him. Still, I don't think Roland would have gone for it if he hadn't actually needed some help with his book at the time. But he did, and she was quite good, as it turned out. They made a lot of progress together. But maybe working for him wasn't as exciting as she'd thought it would be. Or maybe she was *so* interested in him that she felt she needed to nose about in every corner of his house . . . Who knows?' Hedy shrugged. 'I even started to keep an eye out in case anything small and portable went walkabout. But nothing did.'

'Did you ever see her go and talk to Mickey, out in the barn? Or in the village?' Lockyer asked. He remembered the fraction of a hesitation when he'd asked Garvich how she'd got the job with Ferris. The short intake of breath, the blink. She'd lied.

'No,' Hedy said. 'She never went out there, not that I ever saw. Not interested in a random hobo, I guess. Not much in it for her.'

'Right.' Lockyer rubbed his hand along his jaw again. 'Thank you, Hedy. You've given us a lot to work through.'

'Have I?' Hedy brightened. 'Is that good?'

Lockyer and Broad exchanged a look as they got up. Lockyer could tell from Broad's expression that she'd been surprised by some of it. Simple things that the first investigation had failed to note, the worst of which being that it was Paul Rifkin who locked up last thing at night, and nobody had ever asked him if the knife had still been on the drainer. Or if he had moved it.

'I'll let you know as soon as we have anything concrete, I promise,' he said, then thought of something else. 'Hedy, do you remember that song from the eighties, "Voyage, Voyage"?'

Hedy blinked. 'I hate it,' she murmured.

Lockyer waited, but she said nothing else.

'Right, well. Nice to meet you, Miss Lambert,' Broad said. 'And do let us know if you think of anything else at all. Even if it doesn't seem relevant.'

Hedy nodded, but didn't reply. Her eyes followed them, but blindly, the thoughts racing behind them putting a crease between her brows. Lockyer hesitated, looking for something else to say, some way to bring her back to the here and now, to him, before he had to leave, uncertain if or when he'd be back. But there was nothing to say, so he turned and followed Broad to the exit.

*

'I've got it, Guv,' Broad said, after sitting quietly in the car for the best part of twenty minutes. Lockyer had asked her what she'd made of Hedy, and she'd taken a long time to answer. So long that Lockyer had stopped waiting, and gone back to his own thoughts – a persistent and unwelcome one of which was that Hedy hadn't asked *why* he wanted to know about 'Voyage, Voyage'. Was it not a bizarre and unexpected thing for him to have asked? 'The thing was,' Broad went on, 'I couldn't tell if I believed her or not. That was what bothered me about her. You know how some people you just believe, and some you just don't?'

'You're talking about instinct. Intuition.'

'Right. Well, I have no instinct about her at all. Not even an inkling. *Nada*.'

Lockyer absorbed this, then laughed. He couldn't help it.

'What?' Broad said.

Lockyer shook his head. 'Nothing. Gem. You just made me feel much better about something.'

'Oh, right.' Broad was puzzled. 'Good, then, I suppose.'

Back at the station, Lockyer rang Tor Garvich and arranged to meet her again.

'It's a long way to drive, Inspector.' She sounded solicitous, mildly surprised. 'I've got ten minutes now, if you want to ask me whatever it is.'

'I would prefer to speak in person. As soon as possible.'

'Right, well, it must be important, if you want to come all this way just to see me.'

Lockyer heard her amusement, the teasing hint, and

made sure he didn't react to it. 'Tomorrow, if possible, Professor.'

A surprise walk-in to the station meant that Lockyer sent Broad to talk to Paul Rifkin by herself, to ask about locking up on the night of the murder, whether he'd noticed the knife on the draining board, or moved it for any reason, whether he'd heard of or ever met a man named Sean Hannington. Mickey might have told him about Hannington, after all, to explain why he was hiding in the barn. Broad had a theory that Paul might have made things easy for Hannington by secreting the knife somewhere outside for him, as a way to be rid of Mickey without getting his hands dirty. 'There was that unidentified van parked up in the village the night of the murder, Guv. Could've been Sean's, couldn't it?' she said, as she headed out.

The walk-in was Serena Godwin. Lockyer got a call from the front desk, and went down to find her sitting in Reception, looking cool but faintly unsettled, as though she was unused to such surroundings and determined to rise above them. Her figure was rigorously slim. She wore a silk shirt tucked into skinny jeans with a voluminous cashmere poncho and long Dubarry boots, though Lockyer was fairly sure she'd never walked through mud in her life. Everything about her was groomed, clean, contained.

'Mrs Godwin,' Lockyer said. 'This is a surprise.'

'Is it?' She stood up. 'I can't think why, when that woman constable has been harassing me for days. It's hardly a voluntary interview if the alternative is that you never have a moment's peace, is it?'

'We just call our female colleagues constables, these days.' Lockyer guessed she'd come in to save herself the indignity of a squad car pulling up at her front door. Perhaps she'd heard from her brother that this had happened to Paul Rifkin.

'How terribly progressive of you.' Serena looked around. 'Well, I'm here now. I'd never been into a police station before today, Inspector. Who says one can't have new experiences past the age of sixty?'

'If you'll come this way, Mrs Godwin, I'll show you a bit more of it.'

'Be still, my beating heart.' Serena tossed a fold of her poncho over her shoulder as she followed him.

Lockyer, acting on some leftover fragment of schoolboy mischief, took her to interview room four, the grimmest of the lot: it had no real windows, only a tiny horizontal slit near the ceiling; there were several large dents and cracks in the plaster on the walls, and it always seemed to smell of stale sweat. An authentic law-enforcement experience.

Serena peered at the black plastic chair before sitting down, then looked around. 'Glamorous,' she said, with heavy irony.

'I don't think that was at the forefront of their minds when they built it.' Lockyer opened a new tape and slid it into the machine, pressed record, waited for the tone to end. 'Interview with Mrs Serena Godwin, on Thursday, the fourteenth of November 2019. Present in the room, Detective Inspector Matthew Lockyer.' He paused. 'Please say your name for the tape, Mrs Godwin.'

'Serena Evangeline Godwin.' She folded her arms, fingers tapping. 'I hadn't realized this would be recorded. Shouldn't I be cautioned? And given legal counsel?'

For the first time ever, Lockyer saw a slight chink in her armour. 'You haven't been arrested, Mrs Godwin,' he said. 'This a voluntary interview, which you are free to terminate at any time. If you wish to seek legal counsel before we proceed, that can be arranged.'

'Oh, no, no.' She waved a hand. 'I suppose I just wasn't prepared for the level of . . . officiousness.'

'A man was murdered, Mrs Godwin.'

'I'm aware of that. But I'm also aware that the culprit was caught and sent to prison. My brother tells me you're no longer sure you got the right person. He's delighted, of course.'

'Is he?'

'Well, in his own strange way. Of course, a man in his position has no need to fear the consequences of anything.'

'And you think he ought to? Fear the consequences?'

'Don't try to put words in my mouth, Inspector. It's a cheap trick. I merely meant that being so near to the end of one's life is bound to alter one's . . . perspective.'

'Why should Roland Ferris be delighted that we're looking into the case again?'

'Oh, because of his dear little *Hedy*, of course. His pet bird with the broken wing.'

'He's fond of Hedy Lambert, you mean?'

'*Fond* is one word for it.'

'What word would you use?'

Serena thought before answering. 'She's an unfinished project. Like one of his cars that he never got to finish restoring – there's one out in the garage, I believe, an Aston Martin of some variety. There's a touch of Pygmalion about my brother, Inspector. Always has been.'

'You think he fell in love with Hedy?'

'I think he fell in love with his *idea* of Hedy. Of what she might become, under his influence. And, goodness knows, that creature was the blankest of canvases.'

'You didn't like her?'

'There was nothing to either like or dislike, Inspector. You might as well ask if I liked the egg whisk, or the doormat.' Her expression was frank in its disdain. 'Mind you, the doormat was less likely to be hiding any murderous intent.'

'So you believe Hedy was responsible for the crime?'

'Of course she was.' Serena's back was ramrod straight, her shoulders square. 'Roly didn't quite believe it because he didn't *want* to believe it. Men are such simple creatures – like children, much of the time. They cannot grasp why they can't always have what they want.'

Lockyer said nothing, and let nothing show on his face.

'You'll ask me about my brother's will next, I expect,' Serena said. 'And, yes, I do know that it all goes to Harry, bar a few bits and bobs. And I know I get the French house.'

'How do you feel about that?'

'Perfectly sanguine. My brother got the lion's share of our parents' money when they died, and I'm not surprised it'll all go to the next son and heir. It'll take more than a few disgraced media moguls to bring down the patriarchy in families like ours, Inspector. I've never expected to receive any of that money. Luckily, I married twice, and well, to men who had multiple affairs whilst never discovering my own, and who left me amply provided for when I divorced them.' She arched an eyebrow. 'Two can play at the gender disparity game.'

'How did you feel when Harry returned, fourteen years ago?'

'Harry didn't return fourteen years ago.'

'You never believed it was him?'

'Of course not, Inspector Lockyer. I'm not an idiot.'

'Really? Because others have said you seemed convinced, at least to begin with.'

Serena didn't answer at once. She pursed her lips. 'Well, I suppose, briefly, I thought it *might* be him.'

'Why was that?'

'He . . .' She chose her words carefully. 'It was the dog's name.'

'I don't follow you?'

'My brother kept insisting the man knew things, just little things, that only Harry could have known. Things from his childhood – like the headmistress at primary school, who was a harridan of the traditional sort, and made him stand at the front of the hall all afternoon one day, because he'd been naughty somehow. He hadn't as it turned out. Took the blame for another boy. The headmistress wouldn't even let him go to the lavatory, and the inevitable happened, for all to see. She humiliated him. Helen went in the next day and gave her *such* a roasting over it.' She smiled faintly. 'He remembered birthday parties, the village fête, silly things like that. I'll admit it was persuasive. But part of me assumed Roly had been feeding him the answers, consciously or not. But then . . .'

She tipped her head to one side, remembering.

'Yes?'

'Then I went to talk to him one day. I wanted to look him in the eye and ask him something only Harry would have known. Get to the bottom of it once and for all. He looked a lot like Harry, how one might imagine Harry would look as a grown man, I mean, but still I . . . He carried himself so differently. Spoke so differently. I looked him straight in the eye, and asked him the name of his first pet. The question just popped into my head because I'd been asked it recently, for security when I used the telephone banking service.'

'And Mickey knew the answer?'

'He did. And it's not a name one would guess. Harry's first pet was a red and white spaniel named Claypole.'

'Claypole?'

'Yes. After the jester character in *Rentaghost*. It was a television programme Harry loved – Miles too.'

'I remember it,' Lockyer said. 'One of my favourites.'

'Well, there you go. Not a name you'd be able to pull out of thin air. Claypole was a present from Roly and Helen for Harry's seventh birthday, and Harry could not have loved the creature more. My brother was *delighted* when Mr Brown came out with it. *See, Serena?* he kept saying. *See?*'

As she said it Lockyer remembered a photo from one of the montages at Longacres: little floppy-haired Harry, sitting on his heels on a daisy-studded lawn with the puppy in his lap, tail a blur of motion, the boy's face a picture of stunned delight.

'So that convinced you? For how long?'

'Not long. I went away that day thinking it must be him, but I never felt sure. He was just too different from the Harry I remembered, in the ways I mentioned before. And there seemed to be so much else he didn't know, or refused to say anything about.'

'Yet you went along with your brother's insistence that the man in the barn was his son?'

Serena thought before she answered. 'I held my peace for a few weeks, yes. But I would have put a stop to it if it had gone any further,' she said quietly.

'How do you mean, "further"?'

'I mean, *further*. If Roly had actually brought the man into the house, and clothed him, and touted him about the place. If he'd actually tried to bring him into our lives and make us accept him. That would have been quite beyond the pale. As it was, I saw no harm in him having a short spell of . . . happiness. However delusional.'

'In the original investigation, it was you who volunteered a DNA sample for us to ascertain that Michael was not Harry, when your brother refused.'

'Yes. I was angry with him about that – about carrying on with his nonsense when the man was dead. What was the point, then?'

'Well, I suppose the point was that he desperately wanted to believe his son had come home to him.'

'Oh, he *wanted* to. But he never *truly* believed it – of course he didn't! All that nonsense about refusing to come inside the house because of something Harry supposedly said when he stormed out as a child? And what about the fact that the man spoke with a different accent, and seemed to have no idea what had happened to his mother? And why on earth would the real Harry choose to sleep in the very place poor Helen had killed herself?'

'I don't know. To feel close to her, perhaps.'

'Nonsense.' Serena tossed her head back. 'The man was clearly an imposter – well, not even that. Just a hapless simpleton caught up in Roly's fantasy.'

'I wasn't aware that Michael Brown was mentally disabled.'

'Well, you never got to speak to him, Inspector. I did. The man's mind was like a butterfly on a hot day.'

'How do you suppose he knew the dog's name?'

'He must have heard it elsewhere, perhaps from someone in the village. Isn't it obvious? He was a con artist, and people like that do their homework.'

'So he was a practised con artist *and* a hapless simpleton?'

Serena didn't reply, and Lockyer began to suspect that she was far wiser after the event than she'd actually been at the time.

'So you think your brother was playing a game, of sorts?' Lockyer went on.

'Of sorts.' Serena eyed him suspiciously. 'He was lying to himself. But I'm sure we've all done that, at one time or another. When the alternative makes us too sad, or too ashamed.'

'And nobody else broke the spell that you know of? Your son Miles, for example. He knew exactly where the real Harry was all along.'

'Yes, he did.' Her disapproval was obvious. 'He always was wicked. But, no, Inspector. As far as I know, my son never spoke out. And there'd have been quite a scene if he had, of course – I'm sure I would have noticed.'

'And what about on the night of the murder, the night of Tuesday, the twenty-eighth of June, and the preceding day? Did you see or hear anything at all unusual?'

'Nothing. It was a breezy night, as I recall, which always makes it a noisy house – the trees in the garden, and the way the old roof creaks.'

'You're very close to your brother. Very loyal to him, I imagine.'

'Naturally. Our parents died while we were still young, and they weren't terribly warm when they were alive. But we had each other.'

'How do you suppose Roland imagined his game would end?'

'I haven't the foggiest idea, Inspector. Probably with him finally seeing sense, and listening to me. Not with him sticking a knife through the man, if that's what you're getting at.'

'You don't think he's capable of murder?'

'Aren't we all capable of murder? Isn't that what one reads? It's simply a question of the stakes being high enough. And there's the rub, Inspector. The stakes simply *weren't* high enough. Not for anyone in our family. Roland, Miles and myself, we *all* knew, with varying degrees of consciousness, that *that* man was not Harry. He wasn't a threat to us. He was nothing. Certainly not worth going to prison for.'

Lockyer thought about the tears in Kim Cowley's eyes when she spoke about Mickey. He thought about his slim body, with its many scars, bloodless and cold on the pathologist's table. He thought about a damaged young man, his mental health destroyed by years of abuse from chemical substances and other people. Too afraid to even go inside a house. A young man who was possibly a father, though he didn't live to know it. He thought how typical it was for somebody like Serena Godwin to dismiss him as nothing, and how wrong she was.

'Why do you think your sister-in-law, Helen Ferris, took her own life?' he asked abruptly.

'Helen?' Serena echoed.

Lockyer watched her closely, saw the flush that mottled her neck, and the way she settled back in her chair, further away from him. She broke eye contact to look down at the back of her left hand, on which she wore three rings, each with at least one large, sparkling stone. 'That was a tragedy for our family,' she whispered.

For the first time, Lockyer thought he'd managed to move her.

'You were fond of her?'

'Of course.' Serena still sounded distracted. 'Everybody loved Helen. Poor Harry most of all . . .' She trailed off, then looked up, gathering herself. 'Why on earth are you asking about Helen? She died years before any of the rest of this happened.'

'Yes, I know. We're trying to build a complete picture of the situation, to help us understand what happened. Why Harry left, and why Roland was so desperate to believe he'd come back.'

'Well, you'd better ask Harry—'

'Indeed I will,' Lockyer interrupted. 'But I'm asking you about Helen. Do you have any thoughts on what led her to take such drastic action? Did it come as a surprise to you?'

'A surprise? Isn't suicide always a surprise, to those left behind?'

'A lot of the time, I imagine.'

'Well, then.' Serena took a breath, let it out slowly.

'I've been told by somebody who was close to your family at the time that Harry's behaviour had got a lot worse before his mother died, and continued to worsen afterwards.'

'Have you indeed.'

'I've been told Roland and Helen fought a great deal.'

'They fought like any other married couple. It was nothing out of the ordinary, and it was nobody else's business. Whoever's been talking to you about it would do better to remember that.' Her voice rose a few decibels.

'I'm sure that person was merely endeavouring to answer my questions as best they were able, Mrs Godwin,' Lockyer said levelly. 'Which is what I advise you to do.'

'If you take that tone with me, young man, I will simply up and leave.'

'If you up and leave, I might arrest you.'

'Tosh! On what grounds? You wouldn't dare.'

'Obstruction. Let's agree that I'd rather not, but that I might, and talk a bit more about Helen Ferris and Harry, shall we?' Lockyer met Serena's hard gaze with one of his own. 'I am simply trying to understand what went wrong, Mrs Godwin. With Harry and his father.'

Serena made a short, impatient sound. But she relented. 'Truthfully, I'd like to understand that, too.'

'When did it start to go wrong?'

'The moment Harry hit puberty, more or less.' She sighed. 'There was a row about his thirteenth birthday. At the last minute, Roland decided to go to some car rally, even though he'd promised to take Harry out for a special treat. I don't know what it was supposed to have been. Helen begged him not to, but Roland wouldn't change his mind. I happened to be there for Sunday lunch when the news broke. Poor Harry was distraught, and that made Helen distraught, and that made Roland as prickly as a cactus.' She shook her head. 'He really wasn't cut out for modern fatherhood, however much he loved the boy. A century ago he'd have been perfect.'

'How was Helen, generally, at that time?'

'Fine, as far as any of us knew. I can't imagine my brother was a terribly easy man to be married to, but . . .'

She hesitated. Lockyer held his tongue.

'I do remember thinking that perhaps something got broken that day, because after it, Helen was never the same. Or Harry. I didn't see them again for a fortnight or so, and when I did there was . . . something. Something had changed. She had a sort of . . . of *brittleness* she hadn't had before. She seemed closed off, when she'd always been so open. And Harry's behaviour got steadily worse. Nothing seemed to work with the child – not Helen tiptoeing around him, nor Roly bellowing.'

'Do you think perhaps the row carried on after you'd left, that Sunday?'

'You're asking me to speculate?'

'Yes.'

Serena eyed him coldly. 'Then, yes, I imagine it did.'

Neither of them said what Lockyer guessed they were both thinking. That perhaps Roland had lost control, that perhaps he had hit Harry – or hit Helen, and perhaps Harry saw him do it. Hit her, or something worse.

DC Broad was disappointed after her conversation with Paul Rifkin. She phoned Lockyer from the car while she was still parked outside Longacres.

'Not much to add, Guv,' she said. 'He confirms that it would have been him who locked up that night, like every other night, and that he *did*. Thinks he remembers seeing the knife on the draining board but couldn't swear to it after all this time. Denies all knowledge of Sean Hannington, and swears blind he never touched the knife, to move it, hide it or use it.'

'No wobbles, no shiftiness? You believed him?' Lockyer said.

'Yeah. Annoyingly, I did. Again.'

'Which might just mean he's a great liar,' Lockyer reminded her. 'Let's keep our eye on him. Metaphorically speaking.'

'How about you? Did Serena cast any light on anything?'

'She's as adamant as Hedy that Roland isn't the killing type. She says she never truly believed Mickey was Harry, in spite of him knowing certain things about Harry's childhood – which is really starting to niggle me, actually. She also said there's no way any of the three of them would have bothered killing him. Financially speaking, I think she has a point there.'

'So we've moved forwards precisely zero inches today, then.' Broad sounded weary.

Lockyer thought about Hedy not seeming in the least surprised to be asked about the song from the eighties they'd found on Mickey's body. 'Not zero, no. Tor Garvich lied to us about how she got that job at Longacres, and I want to know why. And Serena gave me something.'

'Yeah?'

'Yes. Well, maybe. She narrowed the window on when things started to go wrong with Harry and Roland. And with Helen. It was immediately before or around Harry's thirteenth birthday. There was a huge row – I'll fill you in on it later. But she says Helen and Harry really changed after that. Maureen Pocock wasn't sure when the police came around that time . . . What if it was then? What if it was something more than just a row? What if Helen or Harry called the police – or a neighbour?'

'So . . . we could narrow the search to, what? A two-week window? Around his thirteenth birthday?'

'Let's give it a go. We've got his date of birth on file somewhere. He's forty-four now, so he'd have turned thirteen in . . .' Lockyer shut his eyes '. . . 1988.'

They were both quiet for a moment.

'That's a bit of a coincidence, isn't it, Guv?' Broad said, at last.

'Isn't it?'

1988. The same year that 'Voyage, Voyage' was in the charts.

13

Day Fifteen, Friday

Professor Garvich was as amenable as she'd been the first time they'd visited. She was wearing an emerald green jumpsuit, with orange high-heeled shoes and a multitude of bangles on both wrists. But she didn't move the piles of paper or books for them to sit down this time, and perched herself on the front edge of her desk.

'Tea or coffee? No? Well, I'm dying to know what was so urgent you had to come all the way across—'

'You lied to us, Professor,' Lockyer said.

He watched her carefully, and was aware of Broad doing the same. Garvich's smile faltered, and concern filled her face.

'Did I? I'm not sure I—'

'When we asked how you got the job with Roland Ferris, you claimed to have answered an advert in a magazine or at the university.' Broad sounded almost offended. 'In fact, Professor Ferris never advertised for an assistant. You doorstepped him, and talked your way in.'

Garvich tilted her head ruefully. 'Ah, well. It's a fair cop,' she said. 'Now you come to mention it, I suppose that is more like how it went.'

'Are you saying you misremembered?' Lockyer asked.

'Yes. Or, rather, I suppose I rewrote it somewhat. In my favour. I don't mind admitting to being a crap driver, but perhaps I'm less keen to advertise that I got some of my early career breaks by means of tits and lip gloss.' She spread her hands. 'But there it is. I'm sure as hell not the only one. I wanted to work with Professor Ferris, so I thought I'd just . . . chance my arm. It turned out all right – I think I helped give that chapter on Egbert and ecclesiastic reform some colour. Plus I got to pinch some of our research for my own thesis.'

'Pinch?' Broad echoed.

Garvich raised her hands again. 'Figure of speech. It was all perfectly legit.'

'Are you in the habit of doing that?' Lockyer asked. 'Rewriting history, giving it a better spin?'

'God, aren't we all?' She laughed, but her face fell when neither of them joined in. 'But not about anything *important*. Christ.'

'How did you know Professor Ferris's address?' Lockyer said.

'Well . . . that was also a bit sneaky, I suppose. I saw it on a letter one of my tutors at Southampton had left on his desk. I just happened to see it, I swear! It was what gave me the idea to approach him in the first place.'

'Do you recognize this man?' Broad held out a recent

photo of Harry Ferris, which they'd got from the DVLA. Garvich took it, and looked closely, and Lockyer watched for the blink, the intake of breath. There was none.

'No. Why? Who is it?'

'Harry Ferris. Roland's son,' Lockyer told her.

'Oh, you mean the real one?' Garvich passed back the picture. 'He's shown up, then?'

'He has.'

There was another pause.

'Never met the man,' Garvich said. If she was lying, she was exceptionally good at it.

'And Michael Brown? Had you ever met him before he arrived at Longacres?'

'The man in the barn? No, of course not. He was homeless, wasn't he?'

'A Traveller,' Broad corrected.

Lockyer sighed inwardly. He didn't think she was lying.

'Because Roland's so ill, is that it?' Garvich asked. 'That's what's brought Harry home – for real this time?'

'That seems to be the case,' Broad said.

'It's a strange thought. That someone you know will soon be just . . . gone. Dead tissue, with nothing actually of *them* left inside. Very hard for our poor brains to process.' She folded her arms. 'After your last visit, I thought about giving Roland a call to see if I could go and say a farewell of some kind.'

'But you didn't?'

'I decided he probably wouldn't even remember me – I think my few months there were of far more significance to me than they were to him. But perhaps I will. Couldn't do any harm, could it?'

'I don't suppose so,' Broad said.

'Did you lie to us about anything else, Professor?' Lockyer said.

'No! Now you're making me feel terrible.'

'Hedy Lambert claims she often saw you exploring the house. Going into rooms you had no call to go into, looking at family photographs, that kind of thing.'

'She said that?' Garvich's voice rose with incredulity. 'Well, I've no idea what she's talking about. I mean . . . there were one or two times, early on, when I opened the wrong door to what I thought was the bathroom, and it was a bedroom or whatever. But you've been to that house, right? It goes on for miles – easy mistake to make. And maybe I stopped to look at the pictures around the place on my way to and from the study, but that's hardly a crime, is it? Isn't that why people put pictures on walls? I certainly wasn't *exploring*, or whatever she said.'

Garvich frowned.

'There was one time – I remember now – she actually *told me off* for picking up a photo in a frame! She was literally hovering right there with her duster, ready to polish away every trace! She was a bit nuts, that one.' She raised her eyebrows when she realized what she'd said. 'Well, clearly more than a bit. Perhaps I should count myself lucky all I got was a telling-off.'

'So there was nothing behind your desire to work at

Longacres other than your admiration for the professor?'
Broad said.

'Of course there wasn't. He was *Professor Roland Ferris* – but
perhaps you'd have to be a medievalist to understand. He
was on *In Our Time* once, you know.'

'Yes,' Lockyer said. 'I've listened to it.'

'Well, there you go, Inspector. Doesn't get much starrier
than that.'

That afternoon there was a breakthrough in the search for
Aaron Fletcher. Broad turned from her computer with a
triumphant smile.

'He had a little sister,' she said. 'It would never happen,
these days, but she stayed with the aunt. She was only a
baby at the time their mother was sent down, and the aunt
agreed to have her. Apparently Aaron was too much of a
handful.'

'So they were split up?' Lockyer said.

Broad nodded. 'Like I say, wouldn't happen now. Her
name was Sally, and the aunt legally adopted her when
their mum died. Sally took the aunt's married name. She's
now married herself and goes by the name of Cooper.'

Broad swivelled her screen towards Lockyer – it showed a
Facebook page, a selfie of a woman in early middle age with
a pinched face and very straight hair, striped with blonde
highlights. Next to her was a teenage girl with the same
eyes, wearing false lashes, thick foundation and a pout, the
expression many young girls seemed to make in photos,

these days. As though every shot were an advert for sex, an opportunity to seduce the anonymous masses.

'That's her?'

'Yep. With her daughter, Megan. Aaron's niece. And look here, in her photos . . .'

Broad clicked a couple of times, brought up a picture of Sally with an older man, whose dark hair was turning a grey that made him look distinguished rather than old. He was heavier through the cheeks and jaw than he had been, but still handsome, and Lockyer recognized him at once from the picture Hedy had provided.

'Please tell me he has a Facebook page? And is calling himself Cooper?'

'No, but look in the comment under the photo. Sally's not that tech savvy – she's tried to tag him in the post, but since he doesn't have a profile, it links to the wrong person. Some random old doctor in Florida. But there's a name.'

Lockyer read it. *Amazing to catch up with my big bro, @AaronShawford!! Love you, bro!! xxx* 'Got you, you bastard,' he murmured.

'No idea where he got the name Shawford from, but it hardly matters. We're searching for him now. The PNC, bank records, DVLA, any businesses he might have set up in recent years. Sally posted that picture seven months ago, so hopefully he hasn't upped sticks again. As soon as we find out where he is I'll drop the local boys a line. See if they want to look into what he's up to now. And what car he's driving.'

'Brilliant, Gem. Well done.'

'Coming for drinks later?' she asked, in a tone that obviously didn't expect him to say yes.

'Why not?' he said, surprising them both.

The day – the week – was nearly at an end, but Broad's searches had given Lockyer an idea. He logged into Facebook and searched for Harry Ferris. Nothing came up. Miles Godwin had a page for the estate agency, but no personal profile. Unsurprisingly Roland Ferris didn't have a profile, and neither did Paul Rifkin. Paul was old enough, and had enough of a past, never to have thought social media a good idea. Lockyer didn't bother to look for Serena Godwin. *She doesn't even like to use an ATM.*

Tor Garvich's page was packed, and went back years; her friend list ran to several hundred. Lockyer wasn't surprised. She had the right personality for it – outgoing, flirtatious, someone who loved attention. She'd been an early adopter, a Facebook user since 2005. The very year Michael Brown had been murdered. He went to her first posts from that year. *Tor Heath is feeling bloody glad it's the weekend! Tor Heath is feeling like she'd better get on with some work in spite of the sunshine. Bummer.* Back in the old days, when Facebook prefaced every post by asking *How are you feeling?* Later in the year her posts had evolved, losing the third-person affectation and becoming more conversational. She'd started to post pictures as well. There was one from a festival the weekend before Mickey was murdered. Tor and a friend, their eyes made up into peacock feathers with elaborate glitter paint. The gleam of white teeth, wet hair and skin; tents, banners and a blur of mud in the background. *Best time ever, with my bestie at Glasto! Rain? What rain??*

Other posts were similar, celebrating friends' birthdays and career successes, drily mocking academic life, confirming her attendance at various social and public events. A picture of her dog-grooming flatmate, posing in mock-glamour style on the bonnet of his newly sign-written van, followed by several pictures of his furry clients: neatly clipped poodles, Persil-white Bichon Frises. *The awesome @GazHarris – the man's an artist, people!* Pictures of dogs with expressions of mild outrage in their eyes being cuddled by Gaz, who was a skinny, modish lad with a pierced eyebrow. Nothing about Tor landing a position with the great Roland Ferris, but then, as she'd said, perhaps you'd have to be a medievalist to understand. And perhaps things that wouldn't sound cool or exciting to other people weren't worth posting.

There was nothing in Garvich's old posts that painted her in a different light from the one she still projected. Lockyer moved on. He searched for Hedy Lambert next, but of course she didn't have a profile. The year Facebook had launched was the year Aaron Fletcher had ruined her life, and she was hardly going to have embraced the concept from inside prison. He felt a gathering coldness under his ribs. Social media had become so widespread now that it was hard to imagine life without it. Yet Hedy had bypassed it completely. One more of the many things she'd missed out on. He found himself asking, again, how she could ever hope to rebuild her life. To be happy.

He closed Facebook abruptly, startled by how easily he'd lost an hour to it.

'Come on.' He got up. 'Time for that drink.'

It had been a crisp, dry day, and Broad wheeled her bike to the pub.

'I hope you're not planning to cycle home under the influence?' Lockyer said.

'Don't worry, Guv, I've messaged Pete, so hopefully he'll come and get me later.'

'Good. Wrong time of year for falling in the canal.'

'I'm not sure there's ever a right time for that,' she said. 'Sure you don't want me to come and talk to Harry Ferris with you tomorrow?'

'No, you have your weekend off, Gem. I'd rather give up my Saturday than have to go all the way up to London to talk to him.'

They turned in at the Bell by the Green and Broad chained her bike to the rack outside. A few colleagues were already at the bar. At first Lockyer and Broad kept their distance. It'd been quite a while since Lockyer had joined in the Friday-night drinks. Since the Queen's Head fire he'd been more than happy to go home and not spoil the party. He'd hated the awkward change in atmosphere that his disgrace caused. But perhaps enough time had passed, now, because he didn't detect a ripple, even from Steve Saunders, and it was good to catch up with people he didn't work alongside any more. The bar was loud with Friday-night chatter, music, and chair legs scraping on the wooden floor, and Lockyer soon wished he didn't have to drive.

Broad was a lightweight. After three gin and tonics she was clumsy and her eyes were gleaming. She came over and dropped onto an upholstered stool next to Lockyer, having spent half an hour in stitches, head to head in a corner with DS Ahuja.

'I dread to think what you and Sara have been talking about,' Lockyer said.

'I wish I could tell you, Guv, because you'd piss yourself. But I'm afraid she's sworn me to secrecy. Let's just say it turns out tough guy Saunders has a phobia. And it's a weird one.'

'The mind boggles,' he said. 'You changed your mind about the mascara, then?'

'What?' Broad's face fell, and Lockyer kicked himself.

'I just . . . I noticed you'd started wearing mascara, then stopped again.'

'Yeah.' She looked uncomfortable. 'Pete didn't think it was appropriate. You know, for work.'

Lockyer didn't like the sound of that. 'Not up to him, is it?' he said.

'No, but . . . It made my eyes itch by the end of the day, anyway, and when you rub them you end up looking all emo.' Broad forced a small laugh, then changed the subject. 'So, tomorrow. Are you going to ask Harry Ferris about his mother?'

'Yep. And about what happened back in 1988.'

'I reckon he won't tell you.'

'I reckon you're right.'

'I had a thought, though, Guv – local newspapers. If

there's nothing in the database or the files from back then, now we know the rough date, the local papers might have reported on whatever the police went to Longacres about. If it was even worth reporting, that is.'

'Yes. I was going to wait till Monday morning before asking you to make a start. Didn't want to ruin your weekend as well as your eyesight.'

'I don't mind, Guv. Be easier if I knew exactly what I was looking for, of course. I mean, it might be nothing.'

'It might be nothing. Or it might be something.'

Broad took a swig of the ice melt in the bottom of her glass, crunching the remains of a cube. 'Guv,' she said, but then, 'No, never mind.'

'Go on,' he said. 'What's said in the pub stays in the pub.'

'It's just ...' She hunted out the right words. 'We're spending all this time looking at everyone – looking for a motive. I know I've said this before, but what if we can't find one because there's nothing to find?'

Lockyer didn't reply.

'When we saw Hedy Lambert the other day, she said something that stuck in my head. When she was talking about Mickey leaving the barn sometimes, she said she used to *go to see him*. Not to take him food. Just to see him.' She looked up at Lockyer, eyes serious now. 'And it's obvious she was left to her own devices in that job. In that house. No one was telling her what to do, or paying any attention to what she was up to. Maybe she went out to see him a lot more than anyone realized. Maybe they got a lot closer than she's letting on.'

'You mean, maybe she developed feelings for him?' Lockyer said.

'She said she thought he was a kindred spirit. That she understood him. Doesn't that sound like she was . . . into him? Trusted him? Like she'd trusted Aaron?' Broad paused. 'Would have made it *much* worse when he told her he wasn't Harry. Like you said in the original investigation, Guv.'

'Killing Mickey as a kind of stand-in for Aaron?'

'Something like that. The final straw, you know,' she said. 'Mickey taking the brunt for what Aaron did to her. What I'm saying is, what if it *was* horses after all? Not zebras. What if you were right the first time?'

'If that's the case, it's job done,' Lockyer said. He looked down at the sticky table, with its damp beer mats and greasy crisp crumbs. 'But I don't think so . . . The truth is, I didn't think so at the time.'

'Really?' Broad said. 'Because that's not what comes across when you read the interviews.'

'What does come across?'

'That you . . .' she hesitated '. . . that you skilfully built up a rapport with her, and got her to open up to you. That you were pretty relentless at getting her to talk about her past, and pretty clever about getting her to give up stuff that pointed to her motive for murder.'

Lockyer frowned, but didn't look up.

After a moment, Broad added, 'I don't mean that in a bad way, Guv, just that you went after her, and you got her. It was good police work.'

'And if she was innocent?' He caught the puzzled, faintly

worried look on Broad's face. 'Was it still good police work, to go after her to the exclusion of all other suspects?'

'But if you had doubts, why didn't you say something, Guv?'

'I think because my doubts were as much about myself as about Hedy.'

He wished he'd clammed up earlier.

'Because you'd developed feelings for her?'

Lockyer flashed her a rueful smile. She didn't miss a trick. 'I stopped trusting myself around her, Gem. Considine wanted her for it, everything pointed at her, and I thought if I . . . if I didn't deliver, the boss'd see right through me. The whole force would. And, worse than that, I'd be letting personal feelings get in the way of my work. But now I think maybe I let worrying about that – *rejecting* that – get in the way of my work instead.'

'Do you think she did it on purpose?' Broad said. 'The way she would only speak to you . . . Do you think she sensed something? Sensed she could draw you in? Maybe she knew you had doubts, and thought she could get you to voice them.'

'You have no idea how much I wish I knew the answer to that.' He shook his head. 'You said it yourself earlier on, it's hard to read her. Hard to know if she's honest or not.'

'Are you . . . were you . . . in love with her?' Broad picked up her empty glass again, seeming fascinated by it.

Lockyer didn't know the answer. 'Can you be in love with someone you've only ever spoken to in an interview room? Or standing over a dead body? In any case,' he went on, before she could answer, 'there was *something*. An attraction of some kind. And if I let that cloud my judgement ... If that's what put her behind bars four-teen years ago, and has kept her there while a murderer walked free ...'

'Guv,' Broad said softly, 'even with all of that, it still could have been her. The jury was sure enough to convict her.'

'I know. But I don't think she's a killer. And I need to be sure. Absolutely cast-iron sure.'

'If there's something else to find, we'll find it.' Broad put her glass down and reached out her hand. But if she'd planned to touch him, she changed her mind.

'She didn't really react to being asked about "Voyage, Voyage",' Lockyer said. 'Did you clock that? Not even the faintest flicker of curiosity. And the Ferrises are lying to us. I want to know why. If that turns out to be irrelevant to Mickey's murder, then so be it. But we don't know yet.'

'Another G and T, Gem?' a young PC asked, kicking their table leg as he passed.

'Better not, thanks,' Broad said. 'Got to ride home.'

'I thought Pete was coming to get you,' Lockyer said.

Broad shook her head stiffly. 'He's knackered, he says. And the last time I put the bike in the back of his car, I scratched the paintwork.'

She pulled a comic *whoops* face that didn't quite ring true. Lockyer wondered how tired a nine-to-five mortgage adviser could be. But he didn't ask. 'Never mind,' he said. 'I'll drive you. Just let me know when you want to go.'

'Thanks, Guv.'

He knew he should leave it there, but went on anyway: 'What's said in the pub stays in the pub, right?'

Broad nodded.

'Well, then. It's none of my bloody business, and I won't mention it again, but I don't think Pete appreciates you the way he should.'

Broad was speechless, then jumped at a burst of laughter from Steve Saunders. She turned towards him, grateful for the distraction. 'At least *he*'s left us alone tonight,' she said.

'Yes. Minor miracle. Especially given such a large audience.'

'Perhaps he's finally boring himself.'

'Don't be daft, Gem.'

'No, I guess not ... *Did* you lie to the investigation last year?' she blurted, then quickly added, 'Forget I said that.'

'What have you heard?'

'That you played down how well you knew the perp and his family. That you deliberately concealed knowledge of the son's involvement, his collusion in the arson.'

'Sounds bad,' Lockyer said.

Broad's expression begged him to contradict it.

'I informed the SIO at once that I'd known the Slaters since I was a kid. That I'd gone to school with Kevin Slater and been to the Queen's Head many times. Saunders asked me to look around the pub – what was left of it – and see if I could spot any missing personal items that might have been removed in advance of the fire. I was also sent to Kev's flat to see if I could identify any items from the pub there.'

'And you couldn't?'

'No.'

He didn't say he'd seen the big framed photo montage at Kevin's place the week before. The one that usually hung in the snug, showing beer festivals and darts matches and jubilee and royal wedding celebrations at the pub going back to the seventies, way before there could have been digital copies of the pictures anywhere. It had been tucked into the airing cupboard when he'd reached in to grab a new toilet roll. And, wrapped in a tea-towel, the intricate Welsh love spoon Kevin's grandma had carved for his mother's wedding day. It had usually hung from a nail on one of the pillars by the bar.

Lockyer had asked Kevin why they were there. Asked in a way that made Kevin look away nervously. *Dad said I ought to have the spoon. Too nice for the pub, someone might nick it.* So Lockyer had asked why it was in the airing cupboard, and the conversation had ended there. Tense silence rather than lies. He'd seen Kevin soon after the fire, told him that the police knew about their friendship, and what they would probably ask him to do. When he'd next looked around Kevin's place, accompanied by Steve Saunders, the photo montage and love spoon had gone.

So he had technically only lied by omission. Not that that made it any better. He'd made a snap decision, and had been trying to unpick it ever since. It'd had something to do with loyalty to his friend, but also something to do with what a crime truly *was*: knowing about an arson and attempted fraud before the event, or being bullied by your father into a downtrodden life of petty crime and broken relationships?

And he'd hoped, of course, that by keeping Kevin out of jail while his father went down, he'd be setting his friend free in more ways than one. It was an amorphous – and dangerous – decision for a policeman to make, and he'd sworn to himself it wouldn't happen again.

It hadn't helped that those two missing items, and several more, were subsequently found in a lock-up rented by Bob Slater under an assumed name. And another witness, a regular at the pub, came forward to say the montage had gone missing over a week before the fire. Lockyer was known for being observant, a details man. His claim to have noticed nothing out of the ordinary had begun to look iffy.

'And Saunders didn't believe you?'

'He didn't want to.' Lockyer could hardly blame him. 'Luckily, Considine vouched for me.'

'Still, it's bloody unfair you got into trouble, Guv, not when you didn't do anything wrong.'

'It turned out okay,' Lockyer said, and something in his tone made Broad pause. Or something in the way he didn't say too much about Saunders, or the injustice of it.

She was quiet for a moment. 'You know, some officers are so righteous about being straight. Unbendable. Black and white. But I've always thought that anyone who reckons they'd have no trouble shopping their mum or their other half or their best mate probably just hasn't been put in that position.' She didn't look at him. 'I reckon things'd stop being so black and white if they were.'

'I think you're right, Gem,' he said carefully.

*

Harry Ferris was less tense than the first time Lockyer had met him. He was still cold, and made no secret of the fact that he'd prefer not to talk to Lockyer, but he was less like a tightly wound spring. His anger was better contained. He sat down in a carver and rested the ankle of his right leg on the knee of his left. Folded his arms. A studied pose, which Lockyer thought was probably meant to project ease, or even contempt, but just looked defensive. His clothes were as stylish and crisp as ever. Lockyer suspected he'd never grabbed a pair of yesterday's socks out of laziness or desperation. He imagined Harry Ferris's sock drawer arranged in neat rows, categorized by colour and type.

They were downstairs in a small sitting or drawing room – Lockyer had never been sure of the difference. Upstairs in his study, Roland Ferris was limp and listless, not even able to lift his head from the pillow. Lockyer found this sudden decline alarming. He sensed time ticking away for the old man, and for his investigation. Like Garvich had said, it was hard to imagine everything Ferris knew and thought and remembered, everything he *was*, ceasing to exist. It would happen to everybody, of course, sooner or later. It would happen to his own father.

'He's in no state to talk to you today,' Paul Rifkin told him, shutting the door softly. 'He needs another blood transfusion. I'm taking him in on Monday.'

The sitting room was cold, and had the flat smell of a room that was hardly ever used. The bland scents of the *toile de Chine* curtain fabric and the bricks around the hearth. No lingering human smells. Numerous china plates were displayed on the walls and along the mantlepiece, while various jugs and vases of the same pattern – small pink and blue flowers on a white background – sat on side tables and dressers. Lockyer wondered whether Helen Ferris had collected them.

'Did your mother decorate this room?' he asked.

Harry's brows knitted. He cast a quick glance around it. 'How should I know?' he said. 'I expect so. All this china. It might have come with the house, though, or from my grandparents.' His right foot jiggled, then stopped.

'Do you still miss her?'

'She died when I was fourteen, Inspector. Life goes on.'

'On your fifteenth birthday, in fact,' Lockyer said. 'It must have been very painful.' He remembered getting home after his weekend on Dartmoor. He hadn't owned a mobile phone then, had no idea that his little brother had been murdered while he'd been away. The shock had felt like a physical blow, the pain afterwards so intense that it obliterated everything. He could feel it even now, threatening to derail his thoughts.

'What do you want me to say?' Harry Ferris snapped. 'Are you hoping I'll cry? Yes. It was shit.'

'Do you think it was significant? Her ending her life on your birthday?' Lockyer asked.

Harry just stared at him.

'You didn't read anything into it, particularly?'

'What I read into it was that she was so messed up by then she didn't know what sodding day it was. Of the week, let alone of the year.'

'Yes, you're possibly right.' Lockyer knew, from the coroner's report, that Helen hadn't sought any help from her GP for depression or anxiety, or anything like that. Or for any minor or major physical injuries. But back then mental illness was seen as something to be buried. Something to hide. For some people, it still was. 'Did you feel guilty about it?'

'Guilty? No, Inspector. Not in the way you mean, at any rate. I was a stupid kid . . .'

'You'd been acting up. Getting into trouble at school. Your parents were fighting a great deal. Were they fighting about you, Harry?'

'What the hell is this? If every mother of a stroppy teen-ager killed herself because of it, the world would be in some serious shit.'

'I'm not talking about other mothers, I'm talking about yours.'

'And why is that, Inspector? Why are you talking about my mother?'

Lockyer ignored the question. 'Do you think it's signifi-cant that Mickey Brown was killed in the same place as your mother took her own life?'

'No.'

'No?'

'No. I think my mother killed herself in there because it was easiest. And I think that man was killed in there because that was where he was sleeping.'

Harry's right foot was jiggling again, and this time he was too distracted to make it stop. Lockyer wondered how much effort it was taking to sound so callous.

'Did you know Michael Brown? Or Mickey, as he was called? Had you ever met him, perhaps when you were little? He grew up in this area.'

'No.'

'You're certain? He knew things about you—'

'I'm certain. Never heard of him, definitely didn't know him.'

'Can you explain how he might have been able to find out certain details about your—'

'I can't explain anything that happened here in 2005. I wasn't here. I had no idea any of it was going on.'

'No? Miles didn't drop you a line, let you know Mickey had turned up here, pretending to be you? Having met Miles, I'd say he probably found it quite funny.'

'No.' Harry's tone was stony. 'He didn't.'

'He didn't find it funny?'

'He didn't contact me.'

'At around the time of your thirteenth birthday the police came to speak to your parents. Do you know what it was about?'

'No. I have no memory of that.'

'Maureen Pocock had just arrived to sit with you. The police turned up in a marked car, and you ran away into the fields over the road.'

'You know more about it than I do, Inspector.'

'Why did you run away? Had you seen or done something to make you worried about the police turning up? Were you worried one of your parents might be in trouble?'

'I've already said I have no memory of it happening. So

it can't have been important. I probably ran away because Maureen Pocock used to hug me, whether I wanted to be hugged or not. And she gave disgusting wet kisses.'

'I gathered from Maureen that she was very fond of you.'

'Nevertheless.' Harry lifted one shoulder, but the movement was too stiff and controlled to be a proper shrug.

'Was your father ever violent towards you or your mother, Mr Ferris?'

'What the fuck, Inspector? Violent? No. He was not.'

'From what I've heard, he wasn't the easiest of fathers.'

'He did his best.' Harry looked away, nostrils flaring. 'I didn't always see it that way, but I do now. Not all men are the cuddly bloody picnics-and-Labradors type. He raised me the only way he knew how. It's what most parents do.'

'So why did you cut all contact with him for such a long time?'

Harry gazed across the room, into the shadows of the empty fireplace. 'After a while, it just became a habit,' he said eventually. 'I left because I was angry and grieving over my mother's death, and my father couldn't fix that for me. It was far easier to be angry with him for not having prevented it than it was to work through what I was *really* feeling. So that was what I did. After a few years, life simply carried on. I left it all behind, and it was . . . easier to leave things that way.'

Lockyer recalled something Maureen Pocock had said, about people taking themselves off because they couldn't bear to be seen. To punish themselves, as much as anyone else.

'Do you still blame your father?'

Harry's mouth twisted. 'If he's to blame then so am I. So are all the people who loved her and didn't save her.' Harry stared at Lockyer. 'When someone you love kills themselves, you have to take some of the blame. There's simply no escaping it. You take the blame, rightly or wrongly.'

Lockyer knew he blamed himself for Chris's death. Now Harry's words made him wonder whether his parents blamed themselves too. Murder was not suicide and, unlike himself, his parents had nothing to reproach themselves for. But weren't there always what-ifs?

'Why *are* you asking all this, Inspector?' Harry said. 'How can it possibly be relevant?'

'When we first met you said something that struck me as odd, Mr Ferris.' Lockyer opened his notebook. 'I'd asked you if you could think of any reason someone would want to kill you, and you said, and I quote, "Anyone who knew me well enough to want to kill me would have realized straight away that it wasn't me."'

'So?'

'Why not simply say *no*?'

'You've lost me, Inspector.'

'*Can* you think of a reason why somebody might want to kill you – or have wanted to fourteen years ago?'

'I really hate repeating myself.' Harry exhaled sharply. 'As I said before, no.'

'As far as we can discover, almost everyone who was in the house at the time Michael Brown was killed knew his identity full well. They knew he wasn't you.'

'Well, then.' Harry spread his hands. 'Why are we even having this conversation? I was up in London, totally unaware of what was going on. It was nothing to do with me.'

'The only people who did still believe he was you were your father – and the jury's out as to whether he was truly convinced or merely desperate – and Tor Heath, his research assistant.'

'Never even met the woman.'

Lockyer nodded thoughtfully. 'And there was certainly someone out there who had a motive to kill Mickey, had both motive and inclination.'

'Then he sounds like your man,' Harry said, with the air of someone exercising great patience.

'He does, doesn't he?' Lockyer agreed. 'Trouble is, I don't think it was him. Wrong MO. Plus someone in this house would have to have helped him, and we can't find any evidence that anyone here knew him.'

'"A policeman's lot is a not a happy one,"' Harry said.

'Indeed. It's my belief that you and your father are lying to me, Mr Ferris. Whether or not it's relevant to the death of Mickey Brown, you're lying to me about something important. And knowing I'm being lied to bothers me a great deal.'

'I imagine,' Harry said, levelling his gaze at Lockyer again, 'that that kind of thing must be very hard to prove one way or the other.' His right foot kept twitching, back and forth, a telltale inch either way, until he uncrossed his legs and planted the foot on the floor.

'Oh, definitely. Hard, but almost never impossible.'

'I think we're done here, Inspector. For what it's worth, let me assure you that you're barking up entirely the wrong fucking tree. And I think you should let my father die in peace. It wasn't his fault.'

'What wasn't?' Lockyer said.

Harry blinked. 'My mother's suicide.'

Lockyer stood. 'Word is out about you being home, Mr Ferris. I know you weren't exactly in hiding all these years, but you might as well have been. But you're back now . . .'

'So?'

'So if someone *did* want to kill you fourteen years ago, and they still want to, they know exactly where to find you.'

'What are you saying?' Harry said. 'That the Lambert woman is going to . . . to send someone after me?'

'Hedy? I doubt that very much. I'm talking about the *real* killer. Who I suspect you might know.'

'Oh, just sod off, will you?' Harry stared furiously at the floor, and Lockyer wondered what he was afraid to give away. 'I came down here to spend time with my father, not to play pointless mind games with the local plod.'

Lockyer stayed where he was. 'I'd watch my back, if I were you.'

'Are you trying to scare me, Inspector?'

'Do you think you ought to be scared, Mr Ferris?'

Lockyer saw himself out. He caught Paul Rifkin at the bottom of the stairs, watching him go; his face, for once, unreadable.

Lockyer stood for a while to one side of the house, scanning the locked garages and converted stables, the skylights of Hedy's empty apartment. Then he made his way round to the kitchen window. The draining board beside the sink was fully visible. As the knife Hedy left there to dry, the night before the murder, would have been. The back door was only about five feet away.

He ran through the forensics in his head: the sliver of cling-film, the fingerprint fragments on the cassette of 'Voyage, Voyage' by Desireless. They hadn't turned up any matches during the original investigation, but fourteen years of incidents and arrests had passed since then. Time to chase the lab again.

14

Day Eighteen, Monday

Sunday was a day of rain and early darkness. For hours, the thunder of heavy artillery rolled sporadically across the plain, shaking windows in their frames and cups in their saucers. It was nothing out of the ordinary – there was a lot of live firing within the SPTA, the Salisbury Plain Training Area – but it always put Lockyer on edge. The military was a whole world about which he knew nothing, and yet it lived there, right beside them. He'd walked the fences many times – the red flags flying, the barbed wire and stern warning signs.

Lockyer went to the farm and let his mother feed him crumpets and endless cups of tea. Sitting in the warm, doggy fug of the kitchen, he felt sorry for the soldiers out in the rain. John came in from the barn, put three crumpets on his plate and dropped into the sagging chair by the Rayburn. He noticed the holes in his damp socks where his toes were poking through, and waggled them at his son.

'How are you doing, Dad?' Lockyer asked, when Trudy was out of earshot. He hoped to get an honest answer, but John's eyes slid past him.

'Well enough, son,' he said. 'Found a ewe dropped by the far fence in Long Ground. Could be pasteurellosis . . . I'd had her in the crush the other day.' He shook his head. 'Hope that's it.'

'I'm sorry to hear that. But how are *you*? You gave us a bit of a scare the other day, you know. Not wanting to come inside.'

John still wouldn't look him in the eye. 'Didn't mean to,' was all he said, after a long pause. 'Just a bad day. Got on top of me.'

Lockyer tried to imagine the inner circuitry of his father's brain. Wires sparking, connecting, then disconnecting. Parts with the correct lubricants and electrolytes, parts without. Shifting, sticking, ever-changing. Unpredictable: a computer that might run perfectly well one day, and crash repeatedly the next. He felt powerless to understand, and powerless, therefore, to help.

'It seems as though you're having more of those lately. Bad days, I mean. Might it be an idea to maybe talk to—'

'Now, don't take on,' John muttered. 'I'm all right, Matthew.'

'But you're not.' Lockyer's pulse was ticking in his throat. He'd never spoken so frankly to his father before – it wasn't what they did. He was very aware of the need to get it right.

John didn't reply. He ate his crumpets and drank his tea

in silence, seemingly oblivious to his son watching him and waiting.

'Dad?' Lockyer said. 'I think it'd be a really good idea for you to talk to someone about this. If not me, then maybe the GP, to begin with. There's all sorts of things . . .' His father's blank expression didn't change, and Lockyer's sudden flare of frustration was so intense it drove him to his feet.

He went upstairs to his brother's old room at the back of the house and stood by the window for a while, watching the bloated clouds crawl across the sky. Chris had been a keen rugby supporter – the Exeter Chiefs. There'd still been posters of players on the walls of his room when he died, and a scarf pinned over the bed, a leftover from his early teens. Lockyer remembered taking it all down. Prising the drawing pins out of the wall, balling up old, stiffened Blu-tack. He had no idea how long after Chris's death that had been, whose decision it had been to take it all down, or whether there'd been a discussion. He remembered the numbness, and underneath it, an ocean of pain he was terrified he'd drown in.

On the door were the tattered remains of a rugby sticker that had refused to come away cleanly. The wardrobe was now filled with linen that didn't get used very often, table-cloths and napkins and guest towels, layered with lavender sachets. Chris's desk was still in front of the window, and Lockyer could see him there, hunched over his homework, holding his pen in his left hand in that cramped, awkward way of his. He'd been mildly dyslexic and writing had always made his forehead furrow with the intensity of his concentration. Lockyer would lie behind him on the bed, ostensibly reading a magazine but in fact simply being there. Helping him stay the course, helping with difficult spellings. Keeping him company.

Lockyer felt the heat of anger again. He thought about what Broad had said – that it tended to be a substitute for other strong emotions – and decided she was probably right. Anger was easier than helplessness, easier than despair. It was probably easier than shame and loneliness and fear as well. He went to the door and started to pick at the old sticker again; gouging at it with his thumbnail. Destroying it one tiny shred at a time. Trudy found him there. She patted his hand with a gentle smile.

'Leave it. It'll need a soak to get it off,' she said. Then, 'What is it, Matthew? What's wrong?'

'I just . . .' He didn't know where to start. 'I tried talking to Dad. About his "bad days".'

'Ah.' Trudy sighed. 'I see.'

'It's . . . He's a brick wall.'

'I know.'

'But it can't go on like this.'

'What do you suggest?'

'That we call the doctor ourselves. Ask him to come out and talk to Dad.' He saw the resigned expression on her face. 'You've tried that already, haven't you?'

'More than once.'

'When? Why didn't you tell me?'

'Because he didn't want you to know, love. You know what he's like. If one of his legs fell off, he'd tell you not to fuss.' Trudy took a deep breath. 'He doesn't want to appear weak in front of you, Matthew. And he has to want the help, or it won't work.'

'That's just ... We have to *make* him want help.'

Lockyer heard himself sounding like a child. His mother said nothing. They both knew there was no way to make John do any such thing. He shut his eyes for a moment, and rested his head against the door. Trudy swept a few dead flies from the windowsill onto her hand, dropped them into the bin.

'Kev's in trouble again,' Lockyer said. 'Bob's been making all sorts of new connections in the nick, apparently. He's trying to rope Kev in. Sounds like drugs, maybe stolen goods.'

Trudy turned, her face grave. 'Don't risk yourself for him again, Matthew. Don't risk your career.'

'Isn't that what friends are supposed to do?'

'To a point, perhaps. But what happened last year ...' Lockyer hadn't told her the full story, but she knew he'd stuck his neck out, and it hadn't ended well. 'Has he asked you to help?'

'More for advice, at this stage.'

'I know you love Kev. I love him too. But you're grown men. He can't keep asking you to get him out of trouble.'

'I know. I just ... After last year, I thought maybe something would change. Putting Bob away, I thought things might change.'

Trudy came over and squeezed his arm. 'You can't save him, Matthew. He has to sort himself out.'

'I can't save anyone, it seems.'

'Who else are you supposed to save?'

'Dad. Chris. Hedy Lambert. I just ... I'm ...' He sighed. 'I'm unequal to the task.'

'*Unequal to the task?*' Trudy echoed incredulously. 'These aren't *your* tasks, love, this is *life*.' She looked him in the eye. 'Chris's death was not your fault.'

'I could have stopped it.'

'You don't know that.'

'I do. If I'd been there—'

'Please, stop it.' She turned to the window again, staring out over the plain. 'You'd have laid down your life for your little brother. We all know that.'

'But I didn't.'

'The only person responsible for what happened is the man who stabbed him.' She spoke firmly, but couldn't hide the tremor in her voice. 'You must realize your father and I have to tell ourselves that, over and over.'

'And now Dad ... I don't know what to do. I don't know how to help. And I can't stand it.'

'We'll get there,' Trudy said bravely. 'I don't know where we're going, and it scares me too. But we'll get there, because what else can we do? Just try our best to – to make things better along the way.' She paused. 'As for Hedy Lambert, I'm afraid I don't know what to say.'

'She's innocent, Mum. I really think she is. And I helped put her away.'

'If you made a mistake, then that's what it was – a mistake. Mistakes happen. If she's innocent, you'll prove it.'

'What if I *can't* prove it?'

'If there's a way, you'll find it.'

'And if I do, after *fourteen years*?' He looked at his mother, stricken. 'How can that be justice?'

'Nobody ever said the world was fair, Matthew. People don't always get what they deserve.'

Lockyer knew she was talking about Chris again. About the way they'd been robbed – of their boy, their family, their happiness. Robbed of the chance to look his killer in the eye, and see him punished. He didn't know what he would do if he ever caught the man. He didn't trust himself to be professional, not completely. That anger. But he would have to find a way. Or else step back, and he didn't think he could do that, either. 'It just . . . it's . . .'

'I know, Matthew. I do know.' She put her arms around him. He bent to hug her back, feeling the familiar swathe of her hair against his chin. He'd been taller than her since he was twelve years old. Gradually, the pressure in his head eased, the anger cooled, and exhaustion took its place.

Trudy moved back, held him at arms' length. 'You'll do what's right. You always have. Please, *please* don't tear yourself apart because other people don't do the same.' She shook him. 'I need *you* in one piece, at least.'

He saw the urgency in her eyes, and nodded.

On Monday morning the sun broke out, pallid but painfully bright in a white sky. Broad was late to the station, rushing in with no time to change out of her cycling gear. Her face was flushed, her hands grubby, and she filled the room with the scent of warm skin and hair.

'Sorry, Guv, puncture.'

'Don't worry about it.'

The phone on Lockyer's desk rang. He answered it and immediately got to his feet. 'Kim Cowley's here. You get changed, Gem. I'll see what she wants.'

Kim was standing near the enquiry desk. She looked even smaller, even more fragile, in the hard-edged surroundings of the police station, and she hurried over as soon as she saw him. She held out a blue toothbrush, wrapped in a plastic sandwich bag.

'Here.' Her eyes darted towards every movement, as though Sean Hannington might suddenly appear and catch her in the act.

'Kieron's?'

'Yes.'

'Thank you.'

'Hard for my boy, but he doesn't love Sean, for all he's called him "Dad" all these years. He's bright, my Kieron. He knows bad news when he meets it.'

'I'm glad he was willing to give us this. I hope it'll help.'

'So do I.' Kim looked around again, and suddenly seemed doubtful. 'You *promise* me Sean won't ever know we volunteered for this?'

'I promise. But if Sean *isn't* Kieron's father, how will you tell him?'

'I'll just say I paid for one of those kits.' Her face fell even further. 'But then I guess he'll want to see it – the result – and then he'll know.'

'The report'll come from the lab, not from us. I'll make sure there's nothing on it about the police.'

'Thanks.' Kim hesitated. 'You'll let me know, one way or the other, yeah?'

'As soon as I can, Kim,' Lockyer said, as she hurried away 'And please call us if he gives you any trouble.'

Kim glanced back, but didn't nod.

'It can't help us much with Mickey's case, though, can it?' Broad said, when Lockyer got back to their office.

'The DNA on this toothbrush might be a close familial match to the killer.'

'Yeah, but we don't have any of the killer's DNA from the scene to compare it to.' Broad was standing by their whiteboard with a blue marker pen in her hand, and a few names already written up. They'd never employed the board before: it was a relic of whoever had used the office before them. She looked a little sheepish. 'I just thought it might help. Put some names up, who's got a motive, who hasn't . . .'

'Knock yourself out, Gem,' Lockyer said. 'Anyway, we might be able to use the DNA to get Hannington in for something else. Sweat him, get him to talk about Mickey.' It sounded tenuous, and he felt his frustration rise. A man like Sean Hannington wasn't going to break down and confess to a damn thing because of a stern police interview. 'I'm going to take Kieron's toothbrush up to the lab, and chase them about the rest of our forensics,' he said. 'When you've finished jotting, get online and start looking through the local newspaper archives.'

Lockyer made the drive to the Cellmark lab in silence. No music, no radio chatter. He felt close to something: perhaps an understanding of the crime that had put Hedy Lambert behind bars, or else an acknowledgement of his own failure. The upcoming humiliation of being told to close the reinvestigation and move on. The thought of having to tell Hedy he was dropping the case left him cold with dread. She would stay in jail, hope withering to bitterness, and he would have to find a way to live with that.

But if he found the real killer she could be out within months, and in line for a million-pound payout for wrongful imprisonment since she'd served over ten years. There was her new life, right there. With that money she could go anywhere, do anything, rather than coming out of prison skint and homeless, as she would at the end of her term. He wondered if she'd know where or what she wanted to do. Whether she'd ever dared to dream about that.

Lockyer signed over Kieron's toothbrush, asking for the results as soon as possible, as everyone always did. He spoke briefly to one of the scientists about the prints on the cassette – the crucial chance of newer, enhanced techniques managing to lift comparable prints that had been missed in 2005, and the importance of getting them sent to the Regional Fingerprint Bureau to check for new matches on the NAFIS identification system.

'Please understand, there are serious implications for

those involved if we can find no useful forensic evidence in this case,' he said, trying to communicate his urgency.

'*If* the evidence is there, we'll find it, Inspector,' the scientist snapped.

When he got back to the station Broad was nowhere to be seen, and her whiteboarding adventures didn't seem to have got her very far. She'd separated the persons of interest into two categories: those inside the house at the time of the murder, and those outside. Under the first grouping she'd written:

Roland Ferris. Motive: *found out Mickey not his son. Angry/unstable? MO of murder – assailant physically weaker than victim?*

Serena Godwin. Motive: *? Claims to have known Mickey was not Harry.*

Miles Godwin. Motive: *? Unknown association w. Mickey Brown? Knew Mickey was not Harry.*

Paul Rifkin. Motive: *Wanted rid of Mickey, lied about prison record and army etc. Threat to money/job.*

Tor Heath/Garvich. Motive: *? Believed Mickey to be Harry.*

Hedy Lambert. Motive: *Unstable mind. Projected revenge. To protect Roland Ferris. Outrage about betrayal by liars/con artists etc. MO of murder – assailant physically weaker than victim?*

Under the second, much smaller grouping, she'd written:

Sean Hannington. Motive: *Revenge attack for personal affront/honour. Alleged violent criminal.*

Unknown associate of Hannington. Motive: Acting as his paid/
coerced deputy.
Both of the above: Possible assistance fr. Rifkin/Roland Ferris?
NB unidentified van parked near scene.
Unknown third party?? Local w. past grievance w. Harry
Ferris?

It was a brave attempt to show their progress, but what it mainly did was advertise to anybody who happened to look in that all they'd hit so far were dead ends. Further down the board was a blue smudge where Broad had written something else and rubbed it out. Lockyer squinted at it, and saw the ghost of the word *Forensics*. He almost laughed. She'd clearly decided they had nothing worth writing up under that heading. Perhaps the word 'inconclusive', but that was it.

He picked up the pen and yanked the cap off. Beside Roland's name he wrote *Lying about something. Police visit? Helen Ferris's suicide?* Then he added Harry Ferris's name to the list of persons from outside the house, and wrote the same thing beside it. Had Miles Godwin told Harry about the imposter, back in 2005? Had Harry come back, under cover of darkness? A secret visit, with a secret intent . . . The possibility that Harry and Mickey had known each other, long ago, was also niggling him. The pen hovered next to Hedy's name. He considered writing *not the killing type*, then thought better of it. And he looked hard at the note that the MO suggested a weaker assailant. It *could* also mean that whoever had done it simply hadn't wanted to give Mickey a chance to wake the household. Lockyer took a deep breath.

His thoughts were interrupted by Broad's reappearance, clutching a sheaf of papers.

'Guv, I had to go and get printer paper. Look at this.' She was obviously excited. 'I think I've got something.'

'What – already?'

'Might not be, but isn't it about time we had a lucky break? I started looking two days before Harry's thirteenth birthday in 1988, then went forwards, and here – this is from the *Wiltshire Times* the day after, the thirteenth of May.'

She thrust the printout at him. *Pewsey Girl Killed in Hit and Run* ran the headline. 'Pewsey?' he said. 'That's nowhere near Stoke Lavington.'

'Keep reading, Guv,' Broad said. 'Over the page – this is from the next edition, a week later. Look – here . . .' The story had still been front-page news. Broad ran her finger down the printed column. 'This bit.'

Lockyer read:

> No witnesses have yet come forward in the death of eight-year-old Lucy White, in spite of police and family appeals. A police statement issued yesterday revealed that paint samples taken from the damaged railings indicate that the vehicle involved was old, certainly pre-1960, and possibly a pre-war 'classic car', of a dark green colour (see picture below), and are appealing for anybody in the area who might know of such a car to get in touch as soon as possible.

'A classic car . . .'

Broad nodded. 'Could be why our lot went to talk to Ferris, couldn't it?'

'It could. See if you can find out any more details. Archive, maybe?'

'On it.'

Yesterday morning, 12 May, an eight-year-old girl was hit by a car and killed as she walked home towards Pewsey from a riding lesson in the neighbouring village of Manningford Bruce. The driver of the vehicle did not stop, and is being sought by police. Identified locally as Lucy White, the child's body was found by a passing cyclist later in the day, in the stream by the side of Woodborough Road. An ambulance crew was unable to revive her.

While a formal identification has yet to be made, police say that the girl's family have been informed. The police have issued a statement saying that failure to stop in the case of a fatal accident of this kind is a very serious offence, and that the driver involved will be prosecuted to the full extent of the law should they not immediately come forward and identify themselves. The person, or persons, involved, or anybody with any information, is urged to contact police without delay.

The printout from the later edition of the paper included a grainy colour photograph of Lucy. Lockyer had seen too many like that. Grinning, gap-toothed kids in their best party clothes, hair done nicely but messed up by playing. Families so often supplied a picture taken at a birthday party or similar event, possibly because – back then, anyway – it was when people remembered their cameras, or perhaps because the child radiated such joy on those occasions. All the inevitable tantrums and moments of spite forgotten. Full of sugar, the centre of attention, piles of torn wrapping paper in the background, or with candles lighting their faces. It was either that or the school photograph – too neat, too posed, hands in lap, hair in plaits. But still the sweetness that stung everyone who saw it on the front of a newspaper. All that life taken. All that wreckage left behind. Broken pieces of who people used to be, just like Hedy had said.

Lucy White had had long, light brown hair, a pointed chin and straight, serious eyebrows. The picture had been taken outside, with strong sunshine making her squint. A blue summer dress, the straps tied in bows on top of her skinny shoulders. There was something slightly guarded about her smile, as though she hadn't really liked having her picture taken. Lockyer imagined her as a shy child, an outdoors type. She'd been walking back from a riding lesson when she was killed. Perhaps she'd been the type who preferred being in wellies and a T-shirt rather than a summer dress.

Lockyer sat staring at her picture, lost in thought, for too long. He rejected his gut reaction to go straight to Roland Ferris and confront him with it – with her. It was too much of a leap; they needed more information. Ferris might have had nothing to do with it, but he'd been due to set off to a classic car rally that morning. Lockyer wanted to know where the rally had been, and which car he'd taken, and he guessed that was exactly what the police had gone to Longacres to ask in 1988.

Broad came back with an address for the girl's father, Malcolm White.

'He's still living in Pewsey,' she said.

'Just him?'

'Seems to be. Might be the same house.'

'God, I hope not, for his sake.'

They stopped on Woodborough Road, by the stream where Lucy's body had been found. It was an unmarked country lane, just wide and straight enough for people to drive too fast along as a matter of course. Lockyer pulled over by a field gate a short way past the spot, and they walked back. There was no hump in the road, nothing to mark that it was a bridge other than a stretch of white railings either side. The stream was shallow and only about five feet wide, flanked on either side by the tangled remnants of that summer's undergrowth. Broad stared down at the fast-flowing water, as though trying to picture the abandoned body of a child there.

Lockyer stepped back and looked up. The trees were all but bare now; their leaves lay rotting along the verges. Their branches, black and intricate against the white sky, touched over the middle of the road. Back where they'd parked the car, it was much more open.

'It'd be deep shade along here in summer,' he said. 'Driving into it from that direction, on a sunny day, it'd take a while for your eyes to adjust. Especially if you were wearing sunglasses.'

'You mean it'd be easy not to see a kid walking along?' Broad said.

'All too easy. You wouldn't necessarily have to be driving like a dick.'

Just then a car rocketed past them, doing at least fifty. They exchanged a look, then headed back.

Pewsey lay about seven miles south of Marlborough, a large village with a mainline station into London Paddington. It was popular with commuters who lived in expensive period properties within easy distance of it, in the Vale of Pewsey and across the bottom corner of the North Wessex Downs. It was a beautiful area. Shallow chalk streams wound through marshy meadows, with solitary willow trees leaning over the water here and there. The surrounding hills were dotted with tall stands of beech and oak, and where the land dropped into a deep hollow it was filled with blackthorn that foamed white with blossom in spring, and trapped the frost in winter. The village of Pewsey itself was dowdier, and left to those who struggled to find work and ways to fill their time.

Malcolm White lived in a 1940s ex-council semi on Haines Terrace. It was a plain brick house with a long front garden, an expanse of choppy grass with a muddy driveway up one side and a leylandii hedge, wildly overgrown, along the other. It stood out from its neighbours for its unloved air, and its lack of improvement: no extensions, no loft conversion, no double glazing. Weeds surrounded a 1996 Toyota propped up on bricks, its nearside front wheel nowhere in sight.

A shadow materialized behind the frosted-glass front door, which was then opened by a thin, stooped man in battered jeans and an out-of-date Manchester United shirt. Grey-haired, with the ravaged skin and depleted appearance of the long-term sick, he hadn't shaved for several days and had nothing on his feet. They were pale and off-putting, and his toenails needed cutting.

'Malcolm White?' Lockyer said.

Malcolm's face was slow to show his comprehension as they introduced themselves and showed their warrant cards. Then a wary, haunted look crept into his eyes. 'What is it? Has something happened? Is it Angie?'

Lockyer caught the stench of stale alcohol on his breath. So, not sick in the traditional sense: an alcoholic.

'Nothing like that,' Broad said. We're from Major Crime Review, working on an old case, and we'd like to talk to you, if that would be okay?'

'About what?'

'About Lucy,' Lockyer said.

It was a gamble. Malcolm stared at them with his bloodshot, underwater eyes, before stepping back and ushering them inside.

In the living room, his black leather three-piece suite was worn through to the webbing in places, and had deep, permanent depressions in the seat cushions. Grime and fingermarks were thick on the glass coffee-table and media console. The carpet was deep-pile shag, trampled flat on the thoroughfares, and dirty glasses and cups were scattered about. Lockyer felt his eyes start to itch. Broad coughed, then rummaged in her pocket for a tissue and blew her nose, apologizing. To their relief, Malcolm didn't offer refreshments. He steered them towards the sofa, then sat down on the edge of an easy chair, curling his body against the armrest.

His expression was edgy, almost cringing, as though he expected a blow. Hollow cheeks and eyes, stomach concave beneath his ribcage. He looked half starved, defeated.

'You're looking into Lucy's case, then? Nobody's done anything in such a long time,' he said. 'Years and years.' He ran a shaking hand over his mouth.

'Not exactly, I'm afraid,' Lockyer said. 'We're looking into another case, and we've discovered a potential link to Lucy's death.'

'What link?'

'We've been having some trouble locating the file on Lucy's death,' Broad said apologetically. 'It might take us a while, if it's been . . . archived. We wanted to ask you some questions to help us get an idea of the investigation at the time, if that's all right?'

'Ask away,' Malcolm said. 'You ought to know better than me, though. They were always crap about keeping us informed, but I suppose that's because they never found anything.'

'So, nobody was ever arrested?'

'No. They had a suspect for a while, local bloke who had a bunch of old cars. But he reckoned he'd gone off in the other direction that morning. Nowhere near here. And they never found a car the right colour at his place, or damaged.'

'Can you remember this man's name?' Lockyer said.

'They wouldn't tell us, but I heard it. I used to listen in to the family liaison bird on the phone, only way I found anything out. Ferris, he was called. I've never forgotten it. Like the big wheel at the funfair.'

Malcolm ran his hand over his mouth again, then got to his feet and disappeared into what Lockyer assumed was the kitchen. They heard the rattle of a bottle against a glass, a long pause, then the clatter of the glass on the worktop. Malcolm came back and sat down without a word of apology or explanation. Not that any were needed.

Broad shifted uncomfortably. 'Do you know of any other suspects?' she asked.

Malcolm shook his head. 'No. Said they'd carry on looking, kept on saying that. But they didn't, of course. Couple of months down the line and the family liaison's moved on to some other poor bastard whose life's in bits, and the phone stops ringing.' He shrugged. 'They couldn't find the driver of the car. It was that simple.'

'I can understand that must have been very upsetting for you all,' Broad said. It was the kind of platitude that normally got an angry slap down, but the way she said it, people seemed to believe her.

Malcolm gave another of his weary shrugs. 'Wouldn't have brought her back, would it?' he said. 'Damage was done.'

'Does Lucy's mother still live with you?' Lockyer said.

'Angie? Christ, no. Not seen her in so long I can hardly remember what she looks like. She buggered off about a year after it happened, and I don't blame her. It was my fault, you see.'

'Parents often blame themselves when—'

'No,' Malcolm cut Broad off. 'It was my fault.' He fell silent, and Lockyer began to doubt that he was going to expand. Then he drew a shaky breath. 'She was a sensible kid. Old head on young shoulders. She went where she said she was going, and came back when she said she would. You could trust her not to bunk off, or do anything stupid. She used to cycle to her riding lesson every Saturday, good as gold. Met her little friend there, and then they'd come back together, and play here, at home. Angie always worked Saturdays, in the ticket hall at the station. I'd be here, taking Danny to football, minding Vicky, cutting the grass, getting through the laundry, all that shit. That Saturday, though . . .'

He stared at them, a look of such utter loathing on his face that Broad drew back. 'That Saturday she had a puncture. Must have got it on the way there, so by the time she finished her lesson the tyre was flat as a pancake. That's what she said to me – she rang me from the farmhouse. "It's flat as a pancake, Dad." Wanted me to go and pick her up but I wouldn't. "You can walk it," I said. She didn't want to. Got a bit whiny about it, since she'd be on her own – her friend wasn't there that week, dunno why. "It's no bother," I told her. "It's a couple of miles. You know the way – it'll only take you an hour. Push your bike and walk, and I'll fix the puncture when you get back."'

The shaking wasn't just in his hands now. It had spread to his shoulders, his voice. 'So she walked. Because I'd had a few by then, and I didn't want to risk driving to pick her up. How's that for irony, or fate, or whatever the fuck you want to call it? She walked back because I thought it'd be safer for her. She died because her dad's a piss artist, and a waste of fucking space.'

Lockyer glanced across at Broad. There was no easy response.

'Did Lucy's death lead to the breakdown of your marriage?' Broad asked.

'What do you think? I swore off the drink that day, but I couldn't stick to it. How could I, knowing what I'd done? Seeing how much the other two missed Lucy? And missing her myself, like … like …' He shook his head. 'Hating myself like I did. And Angie hated me too. I could see it. Feel it. Taking the kids and buggering off was the smartest thing she ever did.'

'But you stayed here, all by yourself?' Broad said.

'Where else would I go? For a while I tried to keep in touch with Vicky and Dan, you know, when I was sober. I wanted to let them know they still had a dad who loved them – always would. But I never stayed sober, and as they got older they moved on. Seemed best to let them. I don't see them now, and I never hear from Angie. She remarried in the end, had another baby, I heard. That's all I know.'

'That must have been very hard for you.'

Malcolm nodded. 'But it helped a little bit, you know, thinking that the kids'd started over somewhere new.

Thinking that they were probably happy. They even took their mum's maiden name when she changed it back. Cut me out like a bad bit, pretty much, but it was for the best. Kids can bounce back from stuff, can't they? Not like grown-ups.'

'Yes, I think they can,' Broad said.

Lockyer felt his eyes itch, felt the suffocating atmosphere of dissolution and despair. However much he pitied the remains of the man before him, he couldn't wait to get away from him. His hopelessness felt contagious, a pit to fall into. He'd drowned in his grief and self-recrimination, while Lockyer had managed to cling to the sides of his own.

'What do you do for a living now, Mr White?' Broad asked.

'I cut grass. Do a bit of . . . landscaping for the council, that kind of thing. Weed killing.'

'Would it be possible to see Lucy's bedroom?' Lockyer said.

'How's that going to help?'

'I don't know that it will,' he answered. 'But it might.'

Malcolm waved absently. 'Top of the stairs, second door on the left. I started clearing it out one day. Well, I've started several times, over the years. But then I couldn't bear to. I tried putting it all back. It's a bit of a mess.'

Broad gave Lockyer a glance and got up to follow him. The room was more than a bit of a mess. Two single divan beds were bare, without mattresses, their pine headboards covered with small, glittery stickers. Lockyer felt his gut tighten, thinking of the Exeter Chiefs sticker on Chris's door. Other bits of furniture were piled up – a flat-pack type desk, two chairs, a bean bag, matching pink bedside cabinets.

The wardrobe doors were open, revealing a collection of plastic hangers. Several black bin bags sat about the place, one filled with clothes and sheets, the other with papers and school exercise books, old magazines and comics. A few coloured crayons and pencil shavings had trickled out where the bag had slumped; the headphone wires from a Walkman were knotted up with some purple shoelaces. The curtains were so faded their stripes had virtually disappeared. Posters pulled from magazines still clung to the walls, held up by brittle, yellowed Sellotape. Sun-bleached pictures of horses and ponies competed for space with pop bands – Lockyer recognized Bananarama, Kylie Minogue and Bros, and he half recognized an androgynous bloke with a high flat-top and a lot of make-up. Boy George or Marc Almond, maybe.

'What are we looking for, Guv?' Broad murmured.

'I don't know.' Lockyer kept looking around the room.

'Must have shared with her little sister,' Broad said, glancing at the twin beds. She was silent for a while. 'So I guess we know what the police went to talk to Ferris about.' She clearly thought they were wasting their time in the abandoned bedroom. Lockyer was inclined to agree with her. They headed back to the stairs.

Malcolm told them to see themselves out, but then he got up and followed them, listless but needy.

'Going to help you find out who it was, is it, this case of yours?' he said.

'We can't say for certain, I'm afraid,' Lockyer told him, 'but if we get any new leads we will pursue them, I promise.'

Malcolm cleared his throat and ended up coughing. 'I've blamed myself all these years,' he said. 'And it *was* my fault. But I still wish the bastard who hit her was behind bars. It wasn't right to go off and leave her lying there. Wasn't right to just carry on like she was nothing.'

'No, it wasn't.' Lockyer felt the truth of it right down to his bones. 'In my experience, Mr White, people who do things like this never carry on as though nothing happened. They don't. It stays with them, follows them around like a shadow. Ruins their life, even if they hide it well.' He thought of whoever had stabbed Christopher, and left him to bleed out on the pavement. A split-second decision, a single, disastrous action, both of which could so easily not have been made. He hoped it had ruined his life. God, he hoped it had, because it was all he had to cling to. The possibility of that small shred of justice. 'I don't know if that helps at all.'

'Not as much as seeing the bastard caught would,' Malcolm said. 'Not as much as seeing him punished. The world ought to know he's the kind of person who'd leave a little girl to die on her own by the side of the road.'

Lockyer had no answer to that. He nodded once, and turned to go.

15

Day Nineteen, Tuesday

Before Harry Ferris had gone up to Dauntsey's, at the age of eleven, he'd attended the village primary school.

'Much to my displeasure,' Roland said, when Lockyer rang to ask him. 'It wasn't a particularly good school, but Helen insisted. Said it was important for him to be close to home when he was little, and to have local friends.'

Lockyer remembered Maureen Pocock telling him that Helen had refused to employ a nanny.

'She said she didn't want him growing up entitled,' Roland went on. 'I said he *was* entitled – to the best education we could afford. But she wouldn't budge.'

It was a short drive to Stoke Lavington primary school. Lockyer went on the off-chance, and was shown in to see the headmistress, Mrs Parr, without an appointment. She was a young woman, with dark skin and her hair in braids, touched with scarlet and piled elaborately on top of her head. A general air of kindness and patience.

Definitely not a harridan of the traditional kind, as Serena had described her predecessor from Harry's childhood.

The short walk to her office, through corridors that smelt of socks, pencil shavings, Jeyes fluid and mashed potato, had plunged Lockyer into memories of his own school days. That smell, the chaotic artwork on the walls, and the posters about lending a hand and being kind. Rows of coats hanging on rows of pegs. He'd peered through a classroom door and been shocked by the diminutive size of the children, perched on their tiny chairs at their half-height desks.

'How may I help you, Inspector?' Mrs Parr said, smiling with her eyes.

'I'm trying to find out if a little boy called Michael Brown was ever at this school. He might have been known as Mickey.'

'I see. When would this have been?'

'Sometime between 1980 and 1991,' Lockyer said.

'Well, I can certainly check our records, but I'm afraid you've caught me on the hop today – I'm interviewing a supply for year three in ten minutes' time.'

He handed her his card. 'I'd really appreciate it.'

'I will, of course,' she said. 'Unless . . . You could always just go and look at the photos.'

'Photos?'

'In the main hall – my assistant will show you where, if you like. We have all our school photographs framed on the walls in there, right back to goodness knows when. Certainly before 1980. It might give you eyestrain, but the names are all printed underneath. If one's in brackets, it's because the child was off school that day for some reason, and isn't in the photograph.'

The hall had a slightly sticky parquet floor; tables and chairs stacked to the sides, a high, echoing ceiling, and a smell of boiled onions seeping from a hatch through to the kitchens. Lockyer walked slowly along the line of group portraits, which were banked five high in places, until he got to 1980. He scanned the names, face close to the glass. *Harry Ferris*. The corresponding little boy was sitting crosslegged on the ground in the front row, neatly turned out, hair combed flat. Lockyer would never have recognized him – he might have been any skinny, dark-haired little boy. Mickey's name wasn't anywhere on the list. He scanned 1981 but still no Mickey. The only Michael was a Michael Bloomfield, two years above Harry. But then, appearing out of nowhere: *Michael Brown*. The back of Lockyer's neck prickled.

He scanned the next picture along, and the next. Mickey was there in 1982 and '83, then vanished again. Lockyer stared at his grainy face. Another skinny, dark-haired little boy, squinting into the sun in the first picture, but grinning, showing missing front teeth, in the second. Not sitting next to Harry, but in the same class. Definitely similar in appearance – had anyone noticed at the time? Had the boys themselves? But Mickey was scruffy where Harry was neat; the knot of his tie drooping to one side, his hair standing up in tufts. Lockyer used his phone to take as good a picture of each of the photos as he could, close up, centred on Mickey's face.

From there he went to find Maureen Pocock in the village

shop. *That woman is an elephant, in more ways than one.* Roland had been a bit harsh, Lockyer thought, but he was counting on her memory. Maureen was perched precariously on a high metal stool, filling the space behind the counter. The smile she gave him as he approached was almost a leer.

'Can't keep away, can you?' she said. 'Cass isn't in today.'

'It was you I wanted to see, Maureen.'

She grinned even more widely. 'My lucky day, then, isn't it?'

Lockyer took out his phone and opened the better of the pictures he'd just taken of Mickey. 'Turns out Harry did know Michael Brown,' he said. He handed the phone to Maureen, who put on her glasses and squinted at the screen. 'That was the school photograph, taken in 1983.'

'You know what, Inspector?' Maureen leant closer for a second, then looked at him. 'I reckon I remember him an' all.'

'You do?' Lockyer had hoped as much.

'I'd never have placed the name, not sure I ever knew it, but now that I see his little face . . .'

'Were he and Harry friends?'

'I don't think so. But I wouldn't know what went on at school, would I? Only at home.'

'Did he ever come to Longacres?'

'Oh, yes. He was at one of Harry's birthday parties.'

'Even though they weren't friends?'

'Well, you know how it is when kids are really small. Until he was nine or ten, the whole class was invited. It was what you did. Not a big school, is it? You can't go having a few poor little tykes left off the invite. Helen was adamant about that. Which meant I always went to help her out – twenty-five kids running round your garden is a handful.'

'Professor Ferris didn't get involved?'

'You must be joking! His idea of hell, that. When Harry got older he started having outings and treats instead, and then he'd only invite a couple of his best mates.'

'But Mickey came to one of the earlier parties? You're sure?'

'Sure as sure. It was the one where Harry got the puppy. Claypole. Ha! Daft name. But, then, he was a daft dog. Harry's seventh birthday, was it? Eighth?'

'Seventh,' Lockyer confirmed. 'And you remember Mickey specifically? How come?'

'Well, I'll tell you. For starters, he wasn't called Mickey then. He was Michael, and I remember him because he was on the edge of things. The others weren't too friendly to him, and he seemed shy and a bit . . . nervy. He was new at the school, when the others had all come up together. I had a word with Harry, told him to be nicer to him. He said to me: *But he's got fleas!* Kids, eh? They can be heartless little sods. Michael did smell like he needed a bloody good scrub, mind you. And you could tell from his clothes, his hair and teeth that he weren't looked after properly. He didn't live in this village, so it must have been one of the neighbouring ones – council estate, I'd put money. I remember that gappy grin of his. I kept an eye on him, made sure he got enough to eat at the picnic. Made sure they included him.'

'That was kind of you.'

'Well.' Maureen folded her arms, shifted on her stool. 'Felt sorry for him, didn't I? Looking round the garden at it all, like he'd never seen anything so grand. Tore into his food like someone might take it away.'

She thought back for a moment.

'Then Harry wanted to play Cops 'n' Robbers, so we got them all into two teams. Michael was a robber, Harry was a cop – course he was. The robbers all had to hide while the cops covered their eyes and counted to a hundred, then the robbers had to sneak or leg it back to the den without being caught. The winners were any robbers who made it, and any cops who'd caught a robber – they all got a sweetie.' She cleared her throat, which made her chins wobble. 'Michael made it back to the den. I was standing right there when he made his dash for it – by God, he was fast! I'm standing there and he comes pounding across the lawn, feet flapping, three cops right on his heels, and I've never forgotten his face as he came by me. Panic, that's what it was. Tears in his eyes. Not laughing, not determined to win, nothing like that. He looked scared to death. And I remember thinking, That poor little sod's had to do this for *real*. He's had to run for real.'

She shook her head sadly. 'I made sure he got the best goodie bag at the end of the day. I put extra cake in it – a great big slice. He saw me do it, and that's when I got that grin off him. That big gappy grin, same as in the picture you've got.'

'And I bet I can guess where the den was,' Lockyer said.

'It was the small barn out—'

Maureen pulled herself up short, realizing its significance. 'Oh,' she said, eyes tearing up. 'You don't think . . . Oh, the poor thing.'

The file on the Lucy White case arrived from the archive by courier. It was pathetically thin. The photograph that had been on the front page of the newspaper was inside, folded in half. Lockyer opened it out. In the un-cropped original, Lucy was standing next to another little girl, plain and brown-haired, wearing grubby jodhpurs and a quizzical expression. Lockyer stared into Lucy's face for a long time, then read through the file. At one point he had to stop, lean away from it.

'What?' Broad asked.

'The car didn't kill her,' he said.

'What do you mean?'

'It was estimated to have been travelling at around thirty miles an hour. Lucy sustained two broken legs and a fractured pelvis, various cuts and bruises, and a hard but not serious blow to the head. It might've knocked her unconscious, but none of her injuries were fatal. If she'd been taken to hospital straight away she'd have lived. But they knocked her into the stream and drove off. Lucy White drowned.'

'Shit,' Broad said.

'Yes. Shit.' Lockyer shook his head. 'Whoever it was, it wasn't hitting her that killed her. It was not stopping.'

'Is there anything else? Anything we can use?'

'No tyre tracks behind where she was found, only ahead, so they braked hard *after* they hit her, but not before.'

'Didn't see her, then?'

'Possibly. The accident investigator reckons the car glanced off the railings, sustaining light damage, and came to a complete stop before driving on.'

'So they knew. They *knew* they'd done it.'

'Her bike stayed in the road where she dropped it. So, yes, they knew. Had time to make a decision about whether to go back and check or drive away, and made the wrong one. Lucy had been listening to her Walkman, so maybe she didn't hear the engine. Not that she'd have been able to get out of the way between the railings if she had.'

'Christ. Poor kid.'

Whoever had hit her would have read about her in the paper, Lockyer thought. Seen her picture, known that she had died. He wondered how on earth they'd managed to carry on, to keep such a scar on their soul hidden from the world. How could you possibly function normally, knowing you'd done that? Perhaps the perp had hidden themselves away afterwards, and led a closeted life, surrounded by books ... But no. At that time in his life Professor Ferris had been far more active than now – teaching, speaking at conventions, and festivals, and book launches.

'The paint scrapings from the bridge were the only forensics. The full analysis is here, but I wonder if the actual samples have survived.' Lockyer got to his feet. 'Come on. Roland Ferris had his blood transfusion yesterday. He should be fit enough to talk to us today.'

It was raining steadily by the time they got to Longacres.

It blurred the view through the windows, and made the air smell of leaf mulch and earth.

Lockyer and Broad entered the dying man's study, followed by Harry Ferris and Paul Rifkin, both of them protesting that Roland wasn't well enough to be interviewed. Lockyer made no attempt to be seated. 'Forgive the intrusion, Professor. I'd like to talk to you about Lucy White.'

Lockyer and Broad both saw the name hit home. They saw the way Roland's eyes widened, then drooped, along with the rest of his face. Slackening with shock as he sank back into his pillows.

'Who the hell is Lucy White?' Harry asked. His voice sounded strained, as though his throat were dry.

'I think your father knows,' Lockyer said.

'I do not,' Professor Ferris whispered.

'When I asked you before why the police had come to speak to you back in 1988, you told me you couldn't remember, so it can't have been anything important.'

'Well?' the old man snapped.

'I'd call the murder of a little girl important,' Lockyer said. 'And I find it very hard to believe it wouldn't have stayed in your mind.'

'You're talking about over thirty years ago, man!' Roland struggled to sit up straighter in the bed, his angry gaze flicking from one face in the room to the next.

Paul stepped forwards, partly to help and partly to restrain him. 'Professor, relax as much as you can, please. Lie back.' Roland waved him away but did as he was told. Paul turned to Lockyer. 'He shouldn't be stressed like this, Inspector.'

Lockyer was equally cold. 'Two people were murdered, Mr Rifkin. And another took her own life.' He looked at Harry Ferris, then back at Roland. 'I realized as I drove over here, Professor, that the day your wife killed herself wasn't only Harry's birthday. It was also the second anniversary of Lucy White's death.'

'That had nothing to do with it!' Roland insisted.

'Did you tell her, or did she just figure it out? It was in the local paper, of course, when and what had happened. Plus the car was damaged. It would have needed patching up. Respraying, I suppose, since you left some paint behind at the scene – on the railings, and in Lucy's injuries.'

'That's enough!' Harry snapped.

Lockyer ignored him. 'You'd have had time to do that before the police made it round to see you, wouldn't you? After all, you have everything you need out there in the coach house. Could Helen not cope with knowing what you'd done? Knowing that you'd run that little girl down and not even stopped? Did having to keep such a terrible secret get too much for her?'

'There was no secret! I did no such thing.' Professor Ferris was recovering himself. Recovering from the shock. 'You're wholly wrong.'

'You were a suspect—' Broad began.

'So was every other bugger in the county with a pre-war motor car. They went round *everyone*. What choice did they have? They checked all of mine, none was the right colour, and none was damaged.'

'So you do remember it all. Quite well,' Lockyer said.

'I didn't say anything because it wasn't in the least bit relevant to that other man's death.'

'If it wasn't, why not just tell us?' Broad countered.

'Because it *wasn't relevant.*' Roland set his jaw stubbornly.

'That's not for you to decide, Professor,' Lockyer said. He knew from the file that Roland was telling the truth: the police had been to check on every owner in the area. Their task had been complicated by two classic car rallies that weekend: the one at Blandford Forum, in Dorset, that Roland Ferris had gone to, and another, smaller, one in Marlborough. Wiltshire had been crawling with pre-war models at the time Lucy was hit, from all over the country and even from abroad.

'How can what happened to that girl in 1988 possibly have anything to do with a homeless man getting killed here in 2005?' Harry said.

Lockyer and Broad turned to him. His posture was as defensive as ever. Arms folded, chin lifted. 'We don't know yet,' Lockyer said. 'It just keeps coming up, that year, 1988. The only thing Mickey Brown had in his possession was a cassette from 1988. "Voyage, Voyage" by Desireless. Do you remember it?'

Harry looked perplexed. 'No. I can't really remember what I was listening to then.' He frowned. 'I liked heavy metal, I think – or what I thought of as heavy metal. Def Leppard, Bon Jovi, that kind of thing. Not very heavy at all, in fact, but I thought it was cool.' He looked at his father, with a rare smile. 'You confiscated my Guns N' Roses album, do you remember that? Too much bad language.'

'Did I?' Roland asked. 'I was a tyrant. I'm sorry, my boy.'

'I've got over it,' Harry said.

'Which car did you take to the rally?' Lockyer said. 'And why was it more important than your son's thirteenth birthday?'

'It was a 1947 Rolls-Royce Silver Wraith.' Roland glared at Lockyer. 'Cherry red side panels, jet black everywhere else. And it was important because an American collector had come over for the Dorset fair, and contacted me. He had twenty grand to spend – God knows what that would be in today's money, but it was a lot. And we needed it.' He looked down at his hands on the blankets, pressing his thumbs together hard, jaw working silently. But then he looked at Harry again. 'I wish to God I hadn't gone. I just . . . I thought if he saw it, he'd *have* to buy it. It was a beauty, that machine.'

'I remember it,' Harry said. 'You'd spent so long restoring the thing – a whole year.'

It struck a chord in Lockyer's head too. The picture he'd noticed when he'd first returned to Longacres, of Helen and Harry, down in the yard. He had no idea what a Silver Wraith looked like, but the car in the picture had been red and black, he was sure.

Roland glared at Lockyer. 'I drove straight down to Blandford early that morning, which is to the south-west of here, in case you don't know. And I certainly didn't begin the journey by driving twelve miles north-east, to where that child was hit. But this must all be in the police notes, if you've read them.'

'I like to hear things directly.' Lockyer watched Roland steadily, and the dying man looked back at him, saying nothing. 'And did the collector buy it?'

'He did, which vouched for my presence at the fair. His details must be in there. No idea if he's still alive or not, or where on earth he might be, should you wish to hear it *directly* from him.'

'How did you get home?' Broad asked.

'A friend of mine gave me a ride back to Salisbury in his DB5 saloon. And then I caught the bus, which was a bit of a come-down.'

'Why not call your wife to come and collect you?'

'Well, I did try, but nobody picked up the phone. Probably out in the garden, or in Devizes with Harry, for his birthday tea. Those were the days before mobile phones, Constable.'

'Perhaps she didn't want to talk to you, after the row?' she suggested.

'Perhaps so,' Roland said neutrally. 'Helen didn't like to drive, in any case. She'd have been horrified at the thought of coming all the way to Blandford – or even Salisbury – to collect me. And in light of our falling out over me going in the first place, she'd probably have refused.'

'Why do you think Mickey Brown had a cassette from 1988 in his pocket, when he had nothing else?' Broad asked.

'I haven't the first clue, Constable.'

'I wonder,' Lockyer said. He turned to Harry and Paul Rifkin. 'Would you mind leaving us, please?'

'How long do you plan to keep haranguing him in this

pointless way?' Harry snapped. '*You* ought to be the one leaving.'

'When I've finished. Unless your father would prefer to continue at the station?'

The professor waved a hand at his son. 'Let the man get it out of his system, Harry. He can't have too much more to say, since he's not going to find out anything useful here.'

'You could be the death of him, you know,' Harry said, before leaving. 'Literally.'

With only the three of them in the room, Lockyer pulled a chair up to the bedside. Broad stayed back, by the desk, giving him space.

'I don't think it was a coincidence that that tape was left with Mickey's body. I think it meant something,' he said.

'Is that so?' Roland murmured.

'You wanted to believe Mickey was Harry, didn't you, Professor?'

The old man's eyes turned sorrowful. 'I did. Yes.'

'Right to the very end? Until we did the checks after his death?'

'Yes.'

'You often went out to sit with him, in the garden, in the barn. What did you talk about?'

'For pity's sake, Inspector. What does anyone talk about? I haven't a clue. About where he'd been, I imagine. What had happened to him.'

'About the old days? His childhood? His mother?'

'Maybe, yes, I don't recall.'

'You see ... I wonder if you talked to him about why

Helen killed herself. I wonder if you tried to explain about Lucy White.'

'I've already told you—' Roland's voice shook with emotion.

'I wonder if you told him what had happened that day on his thirteenth birthday. And why everything went so wrong after that for you, and especially for Helen.'

'No. You're quite wrong.'

'And then I wonder if you found out that Mickey wasn't Harry after all. He was an imposter, a Traveller with a prison record and a history of drug abuse. Rifkin knew his true identity. Miles knew where Harry really was the whole time, and Serena had never believed he was Harry.' Lockyer watched Roland absorb this news in shocked silence. 'Hedy knew,' he added.

'Hedy? *Hedy* knew?' Roland sounded bewildered.

'Mickey confessed his true identity to her a few days before he died. She told him that if he didn't tell you she would. And I wonder if she did. Or *he* did.'

'No . . . no, I didn't know . . .'

'Because if you had confessed something to him about Lucy White, only to find out he was not your son—'

'You're spinning yarns, Inspector. Nothing more.'

The old man was breathing through his mouth, rapidly, loudly, his ribcage rising and falling visibly.

Broad shifted uneasily. 'Guv—'

'You'd kept your secret for seventeen years by then. I imagine you'd have gone to *any* lengths to continue keeping it. Did Mickey attempt to blackmail you?' He let that settle for a moment. 'The original investigation considered whether killing him in his sleep might have meant his assailant was weaker, physically. That helped convict Hedy Lambert. But Hedy wasn't the only person in this house physically weaker than Mickey, was she, Professor?'

'Pure conjecture, Inspector. You're wrong about all this.' The old man's eyes were shining and restless, his hands clasped tightly together, fingers white. Lockyer couldn't tell if he was frightened or furious. Or possibly both.

'Using cling-film around the handle of the knife so as to not leave prints . . . That would suggest a sudden impromptu decision, perhaps, a decision made by somebody inside this house.'

'I – I insist you leave now,' Roland said. 'I don't feel well.'

Lockyer got up. 'Very well, Professor. But we will be back to talk to you again. And to Harry.' Lockyer reached into the file he'd brought with him, and found the printout from the *Wiltshire Times*. The one with Lucy White's photo on the front page. 'You hang on to this,' he said.

Roland Ferris looked at it, then away. 'That child . . .' he said quietly. 'I am not responsible for that child.'

They found Harry in the kitchen, standing by the back door and staring out at the barn. From elsewhere in the house they could faintly hear Paul on the phone. Harry stood with his arms folded, not moving a muscle. Lockyer took in the scene and saw the sink where Hedy had so often stood: the draining board where she'd left the knife; the keys still hanging on the nail by the door. Outside, the paved pathway she'd walked so many times, carrying food to Mickey Brown. Or just going to see him, as Broad had pointed out. Getting close to him. Developing feelings for him that were about to be cruelly betrayed.

'You'd really never heard the name Lucy White before?' Lockyer's voice was loud and intrusive.

Harry jumped, half turned, then shook his head. 'No. And my father had nothing to do with her death.'

'Mr Ferris, you were a child at the time. People hide things from their children.'

'I was thirteen.' Harry's voice was oddly toneless. 'I might have been small for my age but I wasn't stupid. I would have known.'

'Maybe you did,' Lockyer said.

Harry glanced back over his shoulder, his expression dark. 'I just told you—'

'I don't mean you knew *exactly*. But I think you knew something – *sensed* something. Perhaps that something was wrong. It was around that time your behaviour changed for the worse, wasn't it? And that usually means something's bothering a child. Was it the change in your parents that was upsetting you, Harry? Your mother, in particular?'

'You really have no idea what you're talking about, do you?' Harry said.

Lockyer saw something in his eyes then, something in the tension of his jaw. He wondered if there was actually something that Harry Ferris longed to be able to say. 'So tell me,' he said.

Harry went back to staring out at the barn. 'There's

nothing to tell. Nothing I care to say, or that's any concern of yours.'

Lockyer moved a few steps closer, to share the view. The worn timber doors sagging on their hinges, the darkness inside that the wan daylight couldn't penetrate. He wondered whether the vision of his mother hanging there had ever left Harry, or even faded. Was his lengthy absence from Longacres simply an attempt to put distance between himself and such a traumatic event? He knew far too well how such a thing could shape the rest of your life. Like losing a daughter to a careless driver. Like losing a brother to a random knife attack. Like being conned into crippling debt by a fake lover, and spending more than a decade in jail for something you hadn't done.

'You did know Mickey Brown, by the way,' Lockyer said.

Harry swung around, angry again. 'I've already told you I didn't.'

'You might not remember him, but he was in your class at school. Just for a couple of years, either side of your seventh birthday. He came to your seventh birthday party, in fact. The year you got Claypole. And played Cops 'n' Robbers in the barn.'

Harry frowned. 'I . . . Are you sure?'

'Completely. Here.' He showed Harry the pictures on his phone. 'He looks so like you. I'm surprised you don't remember him.'

'He doesn't look anything like me. I don't remember him at all,' Harry murmured. 'But my mother used to make me invite the whole class, so . . .' He shrugged.

'You didn't keep in touch with him? Run into him again at a later date?'

'No. I didn't. I honestly don't remember him at all.' Harry's mild perplexity at this failure seemed genuine. 'What happened to him after that? Where did he go?'

'Nowhere good,' Lockyer said. 'I think he came here on purpose, in 2005. He was running away from a very dangerous man. He'd spent his life running from dangerous people, from what I can gather. I think he came here because he remembered it. Remembered hiding in that barn.' Lockyer gestured at it, beyond the window.

Harry turned away. He wasn't interested, Lockyer saw. It didn't matter to him – Mickey Brown didn't matter to him, and had slipped from his recollection as completely as he'd vanished from the school photographs. Longacres must have seemed a different world to a neglected lad growing up in poverty, one who was poorly cared for, poorly clothed, poorly fed. It must have been like stumbling into Narnia. Here was Harry Ferris, with a loving mother, a puppy, a cake three times the size of his own head, living in a house with more rooms than one family could possibly occupy, with a garden like a park – swings, slides. Barns to hide in, trees to climb. A parallel universe of plenty and of safety that Mickey had been allowed to visit for a tantalizingly short time. No wonder it had made an impression. No wonder, years later, he'd remembered that barn, and where the outside toilet was. No way would Roland Ferris have wanted twenty-five small kids traipsing into the house to pee.

Lockyer turned away, leaving Harry to his thoughts.

Paul Rifkin came jogging down the stairs as Lockyer and Broad made their way to the front door. He was still on the phone, but finishing up.

'Yes. Yes, that would be fine, Ms Garvich. Sorry – Professor Garvick,' he said. 'See you then. Goodbye.' He looked darkly at Lockyer and Broad. 'Professor Ferris is exhausted,' he said.

'And yet he's got the energy to entertain another visitor?' Broad said.

'Yes, on Thursday. Little Tor Heath is a professor now herself, if you can believe that. Remember her, Inspector? I bet you do. I wonder who she shagged to get that far.'

Broad bristled. 'Perhaps she earned it by being good at her job.'

'Perhaps,' Paul said. 'But I doubt it.'

'Goodbye, Mr Rifkin,' Lockyer said. 'I expect we'll be seeing you again.'

'Seems to be the way the wind is blowing, yes.' Paul raised his eyebrows. 'Sooner or later, though, you might have to accept that all your digging's turning up nothing because there's nothing to turn up.'

'I doubt that,' Lockyer said. 'Oh, and just to let you know, I'm afraid I was forced to divulge to Professor Ferris that you'd known Mickey Brown's true identity all along, back in 2005. He might want to ask you about that when he wakes up.'

Paul's face drained. Broad and Lockyer left before he found words to express his outrage.

Broad was quiet on the drive back. Lockyer hoped that the next thing she said wasn't going to be that she agreed with Paul Rifkin, since she'd made the same point herself more than once. That they were digging for something that wasn't there. He felt a sinking unease at the thought. But he refused to believe it, even though he knew his refusal was personal, not professional, which meant it had no place in the investigation.

'Weird to think Mickey went there on purpose, isn't it?' she said eventually. 'That he knew Longacres, I mean. Remembered it through all those years of travelling around, changing schools and institutions.'

'And only Maureen Pocock can remember *him* from back then.'

'Just goes to show . . .'

'What?'

'Well, Harry Ferris had it all. That's how it must have seemed to Mickey. But just a few years later it all went so wrong for him, too.'

'Remember that old adage about money not buying happiness, Gem?'

'Yeah.' She paused. 'Would've been nice if things had turned out better for Mickey, though. Wouldn't it?'

Lockyer nodded. *That poor little sod's had to do this for real.* By the age of seven. He couldn't imagine it. How could anyone get away from a childhood like that?

'Guv . . .' Broad said, several minutes later. 'Could the tape not just be a tape? An anomaly, I mean, linking Michael Brown and Lucy White's deaths . . . We've just got nothing concrete, have we?'

'Not yet,' he said.

'I don't see how it could connect.' Broad shook her head. 'That song was big in 1988, the same year Lucy was killed. But that's it. Could be a total coincidence.'

'Same year Harry goes off the rails. Same *day* that Helen Ferris kills herself, two years later.'

'But our guys checked Roland Ferris out at the time of the accident. He *was* in Dorset when he said he was, in the car he claimed to be in. That bloke did buy it off him . . . He's got an alibi, Guv.'

'I know. I've read the 'eighty-eight file. They were especially keen on him because, of all the classic car owners in a twenty-mile radius of Pewsey, *he* had the means to respray one himself, and quickly, if he'd needed to. And they never pinned down what time he *arrived* at the rally. He could have gone out earlier in the morning in a different car.'

'But why would he do that?'

'I don't know – to give it a run? Turn the engine over?'

'Okay, so he goes out early in a green car, hits Lucy, hurries back and hides it, then heads down to Dorset in the Silver Wraith. He gets back in time to repair the damage before we complete the paint analysis and come round to talk to him. Helen can't bear it. It contributes to her suicide, and to Harry leaving. Then Harry reappears seventeen years later, or so Roland thinks. He talks about what happened, then finds out Mickey isn't Harry, and kills him to keep the secret buried.'

'We can't rule that out, can we?'

'So why does he leave a tape that might somehow link to Lucy on the body? I mean, why on *earth* would he do that?'

'Tribute? Token?' Lockyer was quiet for a while. 'Roland Ferris is no hardened killer. I'm sure he felt terrible about Lucy – not terrible enough to go to prison for killing her, but perhaps he wanted to acknowledge her somehow.'

'By putting a tribute on the corpse of a man he's just murdered, who's guilty of nothing except not being Harry Ferris?'

'I— Well. Maybe the tape isn't relevant,' he said, defeated. 'But there's something there, Gem. There's *something* . . .'

Lockyer drove on in silence, frustration growing, his thoughts more and more tangled. He needed clarity: the mindless simplicity of manual labour, or a night-time walk. But for now he could only keep moving the pieces around until he saw the pattern. The inside of his head was as chaotic as Lucy White's bedroom – he thought of the bloated black sacks, the jumbled furniture, the tangled shoelaces and faded pop posters.

'Shit,' he said.

Broad looked at him sharply. They were driving fast along the A361 back to Devizes. Lockyer saw a field gate coming up, hit the brakes, swerved sharply into it. The car behind pulled around them with a blast of its horn.

'What is it?' Broad said.

'The posters,' Lockyer said. He got out his phone, waited for a 4G signal, then ran an image search.

'What posters?'

Lockyer passed her his phone.

'Who the hell is that?' she asked.

'The lead singer of Desireless,' he said.

'That's a woman?'

'She was deliberately androgynous. There were posters of her on Lucy White's bedroom wall – several of them. They were so faded I thought it was Boy George, or Marc Almond. But one of them was that *exact* picture – the flat-top haircut, the black shirt with the high collar, the gloves.'

'Claudie Fritsch-Mentrop.' Broad pronounced the name haltingly. She scrolled down a bit. 'God, she looks different now.'

'It's a link, Gem. I know it is. Lucy White liked that song.'

'How do you know it was that song, specifically? It could—'

'Because that's the *only* song Desireless had a hit with in 1988. The only one she *ever* had, as far as I know.' Lockyer took his phone back, and saw Broad's sceptical expression. 'It's a link.'

'If the song was a big hit, that poster was probably on every eight-year-old girl's bedroom wall.'

'It's a link.'

'Okay. Say it's a link. Say Lucy loved that song. Doesn't make it any clearer how Roland Ferris would even *know* that, or why he'd leave it on Mickey Brown's body. Does it?'

And, just like that, she stole the wind from Lockyer's sails again.

'I know you want Hedy Lambert to be innocent, Guv, but—'

'I *want* her to be innocent? Is that what you think?'

'Is that not . . .? I mean, I know you like her, but . . .' Broad was flailing, and couldn't look at him.

'That's not what this is.' Lockyer took a breath, checked

with himself that he was telling the truth. 'I don't want her to be innocent because I like her. I think she *is* innocent. And I can't have a case as badly botched as this was on my conscience if she is. Botched, in part, *because* I liked her. I just can't.' He paused for a moment. 'This is about me finding out if my instinct – my gut – is worth a damn, Gem.'

Broad still wouldn't look at him, and Lockyer felt for the first time that maybe she didn't believe him. He pulled out of the lay-by in silence.

He sent Broad to the newspapers again, trying to find out if there was some mention of Desireless in any of the articles. Lucy's mother, Angie, had given a lengthy interview about Lucy a few weeks after her death, in the hope of prompting the driver of the car to come forward. There was no mention of the song, but Lockyer left Broad searching for other interviews, other statements to the press or public. Anywhere it might have been mentioned. The tape found in Mickey Brown's pocket probably wasn't Lucy's exact copy: they were available to buy on eBay and collectors' sites. Lockyer thought of the empty Walkman he'd seen in the girl's bedroom. Had whoever hit Lucy got out of the car, found her Walkman on the ground, and taken the tape from it?

Lockyer tried to imagine that: seeing Lucy was still alive, climbing down to her in the stream. Taking something from her, but leaving her there. Unthinkable. He went through the file again to check where the Walkman had been found – on the body, or up on the road with her bike – but nobody had made a note of it. He threw it down in irritation, with himself as much as anything. He was grasping at straws, and he knew it. Broad's questions about the tape wouldn't leave him alone. Surely the only people who would have known whether or not Lucy had liked that song – let alone whether or not she'd been listening to it when she was killed – were her parents, when her things were returned to them, and the police who'd worked the case.

He picked up the file again and read through the names of all the officers involved in the investigation back in 1988. None were familiar.

Lockyer got up and stared out at the drab, rain-streaked trees. He had the office to himself; Broad had gone to get some lunch. He went back to his desk, picked up the phone and left a voicemail for Hedy, asking her to call him. Twenty minutes later, she did.

'Inspector Lockyer.'

'Hedy. Thanks for calling so quickly.' He shut his eyes, picturing her. The delicate tendons on the backs of her hands as they gripped the phone. Her hair pushed behind her ears; the smooth skin of her cheeks; her mouth near the plastic receiver. Her admirable self-possession. He couldn't tell from the way she said his name if she was happy to hear from him or not.

'Well, I had a gap in my diary,' she said drily, with that little bit of bite Lockyer thought must be a hint of her old self, not yet crushed. It made him hope that, given the chance, she could be that person again.

'How are you?' he said.

He could almost hear her shrug. 'It's always the same in

here. Tiny daily fluctuations in the level of shitness, but basically the same. It's good to hear from you. I wish you'd come in to see me, though.'

'I didn't want to lose time scheduling the visit.'

'Why? Have you found something?'

'Maybe. Nothing concrete yet . . .' He stared at the trees again. She seemed so far away; he wondered if she'd ever be nearer. Out in the world. 'I'm getting closer to something, Hedy . . . At least, I think I am.' He heard how inappropriate he sounded, considering where he was, who he was. He checked over his shoulder, but he was still alone. He mustn't be overheard, talking like that. No, he corrected himself. He just mustn't talk to her like that. He cleared his throat. 'Hedy, did Professor Ferris ever talk to you about . . .' Lockyer tried to think how best to phrase it. '. . . about an accident that happened years ago, a road accident, or anything like that? Any kind of terrible tragedy?'

'A terrible tragedy? You mean other than Helen Ferris hanging herself, and Harry leaving forever? Well, not quite forever.'

'Yes. Something else.'

'No.'

'Think, please, Hedy. It's very important.'

'I was only his housekeeper, Matt. I wasn't . . . We were fond of each other, and he talked to me from time to time about all sorts of things, but I certainly wasn't his confidante, or whatever you want to call it.'

Lockyer tried to focus, to choose his words with care, but

her voice reverberated inside his head. It was the first time she'd used his first name.

'What happened? Was there a tragedy?'

'Yes.' Lockyer's instinct was not to tell her. The professional thing would be not to tell her, but he couldn't see any real harm in it. And he wanted to. It was that or end the phone call. 'A road accident. A child was killed.'

'Oh . . .'

It sounded as though she'd shivered.

'Professor Ferris . . . Roland was questioned by police at the time, because paint samples suggested that a classic car was involved.'

He heard another soft intake of breath.

'He was cleared of any suspicion.'

'But you think he was involved?'

'I don't know, Hedy. But somebody in that house besides you had to have a motive for murder and . . . what happened to that child, that's the kind of thing people kill for. Kill to hide, or—'

'Or kill to avenge?'

'To avenge?' Lockyer echoed.

Hedy hesitated. 'Wasn't that what you were going to say?'

'Not necessarily. But if Roland Ferris was involved somehow, why go after Harry Ferris?'

'What better revenge could there be, Inspector? An eye for an eye, a child for a child.'

'Her parents? Roland took their daughter, so they—'

'Take his long-lost son, who he was so delighted to have back home.' Hedy's tone had changed. And she'd gone back to calling him *Inspector.* 'Killing the person actually responsible might seem too quick and easy, as punishments go,' she said flatly.

Lockyer wondered what she was thinking about, or whom. 'I don't know about that,' he said. 'Would a grieving parent kill another innocent person? Surely they wouldn't go that far.'

'Not every grieving parent, no. But some might. The ones who don't manage to "move on" or "find peace" or "closure", or whatever else you're supposed to do.'

Lockyer said nothing for a while. He thought about the man who'd killed his brother. Thought of his parents in the immediate aftermath of it, and now. Had they wanted to destroy the man responsible? Yes, of course. All three of them had, in their own ways – he and his father had both felt the primal urge to inflict pain, vent anger. Trudy had wanted justice, not violence. She'd wanted it never to happen to anyone else; she'd wanted the man caught, and turned onto a different path. Was that a man/woman thing, or a personality trait? Personality, he decided. Women were just as capable of wanting – and exacting – violent revenge as men.

But had any of them come across that man's son or daughter, he didn't think it would have occurred to them to take their revenge by harming them.

'Inspector? Are you still there?'

'I'm still here.'

'Roland never mentioned being involved in a fatal accident, but I've said to you before that he used to make comments about things either being his fault or not being his fault, haven't I?'

'Yes. You have.'

'That was kind of how any conversation like that would go. I'd usually find him looking at an old photo of Helen or Harry, or just staring out of the window, and he'd see me and say something oblique. *It wasn't my fault*, or *Perhaps it was my fault*. I'd ask what he meant, and he'd say *Never mind*. And that was it.' She paused. 'I used to wonder if he *wanted* to talk to me about something, but was stopping himself. I wish I could be more help. I always just thought he was talking about Helen.'

'I think he probably was,' Lockyer said. 'Did he ever keep a diary?'

'Like a "Dear Diary" type of diary? I don't think so. Only a diary of publication schedules and speaking events, that sort of thing, which Paul managed.'

Lockyer couldn't think of anything else to ask her, anything else he could tell her. He simply couldn't let himself say anything encouraging, not when there was still so little that was definite. 'Do you want revenge on Aaron, Hedy?' he asked, surprising himself.

She didn't answer at once. 'It's all a chain, isn't it?' she said eventually. 'A chain of events that leads to a certain point . . . For all our plans and schemes, that's all our lives are, and I don't think we truly get to choose where we end up, or what we end up doing. Our choices aren't really choices. Aaron was a link in my chain, in more ways than one.' She paused to draw breath. 'I hardly ever think about him. I never knew him, after all. He was like – like the generic picture that's already in the photo frame when you buy it. A mock-up. I hope, wherever he is . . . I don't know.' She was quiet for a moment. 'I hope he's not ruining other people's lives. That's all. I hope he found a way to see what it might be like for the other person. What he does to them. That would be punishment enough.'

'Not many people would be so restrained, Hedy,' Lockyer said.

'I've had a lot of time to work through it all. Find acceptance. Closure.' He heard her wry smile as she echoed her earlier words. 'But I *really* want my car back.'

'You're strong, Hedy. I wish I had your strength.'

'I'm not. I might have got to where I am with Aaron, but you haven't asked me how I feel about whoever really killed Michael Brown.'

'Do I want to know?'

'Probably best that you don't.'

'What would you do, Hedy? If they were there in front of you right now?'

'What would I do? I . . . I have absolutely no idea. Probably burst into tears. How's that for strength?'

'Hedy—'

'Chains of events, Inspector. One thing always leads to another. Perhaps if I knew what had led them to that point, to that *moment* of stabbing Michael, it would make more sense. Or any sense at all. And things that make sense are just . . . easier. Aren't they? It's not knowing that drives you mad. Not knowing *why* I've been locked up for so many years. The cause of it.'

Lockyer felt something building inside himself. Like desperation, perhaps even fear. 'Hedy,' he said, 'are you telling me the truth? Have you been telling me the truth?'

And just like that, he made it personal. Personal to him, personal between them.

Again, she took a long time to answer. 'Yes. I always have.' Her voice had no particular tone, no inflection. As unreadable as a mirror laid flat to the sky.

Then there was a rustling as she put her hand over the receiver, and the sound of a muffled voice.

'Hedy?'

'I've got to go, Inspector. Time's up. Will you come in again soon?'

'I—' The call was cut off before Lockyer could reply. 'I preferred it when you called me Matt,' he said quietly.

Lockyer sat back down at his computer and opened a new email from Cellmark. A minute later he was on his feet, calling Broad on her mobile as he strode out of the office. 'Gem, where are you? Meet me out the front. We've got a match on a print from the tape.'

16

Day Twenty, Wednesday

The smell of unwashed clothes and stale alcohol soon filled the interview room, shot through with fresh, anxious sweat. As a significant suspect, Lockyer had brought Malcolm White into a room with cameras, so that they could capture everything — 'achieve best evidence', or ABE. Lucy's father sat on the edge of his seat, his thin body hunched over the table. He looked down a lot, giving Lockyer and the video feed a view of the top of his head. Iron grey hair, cut into no particular shape, dark with grease and sparse across the crown. His legal counsel, called in on his behalf, sat patiently while Lockyer started the recording and they each introduced themselves.

'Mr White, have you ever been to a house called Longacres, in the village of Stoke Lavington?' Lockyer asked.

Malcolm's eyes darted from his solicitor to Lockyer and back again. 'No,' he said. His hands were shaking. Lockyer couldn't tell if it was nerves or alcohol withdrawal.

'Longacres is the residence of Professor Roland Ferris. Have you ever met Professor Ferris?'

'What? No.'

'But you know who he is, don't you, Mr White?' Broad said. 'For the recording, please,' she added, when he nodded.

'Yes. I mean, if . . . if it's the same Ferris you're on about.'

'The Ferris you know was questioned during the investigation into your daughter's death in 1988.'

'Yes. Is it him you're asking about? What's happened to him? Have you caught him?'

'That is the Roland Ferris we're asking about, yes,' Lockyer said. 'Have you ever met him, or his son, Mr Harry Ferris?'

'No. No, I've never met him.'

'Which one?'

'Either of them. Ferrises.'

Lockyer put a photograph of the Desireless tape in front of Malcolm and he looked down at it, head unsteady on his scrawny neck. Then he looked up, bewildered. 'I am now showing Mr White a photograph of item thirteen,' Lockyer said. 'Do you recognize this item, Mr White?'

White looked at Broad, then back at Lockyer. 'Yes,' he said. 'It's a tape. Like a music tape.'

'Do you recognize this particular tape?'

'What? No . . . I don't know.' He picked up the photo, held it closer to his face and peered at it again, screwing up his eyes. 'Didn't bring my glasses.' The picture trembled in his grasp. 'It's a tape. They all look the same.'

'The tape is a music cassette, dating from 1988, of a single called "Voyage, Voyage" by the band Desireless,' Broad said. 'Does that mean anything to you?'

'Mean anything?' Malcolm shook his head. 'No. I mean, I remember that song – Christ, I remember it. The girls loved it. Lucy and her pal, Vicky too. Bloody *obsessed*. They drove us nuts with it, Angie and me. Playing it over and over, making up dance routines we had to sit through five times a day. Danny got so fed up hearing it he pretty much lived with the neighbours for a fortnight.'

'Your daughter Lucy had this cassette?'

'Well, I don't know. Might have been on an LP that they had it. You know, vinyl. Our big stereo in the front room was a record player. We didn't have a CD player back then, I don't think. Did we? When did CDs start?' He looked at his counsel, and at Lockyer, but nobody answered.

'Can you explain how this cassette, of your daughter's favourite song, with your fingerprints on it, came to be on the body of a murder victim at Longacres, the home of Roland Ferris?'

'What? *My* fingerprints?'

Again, Malcolm peered at each of them in turn. His confusion seemed genuine, but that didn't necessarily mean a thing. His jaw hung slack. He looked stunned. Lockyer wondered what effect so many years of drinking had had on his mind.

'The cassette had multiple fingerprints on it, but they'd been rubbed, making them useless for comparison with the database. As though somebody had attempted to clean it. However, whoever cleaned it was in a hurry, or wasn't thorough for some other reason, and a useable partial print has now been found,' Broad said. 'It matches a thumbprint taken from you when you were arrested for driving under the influence of alcohol in 2012.'

Seven years after the murder at Longacres, so the original investigation wouldn't have found a match on the system, even if they'd found the print. There was a pause. 'Can you explain how this tape came to be found on the body of Michael Brown?' Broad asked.

'What? Who the hell is Michael Brown?'

Broad brought out Mickey's prison mugshot and laid it on the table in front of Malcolm. 'I am now showing Mr White a photograph of Michael Brown.'

'What – and this bloke's been murdered?' Malcolm's forehead laddered. Lockyer noticed dark circles blooming in his armpits. The smell of anxious sweat got stronger. 'I've never seen him before! It wasn't me. I don't even know who this is – and I don't know Ferris, either!' He slid the picture away, and Lockyer noticed the way he held it down with the fingers of one hand. As though to hide Mickey's face. Malcolm cupped his other hand across his open mouth.

'So you can offer no explanation for how this tape, with your prints on it, came to be on Michael Brown's person?'

'No! I don't know! I've got rid of loads of stuff over the years. Done some car boots, you know, trying to raise a bit of cash.'

'At the time he was killed, Michael Brown was thought to be Harry Ferris, the son of Roland Ferris,' Lockyer said.

'Thought to be him? What do you mean, *thought* to be?'

'Professor Ferris believed that Michael Brown was in fact his son, Harry. Mr Brown did not correct him in this belief.'

'Didn't Ferris know the difference?'

'Harry had been away for a very long time. Since he was a boy.' Lockyer waited, but so did Malcolm. His watery eyes now shifted restlessly. Lockyer could read nothing in them except the desire to be elsewhere. At the bottom of a bottle, most probably. 'Do you believe Roland Ferris was responsible for your daughter's death?'

'The police never caught the guy who did it,' Malcolm said. 'Never found him. Said there were *hundreds* of classic cars in the area that weekend, and they couldn't trace them all.'

'But Roland Ferris was a suspect. You told me you'd overheard an officer say that.'

'He had an alibi, and he didn't have the right car. So they changed their minds.'

'But did *you*, Mr White?' Lockyer stared at the man. 'It clearly stuck in your mind, that name – Ferris. You remembered it at once when we spoke to you the other day. You're an alcoholic, aren't you, Mr White?'

'It's not a crime.'

'No, it's not. But it can lead to criminal acts. Driving when drunk, for one thing. Violent and unpredictable behaviour being another. Professor Ferris is quite a well-known historian. It probably wouldn't have been too hard to track him down, by word of mouth if nothing else – especially with him being a restorer of old cars as well. Or perhaps you overheard his address at the same time you overheard his name. Or looked at paperwork you weren't supposed to look at.'

'I've got no idea what you're on about.' Malcolm's voice shook.

'Would you like to punish the man who killed Lucy, Mr White?'

'I – I think he should be punished, yes. Shouldn't someone be punished, when they run over a little girl and don't even *stop*?'

'Yes. I think they should. And the justice system let you down, didn't it? It let Lucy down.'

'Yes,' Malcolm said brokenly. He rubbed at his eyes, wiping the dampness across his cheeks.

Lockyer imagined what he or his father might have done if the police had let slip the identity of Chris's killer soon after his death, and not arrested them. Would they have just . . . let it go? Or would they have gone after them? There was no way that could have ended well, but he suspected they might have gone after them anyway. Citizen's arrest. A beating, perhaps. Something worse. The thought made his pulse race. The dark, dangerous temptation of it. How would a drunk person, a person half out of their mind, manage to resist?

'So you took matters into your own hands, didn't you, Mr White?' Lockyer continued softly. 'An eye for an eye – or, in this instance, a child for a child. A son for a daughter.'

'What? I—'

'I think you tracked Professor Ferris down. I think you

found out his son Harry was with him, and decided – whether you were sober or not at the time – to make him suffer the way you'd had to suffer. They'd made it easy on you, after all. Harry sleeping out in the barn with no locks on the doors.'

'You left the tape as a message to Lucy,' Broad added. 'Another way of saying sorry.'

'You're . . . what? This is – this is *bollocks*! I've never even *seen* this bloke before! When was he even killed? I hadn't been out of the house for a week until you fetched me here – only to the offy and back. There must be cameras or something – or ask my neighbours! And how am I supposed to have got to this Ferris's house? I haven't driven in two years. I'm still banned – my car's on three wheels! I just . . . I need a drink . . . I can't think . . .'

'My client needs to take a break,' the solicitor said.

'Interview suspended.'

Lockyer granted the break as much to get some fresh air as anything else. The atmosphere in the interview room had grown fetid and overloaded; it felt thick in his lungs, and was making his head ache. He walked out of the front entrance and stood in the sifting drizzle, feeling the cold and damp revive him. He was angry, and knew it wasn't Malcolm White's fault. It was his own inability to *see*. And it was the gaping holes in their case against White. The CPS would never proceed with a single fingerprint on a tape that Mickey might have picked up at a car-boot sale at any point between 1988 and 2005.

Broad came and found him. 'Want to get back in there,

Guv? See if we can't wear him down? I reckon if he has to go without a drink for much longer we could get him to 'fess up to all sorts of things,' she said cheerily. 'Sorry,' she added, when the joke fell flat.

'What do you think of him?'

'He's doing a good impression of someone who hasn't got a clue. Like assuming the murder must be recent for us to have brought him in. I was waiting for him to mysteriously know it happened in 2005.'

'Me too. Clever not to slip up there.'

'I'm not sure how capable of clever he is any more,' Broad said.

'Me neither.' Lockyer squinted up at the sky. 'But he's got a better motive than anyone else we've found.' He looked down at her. 'Don't you think?'

'Yes.' She sounded guarded. 'But I still think he'd've been more likely to just go for Ferris, rather than Harry. Especially if we're going for the drunken-impulse theory. Killing Harry instead . . . Isn't that more calculated?'

'It is.'

'Plus why suddenly go after Ferris, seventeen years after the hit-and-run? And he's right – the investigation *had* ruled Ferris out for Lucy. Checked all his cars, checked his alibi.' She spread her hands. 'Wouldn't he have come after him straight away, in 1988, if he was going to?'

'I don't know. We don't really know the man. We don't know how damaged he is. Perhaps it took seventeen years for him to realize the full implications of what Ferris had done: not just taken Lucy, but the other two kids as well, and his wife. Things like that fester. You said it yourself, strong emotions often manifest as anger. Perhaps he just hit breaking point. Got desperate to take action of some kind – any kind. And Ferris's name was all he had.'

'Maybe, Guv.'

Broad still didn't sound convinced, and Lockyer wasn't sure he was, either. There didn't seem to be any anger in Malcolm White. Only despair. He wondered whether his own anger – quieter now than it had been – had been the only thing saving him from the same despair, in the years after Chris died.

'How the hell else did that tape get onto Mickey's body?' he said.

'I don't know. Couldn't Mickey have just picked it up somewhere?'

'With White's prints still on it?'

'It's unlikely. But if it'd been sitting in a box of junk, it's possible.'

'I don't believe it.' The drizzle was chilling Lockyer's shoulders and face. Broad was hunched against it, hands in her pockets. 'And why *would* White be so sure it was Ferris that hit Lucy?' Lockyer murmured, thinking out loud. 'Just because the original investigation paid Ferris so much attention? Or could he have found out something more?'

He thought of the Rolls-Royce Silver Wraith that Roland Ferris had driven down to Blandford that day and sold to the American collector. Black and cherry red. He thought of the picture he'd seen in the framed montage in the hallway at Longacres, of that same car. Helen Ferris leaning on it, laughing, a young Harry Ferris at the wheel, hardly tall enough to see over the dashboard. Lockyer shut his eyes, picturing it. There'd been pink blossom on a cherry tree in the background: the photo had been taken in late spring, under a high, blue sky.

'Come on.'

'Where are we going?' Broad asked, hurrying alongside him.

'Back to Longacres. I want to talk to the professor.'

'But what about Mr White?'

'We've got him till tomorrow. He can wait.'

'Shouldn't I let his brief know we're done for today?'

'Until this afternoon, at least. Do it quickly.'

Paul Rifkin had a go at refusing to let them in. He stood with his shoulder in the gap between the door and the frame, face set, chest puffed.

'With all due respect, Inspector, you're taking the piss now. And don't tell me it's a murder inquiry because I know that. Everybody in the whole bloody county knows that.'

'Nevertheless, that's exactly what it is. And one in which you are still a person of interest, Mr Rifkin.'

'A pointless inquiry into a murder that was solved fourteen years ago, is what it is.'

'We would like to speak to Professor Ferris again.'

'It's not convenient.'

Lockyer was unapologetic. 'Well, we could arrest both of you, and charge you with obstruction.'

'Seriously?' Paul sounded disgusted, but moments later he stood back and let them in. Lockyer felt relief wash through him. He wanted to look at the photo again, and didn't want to wait for a search warrant. 'Wait down here while I go and ask if he'll see you.'

'I'd like to ask Harry a few more questions as well.'

'He went up to London first thing. Back later this evening.'

As soon as Paul was out of sight, Lockyer walked a little way down the hall.

'What is it, Guv?' Broad asked quietly.

'Something here . . .' He was studying the picture of Helen and Harry, the Silver Wraith; Broad leant in alongside him. 'Harry must be about twelve there. Twelve, about to turn thirteen. It's 1988 and the car's finished – that must be why they took the picture. Harry said that Roland had spent a whole year restoring it.'

'Okay. So what?'

Lockyer searched the picture. Up close it was grainy, the colours faded but still discernible. The black and red car; Helen's striped blue dress; the pink cherry blossoms; the sun bringing out the brown in Harry's dark hair . . .

'There.' He put his fingertip to the glass, distracted, momentarily, by Tor Garvich's description of Hedy hovering with her duster. In the background, the stable doors were wide open and the bonnets of two other cars were visible in a shaft of sunshine. One a creamy white, the other green. Dark, racing green.

'Oh, my God,' Broad said.

Roland Ferris didn't look at all surprised to see them

again, and neither was he particularly angry about it. What had Serena Godwin said of her brother? *A man in his position has no need to fear the consequences of anything.*

'Inspector Lockyer,' he said evenly. 'What wild theories have you come up with overnight? I'm all ears.'

'We've arrested Malcolm White. Lucy's father.'

'Have you? What for?'

'For the murder of Michael Brown.'

'I see,' said the old man, with the patience one might use with a child. 'And what makes you think he may have done that?'

'The fact that his fingerprints were found here, at the scene. We couldn't identify them in 2005, but techniques have improved. He was arrested in 2012 following a separate incident, so we've been able to make the match now.'

This seemed to shake Ferris. He stared at them in silence. 'Good Lord,' he said eventually.

'And the fact that he had a strong motive, since it was you who ran down and killed his eight-year-old daughter.'

'No. It was not.'

'That photo of Helen and Harry, in the hallway. She's leaning on a black and red car, Harry's at the wheel. Was that the car you took to the rally that day?'

'Yes. That's the one.'

'When was that picture taken?'

'Well, I don't know exactly but earlier that year. Not long before it was sold.'

'In 1988.'

'Yes. Why?'

'I noticed that picture when I first came here a couple of weeks ago, Professor. But I didn't know what I was looking for then. I do now. There's a dark green car parked in the garage behind the Wraith. Looks very much like a match for the colour of the car that hit Lucy.'

Professor Ferris said nothing. His eyes had widened, and his jaw hung slack. He stared at nothing. Into the past, perhaps, into his own memories.

'Bit of an oversight, that. Hanging it on the wall,' Broad said. She glanced at Lockyer. 'Where was that green car when the police came to search your premises, Professor Ferris?'

Still the old man said nothing. He simply lay there, frozen in time. Then he blinked a few times and drew a long, shaky breath.

'You hit Lucy, didn't you, Professor?' Lockyer said. 'The rally, the buyer, that was all cooked up after the event, a hastily constructed alibi. It was one hell of a stroke of luck that somebody at the fair wanted to buy the car – you got a chunk of money, and concrete proof that you'd been there. All you had to do was bully Helen into backing up your story.'

'No.' Roland shook his head.

'What did you do with the car? Did you get rid of it, or hide it somewhere? Or did you simply respray it?'

There was a long silence, then the professor surrendered. 'The latter,' he whispered. 'There was plenty of time. The police took days to come knocking. It's . . . it's still out there now, in the back row of the big barn. It was a complete rebuild, and I hadn't got around to registering it, back then.

The 1950 Jaguar Roadster. It's scarlet now. The bodywork only took the slightest of knocks, didn't even smash a headlight.'

'Well, Lucy White was a skinny kid,' Lockyer said stonily. 'She wouldn't have given your precious Jag much of a bump.'

'Why didn't you stop, Professor?' Broad sounded so disappointed. So angry.

The professor didn't reply.

'Links in a chain,' Lockyer murmured. 'When did you meet Malcolm White? Did he ever come here, to the house? Perhaps to confront you?'

'What?' Roland looked up at last. He seemed to have aged in the past five minutes; his eyes were sunken. 'I've never met the man. He's never been here.'

'Then how was he sure enough of where to find you that he was able to come and kill a man he thought was your son back in 2005?' Broad said.

'I have absolutely no idea.'

'*Think*, Professor. It's important.'

'Why is it important? What does it matter?'

'Because unless we can prove that White knew where you lived, unless we can prove he somehow found out you were responsible for Lucy's death, then Hedy Lambert may well stay in prison for a murder she didn't commit! You remember Hedy, don't you? I understand it'd be convenient to forget about her, but she's been there all this time. Locked up for no reason, because of what *you* did, and the secrets you've been keeping.'

The professor's head dropped again. Lockyer fought to stay calm, fought the urge to shake the man.

'I have no idea how he found this place. How he found me or Harry.' Roland looked up, eyes bright with tears now. 'Are you saying that this is why that man was killed? You're sure of it? To avenge that poor child?'

'It seems almost certain.'

'Dear God,' he whispered. 'Be sure your sin will find you out.'

'But it didn't find *you* out, did it, sir? It found Mickey Brown and Hedy Lambert.' Broad's voice was tight with emotion. 'Two more innocent people. How many lives did you ruin that day, Professor?' She took a deep breath. 'Why didn't you just *stop*? If you'd stopped, she'd have survived.'

The professor made a wordless sound.

'I wonder how Malcolm White felt when he realized he'd killed the wrong man,' Lockyer said. 'Perhaps it's a good thing we have him in custody, now Harry's come back for real. Though I don't think he'd do anything. If he ever had fire in his belly, he doused it long ago.'

'He's a drunk?' Roland said.

'Has been for years, although I suspect it's got worse with time. He blames himself for his daughter's death, you see. He didn't drive to pick her up that morning because he'd been drinking. So that's his big if-only. If only he hadn't had those beers. If only he'd gone to fetch her. I imagine it's been agony for him.' Lockyer was well aware that *if-onlys* could be torture.

'And the mother?'

'We're not in touch with her yet. Neither's Malcolm White. She left him, took the other kids, changed her name. To try to distance herself from her grief, I imagine, but probably because she blamed him too. She started a whole new life – or tried to. You never really get over a loved one's death, though, do you? Malcolm hasn't seen any of them for years. He lost his whole family that day.'

'That's terrible,' Roland mumbled. 'Abominable.'

'Abominable. That's a good word,' Broad said.

'We'll be back later to record a full statement from you,' Lockyer told him. 'I suggest you bend your remarkable mind to how White found you. And found you out.'

He opened the door, but paused on the threshold.

'Guv?' Broad said.

It wasn't my fault. That was what Ferris had always said to Hedy.

He turned. 'What was it you said to me, Professor? That some things about a person should only be known by their loved ones, people who won't judge them?'

Professor Ferris's mouth worked silently, as though he were searching for the right words.

'Your *wife* was driving that car, wasn't she, Professor? *Helen* hit Lucy that day. *Helen* failed to stop. And the guilt made her take her own life, two years to the day after it happened.'

'Yes, damn you.' The old man's eyes filled again. 'Poor Helen! My poor, dear darling ... She didn't like to drive, and she wasn't insured for any of the classics. She certainly shouldn't have been out in the Jaguar – it isn't easy to handle. But it was Harry's favourite. The one that looked most like a racing car. She took him out in it for a birthday treat, to cheer him up, because I'd reneged on my promise to spend the day with them. I'd left them.'

'You mean—'

'Yes. My son was with her at the time. Harry was in the car when Lucy was killed.'

Roland broke down then. His thin shoulders shook with grief. 'I did take the Wraith down to Dorset that day,' he said at length. 'And I did leave first thing in the morning. There was nothing "cooked up" about my alibi. But when I got back in the afternoon, I found . . . Poor, poor Helen. She was distraught, hysterical. She'd simply panicked, you see. After she hit the child she panicked, and drove on. Harry was in a state of shock – they both were. But I must share the blame. She wanted to go to the police but I wouldn't let her. I didn't see how it would improve matters. I was a thoughtless father and an unreliable husband, and it was *my* behaviour that had put them there, in the wrong place at the wrong time. So I must share the blame, but I will not shoulder it all.' He wiped his face with a cotton handkerchief. 'Because I *would* have stopped, Constable Broad,' he said. 'Had I been there, I would have stopped for poor Lucy.'

'We'll need your son to corroborate your story, Professor,' Lockyer said.

Roland nodded. 'But please let me talk to him first. We . . . we swore we would never speak of it. Never again. And we haven't, in over thirty years. Let me prepare him, at least. He loved his mother so very much.'

'All right,' Lockyer said. 'Please ask him to remain here at Longacres when he gets back from London. We'll come over tomorrow.'

'Poor Helen ... poor Helen ... She couldn't stand it. The guilt, you see? Like a sickness. That's how she described it in her letter. A sickness that was devouring her ...' The old man's voice faded into silence.

'So she did leave a note,' Lockyer said. 'May I see it?'

'I – I destroyed it. Not straight away, I couldn't bear to. She ... Even after everything, she had some tender words for me. Words of love. She left it on my desk, for my eyes only. I kept it for a number of years, but then I destroyed it. It was evidence, you see.'

'That's a pity. As you say, it was evidence.'

'Will I be charged? With whatever I became, back in 1988 – an accomplice after the crime, or some such?'

'I have no idea, Professor. Given the time that has passed, and your medical condition, I doubt it. But if I were Lucy's family, I'd certainly argue the other way.'

The old man stared bleakly at Lockyer. 'As would I.'

That evening Lockyer couldn't settle to work on the house, or to food or a book. That same unpleasant surge of emotion he'd felt when he was on the phone to Hedy was still with him. It came and went in waves, rising suddenly, then fading, but never quite leaving him. Chains of events ... *A chain of events that leads to a certain point*, was how Hedy had described life. *Our choices aren't really choices.* She wasn't talking about fate, but the inexorable effect of other people's actions on our own.

He thought about Kevin. About the pernicious influence of his upbringing and, most of all, his father. Any day now Lockyer expected to hear, from Kevin or via the police grapevine, that he was in trouble. Had been caught in possession of drugs or stolen goods – whatever it was his father had got involved with from inside prison. It looked to Lockyer like a simple case of choosing not to get involved, but he doubted Kevin saw it that way. He doubted it felt like much of a choice to him.

He thought about Malcolm White, already on the slippery slope before he lost Lucy, and then everything else. What choices had he had? Perhaps a different person would never have touched another drop. Perhaps a different person would have moved forward, started again, looked for a way to forgive themselves. Thrown themselves into a career in grief or substance abuse counselling instead. But not Malcolm. He was not that person. And if drink and devastation had led him to kill, had he really had a choice?

Suddenly Lockyer saw his own father's collapse, not a world away from Malcolm's but unfolding in slower motion. It had taken twenty years, but it was happening. All that grief, all that helplessness. John, a shadow of his former self, standing alone in a field. And Malcolm, huddled miserably in a cell, trembling from withdrawal and long-term neurological damage. Both were broken men, but neither was a murderer. Lockyer knew it in his gut.

So why couldn't he find that same certainty about Hedy? *She isn't the killing type*, Cass Baker had said. Definitively, adamantly. Yet he had been reduced to asking her – begging her: *Are you telling me the truth?* He *still* didn't know his own thoughts, his own feelings.

He sat down with his notes. Everyone they had spoken to, everything he'd heard and seen and read. He went through Lucy's case file again, with that same sense of having seen something without realizing its significance. One lie didn't mean that everything a person said was lies. A lie could be so deeply buried in the truth that it was all but impossible to distinguish. He found what he thought he was looking for, and did a quick calculation in his head.

His muscles felt tight. He was no longer shocked by the list of things the original investigation had failed to pick up on. Clenching his teeth, he pulled the photo of Lucy from her file. The one the newspaper had cropped. Lucy standing next to the other girl he'd barely glanced at before, gangly, brown-haired. The 'little friend' Lucy went riding with. Now he stared hard at that other girl, searching her face. Stared until his eyes ached. He hurriedly flicked through the typescripts of his 2005 interviews with Hedy, desperate to find the one he was looking for, shamed again by the memory of how proud he'd been that he was the only one she'd talk to. How important he'd felt, how like a fully fledged detective.

DI LOCKYER: *Did you never have any doubts at all about Aaron Fletcher? Not even when he never actually put any money into the joint account himself? That seems very trusting.*

RESPONSE: *I was very trusting. Too trusting.*

DI LOCKYER: *Do you think he singled you out specifically, for that reason?*

RESPONSE: *I don't know. I suppose ... I suppose if you're going to do that to a person – con them like that – you'd have to think you could do it to them. That you could take them in, I mean.*

DI LOCKYER: *So it was random bad luck that it was you?*

RESPONSE: *I suppose so. Although he did always go on about how lucky I was. He grew up in children's homes. I don't think he had a good childhood at all. And he would go on about how lucky I was to have had, you know, a conventional, stable upbringing. A happy childhood. He got that into his head about me, maybe because I got on so well with my mum and my stepdad. But there were shit times, too, you know. I had a sister who died when I was really little. I lost my best friend, and I'm not in touch with my real father. But Aaron just ... glossed over that.*

DI LOCKYER: *Do you think it was revenge, then? For the childhood he'd been denied?*

RESPONSE: *I think it was something he told himself, to justify what he was doing. Make himself feel okay about it. Or perhaps to reassure himself that I'd be fine after he left, since I had my mum. But I don't know.*

Lockyer dropped the transcript and lurched to his feet, feeling as if his insides were filling with concrete. Just as Hedy had described it. The realization that he'd been played by an expert. He ran his hands through his hair, gripped his skull, then yanked on his boots and left the house, letting the door slam behind him.

He walked, God knew where. Uphill, under spreading branches silhouetted by a pallid half-moon. He slipped through banks of their rotting leaves, stumbled across the rutted ground. There was frost in the air, and Lockyer felt icy inside. Was it a lie buried in so much truth that it went unnoticed, or a truth buried in so many lies that it was swept away by them? *The cat there was called Janus, did you know that?* Tor Garvich had said. *After the two-faced Roman god. I remember thinking that was like* her – Hedy Lambert. *Two-faced. One half barely alive, the other half a killer.*

He thought of Hedy in those first few days after the murder and her arrest, when she'd been all but mute. Who knew what her thoughts had been? Frantic, horrified, shut down by shock ... or quietly scheming? Who would ever know? Had she been working out that she'd need an ally – a young detective with whom she sensed a connection? *I suppose if you're going to do that to a person – con them like that – you'd have to think you* could *do it to them* ... He thought of the way her voice had flattened, and turned opaque, when they'd spoken on the phone two days ago about vengeance. About an accident that had happened. A tragedy.

Lockyer walked, and kept on walking. His boots grew heavy with wet mud; his sleeves and trousers snagged on brambles. At one point he was beneath beech trees, feet scrunching through the deep carpet of their fallen leaves. He would walk all night if that was what it took, thinking, trying to find a way to disprove himself. There were questions he could ask, of Malcolm White and Roland Ferris. There were things he could check. One of them might give him what he wanted: a way to make himself wrong about Hedy. Because he was in love with her. He realized it now, and that he might have been in love with her from the first day he'd met her. And the feeling that kept rising up, and threatening to choke him, was fear.

17

Day Twenty-one, Thursday

The expression on Broad's face when she arrived the next morning told Lockyer that he looked as bad as he felt. He was wearing yesterday's shirt, and had mud splashed up his trouser legs from the careless way he'd trudged out to his car in the dark before sunrise. His eyes felt dry, his head oddly hollow. He felt robbed. Like something precious had been taken from him.

'You all right, Guv?' Broad said.

He needed to check something from the first investigation. Which had come first? Them telling Hedy that the victim wasn't Harry, or her saying she'd known as much. And when exactly had Roland Ferris destroyed his wife's suicide letter? Before Hedy had begun working for him, or afterwards?

'Why get in touch with me again?' he burst out. 'Why tell me about Harry Ferris being home, and get me to reinvestigate?'

Broad tipped her head. 'We're talking about Hedy Lambert?'

'She must have known it was a risk. That we might find out about everything. So perhaps . . . she wanted us to.'

'You're going to have to fill me in, Guv.'

Lockyer took a deep breath. His ribs felt heavy. 'Horses, Gem. Horses all along. No bloody zebras after all.'

'You think she did it?'

'But not for any of the reasons I thought.'

'Why then?'

'I think she was Lucy White's best friend.'

He held out the photo of the two girls, and Broad frowned as she studied it. The second little girl, with brown hair and a narrow face. Long nose, grey eyes. Hedy's eyes.

'Shit . . .' she breathed.

She listened while Lockyer explained his thinking, and he was grateful she wasn't the kind of person ever to say *I told you so*.

'Then it *is* strange she got in touch with you again,' was all she said, when he finished. 'Unless she thought you might find out enough to get her a retrial, but not enough to re-convict her. Clearly, she wants out. Perhaps she wants to get to Harry, or Roland, while she still can. Get the right person this time?'

'Yes. She was always really keen to hear about Harry. Whether I'd met him, where he'd been all this time . . . And she wouldn't tell me over the phone that he was back. Made me go in and see her, that first time. Like she was . . .'

'Making sure she still had you on side?' Broad's expression was sympathetic.

Lockyer paused. 'Maybe she just wanted the world to know about Lucy.'

'Maybe.'

'Or I could be wrong. Couldn't I?' It sounded very much like an appeal.

'Well, there are certain things we can check easily enough. And we can talk to Malcolm White again, while we've still got him.'

'Yes.' Lockyer stood. 'Get them to bring him up, see if he wants his brief.'

Malcolm White nodded groggily when they asked if he wanted a solicitor. They sat him in the interview room to wait, his wasted body shuddering, head bobbing on his neck. Broad took pity on him and fetched him a cup of tea and a bacon roll. The three of them sat while he ate it and took a shaky gulp of the tea.

'I need a drink. A proper drink,' Malcolm said weakly. 'It's . . . dangerous to just go cold turkey on it, after so long. I could get ill.'

'You are ill, Mr White. And the sooner we can get to the bottom of all this, the sooner you can go,' Lockyer said.

'You're not allowed to question me till the lawyer gets here,' he said. 'Right?'

'We're not questioning you, Mr White, we're just talking.'

'Not about this murder again . . . Honestly, I don't know the first thing about it.'

'No. I want to talk about Lucy's friend. The one in this picture.'

Lockyer slid the photo across the table, and behind his ribs his heart was thudding. Malcolm picked up the picture, struggled to focus his eyes. He looked at it for a long time, then ran his thumb gently across his daughter's sunlit face. He glanced up at Lockyer.

'You want to talk about Hedy?' he said. 'Why?'

And, just like that, any hope Lockyer had of being wrong vanished.

'When did you last see her?' His words were leaden.

'Christ knows. Donkey's years. She came round a couple of times after it happened . . . I don't know why, exactly. Perhaps she couldn't get it that Lucy was gone. Poor kid. Angie told her to choose something to remember her by, and she went up to her bedroom once or twice but I don't think she took anything.' Malcolm coughed wetly. 'Funny kid. Sweet, but . . . po-faced. She and Lucy were thick as thieves, like they were joined at the bloody hip.'

Lockyer glanced at Broad, whose face showed the same realization as his own. They both guessed what Hedy had taken as a keepsake.

Lockyer waited in a private room as the admin for an impromptu interview was sorted out, pacing impatiently as he watched for Hedy to appear. He hadn't dared let Broad come with him: he felt too exposed, addled, could hardly remember the drive there. And it wasn't an important interview – not in terms of the case. After all, the perpetrator was already serving her time. Every muscle was wound tight as he waited, a churning mass of dread and fury in his gut, in his head. But still that jolt when he saw her, still that urge to drink in the sight of her.

Her face fell when she saw his expression. She approached warily. 'What is it? What's happened?' she said.

Her hair was loose and it swung around her as she sat down; Lockyer caught the scent of it, and it turned his throat dry.

'Hedy ...' He found it hard to speak. Anger simmered inside him, but there was despair as well. Threatening to drown him. 'Hedy, did Mickey really confess to you that he wasn't Harry Ferris?'

'What? Yes.' Her eyes searched his face, trying to decide what was going on. Or trying to see what he knew. 'Yes, he did. Just like I told you.'

'Because I'm pretty sure I told you first. I've checked my notes from 2005, and it seems as though you didn't mention his confession until *after* I'd told you the forensics proved he wasn't Harry.'

'But ... no, that's not right. I don't know. It happened like I told you, several days before he was killed. Five or six days maybe. I mentioned it as soon as we got to it – as soon as you asked me. Matt, what's going on?'

'Inspector Lockyer, please.' Lockyer leafed through the section of transcript he'd brought with him, looking for the snippet he'd noticed, without realizing, back at the start of the reinvestigation. 'You said to me: "He said he wasn't Harry Ferris. He told me his name was Michael." But the victim didn't call himself Michael – he was known as Mickey. Michael was the formal version of his name that the police used.'

'I don't understand. So what?'

'So, surely he would have introduced himself as Mickey, not Michael?'

Hedy was quiet for a while. She watched him, her shoulders set. 'Mickey. Yes. Maybe he did. And I just . . . used the more formal version.'

'Or maybe you got the name from the police – from me – and not from him at all.'

'I got it from him. He told me who he really was.'

'Did you find Helen Ferris's suicide note?'

'What?' Hedy shook her head. 'I don't—'

'You were all over that house. Cleaning, tidying. Searching, maybe? You'd have had ample opportunity to search through Professor Ferris's study, his desk.'

'Search it? For what?'

'For proof. Proof that the Ferrises were responsible for Lucy White's death.' He stared at her and Hedy stared back, eyes widening. In the silence that followed, Lockyer's pulse thumped hard in his ears. He could feel it in the back of his throat. 'Helen's letter would have made it very clear. She ran Lucy down, and Roland helped cover it up.'

'*Lucy?*' Hedy's voice had dropped to a whisper.

Hovering with her duster, like Tor Garvich had said. Ready to clean the fingerprints from the photographs . . . She would have seen the green Jaguar in the background of the picture of the Silver Wraith. Of course she would.

'Did you look for a job there on purpose, Hedy? Did you go and work at Longacres *specifically* to search for evidence so you could find out once and for all?'

'No, I ... I didn't know. *Lucy?* Are you telling me that Professor Ferris's wife killed Lucy White? That the professor knew what had happened, all along? That's ... I can't believe it.' She shook her head.

'Oh, come on, Hedy! The game's up! Am I supposed to believe that it was a coincidence you ended up working there?'

'But it ... it was.' She spread her hands on the table top. Fingers reaching towards him. 'Matt, I didn't ... I didn't know.'

'It's Inspector Lockyer!' he snapped, anger rising. 'Was Aaron the trigger? What he did to you ... He ruined the life you'd managed to rebuild for yourself after the losses of your childhood. Aaron's deception shook the ground right under your feet, didn't it? You couldn't get out of bed for months, you said.'

'Yes. That's right.' Barely a whisper, and still that look of bewilderment on her face. It kindled a flicker of hope that burnt out in an instant.

'It was a serious breakdown. Perhaps I didn't realize just how serious until now. And then you decided to go back to where it had all begun. That's what you told me. Back to the area where you grew up, to start over. Did you think you were putting things right? Malcolm White knew the name Ferris. Did *he* tell you? Or Angie? I know you went round to see them more than once after Lucy's death. Of *course* you wanted to find out if Roland was guilty after all – if he was the first link in the chain of events that left you so *broken*. Broken pieces: that's how you described yourself.'

Hedy shook her head. 'I don't . . . I don't understand.'

'Stop it, Hedy! Just tell me the truth!'

'Tell you what?' She sounded frantic. 'I didn't know any of this – I *swear* I didn't!'

She stared at him, her bottom lip hanging open.

Lockyer slammed the photograph of the two girls onto the table in front of her.

'Lucy White was born in 1980. She was eight at the time she was killed, same as you, Hedy. You were her best friend. You used to have riding lessons with her. You were supposed to go the day she died, but you didn't. Why not?'

'I had to go to the dentist.' Tears welled in Hedy's eyes. 'I was so upset. To miss my lesson, and our Saturday together.'

'The two of you were obsessed with "Voyage, Voyage". But when I asked you about it you didn't ask me *why*. You said you hated it, when really you'd loved it, hadn't you? Spent weeks dancing to it. And you didn't even ask me why I wanted to know, Hedy.'

Hedy stared at him in silence. Lockyer wanted to shake her. Shake the truth out of her.

'I did love that song,' she said eventually. 'But after Lucy died I . . . I *hated* it. She didn't hear the car coming because she had her Walkman on. That's what her mum told me. And I know – I just *know* she'd have been listening to that song!' She drew in a shaky breath. 'You don't know how many times I've wondered . . . if I hadn't gone to the dentist that day, if I'd been with her like normal . . . I made a fuss when Mum told me, but I could have made more of one. Gone after school one day instead.' She shook her head again, slowly. 'If I'd been with her, would she have been in that exact place, at that exact time? I don't think so. And she wouldn't have been listening to her music, either. It could so easily not have happened. I could've prevented it . . .'

She stopped, glassy-eyed, staring into the past. 'I didn't ask why you wanted to know about that song because it made me think of her. Of Lucy. It threw me. I hadn't thought about her in years.'

'Bullshit! You didn't ask because you knew we'd found that song on Mickey's body. You knew because you put it there.'

'What? No, I . . . I—'

'You took it as a keepsake, and you planted it on Mickey when you killed him. And you killed him because you found out the Ferrises had killed Lucy . . . It was a message to her. A token. Something to show you'd finally punished her murderer. But you couldn't let on that you knew the significance of that song because we never went public with it. Only the police knew – the police and the killer.'

He was speaking too quickly, running out of breath. He felt her betrayal deep in his bones. Like a knife that had gone right through him. She had made him believe her – made him believe *in* her.

Mute, stricken, Hedy shook her head.

'You *told* me!' He ground the words out. 'Didn't you? Right back in 2005, you told me the real reason, your real motive for killing Harry Ferris – that you'd lost your best friend, soon after your sister also died. And then you watched me blunder on, oblivious, like an idiot! Trying to work out why you might have done it!'

Hedy shook her head harder. Two teardrops landed on the table.

'And then, when you were certain the Ferrises were to blame, you went for Harry. An eye for an eye. A boy for a girl, a son for a best friend. You'd got fond of Roland Ferris. You'd trusted him. And all that time he'd been hiding the truth. You wanted Roland to feel the pain you'd been feeling all those years. Because I know *exactly* what that pain is like, Hedy! I know it doesn't go away. Did you kill Mickey on impulse, once you'd found proof? And only afterwards realized you'd chosen the wrong weapon – a knife covered with your own fingerprints? Which meant that all you'd have to defend yourself with was a lack of motive . . .'

He dried up for a moment, his throat aching. 'Saying that Mickey had confessed his identity to you, that was the biggest lie of all, wasn't it, Hedy? The crucial one. If you'd known he wasn't Harry, we'd never work out your motive, even if we found out who you really were. After all, you had no connection to Mickey Brown. But you hadn't banked on me.' He lowered his voice, speaking as much to himself as to her. 'You hadn't banked on me, though. Me and my need to find the killer, to deliver justice. To make up for my own . . . shortcomings. Digging up reasons—'

'*Stop*! Stop it! Just shut *up*!' Hedy thumped her hands on the table, hard, making Lockyer jump.

Lockyer looked across at her bleakly. She met his gaze with furious eyes. Wounded eyes. When she spoke, her voice was ragged. 'My dad named me Hedy, after Hedy Lamarr, because he was obsessed with the golden age of cinema. My sister's name was Katy, after Katharine Hepburn. She died of leukaemia when she was seven, and I was five. It was devastating. My parents split up. Dad moved away and Mum and me stayed in Bottlesford . . .' She had to stop, to swallow. 'Lucy was my best friend, and I loved her. When she died I was so upset . . . It was the final straw. My mother sold the cottage and we moved nearer Swindon to be close to my grandparents and make a fresh start. But that was where it ended. Everything else you just said, *none* of it is true. None of it!'

'I don't believe you.'

'It's the *truth*!' Hedy cried.

'It's all just a coincidence?' His tone was acid.

'Yes! They do happen! I had *no* idea that the Ferrises had anything to do with Lucy's death. None whatsoever. And I did love her, but it's not *her* I've thought about all these years. It's my sister.' Hedy rubbed viciously at her eyes. 'A friend is one thing, but a sister is another. I *idolized* Katy. When she died, I felt like I'd lost a piece of myself. And it's always felt like that, ever since. Like something's missing. When you asked me about that bloody song it was the first time I'd thought about Lucy in years, and I felt bad about that. But *Katy* was the first link in the chain, not Lucy.'

Lockyer said nothing.

'I was still just a kid when Lucy died,' Hedy went on. 'I knew nothing about the investigation, or whether they'd caught anyone. My mum shielded me from all that.'

'Maybe when you were little, but you must have been curious about it as you got older. You must have wanted to know.'

'I asked my mum, sure. She told me no one was ever caught. I just . . .' She shrugged anxiously. 'It never occurred to me to try to find out more! If the police hadn't caught the person responsible, how could I ever expect to get anywhere?'

'By going to her parents. By getting the name Ferris, and then a job at Longacres. By digging—'

'*No.*' Her voice shook. 'You . . . you honestly think after what happened with Aaron, after what he did to me, I was in any state to cook up a plan like that? I could barely decide what to wear in the morning!'

'I'm sure it affected you deeply. Made you think about the world differently. Made you act drastically.'

'No. No! I *didn't know*. And I didn't kill Harry – or Mickey! I'm telling you the *truth*. I always have done! I thought you believed me. I thought we were—'

'What? Friends?'

She held his gaze again, eyes gleaming.

'Yes,' she said. 'Friends.'

'Well, we weren't. I'm a fool, and you – you're right where you belong.'

'No, I'm not! I never killed anyone!' Hedy's face twisted with outrage, with desperation. 'Oh, God – I thought you were going to get me out of here! I really did! And now this! *This!*' she shouted, half rising from her chair. Outside the window, the guard paid closer attention. 'I didn't kill him!'

'You were so cold on the phone when we started talking about an accident in the Ferrises' past ... A child being killed. Your tone changed completely. And you were the one who suggested vengeance as a motive,' Lockyer said. 'Why didn't you tell me you knew Lucy White?'

'Why would I? She died over thirty years ago, and you didn't mention her name. I had no idea she was connected to any of this!' She gestured to the files, his notes, then grabbed a fistful of the papers and threw them at him. 'You're seeing things that *aren't there*! So maybe you *are* a bloody fool! You did it before after all – you came up with stories about me, about what I might have done and why. Stories that convinced the jury! But you were wrong before, and you're wrong now!'

'Hedy—'

'You can't really believe this! You *can't*!'

'Hedy, just—'

'I thought ... I really thought you were going to get me out of here.' She collapsed back in her chair, face in her hands, shaking with sobs.

Lockyer watched her in silence.

Then, finally, he left.

If Lockyer had hoped to feel any satisfaction, or righteousness, after talking to Hedy, then he was disappointed. He felt tired, and uncertain. He couldn't stop thinking about her despair at the end – because it had been despair. Slumped in her chair, crying her heart out. Because she'd thought he believed her. And he kept returning to what she'd said about her sister, because it had rung so true. *A friend is one thing, but a sister is another* ... He was all too familiar with that absence, that sense of missing a part of oneself.

In spite of everything, he still wanted to be wrong about her. But he didn't dare let himself hope. *Sibling revelry*. The bond that went beyond love. Love could fade; it could burn out; it could shatter. But the link between siblings was more like something physical – a shared space in the world that could never be filled by anyone else. Chris was the only person he could imagine himself wanting to avenge in that way. *Katy was the first link in the chain, not Lucy*. He thumped his fist hard against the steering wheel, and again, until it hurt. How did she always manage to do this to him? She punched holes in his certainty every time. And coincidences *did* happen. Like Mickey turning up at Longacres on the twelfth of May. Harry's birthday. Or had he known the date, remembered its significance? Had that been what reminded him of Longacres, and sent him there as he fled from Sean Hannington? *That poor little sod's had to run for real.*

Broad was already in an interview with Malcolm White and his brief, going through his official statement. All three looked up as Lockyer burst in, clattering the chair as he sat down.

'Detective Inspector Lockyer has entered the room,' he snapped.

'Guv?' Broad looked worried.

'Mr White, when did you last see either of your other children? Vicky, or Daniel?'

Malcolm looked up, meeting Lockyer's hard gaze with

one wholly empty of hope or expectation. 'The kids?' he said. 'I don't know ... Danny comes by now and then. A couple of times a year. He's got his own business now. Industrial cleaning. Done all right for himself, he has, in spite of having me for a father. Got a couple of kids, but he doesn't bring them. Not that I blame him.'

'And Vicky?' Lockyer said.

'Not seen her in years. I don't know where she lives, even, or what she's up to these days.' He shook his head slowly. 'My little girl.'

'What was she like?' Lockyer asked.

'Like?' Malcolm looked puzzled.

'Yes. When she was little.'

'Like a little girl,' he said sadly. 'A little princess, she was. Lucy was far happier in jeans or her jodhpurs, and being outside. Ponies ... she was obsessed with ponies. Vicky was into all the pink stuff – wouldn't wear anything if it wasn't pink. And she was forever nicking Angie's make-up and plastering it on herself. Playing dress-up, you know. A proper girly girl. She was clever, though. Did well at school.'

'Did she and Lucy get on?'

'Yeah ... I think Lucy got a bit fed up with her sometimes, having to share a room and all that, but, no, they were good. Vicky idolized her, you know? Her big sister. And Lucy was never mean to her, never bullied her.'

Sibling revelry. Katy was the first link in my chain.

'Can you remember *when* it was you saw her, Malcolm?' Lockyer asked.

'Years back. Could be a decade or more ... sometime in

the noughties?' He thought about it. 'Yeah, that's right. I can't tell you what year it was, but Arsenal had just taken the FA Cup from Man U on penalties. It was brutal. She asked me about it – well, commiserated, really. She knew I'd be gutted. And I was.' He looked down, picking at the skin on his fingers. 'I *was* gutted.'

Broad unlocked her phone, did a quick search. She shot Lockyer a significant look, catching up fast, and showed him the screen. '2005,' she said.

'Yeah, could've been,' Malcolm said. 'She looked beautiful. So . . . grown-up.'

'What did she want?' Lockyer asked.

'I don't know. See her old man, I suppose. See if I'd got my shit together. But, then, she'd brought me a bottle, so I guess she knew I wouldn't't've.'

'Did she take anything with her when she went?'

'Take anything? Don't think so. She did go up to their old room. Said she just wanted to see it – it was the first time she'd been back to the house, see, since Angie took her and left. Whenever I saw her and Danny after that it was at a Maccy D's or something.'

'What did she do up there? In her old room?'

'I dunno. I stayed out of it . . . I heard her rustling around a bit. Like she was looking at some of her old things that got left behind. She wasn't up there for long. Didn't like it.'

'You didn't?'

'*She* didn't. She was upset when she came down again. Not crying, but all clenched up, you know? I'd said to her she shouldn't go up there – I'd said it'd only hurt. Lucy was . . .

her hero.' Malcolm took a breath, shut his eyes and turned his face from the memory. 'She should've kept away.'

'But she didn't take anything?'

'Not that I saw.'

'But you wouldn't have seen if it was something small, would you? Something that would fit in a pocket. Or her bag. Like a tape.'

'What's this about? Why you asking about Vicky, anyway?'

'What was she doing for a living, in 2005?'

'I can't remember. She did say. She'd studied . . . It was something clever . . .' His face creased with the effort of remembering. Then he gave up.

'Did she say where she was living?'

'I dunno. She'd changed her name, I remember that.'

'You said before that she took her mother's maiden name after you and Angie divorced.'

'Yeah. Borthwick.'

Broad caught Lockyer's eye, perplexed.

'Borthwick?' he echoed.

'Yeah. Then she changed it again, when Angie remarried. Took *his* name, the new bloke. That was a kick in the teeth, that was. Even after everything.'

'Right. And what was *his* name?'

'Heath.' Malcolm sat up and drummed one finger on the desk, remembering something. 'And it was history she was into. Doing research – a PhD, or something like that.'

Lockyer heard Broad's sharp intake of breath. He sat frozen for a second, trying not to react. Then his head sank into his hands as it washed over him – understanding, relief.

He was suddenly hot, and yanked at his tie to loosen it. He pictured Hedy slumped in her chair, weeping out her anguish. It was unbearable. He looked up at Broad, whose face was alive with the significance of it.

'Tor Heath,' she said.

'Tor, short for Victoria,' Lockyer agreed. 'Vicky White grew up to be Professor Tor Garvich.'

'Who's Professor Garvich?' Malcolm asked, confused.

'Thank you, Mr White. You've been very helpful.'

'Have I? So, what happens next?'

'We'll need to redo this statement, but then you're free to go,' Broad told him. She glanced at Lockyer, who nodded. 'We'll send someone down to go through it with you. Then a squad car'll take you home.'

Malcolm White stared at them in silence, trying to keep up, but Lockyer was already out of the door.

He stopped in the corridor and leant against the wall for a moment.

'Zebras after all, Guv,' Broad said eagerly, as she caught him up.

'Yes. Zebras,' he said, not trusting himself to say anything else.

'You all right, Guv?'

'Hedy, this morning,' he said. His stomach was churning, replaying the scene. That he had believed she was a killer, and told her so. He failed to see how he could ever come back from that. *I thought we were ... friends.* 'I was ... relent-less. Crushed all her hopes.' He shut his eyes for a moment. Broad laid a hand on his arm.

'You had to put it all to her. Get her response.'

'No. I should have waited. Taken you with me. You'd have . . .' He glanced down at her. 'You'd have done a better job of it.'

Broad said nothing, which Lockyer took as tactful agreement. He'd gone there as Matt Lockyer, not as a police officer. He'd gone as any man thinking himself betrayed by a woman, flailing in wounded anger.

'Well,' Broad said, 'it's done now. Did she say something about Garvich? Is that how you made the connection?'

'Not exactly. It was . . . sibling revelry.'

'What?'

'Something my brother used to say. Never mind.'

'Cheer up! You've done it, Guv.' Broad smiled. 'You're about to clear Lambert's name.'

Lockyer nodded, getting a grip on himself. 'We, not me,' he said. 'Come on.'

He straightened, stood away from the wall, and they hurried down to the car.

They still had to prove Garvich's guilt, but surely it was enough. He could still get her out. Garvich's identity, her connection to the Ferrises and Lucy's death, had to be enough to get Hedy a retrial. Only a confession from Garvich was certain to get her conviction overturned, though. The thought was electrifying. 'Fourteen years,' he said, as they pulled out of the station. He glanced at Broad, saw her carefully neutral expression. 'Fourteen years she's been locked up. For nothing.'

'Hang on, Guv,' said Broad, a minute later. They were stationary at a junction: Lockyer had been about to turn towards the main road out of Devizes, west, towards Bristol. 'Didn't Rifkin say Garvich was visiting Professor Ferris today?'

'Shit. Yes.' A thought occurred to him. 'She decided to go when we told her Harry Ferris had come home. When we showed her the photo of him.'

'Do you think she'd go for him again? Try to hurt him?' Broad's eyes widened.

'Yes. I think she might.'

With a lurch, Lockyer swung the car the other way, putting his foot down as Broad switched on the siren and the traffic scattered. 'A "woman's crime",' he muttered. 'And the only person in that house, other than Roland Ferris, who still believed Mickey was Harry.'

'She lied about how she got the job there. And why,' Broad said.

'She did. And Hedy saw her snooping around . . . looking at the photographs. *She* was searching for evidence, and I bet she found it.'

'She had an answer for everything.' Broad sounded embarrassed. She'd liked Tor Garvich, Lockyer knew. But, then, Garvich had made a point of being very likeable. *A proper girly girl.* 'Did Hedy recognize her? She must have met her, back when they were kids.'

Lockyer shook his head. 'No. If she'd realized who Tor was, she'd have said.' Finally, he was certain of that.

*

'Back again, Inspector?' Paul sighed as he opened the door. 'Here to talk to Harry this time?'

Lockyer pushed past him. 'Is Tor Garvich here yet?' he snapped, keeping his voice down.

Rifkin blinked, startled by his intensity. 'Yes, she is. Why?'

'Where?'

'Up with the professor and Harry. Having a coffee and a catch up – hang on!'

Lockyer set off up the stairs, Broad hard on his heels, and they burst into the study without knocking. Lockyer glanced at the bed where Professor Ferris lay, eyes closed, mouth sagging open. Fast asleep, or something more permanent? Harry was by the window, staring out, and Tor Garvich was standing right behind him, her hands hanging loose at her sides. Shoulders high and tense. They both turned at the sound of the door opening, and Lockyer saw her eyes widen. On the desk beside her, well within her reach, was an old-fashioned silver letter-opener. A knife with blunt edges, but a sharp enough point.

'What is this?' Harry demanded, clearly rattled.

'Step away from him, Professor! Now!' Broad said loudly.

Garvich didn't move, and Harry stared down at her, bewildered. She was inches from him: too close. Lockyer stepped forwards and took hold of her wrist.

'Professor Garvich, I am arresting you on suspicion of the murder of Michael Brown, on the twenty-eighth of June 2005. You do not have to say anything, but it may harm your defence if you do not mention when questioned something which you later rely on in court. Anything you do say may be given in evidence.'

'Let go of me!' Garvich snapped. Lockyer dragged her away from Harry and the silver knife, and Broad put herself between them, arms folded.

Furious, Garvich wrenched herself out of Lockyer's grip.

'Don't be ridiculous. Why don't you cuff me? I must be *very* dangerous for you to come thundering in here like *The Sweeney*.'

'I think you came here with the intention of harming Harry Ferris and his father,' Lockyer said.

Garvich said nothing, breathing hard, and in her eyes Lockyer read that he was right. He saw her register her one chance slipping away. Her forehead creased.

'I just . . . wanted to see what he looked like.' She turned to Harry again, eyes raking him hungrily. 'I wanted to see the man who'd killed my sister. And ruined my life.'

'Harry was just a passenger!' Broad said. 'He was only a child at the time – his mother was at the wheel, and she—'

'No. You're wrong about that.' Garvich's voice shook. She kept her eyes on Harry. 'I found Helen's suicide letter.'

'What?' said Harry. 'She didn't leave a note.'

'Oh yes she did, telling your father what *really* happened that day. He kept it hidden, but I found it. She let you drive, didn't she, Harry? Birthday treat, because you were so sad that day. She let you drive, and you lost control. A short distance on a quiet bit of road, but you got excited and went too fast, didn't you? Even though she begged you to pull up. And you hit Lucy.'

Harry Ferris absorbed the words like blows, curving his shoulders against them. Eventually he nodded, abject. Lockyer stared at him, finally seeing the truth. In the photo of the Silver Wraith: little Harry Ferris in the driver's seat, gripping the steering wheel, hardly able to see over the dash. The green Jaguar was the car he'd loved best, the one that looked most like a racing car. Would Helen have been that stupid? That *reckless*? Would any mother? Perhaps so, if they were desperate enough to see their child smile.

'She's right,' Harry said dully.

'And *poor* Helen couldn't handle the guilt. Over Lucy, but over her darling Harry too. The way you changed afterwards . . . the way you went off the rails. She thought it was going to blight your life for ever, and she couldn't cope with that. It was all a "terrible accident", but one that *she* was responsible for. She and the professor. That's what she wrote.' She glared at Professor Ferris, whose deep, even breaths were audible as he slept. 'She let Harry off the hook completely.'

'So Mickey Brown, an innocent man, died because you thought you were avenging your sister,' Lockyer said.

Garvich seemed to gather herself. 'Don't be absurd, Inspector,' she said coldly. 'I didn't kill anybody.'

'Mickey had a son, you know,' Broad said. 'He might have been a bit messed up, but he had a life. A future.'

Lockyer thought he saw Garvich's composure flicker. Just for a second.

'A tragedy,' she murmured. 'But not one I had anything to do with. I went home as usual that day, and my flatmate dropped me off in the morning, as—'

'Yes, you did. But you came back in the night, didn't you? "I didn't drive, back then," you told us. But that doesn't mean you *couldn't* drive. Constable Broad here checked with the DVLA on the way over. You passed your test in 2000, the year you turned eighteen.'

'That was no secret. But I didn't have a car.'

'Your flatmate did. Gaz, with his mobile dog-grooming business.' Lockyer remembered the old pictures on Garvich's Facebook page, one of Gaz leaning on the bonnet of a small white van. 'He had a white van, of the kind seen parked in the village that night.'

'Oh, come off it. That could have been anybody.'

'But it was you,' Lockyer insisted. 'Who else could have put a tape of Lucy's favourite song in Mickey's jacket pocket? We know you got it from your old house when you went to see your father in 2005. Not long after the FA Cup Final, which was at the end of May. So it was after you'd started working here, and before Mickey was killed.'

Again, a flicker of something crossed her face. Some unease or uncertainty.

'It's been puzzling me, that tape,' Lockyer went on. '*Why* the killer would leave something that could potentially lead us to them. But it was because you wanted to lead us to *Lucy*, didn't you, Professor? You wanted the truth to be out, and those responsible to be punished publicly. You wanted it known. But you couldn't do that easily, not without implicating yourself.'

'It's all just words, isn't it, Inspector?' she said, steadily now. 'There's nothing whatsoever to link me to that man's death.'

'There are your father's prints on the tape.'

That hit home. Garvich paled.

'I'm afraid so,' Lockyer said. 'You should have cleaned it better. So, if it wasn't you who left it on Mickey's body, then it must have been your dad. Which would mean it's your dad who's about to be charged with murder. Perhaps you'd like to think about that as we drive back to the station.'

He gestured towards the study's open door. Out on the landing, Paul Rifkin was watching and listening to it all, his expression rapt. Broad stepped closer to Garvich and took her arm, and again Garvich snatched it away.

'There's no need for that,' she said. 'I'm hardly going to make a run for it in these heels, am I?'

'This way, please, Professor,' Broad said, with admirable calm. Garvich crossed slowly to the door. Her hands were flexing, in and out of fists. Her breathing had got faster, and her neck was flushed. Lockyer moved closer to her, sensing a warning.

In the next second Garvich spun back towards Harry. She lunged towards him, raising her arm, but Lockyer caught it in a hard grip before it fell. He held it until she gave up, feeling the shake of her straining muscles, and noticed that she'd been bringing her fist down towards Harry vertically, rather than knuckles first. Not like she'd wanted to punch him, more as though she'd meant to stab him with a knife she'd forgotten to pick up.

'Lucy *drowned*!' she spat at Harry, trembling all over. 'Did you know that? Did they tell you that? Or did you bother to find out when you were older? She *drowned* after you knocked her into that stream.'

Harry stared at her, devastation in his eyes. 'Yes. I know.'

'If you'd stopped she'd have lived! You – you destroyed *everything*!' Garvich's voice was terrible, and so was Harry's.

'I know.'

'He was a child himself, Vicky,' Lockyer said.

'Shut up! That's not my name.'

'Harry?' Roland Ferris spoke weakly from the bed where he lay, all but forgotten. A dying man, watching his only son being torn apart. Harry turned his back on Garvich and went to the bedside. He took his father's hand.

'My children,' Garvich said, once they were in an ABE interview room, and she'd had legal counsel. She looked up at Lockyer in appeal. 'I have to think about them.'

'Professor, I strongly advise you not to say anything,' her counsel reminded her.

'I mean ...' Garvich back-pedalled shakily, '... I mean I need to arrange for them to be collected from school. Looked after until my husband gets home.'

'We've already called your husband,' Lockyer told her. 'Lucky you, to have been free all these years. Free to marry, to have a family and a career. Michael Brown didn't get that. Nor did Hedy Lambert.'

'Oh, I doubt Hedy's noticed the difference,' Garvich said scathingly. 'She was in a prison of her own making as it was. Drab as a dishcloth. Call that living? Because I don't.'

'You can't honestly think it hasn't mattered to her?'

Lockyer said sharply. Broad sent him a warning glance, which he ignored. 'You think she hasn't noticed life passing her by these fourteen years? Don't kid yourself, Professor.'

'*You* seem very bothered by it, Inspector. But then – oh, yes – you were the one who locked her up. I suppose you must be kicking yourself now, if you think you were wrong.'

'I was wrong,' he said slowly. 'Did you recognize her? You must have. There aren't that many Hedys around.'

'Course I did. Even without the name, I'd have known that miserable face of hers anywhere.' Garvich's smile had sharp edges. 'I kept waiting for you to connect her to Lucy, or get her to tell you, but you never did. I couldn't get *near* my own sister for Hedy bloody Lambert, that last year she was alive. Round ours every second of the day, it seemed like.'

'She was Lucy's best friend.'

'She was a leech! Lost her own sister so she latched on to mine, and I was expected to feel *sorry* for her.'

'You didn't like her.'

'No, I didn't. But that's hardly a crime, Inspector.' Garvich folded her arms. 'She didn't recognize me,' she added quietly. 'I kept expecting her to, but she never did.'

'You were younger. You'd changed more.'

'No. It was because she never noticed me. Too obsessed with Lucy. Well, I guess she knows what that feels like now, doesn't she? Being overlooked. And if you ask me, she's right where she belongs. If anyone killed that man because of Lucy, it was her.'

'I don't think so. I don't think anything's as strong as the bond between siblings. She mourned her sister more than she mourned her friend.'

'Maybe. But Hedy's not normal. She never was. It was easy enough for me to find out the truth about what happened. It would have been just as easy for her.'

'I think you were happy to let Hedy go to prison for your crime, and now you're fully prepared to do the same thing to your own father.' Lockyer spoke coldly. 'Hasn't he suffered enough? Or do you think his is a waste of a life as well? A broken alcoholic. Might as well be dead, mightn't he? Or locked up and left to rot.'

Garvich stared at him, eyes furious.

'How did you get into the house when you came back that night?' Lockyer asked.

'No comment.'

Lockyer thought about it. 'Professor Ferris keeps his house keys in that tray on his desk. I wonder how long he's done that. Could be years. People get into habits like that. He had no plans to go out that night, or in the morning. I wonder if you took them when you left, used them to let yourself in and get the knife from the kitchen, then simply dropped them back where you found them the next morning. Before Ferris or anybody else thought to check.'

'*Somebody* could have. The police certainly didn't check – far too busy looking elsewhere.'

'I don't suppose we'd have found your prints on them if we had. Would we?'

'No comment.'

'Shame. If we'd been quicker off the mark we *might* have

found something. If you did as poor a job of cleaning them as you did on that cassette.'

Garvich was quiet for a long while. Lockyer watched her. 'I'm trying to appeal to your conscience, Professor. I think you've got one, somewhere in there – I mean, it's hard to be certain, but I think you have. You're so scathing and dismissive about Hedy Lambert. Calling her a walking laundry pile. Abnormal, someone barely alive. But I think you're trying too hard.'

'I have no idea what you mean.'

'I think you're trying to convince yourself that what you did to Hedy was okay. Because she was a waste of space anyway, and you never liked her, so why not put her in jail, right? Why not let her take the fall for what you did?'

Tor Garvich didn't reply. She stared into the corner of the room with a closed expression.

'Do you know how she ended up working as a housekeeper, and living the way she lived?'

'I know I'm not interested.'

'I'll tell you anyway. She went through university, trained to be a physiotherapist, got a good job, had her own place. She was happy. Then she was targeted by an extremely competent and ruthless conman, who did her out of everything. House, job, every penny. Hedy had a breakdown, and was declared bankrupt. The job at Longacres was her first step towards getting back on her feet. Towards learning to trust people again.'

'Is there a question in there somewhere?'

'There's a question in my mind about whether you feel

any guilt at all about ruining her life for a second time – or third, if you count the losses in her childhood. Because I think you do. I think you *must*. Unless you are actually a sociopath, of course. Well?'

'No comment.' A thinning of Garvich's voice betrayed her tension.

'Did you *deliberately* frame her by wrapping the knife in cling-film, leaving her prints intact? How did you know to do that? Or was it just a fluke? Your prints were on the back door but, then, that was easy enough to explain – you'd been working there for weeks. So perhaps you simply forgot to bring gloves, and had to improvise before you touched the knife. Is that what happened?'

'No comment.'

'You have to think about your kids, you said. But I'm afraid having children doesn't get you off the hook for murder. Neither does having lost a sister in such a tragic, damaging way – and I can't imagine how hard it was having to grow up in the aftermath of something like that. Really, I can't. But not only did you kill an innocent man, you let an inno-cent person lose fourteen years of their life. And now you seem more or less prepared to let your own father live out the remainder of *his* life in prison. So *this* is the person your kids are growing up with as their mother? A selfish, violent person, who wilfully lets others suffer for her actions?'

He stared hard at Garvich, and she stared back, unflinching. But beneath her immaculate make-up, she was pale.

This was what happened, Lockyer realized. This was what happened when the dream came true and you got your revenge. Lives were wrecked. The shockwaves from your act of retribution rippled out, spreading, and ended up drowning things – people – you hadn't even known were there. This was why he should never ever set eyes on the man who'd stabbed Chris. He would step back, if they ever found him. He told himself he would, and hoped to God it was true.

'Why didn't you just tell the police what you'd found out about the accident?' Broad spoke up. 'You could have reported it, and we'd have brought the truth into the public eye. Roland Ferris could have been prosecuted—'

'Seriously?' Her voice rose. 'It took me a matter of weeks to find out the truth about Lucy's death. You'd had well over a decade by then, and what had you achieved? Bugger all. Oh, I know how it goes. The Ferrises are wealthy upstanding members of the community. Couldn't possibly be liars or criminals, could they? And what does it matter if some grubby kid from a dodgy road in Pewsey gets knocked over, right? I expect Roland belonged to the same lodge as your chief constable, did he? Because you lot only gave them the *briefest* of glances.'

'That's not—'

'And Harry? You'd have done *nothing*. You'd have said he was a child, and let him off. But he was thirteen. The age of criminal responsibility in this country is *ten*. He knew it was wrong – you only have to look at him now to see that. He's *always* known it, and yet he's said *nothing*.' Garvich took a moment to get a hold of herself. 'You realize they must have stopped the car to switch drivers before they headed home?' she said. 'So they were out of the car, standing metres from where Lucy was, in the water. Do you think there was a debate? Do you think one of them wanted to go and check, and call an ambulance, and the other said no?'

'Harry might be able to tell you.'

'I was about to ask him when you showed up.'

'That was the part about it you really couldn't bear, wasn't it?' Lockyer said. 'That they left her, and covered it up. That they didn't own up to what they'd done.'

'No comment.'

'They escaped justice. And that's exactly what you did, Vicky.'

'That's not my name!'

'Course it is. Who are you, if you're not Lucy White's vengeful little sister? Vicky White, Tor Garvich. *You're* the one with two faces, not Hedy Lambert. No wonder you remembered that the Ferrises' cat was called Janus. That must have tickled you. And you escaped justice, just like they did. But I bet you've thought about it every day since, just like they have. I bet it's been like a millstone around your neck.'

'No.'

'Professor, I strongly advise—' the solicitor attempted to say.

'No, because, whoever did it, it was *justice*!' she said.

Lockyer shrugged. 'Might have been, of a sort. "Revenge is a kind of wild justice," as Francis Bacon put it.'

'Yes!'

'He goes on to say: "which the more a man's nature runs to, the more ought law to weed it out".'

'Oh? Got a "quote of the day" calendar, have you?'

'And it wasn't Harry Ferris you killed, it was Mickey Brown, and I'm afraid the law doesn't let you off because you killed the wrong man any more than it does because you've got more to lose now than on the night you actually killed him. How did you feel when you heard you'd killed the wrong person?'

'No comment.'

'I expect you felt a bit bad. Shaken up. If you like, I can get Mickey's son and girlfriend to come in, and you can tell them how sorry you are. They live not far away, down in Westbury.'

Garvich looked panicked, and Lockyer nodded.

'It wouldn't be as much fun as dishing out the wild justice, would it?' he said. 'Being on the receiving end of it.'

There was another long silence, which Lockyer was grateful to Broad for not breaking. They sat and watched Garvich. Her expression was mobile now, flying through a series of emotions too quickly to follow. Sorrow, anger, fear, righteousness.

Lockyer took a deep breath. 'Here's the thing,' he said. 'I'm going to charge you anyway. I'm going to keep you here while I talk to the CPS, and I'm going to tell them everything I know. We've sent uniform to your father's house to pick up Lucy's Walkman. Did you think to wipe it down after you took the tape? I expect we'll find your prints on it, to back up our explanation of events. Your *adult* fingerprints, that is. So you'd better call home and let them know you won't be back tonight, possibly not tomorrow night either.

And I'm confident the CPS will come on board, because we *all* know it was you. We all know your father has no idea what had really happened that day, or where to find Ferris, the poor sod.'

He held Garvich's gaze as it wavered. 'The courts take a dim view of people who don't own up. People who drag out a trial, falsely protesting their innocence, people who let others be punished in their place. But if you do own up – especially given the circumstances surrounding Lucy's death – there's a chance of a reduced sentence. A plea of diminished responsibility. You could be out in time to see your kids finish school. Or you can stick to your story, and get a life term. Like Hedy Lambert did.'

Again, he waited. Symmetrical tears welled in Garvich's eyes, stained black with mascara. They left trails down her cheeks. 'Confess, confess . . .' she muttered. She sniffed messily. 'It was such a long time ago. I'm . . . I'm not that person any more.'

Lockyer thought of her standing right behind Harry Ferris, just hours ago, her fingers inches from a silver knife. But he said nothing. There was no way of knowing if she'd have gone through with it a second time.

'The judge might take that into account. But Lucy died seventeen years before you found out about Harry and Helen Ferris. Did that seem like a long time? Something to be forgotten about and let go?'

'No,' she whispered. 'Not at all.'

Lockyer called Eastwood Park direct, rather than leaving a

message and waiting for Hedy to call him back. He stood out in the car park, under the shivering ash trees, kicking at waterlogged leaves on the ground. He wanted to be where nobody could see or even hear him. He felt unbearably tense, almost panicky, like he felt while waiting to hear the jury's decision on a big case. Only worse. This was what he'd wanted, and *not* wanted. He'd proved Hedy innocent, and at the same time proved he was part of a fourteen-year miscarriage of justice.

And now Hedy would be released. Free to do whatever she wanted, go wherever she wanted, and he had no idea what either of those things might be. He had no idea if he would see her again, or what her feelings about him might be now. He had no idea what he wanted them to be. She still left him as rudderless as a leaf caught in eddying water: just hours before he'd found out about Tor Garvich, he'd been convinced of Hedy's guilt. Accused her of being a killer. He felt like an idiot. And he didn't know if she would ever forgive him.

He shut his eyes. Fatigue tugged at his brain. The phone beeped now and then in his ear, as he waited on hold. There was no need to speak to her in person – he could simply inform the CPS, and let it trickle through via official channels instead. He could save himself this particular moment of agony. But perhaps he thought he deserved it.

The line clicked; he heard a rustle. The sound of a door closing.

'Inspector Lockyer?'

Her voice was tight with apprehension. Lockyer opened his eyes.

'Hedy?' he said. 'I'm so sorry.'

She said nothing.

'There's been a development,' he said. And beneath those bland words, his fear gave way to a flare of elation.

18

Day Twenty-five, Monday

Lockyer was finding it hard to concentrate. They'd managed to track down Tor Garvich's mother, Angie, and he'd just left a message on her phone, asking her to call him back. Now he was kneeling on the floor next to Broad's desk – she'd brought Merry in to work again, and the little dog was wagging his whole body as Lockyer scratched his ears and chin. Lockyer jolted upright when he heard footsteps, banging his head on the desk and making the dog flinch, but it was only Broad returning with a tea and a coffee.

He went back to his own desk. They'd had the results from the lab on Kieron Cowley's toothbrush, and Lockyer had already broken it to Kim that Sean Hannington really was the boy's father. There was no match between Kieron and the samples from Mickey's body. Kim had taken the news with a long, sunken silence, followed by a sigh.

'We'll get him for something, Kim,' Lockyer had heard

himself saying, when he shouldn't have. 'And if he's violent towards you, or he threatens—'

'Yeah. You said that already,' she'd said, and rung off.

Now a follow-up email from the Cellmark scientist appeared on his screen, and he clicked it open.

'Something good, Guv?' Broad asked. 'Tell me there's a match on the database.'

'There's a match,' he said. 'You'll never guess, Gem.'

'Looks like good news?'

'The armed robberies in Chippenham, in 1997, the ones we shelved just before we started on Mickey Brown's murder. The saliva sample from the shop counter where the lad got beaten over the head?'

'Seriously?'

'Close familial match,' he said. 'Got the bastard.'

'Bloody brilliant!' Broad burst out, making the dog break cover and come out wagging. She knelt to settle him once more.

'I'll put a report together and send it over to CID,' Lockyer said. 'Finding Hannington might take a while, but as soon as they do . . .'

So some good had come of Kieron giving them a sample, and he was relieved. It almost made up for the fact that Mickey Brown hadn't had a son after all. That he'd died needlessly with nothing to show for his struggles, without leaving any part of himself in this world, and without giving Kim Cowley the means to cut Hannington out of her life, at least until Kieron turned eighteen.

'I've got something else for you as well,' Broad said. Lockyer looked up, and she smiled. 'About Aaron Fletcher.'

'Guv?' Broad said, when she got back after lunch. Her face looked tense, her eyes unblinking. Like she was psyching herself up for something.

'What's up?'

'I know what's said in the pub stays in the pub, and all that . . .'

Lockyer waited.

'I just wanted to . . . It's what you said about Pete. Me and Pete. Him not . . . you know.'

'I shouldn't have said anything. I'm sorry. It was rude, and—'

'No, no, I'm not upset about it. Not . . . Well. The thing is—'

DSU Considine put her head around the door.

'A word, if you're free, Matt.' She folded her arms, eyes sweeping their cramped workspace, the scribbles still on the whiteboard. 'I always did like a long list of suspects up on a board. I'm going to pretend I can't see that creature under your desk, Constable Broad, but my eyesight might be better another day. This isn't doggy daycare.'

'Yes, ma'am. I mean no, ma'am,' Broad said nervously.

Lockyer made to follow Considine, then paused. 'Sorry, Gem, what were you going to say?'

Broad shook her head. 'It's nothing. Forget about it, Guv.'

'You're sure?'

Broad smiled unconvincingly. 'You'd better go. Don't keep the boss waiting.'

In Considine's office, Lockyer pulled up a chair and sat down.

'Well,' she said, 'I've been through your policy book. You've got some pretty ... *big* leaps in there, Matt, I have to say. Intuitive leaps, I suppose we can call them. A bit like guessing at a number in a Sudoku, and hoping that the rest will fall into place. It's a risky way to approach an investigation.'

'I'm not sure that's entirely fair, ma'am.'

'Because things did fall into place?'

'And because I'd have kept trying different numbers until I found the right one.'

'Christ, I know,' she said. 'It's going to be embarrassing, when it breaks. Which will be any day now. The CPS are keen to progress. With Garvich's confession and the new forensics, Lambert'll be out. I'd better make sure my shoes and buttons are polished.'

'I think it presents us in a *good* light, ma'am.'

'Do you really?'

'We made a mistake. We identified it, and we corrected it. No outside influences. No true-crime bloggers or journalists. Just the police, policing ourselves.'

'Hmm.' Considine nodded slowly. 'I suppose that might be the way to sell it. But however you paint it, it was a cock-up. A terrible one.'

'The jury convicted her.'

'We charged her. We put together the case against her.'

'Believe me, I know.'

'We should have looked closer. Looked harder. Not gone for the first obvious suspect.'

'Yes,' Lockyer said again. There was no dodging it. 'But at the time, the forensics backed us one hundred per cent.'

'That's also true. I'll remember that one when the press start laying in – advances in forensic techniques.'

'It might not be that bad, ma'am.'

'It'll be how it is,' she said testily. 'Still. You got the right result, Matt. Well done.'

'Thank you, ma'am.'

'She'll be in line for a hefty payout. But I don't suppose that buys back fourteen years of your life, does it?'

'I doubt it.'

'And you accidentally cleared up three other unsolveds while you were about it. Lucy White, Aaron Fletcher and the Chippenham robberies.'

'Well, not exactly accidentally . . .'

'Yes, all right. Credit where it's due, Matt. Those are the kind of results even people who might have doubted you can't argue with. Keep it up. You and DC Broad seem to make a good team.'

'You've read Roland Ferris's statement? That his wife's suicide letter confessed that *she* was driving the car when it hit Lucy, not Harry. That Tor Garvich misunderstood it somehow.'

'Yes. Tricky one, that.'

'He's lying.'

'I dare say he is. I doubt very much whether Garvich

would have misread something like that. No way to prove it one way or the other, of course, since Roland destroyed the letter. He did destroy it?'

'The search team found nothing. So it would seem so.'

'What does Harry Ferris say?'

'He's coming in tomorrow morning to make a statement.' Lockyer paused. 'He never learnt to drive, you know,' he said. 'Never got a licence, I mean. He takes trains and taxis everywhere.'

'Good job he's a high earner,' Considine said neutrally. 'I suppose we'll know after he's given his statement whether there's anything to take to the CPS. I doubt it'd be in the public interest to prosecute him, even if he insists on confessing.' She shook her head sadly. 'Imagine that, on his thirteenth birthday. What a thing to happen to a child.'

'Damaging,' Lockyer said.

'Catastrophic, I'd say. Still, good work, Matt. Well done.'

'We got lucky with some of it, ma'am.'

'We make our own luck,' Considine said.

Lockyer got up to leave.

'Some of the time,' she qualified, as he reached the door.

At the end of the day, as Lockyer and Broad were leaving, DS Ahuja stood up from her cubicle in the CID suite, threw a Quality Street at each of them, and cleared her throat. Broad dropped her sweet and had to bend down for it, hampered by her backpack with Merry squirming inside.

'Two coppers, three weeks, four solved cases,' Ahuja announced. Other people stood up as well, and there was a scattered, vaguely mocking round of applause. Broad coloured to the roots of her hair, and didn't know where to look. Lockyer, awkwardly pleased, found himself looking at DI Saunders, who sat with his arms folded, not taking part. But perhaps he gave a hint of a smile before he turned back to his screen.

Roland Ferris phoned Lockyer the next morning. He sounded even weaker, even frailer, and had to clear his throat laboriously before he could speak.

'Inspector Lockyer? Good,' he said. 'Harry's just left. He's on his way to you now. I want to ask you . . . I want to *beg* you . . . if he insists on saying he was driving when the girl was struck . . . I want you to . . .' He trailed into silence, as though aware of the impossibility of what he was asking. 'He was just a *child*, you must see that. He's suffered more than enough because of what happened that day – he's suffered more than anyone! Please.'

'Not more than Lucy's parents, I think,' Lockyer murmured. 'Professor Ferris—'

'Arrest me for covering it up, if you want! For leaving them that day when I should have stayed. If a scalp is required then take mine. Poor Helen sacrificed herself, and I'm ready to do the same.'

Lockyer could hear the anguish in the old man's voice, and his effortful breathing – the phlegmy rattle of his lungs. That was new. Hadn't Paul said it was dangerous for him to get ill?

'Professor? Are you all right?' he said.

'No, I am not all right! Foolish thing to ask.'

'Please try not to upset yourself,' Lockyer said. He thought carefully before he carried on. 'Professor, doesn't what's happened to Michael Brown, and Hedy Lambert, and Lucy White ... doesn't it all go to show it's no good trying to bury things like this? They won't stay buried, and lying only makes it worse.'

'Let me do this for my boy, I beg you.' Roland sounded so sad, so desperate. 'I failed him and his mother in so many ways. I've *deserved* to be alone all these years. I know I have. But let me do this one thing for him before I die. Please.'

'It's simply not up to me. It's not my decision to make.'

There was a long pause, filled with the sound of the sick man's breathing. He said nothing more before he rang off.

Lockyer went down to meet Harry Ferris at the enquiry desk. His clothing was as immaculate as ever, but there were dark circles under his eyes and his face was haggard. The anger had gone, and in its place was a kind of bewildered determination. He looked like a man with no idea of what was coming next.

'Mr Ferris. Thanks for coming in,' Lockyer said.

'Shouldn't you have come to pick me up? Arrested me?' A muscle in Harry's right eyelid twitched arrhythmically, on and on.

'No, I don't think so. We're not yet certain who, if any-body, the CPS will want to charge with the unlawful killing of Lucy White.'

'Well, you should arrest me. Charge me. I did it. I was driving the car. I hit her. I didn't have control, and I – I didn't see her.' The confession was delivered in staccato bursts, and at the end of it, Harry swallowed convulsively.

'Let's go and sit down somewhere. Get set up,' Lockyer said. Harry Ferris followed him obediently, head hanging like a child's.

Chains of events. Lockyer thought about the links in the chain, each seemingly innocent, that had led to Lucy's death and so to Mickey's. Helen Ferris's decision to drive the Jaguar that day, her decision to let Harry have a go, on that particular stretch of road, at that hour of that particular Saturday. Her decision – and it must have been hers – not to check on the person they'd hit. Malcolm White's decision to start drinking early that day. Roland Ferris's decision that twenty grand was more important to his family than keeping his word to his son. Mickey Brown's decision to hide out in Roland Ferris's barn, which he remembered from his fractured childhood as a place of safety. Hedy's mother's decision to make her a dental appointment that morning. It could all so easily not have happened, but the decisions had been made, each in the space of a heartbeat, and lives had been shattered.

Lockyer knew he shouldn't say anything, but he couldn't help himself. They were in the corridor, about to go into an ABE room. He stopped and turned to Harry. 'Your father doesn't want you charged with anything. It's his dying wish. He wants to protect you—'

'He can't protect me from something that's already happened.'

'You could let him do this for you. Your mother took her

own life because she felt responsible for what happened, Mr Ferris. And perhaps she *was* responsible, in all the ways that matter. She could have saved Lucy. All she had to do was check on her. Lift her out of the water. Call an ambulance, even if she didn't give her name.'

'She wanted to go to the police. You need to understand that. I heard them arguing about it for days afterwards. But he wouldn't let her. Said she'd be locked up, and we needed her. If he'd let her . . . if he'd let her confess, she might not have killed herself. She might have lived – might still be alive today. And that little girl's family . . . they'd have had some kind of justice.'

'That's why you were so angry with your father?'

'Yes.'

'He'd do anything to make it up to you, Harry,' Lockyer said.

He saw Harry Ferris waver. But then he shook his head.

'No. I need to tell the truth. After all these years of bottling it up. I *need* to.'

Wordlessly, Lockyer opened the interview room door, and they went inside.

It would be Harry's word against Roland's. Roland would say that Harry was lying to protect his mother's memory. Harry would say that Roland was lying to protect *him*. Helen's suicide letter was long gone, and Tor Garvich's recollection of it was fourteen years old, and could hardly be called reliable.

Lockyer doubted very much whether the CPS would take it any further, given Harry's age at the time. But he sat and listened while Harry described every last detail of that morning. How he had pestered and pestered to be allowed to drive the Jaguar; how reluctant Helen was to let him. How he had worn her down. The bright sunshine that day, the deep shade beneath the trees. The way the car had bucked and swerved as he oversteered. That all he remembered seeing of Lucy was a flash of pallid skin, right in front of him, and a flutter of long hair. The clatter as she dropped her bike.

He had no memory of the drive back to Longacres. He remembered nothing else about the day at all, until much later when he heard his parents shouting. Their voices coming up through the floor as he lay in bed, shivering even though the night outside the window was softly warm.

Professor Roland Ferris died at home two days later, from a chest infection; Harry was at his side. *It's a strange thought*, Tor Garvich had said, *that someone you know will soon be just . . . gone.* Lockyer felt that strangeness when he got the news. That all those thoughts and words and memories could just have vanished into thin air. There was a gracious obituary in the *Daily Telegraph*, which he imagined Ferris would have approved of, and at the first reading of his will it transpired that the professor had left Paul Rifkin a generous, if not extravagant, pension. He'd also left the house in France, by the sea near La Rochelle, to Hedy Lambert – much to Serena's disgust. *In case you need a place to go*, he'd written to Hedy. *I'm so very sorry, Hedy. But it's never too late to start afresh.*

Lockyer knew Hedy would be sorry not to have seen

Roland before he died. He wondered if she'd have wanted to go to the funeral, had she been released in time. He'd decided to go himself, but first he had another visit to make: to Angie Heath. Tor Garvich's mother had already spoken to him at length on the phone, describing Tor's troubled teens. How she'd struggled with depression and manic episodes, and got into trouble with drugs and self-destructive behaviour. How she'd been sectioned for a short time after a suicide attempt, and had responded well to medication and psychotherapy. How, since she'd still been a minor at the time, her therapist had shared concerns with Angie about Tor's elaborate revenge fantasies, centring on the person who'd killed her sister and torn her family apart.

Lockyer wanted to hear it in person, and take a full statement. He would get a court order to access Tor's medical records, and track down the therapist who'd treated her. Their testimony would be vital at the trial. He found himself feeling sorry for Garvich, as he made these discoveries: she'd been telling him the truth when she'd said she wasn't that person any more. But she'd still killed an innocent man, and she'd still let someone else take the blame. Perhaps her medical history would help shorten her sentence – it was some consolation.

19

Late February

It was windy and cold the day Hedy Lambert's conviction was overturned on appeal. The press were waiting eagerly on the court steps to capture her first triumphant moments of freedom, but since she didn't want to be photographed the police had arranged to send out a suitable decoy, who was bundled into an unmarked car. Meanwhile, after waiting a good hour, Hedy herself slipped out via the back door.

Lockyer was there to pick her up, as her mother couldn't travel: she'd fallen in the shower and slipped a disc. A couple of Hedy's old friends – Cass Baker included – had also offered to come, offered her sofas to sleep on, but Hedy had turned them all down. She said she wasn't ready yet, and Lockyer thought she meant not ready to slip back into her old life, as though nothing had happened. Not ready to talk about it, laugh about it, analyse it. Answer their questions.

The sight of Hedy walking out of court alone, hair

whipping in the breeze, was somehow shocking to Lockyer. She'd changed out of the suit she'd worn for the verdict, and was carrying a small hold-all, her spare arm wrapped around her ribs against the cold. She didn't have a coat. Her solicitor had bought her some non-prison clothes – jeans that were a size too big, and sat low on her hips, a white shirt and blue jumper. She looked pale in the flat daylight and didn't smile as she approached. If anything, she looked stunned. Frightened. Like the first time he'd met her.

'Okay?' he said. He made no move to touch her, and was carefully neutral in all he said and did. Because he didn't *know*. He just didn't know. 'Ready to go? Car's just over there.'

Hedy pulled some strands of hair out of her eyes. She looked around for a moment, at the laurel hedge and the leafless trees behind it, the handful of gulls wheeling above. Then she followed him, and didn't look back.

She was quiet on the drive west, staring out at the drab scenery as it rushed past on either side of the motorway. There were no signs of spring just yet.

'Have you got clothes in storage? Other things you need to collect?' Lockyer asked her.

'No. Mum gave all my clothes to charity when she moved to Spain,' Hedy said. 'She said they'd be too young for me by the time I got out anyway. I do love her, but she never was especially tactful.' She was quiet for a while. 'She was probably right, though. Who wants to see a middle-aged woman in hipster jeans and handkerchief tops?'

'Thirty-nine is not middle-aged.'

'Not twenty-five either, is it?' Hedy flashed him a rueful smile. 'She wanted to put the rest of my stuff in storage, but I told her to chuck it. I just couldn't imagine . . . There wasn't much, and I couldn't imagine ever wanting or needing any of it again. I think she kept the photos, but that's all.'

'Well,' Lockyer said, not quite able to read her mood, 'it was just stuff, right? Different stuff can be got. Once the compensation comes through . . .'

'Yes.'

'I wanted to say I'm sorry about your sister. Losing her like that, so young. And I'm really sorry for . . . you know . . . getting it so wrong.'

Hedy gave him a long look. He could feel her eyes boring into the side of his face.

'You don't have to talk to me about it,' he said. 'In fact you don't have to tell me anything ever again, if you don't want to.'

'That's true.' She paused. 'But I don't mind. I was only five when Katy died, but I remember her clearly. She used to boss me about but she looked after me too. Smuggled me sweets – and crisps, which I loved but wasn't supposed to have, since I'm allergic to potato. They usually made me throw up and gave me a horrible rash – I wonder now if that was why she gave them to me. But at the time I thought she was the best sister ever.'

'You're allergic to *potato*? I didn't know that.'

'Why on earth would you?'

'No reason, I suppose.'

'My parents divorced after she died. I don't think it was

the only reason, but I think it was the final straw. Dad remarried pretty quickly and started a whole other family.'

'I guess it changes everything. Losing a child.'

'Yes. And losing a sibling. Someone that close to you. Like I said, it leaves a sort of . . . permanent gap. A shadow where they're supposed to be.'

'I know.'

'Yes,' Hedy said. 'You told me you knew what that grief was like.'

'My brother, Christopher. We were grown-up – well, just about. He'd just turned eighteen, I was twenty-one. But still. I'll always feel that gap.'

Hedy looked at him for a moment, as though she might say something else, but then she turned to the window again. Lockyer switched on the radio.

An hour or so later he pulled the car onto the puddled track that led to Westdene Farm. 'Are you all right with dogs?' he asked, as the collies came rushing from the barn, wagging and barking furiously. 'I probably should have checked that first.'

'I love dogs. We used to have them when I was growing up. Shelties.'

Hedy opened the door and the dogs were on her in a flash, paws filthy with mud and worse, bouncing with excitement. Her new jeans were muddied in seconds.

Trudy came out of the house to greet them. 'Down! In!' she ordered the dogs, and they slunk away towards the house. 'Oh, no – look at the mess they've made! I'm terribly sorry, Miss . . . er . . . Lambert.'

'Hedy.' Stiffly, Hedy shook hands with Lockyer's mother. 'Thank you so much for having me.'

'Oh, don't mention it. It's been so long since we had a guest, and I love any excuse to bake. Come in out of this cold.'

It had seemed like the perfect solution. In spite of everything, the farm spoke to Lockyer of home, of safety. Now, looking around, he saw how it might look to an outsider – especially one used to well-ordered, man-made surroundings. The clutter and muck everywhere; the smell of animals; the wet push of the wind; the promise of rain. But Hedy was staring at the wide expanse of Salisbury Plain behind the farmhouse, and her expression was one of naked longing. Lockyer thought of all the time she'd spent locked up and, before that, living her stifled life with Roland Ferris. He wondered how long it'd been since she'd seen the horizon that far away.

'Can I bring in any of your things?' Trudy said, smiling.

'No things,' Lockyer said quickly. 'I thought you might have some bits Hedy could borrow. Toothpaste, you know.'

'Of course.' His mother didn't miss a beat. 'Let's get the kettle on. Then if there's anything you need and we haven't got, we can pop to the Co-op.'

Trudy had given one of the long unused guest rooms a thorough clean, and made up the bed. She'd done her best, but there was no disguising that the candlewick bedspread was decades old, and the curtains were grubby, two inches too short for the window. 'I've been meaning to let them down, but there always seems to be something else that needs doing.'

'It's fine,' Hedy said. Her eyes skimmed the old brown furniture, the framed print on the wall over the bed – of a river running through Scottish moorland – and the matted sheepskin rug to one side of it. Then she looked out of the window. The open grassland of the plain, the horizon now cloaked with charcoal rain clouds. 'It's lovely,' she said.

Lockyer watched from the sidelines, hoping for it to go well without having the first clue what *well* might look like. He felt impatient for something but he didn't know what. They went down and had mugs of tea, buttered scones, and Trudy wasn't in the least bit fazed by Hedy's long silences or her thousand-yard stare. Lockyer had known she wouldn't be, and he loved her for it.

'I imagine this is all very strange,' she said, patting Hedy's arm as she reached for her empty plate. 'But don't you worry about it. Take your time.'

Later John Lockyer came in and nodded at the new arrival. 'You're her, are you?' he said, without rancour or particular interest.

'John, *really*. This is Hedy,' Trudy told him.

'*Samson and Delilah*,' John said. 'Saw it at the pictures when I was a lad.'

'Um, yes.' Hedy glanced at Lockyer, but John had collapsed into a chair and didn't seem to have anything else to say on the subject. 'Any tea left in there?'

'It'll be stewed by now. I'll make a fresh pot.' Trudy stood and reached for it.

So Lockyer watched as his two worlds collided, struck by the strangeness of it. He couldn't relax, felt uncomfortable in his own skin. The only consolation was that Hedy didn't seem distressed. She let Trudy mother her, and answered John's sporadic questions, which came at intervals throughout dinner, and when Lockyer got up to go, she didn't follow him to the door. Trudy came with him, leaving Hedy and John watching the news on TV. The pictures flickered in Hedy's grey eyes, and over her long, immobile face.

'Don't worry about her,' Trudy said, out of their earshot. 'It might take her a while, but she'll get herself sorted. She's a tough cookie, that one.'

'You know all that already, do you?'

'Yes, I do. And try not to study her so closely, Matthew. The last thing she needs is to feel watched.'

'I'm not *studying* her—'

'Of course you are. Goodnight, love. Drive safely.'

Lockyer got a call at lunchtime the following day. He texted Hedy as he left the station to drive back to his parents' farm. A few minutes after he got there, a recovery truck with a Northamptonshire phone number printed down its side also turned into the yard. As it rumbled to a halt the front door of the house opened, and Hedy came out, wrapped in a huge cardigan of Trudy's. She looked from Lockyer to the truck and back again, bewildered. Then, uncertainly, she went closer.

They'd found her Austin Allegro in a garage rented by Aaron Fletcher – or Aaron Shawford, as he was calling himself these days. It'd been given a bad respray, and was now an uneven dark blue rather than the pastel green it had been. But the chassis number confirmed that it was the same car, and the odometer showed that, having got himself to his new location, Aaron had then hardly ever driven it. Too risky, Lockyer supposed, yet he'd kept it rather than selling or dumping it.

The Northants force had searched Aaron's house and found other stolen items, taken from his victims. A child-hood locket, old family photographs. Things calculated to cause the greatest sense of loss. He'd been charged with several counts of theft and was out on police bail. His most recent, and very young, ex-girlfriend had taken out a restraining order against him, as well as lodging a formal complaint of coercive control and attempted fraud by false representation, which was being investigated. Aaron's days of carefree existence were over.

Hedy ran her fingers along the side of the car.

'Hedy Lambert? Sign here,' the driver said, handing her the keys. Once she'd signed he set about unloading the car.

'Are you sure it's mine? After all this time?' Hedy said.

'Yes. I'm sure,' Lockyer said. 'Aaron has been arrested. He's facing various charges.'

'He was doing it to someone else?'

'There have been other victims since you, yes. But I doubt there'll be any more from now on.'

'Good. That's good.' She swallowed. 'Does he know any-thing about me? About where I am, or what happened?'

'Not from us.'

She turned back to the car. 'Awful paint job,' she said quietly.

'You can soon get that sorted.'

'Yes.'

Lockyer was a bit deflated. He'd expected her to be more excited. Happier. But she wore a distracted frown, as though she were trying to work something out in her head. The roar of the truck's engine filled the yard, then faded as it bounced away down the track, turned onto the road, and was gone. Watery sunshine glanced from the car's front bumper and chrome trim. Hedy unlocked it and climbed into the driver's seat. She took hold of the odd-shaped quartic steering wheel, flexing her hands, and pushed her foot down on the clutch, causing it to squeak loudly. Only then did she smile. A wide, joyful smile that Lockyer felt right through him.

'Still smells the same,' she said. 'I was worried he'd've ruined it somehow, but . . .'

'Doesn't seem like he drove it much at all.'

'So why take it? Why not give it back?'

'To have something of yours, I guess. Something that meant more to you than the money.'

'Who *thinks* like that? Who could live with thoughts like that inside their head?'

'Too many people, I'm afraid,' Lockyer murmured. 'Well, now you have wheels again. Real freedom.'

'Yes.' She turned the key. There was a faint click from beneath the bonnet, but nothing else happened. 'Battery's dead.'

'We'll push it into the barn,' Lockyer said. 'Dad's got a charger in there.'

'I'll need to switch out the petrol, too, if it's been sitting for ages.'

'There'll be a siphon in there, and fuel cans.'

'Thank you, Inspector. Matt.'

'No problem.'

'No, I mean, thank you for finding it. For finding *him*. For all of it.' She gave him a look so frank and disarming that Lockyer had to turn away.

'All part of the service,' he said.

'I really doubt that.'

Hedy gazed out across the rising fields to a distant copse of trees. Lockyer saw her eyes glitter. It could have been the wind that filled them with tears, but he doubted it. He wished he knew the right thing to say. She heaved in a huge breath, pressed her fingers to her mouth. 'This is all just . . .' The words were hard to make out. Lockyer saw her shoulders clench, saw how she fought to keep control. 'I just . . . I don't know what to do. How to do any of this any more. How to *be*.'

She sounded so fragile, and Lockyer longed to hold her, to ease it somehow.

'You're strong, Hedy,' was all he could find to say. 'You'll find a way. I know you will.'

Lockyer kept his distance for several days. He didn't want to crowd Hedy, or take advantage of any gratitude she might feel towards him. He certainly didn't want her to feel she owed him anything. The idea made his skin crawl. Equally, he didn't want to promise her anything. He had no idea what he had to offer her, though the urge to offer *something* remained. Something of himself. He was still struggling to separate genuine care for her from his own need for penance. He suspected it was the kind of thing only time would make clear.

At work, he and Broad moved on to unsolved cases of violent crime from the nineties and noughties – anything that looked like it could have been Sean Hannington's work, and where there were forensics that could be re-examined for his DNA, now that they had it. The charge sheet against him was racking up in a satisfying way.

Lockyer resisted calling the farm for news, resisted texting Hedy until she texted him first. But on Friday he caved. *Want to go to the pub tonight? They do good pizza.* He hesitated before pressing send. He had no idea whether or not she liked pizza, but didn't everyone? She replied a couple of minutes later. *Yes, okay. Thanks.*

It was dark when he got to Westdene, and the lights were on in the barn, spilling a yellow glow across the wet concrete of the yard. Lockyer crossed to the doorway, the breeze loud in his ears. Hedy's car was inside, tucked alongside the heaps of tools and greasy machine parts, the sheep-marking paint and animal feed and ancient boxes of rat poison. The floor had a crust of dry mud and baler twine. Hedy and John were under the Austin's bonnet, leaning over the engine, both of them with filthy hands.

'Go on,' John said. 'Hard twist. You won't break it with

those soft fingers.' Hedy had to use both hands, but whatever she was turning finally clicked into place. 'That's it.'

They stood up and rubbed their hands on oily rags, moving in near harmony, both quiet, both considering. The sight of them together like that, working side by side, was almost painful to Lockyer. But deeply pleasing too. He knew he should announce himself: they wouldn't see him in the dark beyond the doorway, wouldn't hear him above the wind. But instead he stayed silent, stayed still.

'Well,' John said eventually, 'Just about ready to roll, I'd say. You'll need to get those bushes seen to, mind, else she might shake herself to pieces.'

Hedy nodded. 'I will.'

'Good girl.'

It was what John said to the dogs, and to Trudy, and to the ewes. He'd accepted Hedy into that circle, apparently – things in his care. He'd appreciate her quietness, Lockyer guessed. The way she never hurried. John shut the bonnet with a bang and cleared his throat. 'You can't let things linger, see,' he said, looking down at his hands as he rubbed them again. 'Does no good. Fix it if it can be fixed, but if it can't . . .' he shrugged '. . . get shot of it. No good hanging on to rubbish. Broken things.'

Hedy gazed at John. 'Hard to do that, sometimes, though,' she said.

'Hard enough, but it's the only way. Else sooner or later you find out you *can't* get rid. You find it's too late. Gets attached, like it's part of you. So you've got to *try*, do you hear?'

'I hear,' Hedy whispered.

'Good girl.'

Lockyer backed away quietly, returned to his car. He waited a heartbeat, two. Feeling that grief, that pleasure; so bittersweet. Then he slammed the door loudly and approached the barn again, calling a greeting.

He took Hedy a couple of miles up the road, to the pub in West Lavington. It was busy, with the Friday-night drinkers clustered around the bar and most of the tables occupied by diners. Hedy chose them a spot near the fire.

'I never used to feel the cold. Now I'm freezing the whole time,' she said.

'Perhaps you just need to reacclimatize.'

'No. It's old age. Your mum was telling me.' She smiled to show she didn't mind.

'Is it all right? Staying there?'

'Of course it is. It's great. I'm very grateful.'

'You don't need to be—'

'Prison hasn't turned me into such a pleb that I can't be grateful to be welcomed into someone's home, Matt.'

'No. I know. I just meant that she likes having you there.'

'And your dad?'

'He likes it too,' Lockyer said. 'He likes you.'

Hedy shot him a quick smile. 'Harder to tell with him, isn't it?'

'He's a master of non-communication. I think it's doing him good, having you in the house.'

'Well. Great.' She took a sip of her drink, a Diet Coke. Lockyer had said nothing about her ordering something non-alcoholic. It was none of his business. 'I took the car out for a spin. Just a short one.'

'Yeah? How was it?'

'Just the same,' she said. 'It steers like a shopping trolley, God love it. There are more cars on the road than I remember.'

Lockyer nodded. 'All the time.'

'Your dad's been such a help. He even changed the brake fluid for me. I didn't have the heart to tell him I could do it myself. He was having too much fun grumbling about how women know nothing about cars.'

'Sorry about that. He has to complain when he helps someone, so they don't guess how much he likes doing it.'

'Well, I've enjoyed it. He's a kind man.'

'Yes. He is.'

Hedy looked at him for a moment. 'A sad man, too,' she said.

'Yes. We're . . . trying to fix that.'

Hedy didn't answer at once. Then: 'It won't be easy.'

'No.'

Lockyer changed the subject. 'So, now you have wheels, where will you go?'

'I don't know.' Hedy looked down at the fire beside them. It lit her eyes with shifting orange light. 'To see Mum first, I suppose.'

'In Spain?'

'Near Almería. She lives in one of those awful expat encampments on the edge of a town. They all have a pizza oven, and a pool with the developer's logo tiled into the bottom. It's such a cliché. I want to see her, but I definitely wouldn't want to move there.'

'It might take a while for the compensation to get sorted out.'

'I've got a little bit of money. I started putting fifty quid of my pay packet into an ISA when I was working at Longacres. It's not a lot, but it's been accruing interest all this time. I've been into the bank to open an account, and get it transferred. There's a few hundred in there now, enough for a cheap flight to Spain. Enough for several tanks of petrol and—' She broke off. 'And then I don't know what. Or where.'

'You own a house in France now,' Lockyer reminded her. 'You could live there. Or at least take a holiday.'

'I could,' Hedy murmured. 'I don't speak French.'

'You'd soon learn,' he said. 'And the French are well known for being friendly and welcoming to clueless English settlers.'

Hedy pulled a face. 'It was a kind thing for Roland to do, though, wasn't it?' she said. 'To think of me after all this time.'

'I don't think he ever *stopped* thinking about you. In fact, I think he was always a bit sweet on you – just in that wistful, non-randy way old men sometimes are. And I don't think he ever really believed you were guilty.'

There was the same awkward, empty beat that always followed any mention of her guilt, her innocence, her time in prison. Lockyer's part in putting her there was the elephant in the room.

'I wish I could have seen him again,' Hedy said.

'He'd have liked that.'

'What do you think I should do?' she asked abruptly.

'Me? How can I possibly say?'

'I don't know. I just thought you might have an opinion. On me moving to France. Or not.'

Their food arrived and Lockyer was grateful for the distraction. Was she asking for a reason to stay in England? In Wiltshire? He wasn't sure, but perhaps she had been. She reached for her drink and rested her hand there, fingertips smearing the beads of moisture on the glass. He could reach out and touch her skin for the first time. He thought back. Yes, it would be the first ever time. They ate in silence for a while, then talked about other things – places they'd grown up, places they'd been and never been. Neutral, seemingly safe topics that nevertheless kept sending them crashing into all the years she'd lost, and the strange territory of how they'd come to know each other.

'You're different when you're not on duty,' Hedy told him.

'Am I?'

'Yes. As "Detective Inspector Lockyer" you're very decisive. Forthright. You don't hold back. When you're just Matt, you don't say much. You seem less sure of yourself, more of a closed book.'

'Well.' Lockyer shifted uncomfortably. 'When I'm at work I've got a job to do. I know exactly what I'm supposed to be doing.'

'And you don't when you're not at work?'

'Not usually, no. Unless we're talking about DIY.'

'We're not,' she said. 'So your badge is your talisman? It gives you the courage to do what needs doing, say what needs saying?'

'I suppose you could put it like that.'

'A bit like Dumbo's feather.' She smiled. 'You know, the feather the crows give him, so he'll believe he can fly?'

Lockyer raised his eyebrows. 'You've got me sussed.'

'So which is the real you?'

'Both.'

Hedy nodded. 'One's got a job he knows how to do, and the other . . .'

Lockyer held her gaze, feeling as if she could see right through him. '. . . is just going along, hoping to get things right at least half of the time,' he said.

At the end of the evening they walked out to the car side by side. A fine drizzle blurred the pub's lights and caught as tiny droplets on their hair and clothes. Hedy put her hand on Lockyer's arm as he reached into his pocket for the car key. She looked up at him, but didn't speak. The moment hung.

'We don't really know each other,' Lockyer said quietly. 'Do we, Hedy?'

'Oh, I don't know,' she said, with the ghost of a smile. 'I don't know how much more I need to know about someone who'd let me borrow his family when I needed one. Someone who'd admit a mistake, and put himself on the line to make it right.'

'How can it ever be right, Hedy?'

'I don't blame you.' She stared at him keenly, as though

trying to make him see. 'I know you must think I do, but I don't. You did your job. The evidence pointed to me. I'm – I'm not angry, and I'm not harbouring any weird feelings about it. About you. In case you thought I was.'

'I sat opposite you and called you a killer. Just a few months ago. I believed it. Not for long, but I did.' He could hardly imagine it now.

'You did.' Her face fell, doubt creeping into her eyes. 'But I could tell how much you hated to think it. How much it hurt you.'

'It did. And I *did* hate it.'

'Well, then.' She smiled again. 'It was still you who got me out. Who agreed to look into it all again.'

'I don't want you to be grateful to me.'

'I'm not sure I can help it.'

'Can't you just see it as me finally doing my job *properly*? I don't think I can stand for you to feel grateful. Not to me.'

'All right. Then I don't,' she said, and he didn't believe her. But his hands moved without waiting to be told, cradling her face as he bent forwards to kiss her.

The call came while he was at his desk the next day, still with the taste of Hedy on his lips and tongue.

'Matthew? It's Mum.'

'Is everything okay?'

'Yes, we're fine. I just . . . I thought you'd want to know. It's Hedy. She's gone.'

'What do you mean, gone?'

'Well, gone. She spent the morning letting down the curtains in her room – did a very neat job of it, too. Then she packed up that little bag of hers and drove away in the Austin. It just . . . it seemed rather sudden. She's not ducking out on anything, is she?'

Lockyer sank inside. *Only on me*, he didn't say. 'No. No, she's free to do what she likes.'

'But you thought she might stay longer?'

'Yes, I suppose I did.'

'You wanted her to, I can hear it in your voice. Oh, Matthew. I'm so sorry.'

'Did she say anything about her plans?'

'No. She thanked us both very much, said that staying with us had been exactly what she needed to get that *other* place out of her system. So that was nice.'

'Yes.'

'You gave her back her freedom, Matthew, not just her car. I hope you're at least a little bit proud of yourself? Even if this isn't the outcome you hoped for.'

'It's fine, Mum. Thanks for letting me know.'

Lockyer rang off and stared down at the paperwork on his desk. Across the small office, Broad cleared her throat.

'Everything all right, Guv?' she said, when he didn't look up.

'Yes. Fine.' He kept his eyes down, though he wasn't reading. He was trying to work out what he was feeling, and what it meant. *You gave her back her freedom.* And she'd taken it and run. He sat with it a while longer, then took out his mobile and started a message to her but abandoned it without pressing send. She was free, and she'd chosen to go. The more he thought about it, the more that was all there was to it. She knew where to find him. If she ever wanted to.

'Has Hedy gone?' Broad kept her voice down. She was the only one Lockyer had trusted with the information that Hedy had been staying with his parents. He looked up, and saw her face full of guarded sympathy. 'World's her oyster now, I suppose,' she said gently.

'She said she might go and see her mother in Spain,' Lockyer said. He looked away out of the window, at the grey sky and the wet ground and the bare, freezing trees. He could hardly blame her.

'Spain? God, I would. In a heartbeat,' Broad echoed his thoughts. She gave him a rueful smile, lips pressed together, a smile of solidarity. 'Perhaps she'll be back,' she said.

'Perhaps.'

'You could always just . . . call her? Tell her how you feel?'

Lockyer smiled wanly. 'I'm not sure it would do any good. And I think she already knows.'

'Oh.' Broad thought for a moment. 'Well, it couldn't hurt to try, that's all I'm saying. I mean, if you haven't actually *told* her . . . Best not to assume, with things like that.'

'Told her what?

'That you . . . want her to stay.'

Lockyer stared at Broad, hearing the words *love her* hovering unsaid. 'Is it that obvious?'

'No, I just . . . There's obviously something there, Guv.'

Lockyer didn't answer. Broad's tone was almost wistful;

careful, or caring. She coloured slightly under his scrutiny, and turned back to her work.

Later in the day Lockyer realized that Hedy's passport would have expired while she was in prison. She couldn't go to Spain, at least not right away. He sat up with a jolt and reached for his phone again, but put it back down. It was none of his business. He was not responsible for her, had no hold over her. She knew where he was.

When he got home that evening it was to roam the house again, moving from room to room, mentally cataloguing the work that needed doing with the same disjointed apathy he'd started to feel before. The same feeling of pointlessness. He drank a beer, made some supper, drank another beer. The house was too empty, and not knowing where in the world Hedy was made him feel lost. Since the day he'd first met her, he'd always known where she was. Until now. The darkness pressed in at the windows, and when his phone rang he leapt to answer it. But it was Kevin, so he let it go to voicemail before playing the message back on loudspeaker. His friend's voice echoed around the bare kitchen, breathy and taut.

'Matt, it's me. Can you call me back? I need to . . . It's just there's a bit of a situation brewing here. I've got into a bit of a bind . . .' At this point Kevin attempted to laugh, but he was too rattled and it just sounded weird. 'I know you told me not to get involved but . . . Look, can you just call me back, mate?'

Lockyer left his phone on the kitchen table. He pulled

on his coat and went to the back door for his boots. He would walk. The night was very still, but there was always a breeze on the plain – up on one of the ridges, with the twinkle of distant lights below, and the fainter smattering of stars above. The black silhouettes of hawthorn trees and hunched thickets of bramble; all the night creatures about their business. He would go out into that wildness and let the wind blow right through him. Maybe then he wouldn't feel so empty. It was the only thing he could think to do, because otherwise all he felt was the absence of *her*. The shadow she'd left behind.

He wrenched open the door, then pulled up short.

Mrs Musprat was standing on the step, one hand raised to knock. Her mouth was open, the whites of her eyes gleaming. Like she'd seen a ghost.

'Christ!' Lockyer swore. 'You scared me half to death, Mrs Musprat.'

The old lady said nothing, but nodded vaguely. Her peculiar, faintly goaty scent drifted in over the step.

'I was just on my way out,' Lockyer said.

'I need to talk to you. Got to tell you something,' she said. She took a deep breath and squared her shoulders, but her eyes remained fearful.

'Can't it wait till tomorrow?' He looked at his watch. 'It's half past ten. I was just—'

'You're a copper, ain't you?' she snapped. 'Well, then. There's – there's something I've *got* to tell you.'

Lockyer hesitated. He wanted to turn her away: he didn't

want to hear it, whatever it was. Not just then. But he was a copper, and the look on her face was making the back of his neck prickle. He opened the door wider, and stepped back to let her in.

ACKNOWLEDGEMENTS

Sincere thanks to Guy Turner, Major Crime Review Officer for Wiltshire Police, and to PC Jenny Freeman and DI Simon Childe, also of Wiltshire Police, for all their help during the writing of this novel. All inaccuracies (and procedural improbabilities) are entirely my own.

A huge thank you to my brilliant agent, Mark Lucas, to Niamh O'Grady at the Soho Agency and my dream team of editors, Jane Wood and Florence Hare, for their enthusiasm, ideas, and determination to get the best from this book. Also to the whole team at Quercus for their skill and dedication. DI Lockyer could not be in better hands, and I am so grateful.